Irene T

The Chateau

Best Wishes

Irene Taylor

Matador
5 Weir Road
Kibworth Beauchamp
Leicester LE8 0LQ, UK
Tel: (+44) 116 279 2299
Fax: (+44) 116 279 2277
Email: books@troubador.co.uk
Web: www.troubador.co.uk/matador

ISBN 978 1848763 289

British Library Cataloguing in Publication Data.
A catalogue record for this book is available from the British Library.

Typeset in 11pt Book Antiqua by Troubador Publishing Ltd, Leicester, UK
Printed and bound in Great Britain by TJ International Ltd, Padstow, Cornwall

Matador is an imprint of Troubador Publishing Ltd

To Alexander, my husband and Stuart,
my son for filling my life full of love and laughter.

To David, my brother, always in our memories.

WIN A WEEKEND IN FRANCE

Return flights from UK.
3 nights accommodation in a prestigious Logis de France.
Dinner, bed and breakfast ir ᵈed.*

What you have to do…

Name all French rivers refer͓   ͓ne book and send your
answer to the website desⁱ   ͓ow.
    If there is more thaʳ   ͓ect answer a draw will be
made and the winner'   ͓sted on the website.
    Thereafter arraʳ   ᵥill be made for dates of the visit
convenient to alⅼ

To enter this   ͓ompetition please email your answers to:
                        ͓_chateau@hotmail.co.uk

*Terms and conditions.

Offer of weekend to maximum value of €1,200.

Hire car available for duration of 3 nights stay.

One entry per household.

Date of draw to be advised on website.

Weekend visit to be taken no longer than 12 months after winner announced
and confirmed.

Prologue

THE SUMMER, FRANCE, 1999

Freedom is not possible for me now. I have been imprisoned by events in mind, body and soul. Hope is vanquished, the future bleak, I am locked in a horrendous hell: but two days ago I was in Heaven. I laughed with my lover then, I shudder at the contrast now. My memories of us are mellow, meandering arms entwined through the glorious garden enticed by the perfume of primulas, the tubular petals of their dancing heads welcoming our presence bowing in the mid-summer breeze; the aroma of magnolias murmuring mutedly together nodding 'bonjour' as we passed by.

If only I could translate the nightmares that choke my thoughts now into the joyful reality and dreams then, I might find some happiness again. But that is foolish childlike naivety. Events have murdered such thoughts and me.

But have they? Why should I allow this to happen? Do I not have the control now over this man's arrival in my life, even to manipulate these events and determine my own destiny? After all I am independent, financially sound with my career at its epitome. I have a strong and loving family, the Sinclair family.

No this man will not destroy me.

I must, I will survive.

Chapter One

March arrived with joy and exited in despair. In just 14 days my family disintegrated, torn asunder and I was the culprit, the only one to blame.

How vividly I recall the middle of that month. I was at home on Easter vacation from my studies at the University of Glasgow and I was angry. Angry with myself because I was running late, which was unusual for me.

Normally well organised I could not believe I had allowed myself to preside over the recent chaos.

Frustrated I seated myself at the table in the pine panelled kitchen of my home, "Marchmont", and swallowed some of my long abandoned instant coffee. It was foul and I emptied the remaining contents of the mug down the sink in disgust.

This house, "Marchmont", was my home, a handsome Georgian building situated in a small village near Perth in central Scotland. Perth was considered "the gateway to the Highlands". How I loved my home having grown up in its warm, loving environment with Papa, Maman and my ten year older brother, David, all of whom I adored.

Papa was Scottish, Maman French: they had met at the

1

Sorbonne during Papa's doctorate year – a *coup de foudre*, love at first sight and they had never parted.

Suddenly my reverie was pierced by the shrill tone of my mobile. I glanced at my watch, 2.30 pm and still shopping in the town to finish before my parents returned this evening.

I swore aloud in French and picked up the receiver.

"Hi Caterine! How are things?"

My mood changed as I recognised my best friend's familiar tones. Shona Carruthers and I had toddled together accompanied by our respective proud mothers presented to the local nursery school in prime condition; we often departed in a different fashion, re-emerging with shoes scuffed, knees plastered and occasionally torn or damaged clothes despite valiant efforts from nursery staff to restrain us from our tomboy antics. Over the years not much had changed!

"Shona, I'm in a mess. I promised myself I'd prepare a special dinner for Papa and Maman after their week in the Borders. Of course I was an idiot trying out a different pastry recipe for the mushroom pie. It was a disaster so I reverted to the old one. But it's cost me a lot of time."

"Can I help, Caterine? I'll come over soon" Shona asked anxiously.

"Thanks a lot but not really. I'm shopping in Perth and leaving now. Can I call you later?"

"Sure, no problem. I'm home tonight, working on a French essay to be handed in after the Easter hols. Just a minute" Shona laughed, "you're the one who's bilingual you should be helping me! Bye!"

I was still chuckling at the remarks as I grabbed my bag and Maman's list, racing down the drive, gravel flying in our old family jalopy which I had inherited after passing my driving test.

Fifty minutes later, items purchased, dumped in the car boot, I departed the main car park. The weather was foul, heavy rain, high winds, dark and dismal: however I was optimistic. Just ten minutes I thought, an indulgence. Pulling my anorak hood over my unruly long hair, I hurried across the square to the adjacent street and my sanctuary, the local antique shop and auction house. As always its magnetism pulled me into its mesmerising interior.

Gordon McArthur, the proprietor and chief auctioneer, greeted me in the hall. His family and mine were old friends.

"Well, young lady, how are you coping with those studies in Fine Arts? A very demanding course as I understand it."

I was taken aback and replied.

"Not really Mr. McArthur and anyway I find all the subjects fascinating."

"Well Caterine, that means it's in your heart and that's what counts. Now, can I help you today or is it just a wander round?"

I hesitated. "Where's the little Scottish oak chair I admired last week? I don't see it."

"Sold, Caterine, yesterday. We'd an exceptional response to the March auction. Business has been brisk."

"To a Scot?" I asked anxiously.

"I'm afraid not, young lady. To my dismay it went to a foreigner and at a bargain; a tenacious negotiator."

"Oh no, that's terrible. It should have stayed in Scotland where it belonged." I exclaimed.

"Unfortunately, Caterine, the destination of these items is out of my control" Gordon McArthur replied shaking his head "I'm as upset as you are."

Driving back to Marchmont, still pondering about that exquisite chair I rounded a country road bend to be met by a horrific sight, a man in the adjacent field was flailing a whip at a little pony its cries of pain surmounting the sounds of whistling winds and battering hailstones.

Stamping on the brakes, our old jalopy skidded in protest to a halt and I narrowly avoided the ditch. As I jumped over the small border fence I started shouting,

3

"Stop it, stop it, you're murdering that animal." But he ignored me, lifting his arm higher to inflict even more suffering.

Reaching this fiend now I grasped his wrist trying to wrestle the whip from his grasp. We struggled probably for only a minute but it seemed an eternity. I was taller but he was stronger, eventually turning the whip on me striking me relentlessly on my back. Even through the padding of my ski jacket I felt the stinging pain of his blows, I found myself faltering, but kept twisting away from him to lessen the target of his attack.

I remember thinking "I must win or the little pony will die."

With one final effort I turned to confront him and used a trick David had told me about self-defense.

I spat in his face, in shock, he hesitated and I used my major asset. With all the force I could muster I kicked him with my size seven boots and caught him in the groin.

"Bloody hell" he yelled putting his hands down to protect himself and dropping the whip. I, in turn lost my balance, ending face down in the muddied field. Fortunately, he fled.

"Caterine, are you OK? What a fight." It was farmer Black, our neighbour.

"Fine Jimmy" I gasped scrambling to my feet "just a little breathless."

But there was no response as he stared in shock at that poor bedraggled creature.

"My God it's Daisy, the children's pony, stolen last month. She's half dead" throwing his arm round her dirty, matted apology for a mane.

Acting swiftly I replied

"Right, phone Andy's surgery and I'll call the police to report the incident."

Soon Daisy was being led gently to the sanctuary of one of the farm's barns.

Andy Cormack our Perth vet arrived within minutes. I

knew him well having worked in his surgery on several school holiday jobs to earn extra pocket money.

"Well" he said shaking his head "she's in a sorry state poor girl. I've given her an injection for her general condition and left ointment for those weals. With rest and loving care which she'll receive here in abundance, Jimmy, as I know, Daisy should make it. Fortunately, she's young, an old horse no chance."

"One of the family will sit with her during the night. We'll take turns" Jimmy said, stroking the pony's scraggy neck.

"Just as I thought" Andy replied "any change in her general condition, call me anytime. Otherwise, I'll return tomorrow morning."

Despite Jimmy's entreaties for me to join him in a "wee dram" to calm our jagged nerves, I declined, smiling to myself. Jimmy, by repute, was a master of hosts with his "wee malt whiskies" usually treble the standard bar measure!

When I returned to Marchmont it was 6 pm. Papa and Maman were due in an hour.

Despite my aching back, I moved fast: ratatouille and mushroom pie in the oven to heat and then stairs taken two at a time to my bedroom.

Looking in the mirror, even I was shocked. Heavens what a mess! Of course, unlike Maman, I was no beauty, but my hair was mangled and muddied and my pale angular face looked like some dusty canvas covered in brown and red irregular spots. Then I realised a cut above my hairline together with the grime had created this ghastly image.

My body was put in the shower and my hair gingerly into shampoo and I prayed for time: the gods heard me. I received a text message from Maman. Atrocious weather conditions and major road works meant they would be delayed by an hour.

I made sure I benefited from that additional time.

Suddenly a commotion as the back door clattered open, the

wind bouncing it against the grey stone porch wall and my parents announced their arrival home.

"Heavens above, Véronique" I heard Papa's exclamation "the storms have increased in intensity since the Borders!"

I ran to welcome them, coats and boots dispensed in the back of the porch to dry, they greeted me with hugs and kisses. Then everyone spoke at once. As usual Maman took command and soon we were relaxing in the sitting room luxuriating in the warmth of our open fire and its merrily burning logs.

While Papa poured our aperitifs Maman remarked "you're looking pale, Petite, feeling all right?"

"Fine Maman" I replied hastily, knowing how observant she was "just annoyed, I was disorganised today and then suffered a soaking in torrential rain in Perth."

"Unbelievable conditions" Papa agreed handing us our glasses "the roads were more like rivers."

My dinner to my satisfaction was well received.

"Petite, with that paté starter and then the mushrooms, you'll soon be challenging Maman!" Papa announced as he cleared his favourite Roquefort cheese from his plate and finished his claret.

"You're right there" Maman smiled "I'll need to raise the standards!"

As we were taking our coffee, we heard the doorbell.

"I'll get it" Papa said muttering under his breath as it was after 10 pm.

It was Jimmy Black's voice I recognised in the hall.

"My God" I thought "it's Daisy, she's dead."

"Véronique, Caterine, my apologies as I've just expressed to Angus but it's a special mission."

He turned to me smiling.

"Daisy's on the mend, Caterine, we're all sure, even after a few hours: she recognised the children and starting to eat. What can we say except you saved her life."

I was embarrassed, for once, lost for words.

Papa and Maman looked bewildered as I glanced at them.

"What are you talking about Jimmy?" Maman asked.

"Yes, what about Daisy? What's happened?" Papa added.

Now Jimmy looked bewildered.

"Didn't Caterine tell you?" He was aghast and reiterated the whole story adding "Caterine, you and Shona were rogues as schoolchildren on the farm, all the pranks, the tree climbing and as for that assault course you designed. Still gives me nightmares thinking about its hazards over the river."

"Why Jimmy" I teased him "Shona and I completed it, the boys didn't."

"I'm well aware of that, young lady, my farmhands have never lived it down – shamefaced to this day!"

We all laughed at the memory.

Jimmy took his leave.

"The children will call tomorrow to thank you personally. High spirited, determined, even obstinate you may be but conceited and selfish you are not. As for saying nothing about what happened today" he shook his head as he was leaving, ...!

Maman came over immediately to me as Papa looked up,

"So that's why you're so pale. Are you hurt? What about your back?" She enquired anxiously.

"It's nothing Maman, just a little stiff."

"Well, let me look at it Petite" she insisted almost marching me despite my protesting to the bathroom.

"There's no skin broken but bruised". I received the iodine treatment.

I smiled at the familiar nickname for me 'Petite', it was ludicrous. Heavens, I was 5'10" one inch taller than Maman, but still the name prevailed!

The next day, Sunday, was the beginning of a flurry of activity: the preparations for a family party to celebrate my 18th birthday the following weekend. For my friends a disco had been booked in Perth before my return to university in early April.

Maman and I had already discussed the proposed menu for my party and so now it was just a question of implementing it. We set to work.

Papa suddenly had become ensconsed in his study!

On that Sunday, just before lunch I was reorganising some books in my bedroom when my mobile rang.

"Chérie, I dreamt about us last night."

"Grégoire" I replied, "you're teasing me, you'd only dream about your favourite football team!"

There was silence.

"I was serious, Caterine, only if I described it to you, you'd be shocked!"

"Grégoire, now you are being flippant!" We laughed, chatting for several minutes.

"I'm so looking forward to next weekend, the family party and being together. Take care, chérie, I love you."

"I love you too" I replied and we said "au revoir".

I curled up on my bed as my thoughts wandered.

Grégoire Jourdain – not just my boyfriend but also my cousin, the son of Tante Sylvie and Oncle Thierry, Maman's brother.

We'd played together as children with his younger sister Marie-Françoise at "Acacia", the old farmhouse south of Orléans which had been owned by our family through the generations and we had shared many memorable holidays. Then last summer we had fallen in love. Incredible.

There had been an incident in the local stables where Grégoire had halted a runaway horse. I had looked at him in admiration and he returned my gaze. I found I could not look away. Embarrassed I had escaped to walk in the surrounding woodland but Grégoire had followed me.

"Caterine, why are you running away?"

I had halted at hearing his voice, heart hammering, breathless.

Then I had felt his hands on my shoulders, turning me round gently, lips firmly on mine.

That was the beginning of my first love affair.

"Caterine, lunch is ready" Maman called from the hall and my mind returned to reality.

It was over lunch that the crisis occurred.

"Petite" Papa began "Maman and I are very proud of your efforts to save Daisy; it showed much courage but also somewhat foolhardy. Take some advice from both of us. If confronted again with a similar hazardous incident, use your phone and call the police. Don't put yourself at risk or in any danger."

He and Maman lifted their glasses of sparkling water, as temper roused (inherited from Maman) I responded

"Risk, danger! What are you talking about?

How dare you accuse me of, what was it, being foolhardy.

You, Papa, an eminent historian in demand worldwide but also a renowned mountaineer, conquering the North Face of the Eiger at 32. Is that not risk, danger even foolhardy with a wife and baby son waiting fearfully in the background.

And Maman a respected children's writer of anecdotal stories about animals and president of the Scottish League of Cruelty against these vulnerable creatures.

What would you have done in my circumstances. Calmly phoned the police when a defenceless pony was being whipped to death.

You still treat me like a child. Well I'm not I'm a woman. At 18 in Scotland I could have been legally married for two years with children, perhaps even the responsibility of a pony." I added sarcastically.

"Excuse me" and I left the table, exiting by the patio doors to the garden.

Of course I was miserable perched on my special stone seat in the rose arbour, in mental discomfort. "I should have kept my temper" Papa and Maman were thinking of me and I loved my parents so much.

All the care, concern and guidance over the years, combined with a first class education, sporting opportunities, encouragement when I was in low spirits plus so much laughter, fun at home and always surrounded by unconditional love.

"Petite" it was Papa's voice.

I turned round.

"I'm sorry" I began but he interrupted me "you will not apologise. It was Maman and I who were wrong. We were coming to speak to you together but she had to answer the phone."

Papa sat down beside me and took my hand in his "you were right. You're not a child and we belittled you."

"No, Papa" I protested.

"Yes, Caterine, but let me explain. David was our 'before' and you our 'after'. You know about the trauma of Maman's miscarriages when we were eventually advised by medical experts there could be no more children. Then you arrived out of the blue six years later and so we wanted to keep you as a miracle baby and forgot that this baby would still grow up."

I stared at him but said nothing sensing more.

" 'Before' and 'after' such little words in the English language but so significant.

After birth, the membrane of life; afterglow the vibrancy and joy of spent lovers and aftermath the consequences of what went before."

He kissed my cheek.

"Come on let's join Maman and her chocolate gateau."

On reflection as events unfolded what a poignant moment that was as he took my hand.

The remainder of that week evaporated rapidly: foodstuff stored in the freezer, my birthday cake baked by Maman, iced, dominated by the marzipan figure of my beloved three quarter bred grey, Tiger: the snooker room in the basement devoid of its table was set up for some family dancing, decorated in Scottish and French emblems to celebrate the "Auld Alliance"!

At Friday lunchtime, I arrived back at "Marchmont" from returning some books to the local library, to be met by the front door opened wide. I was startled and then saw him "David" I shouted "you're early, supposed to arrive this evening" but he grabbed me before I could find out why, spinning me round in the air and finishing with his traditional bear hug.

"Put me down!" I gasped "I'm too tall now."

"Nonsense" my brother replied "you're still my little sister.

David was 6'2" with dark blonde hair and deep grey eyes inherited from Papa. Perhaps not conventionally handsome, he possessed a striking personality, however and a droll sense of humour. I adored him.

"Come on" he added putting his arm round my shoulder.

"It's time to meet Alix."

Suddenly I remembered, the new girlfriend. David had told us about her last Christmas. Papa inadvertently had introduced the subject while discussing my brother's appointment to his mercantile bank's head office in Zurich.

"New job going well David?"

"Yes, Papa, settling in now. The boss is a little tetchy but I can cope with that. The apartment I bought in November was a bit of a bargain. It's appreciated 10% already."

"Heavens," Maman had replied "what a sound investment."

"Are you skiing as usual with your pals in the New Year?"

David had grinned and said

"Skiing yes, but with my girlfriend, Alix. She's an

interpreter. We met at an international conference. The only problem is" he hesitated "she doesn't speak English."

I can still recall the silence over our coffee and mince pies as three pairs of eyes stared at him incredulously.

"What on earth do you mean" Papa exclaimed "an interpreter not speaking English. That's preposterous. What nationality is she?"

Looking round us all with an amused look on his face David had replied

"She's a Scot!"

And so as the result of a fortuitous earlier plane flight I was the first member of our family to meet Alix McCallum.

"Caterine" she smiled coming out to greet me in traditional French fashion.

"What a pleasure to meet you at last. I can assure you I didn't believe a word about those outrageous tales David had told me" and she winked.

"Just a minute" David interrupted "what tales about Caterine?"

I laughed liking her immediately as did Papa and Maman when we all chatted together during dinner.

"David and I did not get off to a very promising start" Alix informed us over coffee in the sitting room. "He asked me to translate some English into French and then corrected my grammar!"

"Heavens Alix, it was a joke and in private. I'll never forget your response, called me a conceited arrogant prig" my brother replied shamefaced.

All of us burst out laughing.

Maman and I, however, instinctively exchanged glances. David, this time, could well have met his match!

That evening snuggling up in bed I hugged my duvet; birthday party with my family tomorrow sharing it not only with Papa, Maman and David but also Oncle Thierry, Tante

Sylvie, Marie-Françoise and Grégoire: then a thought, also Alix. What a surprise she was and such a contrast to the giants in our family: petite, small boned with a luxuriant head of raven curls cascading onto her shoulders and exceptionally pretty. Alix resembled in physical appearance, what was it? I thought carefully then the image formed – a classic china doll.

Then I found myself chuckling. How ridiculous! With her brain, wit and forthrightness this porcelain figurine was well protected by a mental suit of armour inherited from her Scottish ancestors.

I fell into a dreamless sleep unaware of the nightmare on the horizon.

On the following morning, Saturday, I was standing impatiently in the arrivals hall of Glasgow International airport awaiting the appearance of our French family.

Papa had driven me in his more luxurious version of my jalopy while Maman finalized details of the dinner menu. David and Alix had disappeared to visit the Perth shops.

"Where are they?" I thought. The Air France flight had landed five minutes early at 10.10.

"Grégoire" I cried as suddenly I saw him and raced forward to be gathered in his warm embrace, a kiss on each cheek but with a naughty comment in my right ear which caused me to giggle.

Oncle Thierry and Tante Sylvie were on Grégoire's heels and under one hour later we were munching Maman's fruit scones over a traditional pot of tea at "Marchmont".

"How's the golf Thierry?" Papa asked, hastily trapping a currant before it escaped his mouth!

"Much improved since my retirement, dropped two on my handicap, I'd be wary at our next encounter Angus. I'm just one match down and confident of leveling the score."

"Nonsense, Thierry, you'll have lost your edge: too early to leave Air France as a senior pilot in your mid-fifties. The brain stagnates, body languishes: anyway I've developed a new putting technique. If you want I'll give you a lesson!"

And so the banter continued, as always and all weekend, as I remember now, casting my mind back to those 18th birthday celebrations.

Every time I think about that weekend it is like a photo album: snapshots of incidents, fun, laughter and music as after Maman's dinner we had retired to the snooker room and literally "danced till dawn."

Before dinner I had received my birthday presents. Papa and Maman had already given me a very generous cheque funded by an endowment policy taken out after my birth. With advice from Papa and David I had set up a share portfolio which David would monitor for me until I gained more investment experience. I had felt humbled and privileged.

Now on that Saturday evening, aperitifs served, my uncle and aunt presented me with a large box swathed in jade green, my favourite colour.

"It's brilliant" I gasped as I saw the contents, black riding boots, beige breeches and a helmet covered with the same colour green silk as advertised by the wrapping.

From Grégoire I stared in disbelief at the silver locket with a photograph of us inside taken at "Acacia" last summer when we had fallen in love.

Trying to hide my tears of emotion I ran over, "Thank you so much. I'll treasure it for ever" I stumbled out, a little embarrassed in front of the family.

Grégoire, however, had other ideas. Picking me up he planted a very special kiss on my lips, to which we received a burst of applause.

To my surprise Alix came over to offer me an exquisitely wrapped box.

"Congratulations on your 18th birthday" she said "it's a new chapter in your life. Don't waste any of your future time." In retrospect that was a poignant statement.

Inside the box was an atomizer of my favourite perfume.

"How did you know that this is my favourite? Did David tell you?" I exclaimed.

"David, perfume brands! You must be joking Caterine, he still can't remember mine, although" she grinned "I've reminded him often enough. No, I asked the oracle, Maman!"

But no present from David. That puzzled me a little.

Aperitifs consumed, David rose slowly, yawning.

"Well, Petite, I'd almost forgotten about my gift, it's in the garden" and he departed.

I was taken aback, "the garden" I thought "could it be a rose bush to plant for the future. It was my favourite flower after all."

Moments later David returned dragging behind him our oldest rusty wheelbarrow which I recognized from the mangled state I espied under the voluminous white sheet with which it was covered. Protesting volubly with rattles and squeaks the apparatus declared its displeasure at having its retirement from the garden shed so rudely disturbed.

"It's the rose I was sure" I thought, then alarm bells rang, knowing my brother's humour.

"What's happening David?" then turning to face everyone.

"It's a joke, you're teasing me!"

"Caterine" David addressed me face solemn. "It's no joke. Eyes closed, please. Count to five, then open them."

I smiled but closed my eyes.

"One, two, three, four, five" opening them still amused.

The amusement turned to disbelief. That garden wheelbarrow still shocked from years of labour stood smiling before me, bedecked in fancy paper ribbon and a bouquet of flowers: but that was the least of it. In the middle almost grinning at me was that exquisite Scottish oak chair.

I stared again dumbfounded, then remembered.

But it went to a foreigner, a bargain at auction. Why is it here?

David came over to kiss me.

"Happy Birthday Petite. Maman knew from Murdoch how much you loved the chair so she went to the auction and bought it for me to present to you. Bravo Maman!"

"A pleasure David, but I'll add this comment – the next time I see Murdoch I'll take him apart. Saying to Caterine the chair had been sold to a foreigner and me with a Scottish grandmother." She hesitated "as for a bargain, well I did a bit of haggling!"

Everyone laughed aware of Maman's tenacity but I was I recall still standing nonplussed.

"Hey, Petite, don't you like it? Shall I take it back?" David inquired.

"No way, no way" I shouted as I ran over to kiss him tears re-emerging in my eyes.

He lifted that antique chair out of the wheelbarrow and placed it on the cinnamon carpet. I touched the oak relishing the quality and the love which had been endowed in its creation.

The cork erupted, champagne opened to embrace a memorable party.

On Sunday after "brunch" at 11.00 am, Grégoire and I went for a long walk in the adjoining woodland bordering on Jimmy Black's farm. There was of course another reason "Marchmont" with its five bedrooms could not accommodate the whole family of eight plus Alix unless we had resorted to unconventional sleeping arrangements!

Therefore plans were put in place similar to previous years whereby my aunt, uncle, Grégoire and Marie-Françoise including any other guests took advantage from farmer Black to overfill into a cosy well appointed cottage on his land, let out from time to time over the summer tourist season.

As I had serviced it during school holidays to earn extra funds, I still retained a back door key.

It was a passionate hour but for Grégoire, not passionate enough!

"Come on Caterine, we're not going to do anything irresponsible, I just want to feel your skin next to mine" he murmured mouth caressing mine, hands moving under my angora sweater, brassiere expertly unhooked, exploring, seeking, finding.

Every part of my body tingled, alive with sensations I never knew existed. Now I was half naked pulling open Grégoire's shirt, burying my head in the dark hairs of his chest desperate for more, much more.

"No!" I cried out "that's enough," pulling my sweater down flushed, breathless, escaping to the loo.

Body still throbbing, I looked at myself in the mirror: face crimson, sweater askew and my hair wild, a tangled mane. I restored some order, bathed my face and apprehensively returned to the lounge.

Grégoire was sitting back on the sofa, flicking through some magazines arranged on the walnut coffee table. He looked cool, almost debonair, certainly unfazed. I was furious. Pent up emotion and frustration manifested itself in a loss of temper.

"Is that all you can do, read a magazine as if nothing's wrong" I said voice rising "after what you were trying to do!"

Grégoire turned towards me and sighed.

"I was only doing what we both wanted, chérie."

"What do you mean by that. You don't know what I wanted." I protested standing beside that little table strewn with its reading material and boasting as a centre piece a handsome poinsettia plant.

Grégoire rose walking to the window to open the drawn curtains, our basic precaution.

"Petite" he replied using that absurd family nickname, a further irritation for me.

"I do know what you wanted, your body was vibrant, trembling but I'd forgotten you're just 18 and inexperienced while I'm 23 and not. Perhaps I moved too fast but it can wait."

Incensed at what I saw as a patronizing attitude I erupted.

"Merde, Bloody Hell. Who do you think you are" I hesitated casting round my mind for a name and finding it "James Bond?"

Flashing one of his disarming grins, Grégoire replied.

"Not exactly, but you're still a virgin while I'm not. That's the difference."

I stared at him dumbfounded as realization struck home. What a fool I had been. I saw myself as a woman, but not enough woman for him. Sinking into the sofa I felt completely deflated.

"Yes" I murmured "I see."

There was silence.

Trying to regain some dignity I said.

"OK. I understand. I'm sure you'll find someone else soon enough."

Before I could finish he was pulling me up from the sofa, arms around me, kissing away the tears before they took hold.

"Caterine, chérie, you didn't listen. You're the one I want. I told you. I can wait."

Fingers entwined we wandered back to "Marchmont".

That night, in the shower, I thought about the incident. Heavens, we were approaching the last decade of the 20th century. Social values had changed and women emancipated, academically and financially independent. I'd put myself on the pill and also consult Maman; she was liberal in her thinking and I knew she'd agree.

I recalled a conversation with her when I was 16 and had just read some current sexy best-seller literally under the bed clothes.

The next day I had asked her boldly about love: the mental and more importantly as I saw it, the physical element of the mysterious union between man and woman or was it woman and man?

Maman was not fazed.

"With lovers it takes time Petite" she had told me "like playing the finest of musical instruments. You have to practice become attuned find a common rhythm specially for the woman. More sensitive to timing more than the man" she had smiled at me and continued : "Of course sometimes that sexual chemistry ignites and then there is no adjustment an indescribable explosion of desire and lust."

Maman had come over to the sofa where I was sitting putting her arm around me. "Such a little word 'love' yet probably the most complicated in our language. The ideal of course for a man and a woman is to love and be in love with each other plus one other addition to the equation"

"What's that?" I asked looking into those large aquamarine eyes.

"A dash of wicked lust" and she winked.

We collapsed in mirth. How close we were then.

On Tuesday morning, all the family gathered together at Papa's request. He was seated in his favourite chintz armchair its pattern depicting images of Scottish heroes in ancient folklore, brown brogues resting on the worn footstool inherited from Grandpa Sinclair.

"Right, everyone" he began staring down at his jade green personal organizer, a Christmas present from me.

"Thierry, you're off tomorrow and Véronique's driving you to the airport?"

"Yes, Angus, stopping over in Paris," he hesitated adding

with a pained expression "the ladies have planned some shopping! We'll return to our Bergerac farmhouse on Friday. Thanks again for the use of your Montparnasse apartment. It certainly saves on hotel bills."

"Nonsense" Papa replied "we've benefited from many low flight prices which you've advised us of in our travels."

"And Alix and I leave tomorrow also" David confirmed "two days in Invernesshire with her family and back to Switzerland on Friday afternoon for the Easter weekend."

"So that leaves you and me, Petite, toiling away at our chosen profession while other family members pursue their pleasures!"

"Yes" I sighed in response "but some of us must work so they can afford to indulge them!"

Papa laughed amid much protesting.

He and I were travelling on the following morning by train together to Stirling; he to a lecture course he was conducting and me to an external university seminar to be held at a hotel just outside the town.

"Well" Papa continued "I think I've found, hopefully, some pleasure for you, Caterine."

I turned to face him in anticipation.

"Half an hour ago I received a phone call from a former university friend of mine, Peter Strang. I had found out he had become a director of Dunn's the renowned Fine Arts house with its HQ in London. Hearing of your aspirations, he's invited both of us for lunch on Friday to discuss future options for you. Coincidentally, he lives in Doune, just outside Stirling."

"Papa, that's brilliant" I cried out running over to throw my arms round his neck enveloping him in a hug.

I looked over at Maman who was smiling. She had known already.

Lunch was a diverse effort: David and Alix were visiting

mutual friends, my uncle and aunt had invited Papa and Maman to eat at a local gourmet restaurant while Grégoire and I were to dine with the Black family, with their guest of honour in attendance on the lawn, the pony Daisy!

The evening started energetically at 5pm with the singles' final of our table tennis competition. The doubles had been won, surprisingly by Papa and David beating Marie-Françoise and Grégoire. The singles' final was between my brother and me: I was determined to wreak revenge.

It was very close, best of three games, we were one each and deuce. As David and I changed ends Grégoire whispered some advice and I took it, after fortunately winning the next point which was crucial.

"OK, David, that's it, game over."

"What do you mean, there's another point to play" he replied irritated.

"Yes, I know, but you're tensed up. I can see it, unlike you, normally so relaxed."

David muttered under his breath and served: straight into the net!

What fun and laughter for everyone including my brother. My prize was a bottle of Papa's vintage champagne!

The meal that evening after our extravagant lunches was a light supper of vegetable consommé, plus cold cuts, salmon mayonnaise and salad.

Just as we were gathering for our traditional aperitifs I heard the unusual tone of the hall phone.

"I'll answer it" David called as Papa continued to prepare our drinks.

Several minutes later David appeared looking very concerned.

"That was Gildas. He can't come with Isabella to spend Easter in Switzerland."

"Why not?" Alix exclaimed "What's the problem?"

"They've just received a message that his younger brother, you all remember Frédéric, suffered an injury to his head and leg during a rugby tournament in Toulouse. They're en route there now. Isabella phoned from the car."

"My God" Papa and Maman exclaimed together with Maman adding

"Have they no details, none at all?"

"Sketchy" David replied "although Gildas told me Frédéric has regained consciousness and appears lucid, so that's a relief, but as for the leg injury, no more information. I've told him we'll call tomorrow. They'll only arrive in Toulouse late tonight."

Papa came round with his tray of drinks, serving all of us.

"I suggest a toast. To Frédéric, a speedy recovery."

We all said. "D'accord, santé!"

I sat pondering for a moment about this man Gildas and his wife Isabella. After their meeting at a European environment conference, David had become close friends with this French count. Papa and Maman had stayed last year in his historical chateau on the Loire and returned in raptures at the welcome and hospitality. As yet I had not met him or his wife.

"You like this man, don't you David, you too Papa" I announced suddenly, interrupting family chatter "and yet neither of you is a fan of the aristocracy. Why?"

Papa and David exchanged glances, smiling, Maman, usually vociferous stayed silent.

"Well, put it this way" David said, "Gildas does not consider himself an aristocrat. That to him would be laughable. He's a businessman, entrepreneur, albeit shouldering his father's mantle earlier than anticipated and very successful at it as I've heard!"

David lifted his glass of malt whisky as if the subject was closed and turned to speak to Alix.

I glanced at Grégoire, regarding me keenly and continued my probing.

"What do you mean, doesn't regard himself as an aristocrat. He uses the title, Conte du Gilbert, it's on his notepaper, thick, white, starched notepaper. Maman showed me his last letter to the family"

There was a pause in the proceedings, then Papa intervened.

"Petite, why should Gildas not be proud of his ancestry? His forefathers walked in the footsteps of the kings of France. Are we not fiercely defendant of the realms of Alba and our Scottish heritage, proud of our Scotland as he is proud of his France?

I give you all a final toast – The Auld Alliance!"

Putting my glass down again I noticed Maman leaving to lay out the buffet supper in the dining room.

Rising to help her, I knocked over the small table on which my glass rested. Consequently the vermouth spilled onto our relatively new cinnamon carpet casting a blood red stain.

"I'll get it" I cried out, responding immediately. With sponge soaked in vinegar and water I caught the damage in time. The incident was forgotten : that was a mistake as it was a warning, but lost by me in the annals of time.

On Wednesday morning after a very early breakfast of porridge, eggs, tea and toast we said our farewells. Grégoire and I were not so sad as usual, because he would be returning in two weeks for my disco party.

By 10am, I was immersed in my seminar studies at the hotel while Papa was commencing his lecture programme at Stirling University.

My course, which was on option for second year Master of Arts Studies, was more demanding than I or my fellow scholars had anticipated. I relished that challenge, however, and found the preparatory work undertaken by me prior to the seminar was a bonus: to my surprise I achieved an A+ on the final test.

That work was important, even critical, not so much for me

but more for Papa. He had always assumed my studies would be in the sciences where I had shown promise at school. His vision had been a family quartet: he, the historian, Maman, the philosopher, David, the financier and me, the scientist. When I announced my career plans one of the quartet's strings had been broken!

I smiled to myself at this memory pulling my hotel bedroom curtains more closely together. It was a vile night, storm winds and heavy downpours, hailstones rattling against the window panes.

Yawning, I clambered into bed putting out my table light, looking forward to returning home, the disco and my university summer term. Events changed everything.

Sitting in the hotel foyer the following morning, rucksack beside me, I glanced at my watch 09.45. Minutes before Mr Strang was collecting me. As I was leafing through some fashion magazines, chaos erupted in the vestibule and a young boy, ten or eleven years, raced towards the reception desk, screaming.

"Dad's on fire, do something, an accident, we need a doctor, an ambulance." He started sobbing hysterically.

The hotel manager was at the desk and wasted no time, albeit unsure of the circumstances, in phoning 999.

Grabbing his mobile, he told his assistant:

"Jack, keep in touch while I determine the location and give directions to the emergency services. Find out through the intercom if there's a doctor registered as a guest."

"Come on young man, take me to your Dad."

"I can help" I shouted running with him to the door "I've first aid training."

"Right" he replied "let's move fast."

Sealed in my memory for life, I shall never forget that scene of horror.

In a field less than a quarter of a mile from the country hotel we found the burnt out wreckage of a vehicle with a man kneeling beside it, rocking backwards and forwards moaning with pain.

"Daddy, Daddy" the boy cried out.

"I'm all right son, I'm OK"

"Thank God" I thought as we reached him, although his hands were badly blistered.

Father and son clung to each other, the boy sobbing.

The hotel manager responded to his mobile confirming the location of the accident.

"Help is on is way" he assured the boy's father, just a few minutes. You've had a lucky escape."

"Escape? That poor bugger had no chance to escape. Burned to death in front of my eyes. I tried to save him, never forget his screams of pain as the flames enveloped him. It could have been us, my son and me. We were following him, then rounding the bend saw the fallen tree. He swerved immediately but the car skidded, through the hedge, somersaulted and burst into flames: he was cremated alive. What a hell of a death!"

In abhorrence, the manager and I turned to look at that charcoaled wreckage. Together, without a word spoken, we recognized the outline, blackened embers of a human corpse.

Out of the driver's window hung a charred branch as from the tree, its twigs grotesquely twisted in five points like a human hand.

In fact it had been a hand but now all that was left was a gold signet ring. A ring which had survived that inferno.

That signet ring belonged to my Papa.

Chapter Two

Perhaps it is a cliché but, on reflection, life was never quite the same again.

Papa, it transpired arrived at Peter Strang's house early, his morning lecture cancelled owing to a power cut at the university. Planning a surprise he had borrowed Peter's car to collect me personally.

David returned from Invernesshire immediately while Alix remained with her parents.

"I could not intrude on the depth of your family's grief" she had told my brother "but if you need me I'm here."

Oncle Thierry, Tante Sylvie, Grégoire and Marie-Françoise arrived at their Bergerac farmhouse on Friday at lunchtime and literally reversed their tracks on receiving the news. I understand from Grégoire's description to me later, none of them took time to sit down.

I fell into his arms when they reappeared on our doorstep late that same evening.

"I've no words chérie," Grégoire had said softly voice muffled clasping me in his arms trying to qualm his own emotions. I had rested my head on his chest my tears brimming over creating damp circles on his blue cotton shirt. All the family had been contacted but uncle Fergus, Papa's brother and aunt Bebe who were on a touring holiday in Australia. It was several days before David reached them with the tragic news. They booked on the first flight available.

David and I were desperately worried about Maman. Icy cold to our touch she remained for the most part motionless as a statue not a tear shed. We consulted our family doctor but she refused to see him.

"Your parents were very close?" he enquired of David and me as we sat in his surgery.

"Exceptionally" my brother replied.

"Then I can offer you only my deepest sympathy. There's no medical cure."

"Time?" David looked up hopefully.

"Perhaps the only one. It depends. You see she's lost direction living in a vacuum, feeling nothing. There are many forms of grief. I'm afraid your mother is wandering down a …" he hesitated "difficult path."

In fact the word was dangerous but he refrained from using it. He shook his head "I wish I could be more encouraging."

David and I left the surgery with me in tears and him, arm around me, grim face set in silence.

At the private service for Papa where family members and close friends had gathered I stood next to David on one side of me and Grégoire on the other both holding my hand, their support staunch knowing I wanted to be dignified for Papa. The swift thrust of throbbing pain I felt on seeing Papa's coffin just like a dagger blow to my heart still sears my memory.

Maman could not attend.

For some illogical reason during that service I recalled my discussion with Papa in the rose garden at Marchmont when he had apologised to me over the circumstances of Daisy's rescue.

"Before and After" he had reflected "words of two syllables

in the English language but of such poignancy in their simplicity and in their compounds."

How right he had been in his wisdom.

Consequently David's life and mine for those insane weeks following the death of Papa fell into two categories. "Before and After." Maman remained in "before" warped in time unable to commit. David and I were forced to commit immerged in the aftermath.

The world goes on, family, friends, with colleagues in tow, paid their respects, issued their sympathy and left to look after their one lives and why not, they too had their loved ones, jobs and responsibilities. That's life but for David and me it was war. That was what we were waging, a war of emotional attrition facing the enemy of appeasers from within and outwith the family who thought Maman should be placed in some form of institution of a recuperating nature or "aftercare" as one member described it in some attempt at euphony. We were appalled.

From Oncle Thierry and Tante Sylvie with received a magnanimous gesture; a retreat for Maman with loving care and attention at their home in Bergerac. It was agreed by all of us that she might benefit from the environment of their 18th century farmhouse nestling in woods, east of Bordeaux.

Therefore when I returned to my Glasgow university studies in April, Maman was living in France.

Further, there had been another development.

During the first year of our degrees, Shona (who was reading French and German) and I stayed in the students halls of residence, then shared a flat in Glasgow's west end – we nicknamed it "KG". The rental had been nominal as ironically it was part of a family legal dispute over a contested estate.

"I suggest you buy it, Petite, now I've discovered the sale details, a sound investment" David had advised me.

We were sitting in the apartment the day before my return

to the university. David was departing for Zurich the following morning.

"But buying it using Papa's money. I'm not sure that's right," I replied voice faltering.

David turned from the bay window overlooking the Botanical Gardens.

"It's your money, Papa's legacy to you and how he would have wished you to invest it wisely"

"Property, young man that's what you buy, bricks and mortar" Papa always told me.

"He was astute on that score, hence the plans: keeping Marchmont as our family home and Montparnasse plus my intention to purchase another apartment in Zurich to rent out."

"If you say so David. I'll always follow your advice."

My brother grinned: "No Caterine, consider it and then make your own decision. Sometimes it's the hard way but the only way to learn. Now on a practical note the family will chip in with bits of furniture etc. everyone's attic is groaning under the excess. Just think of Marchmont. You can trawl the second hand shops with Shona but remember one rule, no woodworm."

I laughed "no way, anything we might buy will be checked out. Promise."

"OK" David replied smiling. "Of course Shona's rent will pay for your living costs and if I feel generous I might just contribute to the carpets and curtains. Sounds a good deal to me. Agreed?!

I stared then realised what he had said and ran over to give him for a change my effort at a bear hug. We laughed together as he lifted me up spinning me in the air. I loved him so very much. God forbid if anything happened to him.

That same evening David treated me to a pre-theatre dinner and an evening of classical music at the glorious Glasgow concert hall. It was a varied programme, Mendelssohn,

Moussorgski, Sibelius, Dvorak, Vivaldi and Beethoven, a plethora of pleasure.

We stayed overnight with the former head of my brother's law faculty Professor Corbett and his family.

The professor informed me: "Don't believe a word David tells you Caterine. Far from a model student he was always causing ructions as president of the students' union or burying opposing team members in the rugby matches, that I can applaud but also on several occasions lurking suspiciously with some female counterpart in the cloisters. Usually to everyone's envy the best looking."

"Now just a minute" David began looking alarmed but he was drowned by everyone's hysterical laughter.

Unexpectedly for me, the summer term of my second year became a titanic struggle about mind over matter. On the first few days my friends were confused not wishing to upset me and not knowing what to say. I received hugs from the females and sympathetic glances from the males with the occasional pat on the back, but everyone seemed bereft of words. I felt like an outcast.

"They don't know how to handle it" Shona told me on that first weekend we spent at K.G.

"What do you mean" I retorted "Papa's dead, killed in a car accident. Can't they just say 'sorry'!"

I was washing up after our lasagne supper which I knew was below par, prepared by me without any interest in cooking it.

"Caterine, your Papa was an eminent man, renowned worldwide as a historian and a mountaineer. There has been unprecedented publicity, all over the media. Look what you have to endure. Television crews parked at Marchmont, family history recounted in the press, you mum's depression and that horrendous photo of the car wreckage" she stopped suddenly.

"I don't need photos" I reminded her "I was there."

"My God, what am I saying, I'm so sorry" Shone started to sob.

Tears streaming down my own face I ran over to hug that stalwart friend of mine. We clung together with images of times past and present vividly in our minds.

In silence we retired to our bedrooms.

However I could not sleep, fear engulfed me: not again, surely not again that nightmare! It occurred always at the weekend and always on a Friday. Strangely, the car wreckage was not the picture I saw: it was Papa's smiling face distorting in horror as it slowly, so agonisingly slowly became enveloped in flames.

And I was responsible no doubt about it, even the press had highlighted it. I remembered the quote verbatim as if I was not already aware of it.

"How specially tragic for Caterine Sinclair that her father drove personally to collect her on that unfamiliar route which the locals with knowledge of past storm hazards would have avoided!"

On that Friday evening I managed to waken before I started to scream.

By the middle of May I was becoming concerned. My class exam marks had fallen from consistent "As" even A+ and A++ to B-. I was malfunctioning, distraught and alone at K.G. Shona by spending a month in Germany as part of her degree course.

Naturally David phoned me constantly as well as Tante Sylvie to advise me of Maman's progress. In fact there was none. And Grégoire, dearest Grégoire, how I longed to be in his arms again.

"Chérie, how are you coping? What about your work?" were his constant entreaties.

"Fine Grégoire, I'm OK chéri" I told him the same lies I told David.

It was at this critical time I received a message to visit our Faculty head of staff, Professor Donald Cameron. An appointment was arranged ironically on a Friday at 5pm. As I walked to his rooms after my English antiques seminar I reflected about this unusual man and his vision which had prevailed to create the Masters Degree, a new development at Glasgow University. It combined the faculties of Fine Arts and Art History, specialising in the history of antiques including ceramics, sculpture, paintings, architecture as well as ancient Egyptian and oriental antiquities.

It was a vast subject and opposition had been encountered as to the wisdom of its foundation but Cameron was tenacious. The youngest Dean of any faculty in a UK university, his vision became reality.

"Miss Sinclair" he greeted me "please be seated."

He was not at all handsome, plain almost, thin featured, narrow faced with a mass of unkempt blond hair emerging from his scalp in shock waves, yet a film star smile. You forgot everything when he smiled but an act rarely performed. He was a task master. All the students were in awe of him for he commanded total commitment, no prisoners taken. Unknown to me on that day he became a major influence in my life.

Blunt as always he came straight to the point.

"Your class exam marks have slumped dramatically recently. Can you explain why?"

My heart sank as I had anticipated the question but had no answer. To have blamed my guilt and my grief would have been gutless lacking in character.

"I'm not sure" I stuttered "I seem to lack concentration."

There was a silence as Cameron walked over to the stained glass windows which looked onto the university cloisters.

"Perhaps lack of commitment might be more accurate" he replied turning to face me.

I swallowed, unable to offer any response and desperate not

to dissolve into self-indulgent tears and make a fool of myself.

He continued "Miss Sinclair, I do not wish to raise the subject of your family tragedy. It has been well documented by the media, bloody ghouls, all of them."

I was taken aback, never heard him swear.

"Suffice to add, I never had the honour of meeting your father, knew him only by repute, an exceptional man. From my observations you may have inherited some his talents. I stress the word 'may'. However, you will never find out if you dwell in the past. Let me offer you some advice. Look forwards not backwards, just like an experienced mountaineer and scale those horizons as did your father."

He walked forward and shook my hand.

"Good luck in you future studies."

I left his rooms in a daze, nonplussed. He was indeed a very unusual man.

Returning to K.G. I slumped into an armchair of the suite which I had salvaged from the Marchmont loft.

"What had prompted Professor Cameron to take the trouble to offer that advice. Then I remembered his introductory lecture to my class as first year students. It had been a revelation, unorthodox its summation in similar mode.

"In this faculty there is a dress code" he announced. Every pair of male and female eyes opened if possible in further astonishment. "Jeans of any description are banned"

"Silence" he barked at loud verbal protest holding up his hand to stem rebuke.

"Male students will wear trousers, shirts, collar and tie, jacket or sweater optional. The kilt, of course, with similar accompanying apparel, is most welcome."

A few titters of laughter rippled through the lecture hall from their female counterparts seeing the utter disbelief on the faces of their male colleagues. This amusement was short lived!

"Female students, however, will not wear trousers. Skirts and blouses or dresses at your liberty, jackets or sweaters optional. Once again kilts in the form of kilted skirts welcome." Stunned silence prevailed.

"I will add" he continued "that the rule of no trousers for female students is not from any warped desire of mine to view the limbs of the female anatomy. With respect, I would doubt if any pair of legs here is of a high enough standard to merit a second glance from me."

Gasps now from the conceited female students' element.

I found myself amused.

Cameron continued "The reason for this code of dress is simple. You will be studying subjects by Masters of the Arts. We owe it to them to reflect these high standards in our apparel.

Finally and perhaps most importantly the main door of my rooms is always open for any problem academic or otherwise. Make use of it. If justified your concerns will receive my full attention."

That statement interested me, profound, perhaps the measure of the man.

"For all of you I wish a studious year, a year also of pleasure in your work and a year of which you will be proud."

He nodded his head as in a formal bow and withdrew.

Afterwards, an outcry, rebellion and a meeting with the President of the Students Union where outraged protests were voiced.

"This is ludicrous, a dress code! For heavens sake, we're nearing the end of the 20th century, not the beginning. Who does he think he is? Some kind of God!" exclaimed a glamorous, natural blonde dressed in an aquamarine wool designer trouser suit.

"A skirt. I've only brought trousers" wailed a second female student clothed contrastingly in a well-seasoned grubby brown example of her wardrobe.

"No jeans, he must be mad, that's all I wear" was the general male consensus.

The President a Senior Honours Law student and favourite for the Faculty department top prize answered succinctly.

"Challenge him at your peril. Speaking from bitter experience, I can assure you Cameron will win!"

Consequently, we became the best-dressed Faculty at the university. After initial jibes and ribald statements, criticism from other Faculties died. Standards were set and we became an elite not by privilege but by merit, respected, the Faculty of Faculties of which we all became proud.

Cameron had won!

On impulse, after these reflections, I rose walking purposefully to the kitchen. Opening the fridge I removed that bottle of vintage champagne which I had won at Marchmont, uncorked it and chose a crystal champagne flute, a set of which had been an 18th birthday present from Shona and her family.

Returning to the lounge I said out aloud

"Santé Papa". During the following hour I downed all of it.

The nightmares disappeared but unfortunately the guilt remained.

Towards the end of June I received my 2nd year exam results. On the six set papers spread over three days I achieved straight A's : three with A++. I sighed with relief. I was back from a virtual abyss.

The following day on the eve of the end of term Shona and I set about cleaning the flat and emptying the fridge prior to our departure on vacation.

"I'm so excited" Shona exclaimed "spending a week with Gerald (her boyfriend who was studying medicine in London). It'll be super to have time to ourselves without parental interference in the south of Spain."

"Well" I replied "not too much sangria or you might find yourself in the local surgery, nursing a hangover!"

There was a pregnant pause.

"And you Caterine, back to France. Any better news of your Mum. I didn't want to ask" she hesitated "you've said nothing."

"Nothing to say, Shona, no change. But it's early days, just a few months. We must give her time. Come on we've work to do and then make final arrangements for our dinner out tomorrow."

"OK, let's get moving!" she smiled.

Whistling I tried to sound cheerful but the truth was David and I were very worried about Maman.

At this point the phone rang and I answered it.

"That was Professor Cameron. Wants to see me. Heavens what is it this time?" I exclaimed exasperated.

"He could have spoken to me after this morning's final lecture!"

"On you go, I'll finish up" Shona replied.

Muttering to myself, I grabbed the cotton jacket for my trouser suit and set off for his rooms.

"My God" I thought en route "Cameron's dress code, no trousers for female students. Just too bad, I was not returning to change!" This was after all leisure time.

"Miss Sinclair" he greeted me "what a fine June day to bless our magnificent university and exceptional Scottish countryside."

I muttered agreement, astonished. He was almost jovial,

In fact, today, well dressed as always in a three piece beige linen suit sporting a spotted maroon tie with matching handkerchief; he actually looked dapper.

"It must be a woman" I thought "or perhaps a man?"

At 32, I knew he was unmarried.

"Please be seated. Well it was a close call but you responded in time, exam results just good enough."

Just good enough! Heavens, although I'd told no-one, not even Shona what the marks were, in fact I'd played them down, I knew they were the best in my year."

"I think the news deserves a celebratory drink. Which malt is your preference?" he asked opening an antique cabinet which contained at least 30 bottles, in actual alphabetical order, of an incredible array of Scottish whiskies.

I began to wonder if I was dreaming.

"Keep calm" I told myself. I knew he was considered somewhat eccentric but this was ridiculous.

"Talisker" I replied amusing myself "he can't stock it." But he did.

"Excellent choice from the Isle of Skye. I'll join you!"

Handing me my glass, he raised his own.

"Slainthe, you're the first recipient of the Gilmour bursary."

Before I could absorb what Cameron meant, he continued.

"Of course, much extra work is involved but your pursuit of it means a Doctorate will be at your fingertips just four years after commencing this course."

I was dumbfounded. Everyone had heard of Bartholomew Gilmour: a millionaire businessman and native of Glasgow, he was also a philanthropist and patron of the arts. In learning of the plans of Donald Cameron for this Masters Degree, he had lent his considerable eminence to the cause; however I was completely unaware of his funding for this or any award.

"I'm very honoured, thank you" I stumbled out. "Have you any information about the format?"

"Yes, of course" Cameron replied pulling out a dossier from his desk, with a sheaf of documents, albeit impatiently.

"Peruse these tonight and if any doubt consult your family and me again. Gilmour and I concurred on choosing you. There's no other candidate."

Shaking my hand, he flashed his Hollywood smile "I await your confirmation tomorrow."

Shona and I studied the details when I returned to K.G., very excited.

It was a superb opportunity, university fees paid, free

travel and accommodation throughout Europe to specialist courses, further studies and research. The work load was immense but the rewards phenomenal. I phoned David. He was thrilled for me.

There was a problem, time – no time for anything or anyone else.

I also phoned Grégoire : he was generous in his congratulations but very aware of the restrictions for us.

Shona and I said our farewells at Glasgow International airport.

"Take care, Caterine. Give my love to all your family."

"And mine to yours" I replied as we hugged each other. "We'll keep in touch during the summer."

Just after checking in at the British Airways desk for Bordeaux, the nearest airport for Bergerac, I heard myself being hailed.

"Miss Sinclair, Caterine Sinclair!"

I turned in surprise which changed swiftly to horror.

Three men were running towards me whom I did not recognise but their equipment was instantly familiar.

Abandoning my trolley I raced for the Internationals Departure gate. I was fast, 100 metres school record holder, but was impeded by the combination of increasing passenger traffic plus my cumbersome briefcase containing weighty literature presented to me by Professor Cameron.

"For God's sake" one elderly man shouted at me as I pushed past him in panic "you youngsters nowadays have no respect" but I kept running, ignoring the comments and expletives in absolute desperation.

Suddenly a man blocked my path offering no escape.

"Miss Sinclair, your problem is being taken care of. I'm the Airport Manager. Please come with me."

Breathless, I stared at him and then the identification badge on his lapel. I turned round. My erstwhile pursuers were surrounded by airport police.

Minutes later I was seated in his private office sipping a welcome espresso while he issued instructions on the phone. I felt weak, hand trembling, but so relieved to be rescued, but why?

"Miss Sinclair" the manager addressed me, "I knew your late father who passed through this airport frequently on his travels. He was an exceptional man: brilliant of mind, but also of spirit and a gentleman, rare in someone with his talents, from my experience.

Inadequate as it may sound, I can offer to you and your family only our deepest condolences from myself and the Glasgow Airport personnel."

I swallowed, blinking away those childish tears stuttering "Thank you and for rescuing me."

"No need to apologise. Unfortunately, your departure date coincided with a European cup tie, hence the camera crew. Unfortunately you're easily recognisable."

There was a knock at the door.

"That's Ian, my deputy. He'll escort you to the V.I.P. lounge and here is my card. In future please advise me if you or any members of your family are travelling via Glasgow Airport: I will ensure you receive the same service."

I was still in shock when we reached the V.I.P. lounge. Ian smiled to me sympathetically as he installed me in a corner chair.

"Anything else, Miss Sinclair, coffee, tea, a sandwich?"

I was about to choose when a word entered my mind, a word used by both Professor Cameron and the airport manager to describe Papa, that word was "exceptional". What answer would Papa have given in these circumstances? I asked myself and I knew.

"Thank you again, Ian, for accompanying me here but you've more important duties. I'll just help myself."

Standing up, I wandered nonchalantly over to the buffet

table, as if it was an everyday occurrence and to the other occupants' astonishment, all male, I poured myself a glass of champagne.

That could have been the day when the seed of ambition took roots.

I'll always remember that summer of 1989 as a paradox. The climate was stifling, oppressive and hot as the proverbial Hell; but our family Hell was the opposite. Greetings, once so warm turned cool, conversation stilted, unnatural and Maman remained like a pale marble statue, cold, immovable.

The events over that period following our appalling tragedy cast such shadows of sorrow that hope and light were extinguished for all of us. We were rendered lifeless as a family, like puppets with taut strings incapable of any animation.

During my visit to Bergerac the strings began to snap.

"Come on, we must find some solution, David. We are at our wits' end. Tried everything."

It was Oncle Thierry speaking.

I peered out from my sanctuary on the curtained window seat, two days after my arrival, where I had been toying with a book. He was running his fingers through his bushy grey hair very agitated.

"Thierry, I've consulted specialists after specialists. You know that. You've seen most of them here. Plus I've Caterine to consider and the administration of Papa's estate. The family lawyer is an idiot, out his depth. He should have been dumped years ago. Papa was far too sentimental."

"I still think you could have done more." Uncle Thierry continued looking exasperated.

"Such as what? Give up my job? Unlike you I've a living to earn."

"Just a minute David. I resent that. We've had to cope with Véronique. God knows we love her dearly but Sylvie is exhausted and"

"Please Thierry" Tante Sylvie interrupted looking anxiously from my uncle to my brother.

"You know you are" Oncle Thierry retorted voice roused "it's all over your face. We need a private nurse."

"Then bloody well get one and don't worry you won't be picking up the bill" David shouted in anger pacing up and down in front of the 18th century fireplace. "We can well afford it. But Maman's not staying here. I'll find a solution. God forbid if it's an institution."

"Never" I cried out pushing back the curtains and emerging from my hidden corner. "I'll look after Maman. It's my fault Papa's dead.

Everyone stared in total shock at my unexpected appearance. Although trembling I stood defiant centre stage. Then I could not contain my pent-up grief dissolving into tears stumbling into David's arms as he ran to catch me in his familiar bear hug reminiscent of earlier happy times.

"My God Thierry it shouldn't have come to this."

"I'm appalled David and apologise …… it's my fault."

"Rubbish. I'm equally to blame" my brother replied.

During these family exchanges I tried to regain some composure. How selfish of me to create more trauma and exacerbate the present circumstances.

"I'm sorry for the outburst" I began

"Nonsense" Oncle Thierry interrupted "we're all a little overwrought. Come on Sylvie let's open that special cognac. We'll all benefit from it! It's in the cellar."

David, arms still round my shoulder, grey eyes looking concerned added, as my aunt and uncle departed.

"Caterine, you must not blame yourself for Papa's death. He was killed in a car accident, a tragic accident, after atrocious weather conditions; no one could have avoided that lightning damaged tree."

"Yes, David, I know" I replied but the guilt remained.

Over the cognac decisions were taken. Maman was to return to Marchmont with my uncle and aunt in charge while a specialist, Dr Callum Baxter, recommended to David would oversee her treatment.

"And now our surprise, Petite" David announced.

"What's that?" I asked.

"Tomorrow, you and I are off to Acacia to meet mutual friends joining us for a week."

"What friends? Who are they?"

"Alix and Grégoire" he replied grinning.

That night I slept well.

It was indescribable, that feeling, when I saw him again loping stride, wavy dark hair and mischievous grin. David and I collected Alix and him from the local station and I almost, not quite, but almost felt happy again. We all hugged each other and chattering together drove back to that family farmhouse. Grégoire and I were left, deliberately, to our own devices. We played tennis, swam in the pool, went horse riding at the local stables and walked for miles along those secluded country lanes.

"I've missed you so much Caterine chérie, sorry I couldn't be at Bergerac last week but my science course was compulsory, critical for my degree."

"Yes I know Grégoire and you've always been in touch, such a support, I don't know how I'd have coped without you, David and the family."

We spent three days of perfection together at Acacia then circumstances dramatically changed.

"Right" David shouted "We're off and lunching at the golf club. Should return about 6pm." "Enjoy yourselves" Alix added smiling.

I was concerned. Grégoire had been in an odd mood it had developed late the previous evening and that morning he had been quiet, almost the Scottish 'dour'.

42

"All right Grégoire?" David had asked him at breakfast, as Alix and I cleared the plates.

"Pardon. Oh yes" he had faked a grin "just mulling over the summer course. Probably I could have done better."

"I wouldn't worry. You'll always give it your best shot. Don't waste time in morbid post mortems. More coffee" David had enquired. Grégoire nodded and I had poured everyone another cup.

After David and Alix left I washed up the breakfast dishes, tidied the kitchen and loaded the laundry into the machine. Grégoire had disappeared.

Had I done or said something to upset him. Usually we discussed everything. Heavens I thought he can't really be concerned about his course. Glancing at my watch I saw it was almost 10am, I studied the bookshelves choosing a volume on Renaissance painting and wandered out to sit under the oak abri on the west side of the park removing my t-shirt and shorts ready to jump into the pool in my bikini if it became too hot.

About an hour later Grégoire appeared

"Hi, I was looking for you. What are you reading?" He seemed back to normal and I was relieved.

"Oh, a boring book, not for a budding scientist like you" I smile "on Renaissance architecture."

"Really? Many illustrations?"

"Of course" I replied pointing out some of them to him.

It was another very oppressive day, tiny black flies had appeared punctuating the hazy atmosphere like a moving mass of commas and semi-colons. The emerald lawn surrounding the white patio flagstones had been eroded now just a patchwork of faded shades, apologies for green some areas turned already light brown parched desperately seeking some moisture from that unrelenting cloudless sky.

"Mon Dieu, it's hot" Grégoire said. Rousing himself from

his recent lethargy he jumped up suddenly: "Come on. I'll teach you the butterfly like I promised."

"OK" I shouted diving in after him racing up the pool refreshed by its shimmering water although it must have been at a temperature of 30 degrees C.

"God it's difficult" I gasped after my third attempt at a length.

"Use more arm power and your legs are still slowing you down" Grégoire called from the deep end. I paused breathless stretching my taut muscles and adjusting my bikini top not designed for such flagrant physical punishment and my generous 34 D cup. This time I nearly completed the length Grégoire catching me laughing as I became submerged again.

"Not bad, not bad at all. Right one more swim to the shallow end and then take a rest. Remember more arm power."

Muttering to myself I set off again. I made it! Grégoire was swimming alongside me and he stopped just before the steps at the shallow end.

"Well what about that" I said turning to face him grinning broadly.

He was staring at me with an expression I could not fathom. Suddenly I realised I was half naked my bikini top floating merrily past me to land and sun itself on the pool step. Grégoire pulled me towards me "Mon Dieu, you're gorgeous" his hands everywhere, mouth finding mine and I responded, arms thrown round his neck, skin next to skin, flesh against flesh. We fooled around together in the water with him chasing and then catching me a woman prisoner gasping and laughing as his hands and mouth explored my body again.

I felt a release, a freedom I had never known before flirting with and teasing him floating on my back and then diving down pretending to evade him and soon surrendering again to his touching explorations.

"Love you Chérie, want you so much."

"Me too Grégoire, me too" I replied kissing him again and again at the diving pool steps leaning forward provocatively so he could caress my body his head now buried in my breasts. I thought I was in heaven but I was actually approaching hell.

He pulled me into the water again and I raced ahead but he grabbed me. I turned laughing as he pressed himself against me hand inside my bikini pants trying to pull them down. Then I quickly realised he was naked swim shorts off.

"No Grégoire no please" I panicked pushing him away and swimming in a fast crawl to the shallow end breathless gasping staring at the abri in confusion. It had gone too far.

I closed my eyes as I heard him shouting at me voice raised in anger.

"You're just a tease, not interested in a man. Forget your university career. Join a bloody convent." He yelled finally as he ran from the abri into the house. I remember shivering despite the temperature shaking, shocked and semi destroyed. On reflection I'm not sure but maybe that's when my decision was made.

Of course we made up both apologising before David returned.

"I'm sorry Grégoire, just in a bit of a mess this year trying to get things right and also for us".

"Caterine, it's my fault. You've had a rotten time and I'm too impatient. Dreadful what I said. I was just so frustrated, wanting you so much."

Then the mischievous grin "One thing I can confirm"

"What's that?" I asked anxious again.

"With that body you'll never enter any convent." We laughed together and set off to prepare dinner, David and Alix were due back in an hour.

Later as I lay in bed I found Grégoire's description a confidence booster. I knew my body was an odd shape, out of proportion, no French model but Grégoire genuinely liked it and I loved him all the more for it.

Hugging my pillow, I turned over to dream of haute couture, the catwalk models and Paris, my favourite city in Europe. Unknown to me at 18 Paris was to become a major influence in my life.

Five days later we said our farewells. Grégoire returned by train to Bergerac, while Alix, David and I checked in at Charles de Gaulle. She flew to Zurich, my brother and me to Glasgow International airport. This time the manager was warned in advance!

Collecting the family jalopy we drove to Marchmont. The weather was cold, damp and uninviting although the forecast had predicted some sun. It never appeared; perhaps that reflected our mood.

Conversation, lively at Charles de Gaulle descended into anecdotal commentary during our flight culminating in silent despair before arriving home. Both of us fearful, deeply concerned for Maman.

David slowed down as we approached the house.

"What do you think, Caterine, the main gate or through the farm?"

I hesitated remembering all too vividly those imprisoned months when the media appeared permanently camped on our doorstep.

During that period we had accessed Marchmont through the adjacent field by a side gate parking our vehicle at the Blacks'farm. In fact this field belonged to our family home. Jimmy Black had approached Papa after he bought the property asking if he could rent it for grazing.

"Certainly not" our father had replied "I've a better proposal."

As a result Jimmy paid no rent and we received free milk and eggs plus a discount at the farm shop.

"Slainthe!" They came to the agreement over several malts!

"The farm" I answered, recalling my experience at Glasgow airport. It was a paranoid reaction but the safer option.

As it happened I was subjected to much media attention in my future life, thankfully, I was unaware of it at that time.

Oncle Thierry greeted us at the rear porch.

"You're both looking fine" he smiled at us falsely cheerful.

"Come and join our little family."

Maman was seated in the conservatory which faced south, the late summer sun had now appeared casting a warm cloak over the linen tapestry covers depicting events in Scottish history from ages past: but its glory failed to touch Maman. Even before she turned to greet us I saw there was no change. She sat shrunken in that chintz chair which seemed too large for her shrivelled frame. I bent over and kissed her pale chilled cheeks, her face gaunt and her aquamarine eyes now colourless, seemingly sightless with no hope of that enigmatic smile so beloved by us all. Fear and great sorrow for her pierced my heart and I remembered the last occasion I had felt like this. It was my first sight of Papa's coffin. I looked up at David my thoughts mirrored in his eyes. Maman stirred and then slowly recognised us.

"David, Caterine" stretching out her limp arms to embrace us both. She hesitated as if to form a sentence, such a testing task. "I had forgotten about your visit. I'm sorry."

I turned away pretending to admire that tranquil view of the Scottish countryside. Tears pricked my eyes as I gazed at our garden and in the foreground Papa's rose arbour with its columns of colour: apricot blending to other pastels, with interspersions of cream, soft lemon and virgin white transforming into those larger classic bushes of claret red and royal mauve. How Tante Sylvie had cared for those blooms I thought.

Meanwhile David replaced me kneeling beside Maman

speaking softly saying nothing in particular and so in fact saying it all.

We sat down to tea and despair.

After dinner Maman retired early little eaten less said. She tried. David and I knew she tried but it was pathetic to witness. She of that clever, witty turn of phrase could find nothing in her broken mind, her thoughts in pieces. It reminded me of one day seeing the beauty the workmanship the years of skill required to create some priceless piece of porcelain Sèvres or Limoges and the next to discover it shattered irreparable its ruptured remains on some funereal floor.

"We're at our wits ends" said Oncle Thierry running his fingers nervously through his bushy grey hair in a familiar gesture. Mr. Baxter saw Véronique this morning. He pointed out it's over four months since Angus's death as if we needed reminding, I wish Sylvie and I could have achieved more over those months in France. To see her like this, mon Dieu. For us it's devastating enough but for you."

He looked at us with such helplessness that I ran over from where I had been seated and kissed him tears in my eyes unable to speak.

"Oncle Thierry, Tante Sylvie" David said "no one could have offered Maman more. You provided her with love care and security. Caterine and I can never repay you for your efforts no money could buy. However we can't prevail on you much longer. As you know Caterine and I have a meeting with Mr. Baxter tomorrow afternoon and then we can decide the future plans. After all this was a temporary arrangement."

"David" Tante Sylvie interrupted "Thierry and I will stay on certainly for these coming months, this is no duty for us. It's love. Neither of us will be defeated. Somehow some way we must save her for you, for us but most of all for herself."

"Quite right" added Oncle Thierry "and anyway I need

more time to knock another stroke off my handicap." It was the first time we smiled since our arrival.

The consultancy rooms of Callum Stuart Baxter were housed in a Victorian drab grey sandstone edifice. I remember clearly the approach to that building with open fields to the south, the mid-afternoon sunshine smiled down on our car and then a turn north and the warmth evaporated sun gone as we parked outside that austere building: a devil of contrasts a sense of foreboding.

The receptionist greeted us and we followed her into a small anteroom with a tray prepared for self-service tea coffee and biscuits. By common consent the tray was left untouched.

After a few minutes Mr Baxter appeared and David and I shook hands with him.

"Good afternoon" he said in his usual abstracted manner "please join me in my consulting room."

He was a small dapper man about mid-forties dressed in a three piece dark blue suit pale blue shirt with white collar and rather startlingly sported a spotted red and white handkerchief in his jacket pocket. His head was an advert for some shampoo company a shining sheen of jet black hair so perfectly groomed one might have thought at first that is was a wig. And yet he wore this distracted expression like some absent-minded professor quite in contrast to his sartorial standards but his reputation preceded him.

"And how did you find your mother yesterday" he enquired of us but looking at David not me.

I was agitated and blurted out "Just the same despite all the care and help from my family". Personally I thought he should have achieved more.

Turning to David, Baxter enquired "And you Doctor Sinclair?"

"Actually a degree worse" David replied his voice sad in tone. I was shocked taken aback we had discussed nothing of this and yet we were so close. I stared at him, I remember, astonished but his concentration was focussed on Mr. Baxter.

"I agree" he responded "unfortunately we've little time left." I felt numb, Baxter stood up suddenly and walked to his filing cabinet closing one of the drawers in its grey frame which scarcely seemed open. "Of course you might prefer to take a second opinion. I'm not a patron of the conventional school of medicine. I've examined your mother and consulted the other specialists who have treated her." He shook his head repeating "time's running out".

I thought that the man must be an idiot. Why no suggestion of some solution some cure.

"Mr. Baxter the family consulted you as our father held you in high regard, we require no second opinion" David did not even glance at me and I found myself trembling with foreboding.

The doctor cleared his throat.

"Your mother has descended onto a treacherous path and the drop is gaining momentum. In my opinion drastic action is required to arrest this precipitous fall a form of shock treatment."

He looked up as I gasped "No, not physical but mental to jerk her back to reality which she's abandoned. But my strategy is risky and I can offer no guarantee otherwise" he stopped.

"Otherwise what?" asked David quietly.

"Otherwise" repeated Mr. Baxter "she'll fall into the abyss and an institution."

"Never" I heard myself cry jumping up. "Never, I will take care of her, everyone knows it".

Before David could remonstrate we were both rendered motionless at Mr. Baxter's words.

"That's what I hoped would be Miss Sinclair's response. Please sit down both of you and let me explain my plan."

It took another hour. My brother and I prayed it was worth it. There was no guarantee.

Chapter Three

In mid-September David and I were to attend a memorial service for Papa at Eglise Saint Paul in Paris with a reception afterwards at the British Embassy. I hated it. Most people present were I suppose sympathetic but others those professional memorial service attendants seemed to me to be sycophants so insincere. The reception room with its marble entrance staircase was amass with people clustering in conversation. It revolted me. How false were those chattering classes. What did they really care know or understand about Papa. I stayed glued to David mingling as best I could. After all it was in Papa's memory viewed as an honour a tribute. I hated it. Suddenly I was aware of a change in the tone of those droning decibels. Looking up I saw a couple descending the staircase. The man was very tall and even at this distance an imposing presence with unfashionable longish dark hair. His female companion it turned out to be his wife was also tall of stature couture slim with shimmering ebony hair resting heavily on her shoulders.

"Why" David exclaimed "it's Gildas and Isabella". Before I could gather my thoughts the couple was standing beside us. David introduced me.

"Mademoiselle your Papa spoke often to me about you" the count addressed me. "He was very proud of your achievements. I'm sure you'll move forward on the path he paved for you."

He regarded me with cool sea green eyes incredibly green eyes and I realised in his hair I had been mistaken. It was red, dark red, like burnished copper. So this is the great Gildas I thought. I took an instant dislike to him.

The countess suited him I thought. She was a beauty all right and she knew it, the luxuriant black hair perfectly groomed like the hood of a silken evening cloak surrounding her head. She smiled politely at David and me muttering some pleasantries. Before moving on Gildas added "David, Isabella and I were very upset at our absence from Angus's service. It was a tragic irony Isabella's grandmother died on that day."

"I know Gildas's great sadness for both our families."

After they departed David turned to me.

"Well" he enquired his face more animated than I had seen it for months. "What do you think of Gildas and Isabella." I was silent.

"Why Caterine, what's wrong. What's the problem?"

"I can only give you my impression" I answered "and my impression is of two sanctimonious bastards" looking up at David's astonished face. Looking back I can confirm now I was not entirely wrong.

Towards the end of the luncheon reception, my duties performed, I sought out Grégoire, a guest with Oncle Thierry, Tante Sylvie stayed at Marchmont with Maman despite our brother's protest.

"No David, thank you but I insist. Thierry will represent me and with respect I think Angus would have preferred I stayed with Véronique." There was no defence.

"Merde, bloody hell" I muttered to Grégoire on finding him "I can't wait to get out of this place. I feel I'm suffocating."

Grégoire put his arm round my shoulders shaking his head. "God knows Papa and I find it an ordeal. It must be horrendous for David and you."

Thankfully just one hour later we returned to the sanctuary of our Montparnasse apartment. The ordeal however was not yet ended: at least for David and Oncle Thierry.

They had been invited to a memorial dinner that evening at the Sorbonne, a further tribute to Papa including numerous speeches. David was giving a reply on behalf of the Sinclair family. Grégoire and I of course were not included, thank God, on the honoured guest list.

We spent a quiet afternoon all together few words exchanged, each of us immersed in private recollections.

"Well Caterine, will I pass?" Oncle Thierry appeared downstairs in his dinner suit.

"Damned problem with the trousers, I had to use the second waist button, I need to take more exercise, golf perhaps?" and he winked.

I knew he was trying to lighten the proceedings and I smiled. "Handsome Oncle Thierry, even dashing" I quipped desperate to match his mood.

"Only one comment Papa" Grégoire added. "You can't afford to eat." There was false laughter.

"What's the joke" David asked emerging from the hall and his phone call.

"Papa's just squeezed into his suit" Grégoire said "It's a barren meal tonight."

"Don't worry Thierry. I'll manage your portions."

"No chance David but I might give you the dessert."

David then turned to Grégoire standing next to me at the fireplace. "Your Papa and I joined forces Grégoire, robbed the bank in fact" he smiled but I saw how tired he looked, unusual for David, face greyish etched I suppose with strain and sorrow.

He walked over and handed Grégoire some French francs.

"What's this, I don't understand" Grégoire replied confused.

"It's for this evening" Oncle Thierry said. "I'm buying the wine and David the food. Tale yourselves off to that little restaurant opposite the Parc Brassens and relax. It's been a trying day."

Actually I thought 'tortuous' more appropriate!

"It will be late before we're back" David reminded us "probably around 1am. So don't wait up." He collected his set of house keys from the rosewood hall table with its golfing key ring. I swallowed, a lump in my throat, a present from Papa.

It was kind of them and so we set out just after 7pm trudging along both of us low in spirit to the speciality seafood restaurant with its distinctive blue shutters on the other side of the Parc. The evening typified our mood, damp, gloomy with the odd spot of rain not the usual September in Paris.

"I'm not very hungry Grégoire" I sighed as we settled down in a corner table next to the special feature, an open log fire. We were lucky. It had been a cancellation. I was also apprehensive for other reasons.

"Nor me" he replied lamely. "A rotten day bad enough as I said earlier for Papa and me but you and David" he shook his head.

"Should I tell him now" I thought. No I'd wait till later. For several moments we sat in silence. Suddenly there was a burst of music, a piano accordion leapt into life from a corner of the restaurant where a local trio were nestling almost unseen. It jolted us out of our morbid reverie.

"Come on" said Grégoire brightening "after all this is on the house. What about a crudités starter and then I'll order one of their seafood specialities for two." I nodded thinking how lovely he was with that mischievous grin. "OK, you choose but give me the wine list. I'm the connoisseur, remember. What would you prefer Monsieur? Bordeaux or Burgundy?"

We laughed together genuinely for the first time that day.

We ordered a house cocktail feeling very sophisticated and then my claret. Recent and past memories dissolved with the aperitif and the wine. At last relaxed appreciating the simply prepared quality food.

Papa's words drifted into my thoughts "Make the most of life my Petite. You've only one shot at it. Harness your talent. You're fortunate to have many. Don't waste time it's too precious." I remembered his words, the deep grey eyes inherited by David wisdom shining out of them in that animated face hand clasped round his unlit pipe. And so over coffee I told him. Grégoire stared at me coffee cup en route to mouth replaced on the saucer untouched. His expression what was it as I look back now? Surprised is not accurate but shocked too much: probably somewhere in between.

"When?" was his only question I gave him my answer.

Bill paid, hands clasped tightly, we hastened back, when we arrived at the apartment I can recall it was exactly 9.15pm.

It started in the hall the moment the door clicked shut. Light on then off. Hands and mouth searching, seeking, finding with bodies trembling, clothes discarded then grabbed haphazardly as we clambered up the stairs pulling at each other, pent up frustration over months hotting up like an awakened volcano desperate for escape. It finally erupted as our bodies crashed together onto the bed, fevered flesh invited and inviting rocking as one in time honoured lovers mode, together in ecstasy. Ecstasy for Grégoire but nothingness for me.

"It was gorgeous wasn't it chérie, gorgeous" Grégoire murmured.

"Yes yes" I lied what else could I say.

"Love you so much".

"Love you too" I replied.

We kissed once more drifting off as we clung together for longer then we should.

"Grégoire" I whispered "it's after midnight. You must go please. David and your Papa are back soon."

"Yes sorry chérie" Grégoire murmured sleepily slipping out of the bed.

In the shadows of the room I saw his silhouette like a penumbra from a light cast by the window through the azure chintz curtains pulling on some clothes gathering the others and then kneeling by my bedside for a final kiss stroking my hair whispering lovingly again before he left for his own bedroom.

Alone I lay back against my pillow pushing my hair off my face attempting to trap it behind. Incredibly I was trembling and pulled the duvet up to install some heat into my body trembling from shock and disappointment not from any saturation of desire. Why? What went wrong?

I had been so turned on nerves tingling body aroused aspiring to its crescendo then the high note lost flat the result was an instrument abandoned un-tuned.

I tried to sleep but could not, images monopolising my mind. Those numerous holidays with my cousins as children family photographs Grégoire transformed from boy to man, my awareness of and my attraction to him. Then our relationship boyfriend and girlfriend to lovers. What was wrong?

"It must be me" I thought. "After all Grégoire's experienced, I'm not."

Then I remembered Maman's words to me several years ago when I had asked her about making love.

"It takes time," she had told me "especially for the woman, although sometimes the sexual chemistry ignites immediately into an indescribable explosion."

"Give it time" I told myself as, eventually, I drifted off to sleep.

After the memorial service I returned to Scotland and my university bursary course. The workload exceeded even my expectations, but failure was not an option. Life had developed another dimension for me. This manifested itself in one emerging characteristic which had taken root in that Glasgow Airport V.I.P. lounge, ambition, raw, ruthless ambition. I was determined to fulfil my promise to Papa and pursued this ideal relentlessly. It took the form of a vendetta against the circumstances contributing to his death for which I considered myself responsible.

One evening in the middle of that autumn term, I was sitting down on the lounge sofa, having just finished a hastily heated tin of soup. Two hours later I was found by Shona stretched out, sound asleep, lecture notes either squashed beside me or strewn in disorder on the carpet.

"Caterine" she said quietly touching my shoulder "this is ridiculous!"

"What?" I mumbled sleepily.

"Cameron's worse than a slave driver. I think I'm working hard until I look at you. You must discuss this pressure with your family. You're mentally and physically exhausted."

"Nonsense" I replied now fully awake, but irritable, "I'm fine."

An argument ensued but I was resolute; however I decided to ask Professor Cameron's advice.

"Stubborn, Miss Sinclair, as I anticipated. You've wasted time."

"Pardon, what do you mean?" I replied thinking "is Cameron mad?" I was trying to save time to study more!

"You should have approached me earlier."

At this response my temper roused itself. Forgetting I was addressing not only my Professor but the youngest one of any university situated in the UK, I erupted:

"Earlier! When? Phoned you during the night when I

couldn't sleep with images, dates, configurations pervading my mind in chaotic confusion? Don't you think as you nominated me for this damnable bursary, it's you who should have approached me!"

There was silence.

"My God, what had I said!" I sank into his leather upholstered sofa, appalled.

Cameron, however, was unfazed.

"I think, Miss Sinclair, your sentiments only re-affirm mine. You should have consulted me earlier. Let me offer you some solutions."

Over the following months and actual years of my future career, I followed his academic Bible learning the method of "fast reading" discarding of minutiae and the capacity of fact absorption decompartmentalised in the mind.

By the time of the end of term exams in December, I had regained a voracious appetite for the bursary course and devoured it like a forbidden meal.

It worked. Callum Stuart Baxter's strategy worked. All the family owe that doctor so much. Maman's life no less and for her a new dawn.

It was slow but her determination our encouragement and the loving care bestowed by Oncle Thierry and Tante Sylvie were the winning recipes. Nine months after Papa's accident Maman now looked more like Maman. Physically and most importantly mentally her strength had returned. She was back from the abyss. On our visits to Argyll and Marchmont David and I found that laughter had returned to the house. At last she allowed its remedies to re-enter her world rediscovered as she remembered her beloved Angus, the happy times and even some of their battles! It was the breakthrough, the recognition he was dead.

That Christmas of '89, albeit tinged with sadness became a family celebration after Maman's words to us over aperitifs.

"Thank you all for your efforts and putting me back on the rails. I give you a toast."

"Slainthe and Santé! To all the Sinclair family's future!"

And as my 19th birthday approached on the 19th March some more happy news, David was to be married. Perfect!

This was the news which really spurred Maman back into her organising mode and made everyone happy, two celebrations for the family and friends were to take place, one Scottish and one French of course. Maman set about making both memorable for David and Alix, his fiancée, with their willing cooperation.

The Scottish engagement party took place at Marchmont. David and I had been somewhat apprehensive. After all Maman was mixing for the first time with large groups of people albeit known to her for the most part family and friends but all aware of her illness, her mental depression. We consulted Callum Baxter again.

His comments "This will be further therapy for your mother. She'll lead the way."

He was right. Maman was a star. Pale and still thin but elegant, growing taller as the evening advanced, thanking guests, mentioning Papa and mingling with no self-consciousness.

David and I were astonished and then realised she had found after Papa a new horizon in us. God forbid if it went wrong.

Paris was different but equally rewarding. A larger affair than initially anticipated the Montparnasse apartment was too small to host such a party. Maman had looked at other venues when suddenly she received an offer from the Sorbonne to use one of their smaller reception rooms. It was a gesture for Papa. I am sure she shed a private tear although we never saw it but she accepted.

David and I thought Maman made a special effort for the

Paris party because she knew she had been absent from the memorial service. She now paid her tribute to Papa at the Sorbonne celebration. Dressed in a couture creation of silver and black, Papa's favourite colours for her, she shone again if possible an even bigger star than in Scotland. She had arranged her hair swept up in that style peculiar to her, ageless and elegant. It had maintained its claret colour albeit diluted a little by an accompanying rosé maturing gracefully in the fine French tradition of Château wine.

Mon Dieu" Grégoire said "what a transformation in Tante Véronique!"

"Yes" I replied "unbelievable and Alix looks so lovely in that cerise D'Aquin gown. It seems to reflect her joy. She's glowing."

"No wonder David can't take his eyes off her, just as I can't from you" Grégoire replied hands clasping mine. "Do you think you can organise things tonight like we discussed?"

"I think so" I said "Maman will go to bed early. She still tires easily. Your Papa and Maman are staying with your other cousins while David and Alix are going on to a cabaret spending the night with friends. No problems I'm sure, none at all". It was said light-heartedly but I was apprehensive, very apprehensive, for different reasons from Grégoire.

"I'd better mingle and find Maman. Come on see you at the buffet."

"OK" Grégoire grinned. "Can't wait for tonight."

I wandered round, a word here and there, to family and friends. Maman was on the other side of the reception room moving, no gliding, again amongst her guests as I remembered her: a credit to Papa, to us but most of all to herself.

Pausing for a moment to admire a Monet print on the west wall I was startled from my reverie by those cool almost formal tones.

"Caterine, how are you? Delighted we're meeting again

under much happier circumstances." I turned immediately recognising the voice. He stood there those green eyes I remembered from Papa's memorial service regarding me quizzically. This time he appeared to be without his female alter ego.

As he addressed me in French it was rude of me to give my response in English but for some obtuse reason I did just that.

"Yes, it's a major family celebration" I replied.

If Gildas was surprised by my change of language he showed no sign of it.

"Of course it is and I wish you many more of them especially with Maman returned to such good health."

I was the one who was surprised even astonished. Not that he replied in English because I already knew he was fluent but at his accent. There was none. If I had not known he was French I would have presumed him British.

"Gildas, how are you, saw you arriving but where's Isabella" it was David appearing on cue more by design I was sure than hazard.

"Her sincere apologies David. Isabella's in Switzerland as part of a charity delegation. I'm afraid she couldn't call off."

"Of course not. We'll meet up soon I'm sure, please give her our warmest wishes."

"I will David" Gildas replied "by the way I didn't know you knew my cousins."

"Do I?" David asked looking taken aback.

"Well they're both here Jacques and Philippe."

We followed Gildas's gaze to see two men waving over to him. They were both striking looking, one as blonde as the other dark. Gildas raised his right arm in acknowledgement.

"Oh yes of course I recognise them but don't really know them. They're friends of Alix."

"She's a lucky lady to escape their clutches" Gildas replied almost seriously "they've quite a track record."

"No chance Gildas. They couldn't compete against me so handsome and debonair."

We laughed.

"Now tell me" David continued "what have you been up to?"

As they chatted I had time to regard Gildas. He was at least two inches taller than David and very broad. The copper hair still longish but not one strand out of place: beige checked bespoke mohair suit, light tan coloured shirt, sporting a silk tie with an unusual motif which I vaguely recognised. That was it. "GduG" was part of the family crest Gildas du Gilbert. I had seen it on his notepaper. What arrogance I thought everyone already knew who he was. And the shoes, I glanced at them, maroon brogues polished like the proverbial glass. Probably checked his reflection in them I thought, much to my amusement. Manicured to perfection that was the phrase that sprang to mind.

Then I heard my name "I was just saying to Caterine how well Véronque looks."

"Yes, a miraculous recovery" then David grinned.

"Right Gildas come and join all of us in a glass of champagne". With his arm round my shoulder he announced "let's go".

It was almost a charge. David on my right, Gildas on my left. I felt like one of the three musketeers only I was unsure which one.

David spoke to me just before the evening ended. "It was uncommonly impolite of you to reply to Gildas in English. Why?"

"Well, why not! He speaks it fluently and with no accent, unusual" I had added.

"Not really" David had replied "Gildas spent several of his teenage years at school in England. With the discipline there any French overtures would be quickly silenced. What I don't understand is why you dislike him so much."

"I don't know" I had replied "I find something disturbingly detached about him" hesitating for several seconds I had added "like some distant demeanour on a darkling shore."

David burst out laughing shaking off his annoyance. "Honestly Caterine your imagination. It's worthy of a Machiavellian play. Let's find Alix, Maman and the family. The party's coming to a close."

Arm in arm we mingled again but I knew the shadow of a ghost had crossed my pathway touching my mind, my body and even my soul.

At Montparnasse that evening after a light supper Maman announced yawning "I'm off. Apologies Grégoire but I'm rather tired, a long day."

"Please don't apologise Tante Véronique. If I may say so you were a triumph : elegant and attentive, the perfect hostess, just as I remember you."

It was said with sincerity.

"I'm flattered Grégoire, thank you. Now enjoy your evening. Breakfast, 7.30 as usual." She came to kiss both of us. "Bonne nuit, good night."

Grégoire and I washed up the dishes and taking our glasses of wine went into the salon to listen to some 80s hits and then Grieg's Peer Gynt suite. Grégoire his arm around my shoulder was very relaxed. There was the occasional kiss but low key in confident anticipation of the hours to follow. In contrast I was tense anxious trying to appear like him head on his shoulder listening to the music. When the Peer Gynt suite Number Two ended Grégoire said "well it's after 10.30. Shall we call it a night" grinning at me, kissing me again, mouth gentle on mine. Lights turned off we went upstairs.

He was so kind, considerate but the nothingness remained. I decided it was due to my feelings of guilt. Maman in the same house although we were separated by three bedrooms and the master en-suite bathroom.

It was wrong against what I understood as a moral code. She was in ignorance when I should have confided in her. Under different circumstances I would have asked her advice but she had been so ill and I had acted on Papa's sentiments "don't waste time", after all his time was cruelly cut short, taken too early from him.

Then I recalled the holiday that Grégoire and I had spent last New Year, it was a weekend spent skiing in the French Alps with Marie-Françoise and her boyfriend José, staying in a small two bedroom chalet owned by José's parents. We all knew the score before we arrived.

For me excited at seeing Grégoire again geared up, anticipating the holiday and certainly relaxed, I had returned on the 3rd of January, confused, uncertain and concerned. Nothing had changed. Surely guilt was not the answer now.

"Well" Maman said next morning at breakfast "thanks for collecting the bread Grégoire. You were certainly up early. I heard you whistling en route downstairs."

"Mon Dieu, Tante Véronique, did I waken you, I'm sorry if I was noisy."

"Don't be ridiculous, I was just delighted you felt so energetic. It saved me my walk to the boulangerie. Come on have some more bread and try my raspberry jam. What about another coffee." Grégoire grinned "I'll accept everything on offer. I'm famished." Turning to smile at me.

In contrast I felt unsettled, queasy and ill-at-ease. I had woken with a headache and little appetite for any breakfast.

"Are you all right Petite, you've not eaten much" Maman asked anxiously.

"Fine thanks" I replied "too much indulgence yesterday, probably the champagne" Grégoire grinned at me and winked.

Maman smiled "Well next time you won't take so much. Now let me see. We're all meeting here at noon, David, Alix, Thierry and Sylvie for a family rendez-vous and then you're off to Scotland

Caterine. Your flight's direct isn't it? No London transfer."

"No Maman I arrive at Glasgow airport 6 pm local time and take a taxi to KG. The students' rate's quite cheap.

"Right" Maman glanced at her watch "it's just 8.30. Take some time to yourselves. I've letters to write and a few phone calls. See you here at noon."

Grégoire and I walked together hands clasped. He was animated joyful passionate chatting about his studies aspirations and his plans for the future. We sat in the Tuileries gardens, in the same genre as the other lovers.

"Caterine chérie" Grégoire said "I love you so very much but I can offer you nothing just now, not until I graduate and find a job."

I nodded not really listening looking out over the gardens desperate for an answer to my numerous questions.

"Please tell me you'll marry me. I want you so much for ever. I'll look after you always. Please marry me."

"Pardon. What did you say?" I asked returning to some form of reality staring at him.

"Chérie please say you'll marry me."

Of course that was it. That was the answer: marriage, just like Papa and Maman, everything will be all right. I turned arms thrown around his neck.

"Yes Grégoire, yes of course I'll marry you" what a fool I was.

As we returned to Montparnasse we talked constantly plans sketchy but one point certain. This engagement was our secret for the moment part only of our long term plan.

"What a fabulous few days" David said as the family sat in the salon at Montparnasse with coffee after lunch. "Thank you Maman for your planning your organisation and your expertise."

Maman smiled in reply "It has given me back my happiness."

Just before everyone was preparing to leave for their diverse destination David announced "An invitation to all of you from Gildas to spend a long weekend in July at St Roche Rivière. It's the first weekend actually, Alix and I have already accepted. What do you all think?"

"I'd be delighted" Maman replied "how thoughtful of him."

"Sylvie and me too" said Oncle Thierry. "We've no plans until August and would love to see the place. What about you and Caterine Grégoire?"

"Damn it we can't Papa. We've booked Acacia with Marie-Françoise and José. The four of us got on so well over New Year we thought we'd spend a couple of weeks there in the summer. And we arranged it from the first weekend in July."

Grégoire turned to David "Would Gildas and Isabella be upset we can't come? Caterine and I had no idea about the invite."

"Don't be ridiculous he's not like that. I'll confirm who'll be present and that's it. Come on Alix we've still packing to finish."

And so the family dispersed. That same evening I flew to Scotland to recommence my studies.

Chapter Four

That year in the month of June I received my First Class Honours Masters Degree from the University of Glasgow. On my "fast track" course this was achieved at least one year ahead of my peers.

What an honour it was and so nostalgic to be seated with all those other graduates in the Bute Hall recalling how I was continuing a tradition established by my grandfather, continued by my father, maintained by David and now repeated by me. As the organist commenced the traditional academia anthem "Gaudeamus Igitur" I stood proudly as the Chancellor of the University headed a procession of academics including the Chaplain, the Clerk of Senate and the Deans of Faculties into the awe inspiring Bute Hall.

Dominating the proceedings as the voices of the congregation swelled in celebratory song was the old silver gilt mace, symbol of the University's authority. It is carried traditionally by the Bedellus. Of all my family, only Maman attended. Donald was present of course as a Faculty Dean.

It had been quite a battle!

"This is preposterous, unthinkable!" David had exclaimed over the phone from Zurich. Alix and I must be there with a family celebration afterwards, whatever is Maman thinking about, never mind you."

"David, please" I remonstrated "let me explain."

It took several phone calls but eventually and reluctantly he bowed to my request.

Consequently, it was Maman, Donald and I who shared a quiet dinner, after the graduation ceremony.

The reason for no family was simple. My goal was my doctorate and with a special distinction. This Masters was but a stepping stone.

After that Professor Cameron (Donald in private) and I became 'mates.' Still a taskmaster, no prisoners taken, but more approachable and what a mind: a walking encyclopaedia about the world of fine arts and his specialisation because at his academic heights one would imagine he had a particular area of expertise. For example for a dissertation, Masters, PhD but I was wrong. His 'specialisation area' encompassed all! It was unbelievable. No surprise now why he was held in such high esteem inside and outside the academic world. He recognised my ambition and made it (I think in retrospect) a personal crusade to 'fine tune' it ruthlessly, so I could pursue my goals. His guidance was indispensable and his knowledge I grasped with a passion which I could physically feel.

The following day, Maman and I flew back to France and Montparnasse where I received my graduation present from her. It was twofold: firstly, a day's shopping in Paris for several outfits of clothes and a new set of luggage.

The second part was a month's holiday with her, visiting Uncle Fergus, Aunt Bebe and their families now living in Perth. Not Perth Scotland, but Perth, Western Australia. How lucky I was! Their house was situated near the exceptional King's Park overlooking the Swan river west of the city, the capital of that part of Australia.

It was one of the older properties, originally constructed at the turn of the century by a local entrepreneur; very handsome and spacious, it was designed to complement the Mediterranean type climate. Uncle Fergus had undertaken a modernisation programme but retaining the property's character and graciousness. Maman and I loved it.

What amazed me was the verdure, the plants and shrubs in the family garden, such splendour.

"Remember Caterine" Uncle Fergus informed me, eyes twinkling "we're in Perth, not Alice Springs!".

On reflection it was a very special holiday. Why? Because what it offered me was a definitive dichotomy, a break from my past studies and preparations for the future ones to come; also it defined my future with Grégoire.

The months of July and August were more intensive academically than I had anticipated which required a call to him.

"You mean Acacia's cancelled. We can't spent two weeks in July as planned." He responded on my mobile, voice raised in anger.

"I'm sorry chéri, but I'm running out of time."

"It appears you've only time for your bloody books" Grégoire replied "none for me" and he cut off the connection.

I sat down in the lounge at K.G. very deflated and also concerned. Was I being selfish to devote so much time to my studies? But Grégoire had committed himself to academic endeavour, like me, over many years. Having completed a year as a scientific graduate trainee with a multi-national organisation in Bordeau, he was being appointed to their Paris HQ at a junior manager level. Surely he did not begrudge me similar success!

The phone bell shrilled, Grégoire!

"Sorry, chérie, I was far too hasty. You said you can spend a long weekend at Acacia. Which one is best?"

We chose the last weekend, four weeks before David and Alix's wedding in mid September.

It was as always an idyllic setting. We played tennis, luxuriated in the pool and dined on local produce, sharing the cooking.

There was fun and laughter but sexually for me nothing changed; the nothingness remained. I was in despair so I pretended my passionate response – an act as read in books.

Frankly even when asked now I hesitate to answer the question. What happened to the two years following that Australia holiday. They just seemed to evaporate. Possibly the main reason was the European travel but there were others.

"Well," Donald enquired, "firstly what's the specialised subject to be and secondly the decision about your thesis."

I smiled at him. It was the beginning of September and we were sitting in his rooms at the University of Glasgow, sharing coffee and planning my two year doctorate course in detail.

"You already know the answer to the specialist subject Donald, paintings."

"And the second" he asked eyebrows raised. I told him.

"Not possible Caterine" he barked standing up now frowning.

"Have you taken leave of your senses. The doctorate you are attempting is an advance PHD, traditionally a three year course. For you, it's only two on this schedule. Your dissertation subject is quite unacceptable, taking another year at least. No, you must change it. There are many options open to you for example"

I interrupted him: "No Donald, this must be my decision, albeit a high risk strategy and anyway my thesis is already under way."

September arrived with its hues of pink and rosé maturing into russets and reds, bronze colours of the autumnal season. David and Alix were married in a simple but moving service in our local village church.

Alix's gown was a surprise to everyone except me as her chief bridesmaid. It was in contrast to her classic professional style and neither white nor cream. She advanced down the aisle in a crinoline creation of pale oyster, her luxuriant ebony hair caught up in romantic ringlets, the archetype virginal porcelain figurine. Following her down the aisle with myriad cousins in tow as train bearers I had difficulty hiding a smile imagining David's astonishment on seeing his demure bride in her late 19th century creation.

We repaired to Marchmont and a reception for family and friends, a small marquis erected on the south facing lawn. It was an exceptional family reunion which included Uncle Fergus and Aunt Bebe and all our Australian cousins. Gildas and Isabella amongst other European friends were also guests, a prominent presence. I observed Isabella from a distance. In my opinion she had chosen an inappropriate outfit for a wedding: white chiffon cut in contours to her designer body difficult and expensive with such a fabric. It was edged in black like some testament to a fallen virgin I thought amused.

"Caterine chérie you're in dreamland" Grégoire laughed taking my hand. "Let's get away from this crowd, come on."

We walked through a narrow hibiscus passage way to a shrubbery area we knew well, sitting down together on the old stone garden seat.

"Can't wait for tonight chérie. Love you so much". Strangely I'd found myself a little irritated and pulled away as he tried to caress me.

"It's not possible tonight Grégoire" I replied standing up.

"What do you mean, why not?"

"It's just not practical too many of the family staying and then there's Maman."

Grégoire also stood up "What's Maman got to do with it" his voice raised now "She was there in Paris at Montparnasse after David's engagement party."

"Yes" I replied "I know but this is different."

"Different?" he retorted angrily. "Why? What are you trying to do. Pretend you're still a virgin just because all the family's present."

I was now frustrated and furious. Turning to face him I snapped "I wish I were because you're a lousy lover" pulling up my long dress I ran as fast as my high heeled shoes allowed me to the back door of Marchmont and the sanctuary of my bedroom.

"My God I should never have said that" I thought aloud. "How cruel and unfair."

I glanced in my mirror. What a sight, flushed face and hair wild dishevelled. As I attempted some repairs there was a knock at my door. Maman, I thought, she'll be furious at my disappearing on David's wedding day.

"Just coming" I called running the tap in my washbasin as a distraction and gulping some water. Trying to smile I pulled the door open.

"Am I Caterine, am I?" Grégoire stood there ashen faced, hazel eyes reddened staring at me. I felt so guilty and gathered him in my arms as he started to sob.

"Sorry chéri, nonsense what I said, forget it, I love you too."

As I realised later it was at that moment our relationship changed.

Two days after the wedding celebrations, Maman and I were alone at Marchmont. David and Alix were en route to their honeymoon destination, Barbardos, while Uncle Fregus, Aunt Bebe and our cousins were on a Scottish sight seeing tour accompanied by Oncle Thierry and Tante Sylvie.

Grégoire was going back to Edinburgh completing a work experience course organised by his company's Paris headquarters.

"It's brilliant" Grégoire had explained during that weekend in July at Acacia.

"I couldn't believe it when I was the one offered the choice of London or Edinburgh, since I was competing with four other bilingual students. I think they were surprised I decided on Edinburgh but Scotland's where my heart is!" kissing me tenderly.

I had responded hugging him, but in my mind I was already disturbed.

Reflecting on developments I was even more concerned. The balance of our relationship had changed. As I re-arranged my university notes in my bedroom I was in a pensive mood.

"Coffee and scones in the conservatory, Caterine" Maman called.

Whistling to sound cheerful, I went downstairs. My perceptive mother was not fooled.

"It's not working out with you and Grégoire, is it?" she asked as she poured out the coffee from the porcelain percolator.

I looked up at her still lovely face and shook my head staring down at my cup.

Then she added "Mentally or physically?"

I looked up again not really surprised.

"So you know. I should have told you."

"No, Petite, you made your decision when I was not there to guide you although I would have made the same one."

Putting her arm round my shoulder, she said:

"You must tell him."

"I can't hurt him, Maman, he's so kind and considerate."

"You hurt him more by staying silent. You've moved on. He's not the man for your future life. I've seen the signs and most recently at weekends here, when Grégoire has returned from Edinburgh on his work experience course. He's a fine young man and I love him dearly as my nephew. But you've been together for more than two years. Mon Dieu! What if he's planning marriage! At least you've not made that commitment otherwise to have continued the relationship would have been heartless."

She stopped at my intake of breath.

"Caterine, not already! Has he asked you?" she looked aghast.

Trembling, I told her the whole story.

A row erupted with me in defence, Maman on the attack. I lost.

"May I remind you as you did to your father and me that you're a woman. Act like one and tell Grégoire the truth."

"How? Admit I made a mistake?" I replied struggling for other options, or easier solutions.

"Don't feel sorry for yourself Caterine. Your betrayal was no mistake. Tell him what you've told me, sexual incompatibility and you lied to him faking your response."

A phone call later I was trudging through Jimmy Black's farm pastures, my mind in turmoil.

This cottage where I was meeting Grégoire had became our retreat used discreetly during the previous two weeks when we knew it was vacant of family members over the hectic period of David and Alix's wedding celebrations.

I knocked at the door, a letter in my other hand.

It was worse than I had feared. Grégoire, unsure of the reason for my visit earlier than planned, was at first anxious, then apprehensive followed by confusion and then utter disbelief.

"Merde, Bloody Hell! At worst from your tone on the mobile I thought you might be pregnant. But we would have married. I'd have taken care of you, but this" turning away in pain after I stumbled out the words.

I collapsed in tears on the sofa to supplement his sobs as he ran from the room.

The letter I left on the walnut coffee table. This time the poinsettia plant had been replaced by a cyclamen. Ironically, it was withering.

The letter read.

My Dear Grégoire,

The arrangements for your accommodation during the remaining two weeks of your course in Edinburgh have not changed.

You are very welcome at Marchmont and I shall enjoy your entertaining company.

Caterine will be staying in K.G.

With love.

Tante Véronique.

It was not the banishment it might have appeared. Maman and I agreed it would be unjust even cruel to change the original plans for Grégoire.

In my intensive study course I was already spending four days a week in K.G. attending Glasgow University seminars returning on Fridays for a long weekend at Marchmont. It meant I absented myself only from that following weekend.

At the end of September Grégoire was joining his parents in Invernesshire, work experience course completed where we had been looking forward to another family reunion at Graham McCallum's (Alix's brother) 21st birthday party.

As I arrived at Marchmont on that last Friday in September, I was dreading that reunion.

With a welcoming hug on the doorstep, Maman greeted me.

"Well, Petite, how are you? You've sounded fine on the phone."

"Not bad" I replied "felt a little below par yesterday but I suppose that's delayed reaction. More important, how's Grégoire now?"

"Out of the woods and in better spirits although still a little shell shocked. As I told you on the phone, we had several long talks and I phoned Tante Sylvie. That prepared the way before Grégoire gave them the news."

I groaned "what must they think of me."

"Caterine, Thierry and Sylvie understand, 'c'est la vie', you're both young, life and careers ahead of you. Take advantage of the opportunities which present themselves. You burden yourself with guilt. That's wrong. I'm the guilty one."

I looked up from the footstool inherited from Grandpa installed traditionally beside the open fireplace. It was still sporting the logs but in September unlit without their merry cheer.

" I don't understand why you feel guilty. You've helped so much with me and Grégoire."

"I'm referring to Papa, that's my guilt, I let him down'"

"No, Maman" I protested jumping up to put my arm round her on the sofa.

"Yes, Caterine. I was a prisoner in a dark cell, in atrophy, wasting away, physically gradually but mentally rapidly into the abyss."

Then David confronted me at Marchmont, informing me in harsh words that you were surrendering your studies to care for me. It was the further shock I needed jolting me back on the road to reality; a slow arduous process of finally unlocking my mind."

There was silence. Maman's eyes were blank as dark memories pervaded them, but within seconds she snapped into the present and action.

"Right, let's pack for our trip to Inverness tomorrow and then have dinner. By the way I've purloined a bottle of Papa's favourite claret from the cellar. I'm surprised he left it behind."

I stared at her and her attitude. We hugged each other, but no tears. They were past: left behind.

On the following afternoon when Maman and I arrived at the McCallum's grey sandstone Victorian mansion situated on the outskirts of Inverness, I was feeling decidedly seedy again.

Maman had asked me at breakfast:

"You're very pale, Petite, not feeling well?"

"Just a bit of a headache" I had replied.

In fact I had awakened feeling rotten; a headache which seemed to stretch down my neck while my stomach was bloated and queasy. I had thought it might be a form of PMT as I was overdue.

"Right" Maman had stood up from our pine kitchen breakfast table, "some aspirin and one of my herbal teas. That will do the trick!"

Unfortunately this remedy for once failed to work.

As I was changing for the party in one of the guest bedrooms I found myself staring at my reflection in the free-standing mirror. At 5'10" I was too tall, limbs slim certainly but hands and feet too large, shoulders too narrow and broad breasted, 34D cup, completely out of proportion with my hips I sighed.

As for my hair it was a shadow of Maman's rich claret colour, a faded red and unruly, far too long now I realised. Why had Maman not suggested I wore it up tonight?

Everyone knew of course about the split up between Grégoire and me, it was common knowledge. David had tried to console me with kind words of comfort when we had met at the McCallums.

"I know the feeling, completely down, empty, lost."

"But I feel so guilty" I replied. "It's bad enough for me but Grégoire did not expect it. How must he feel?"

David looking at me, arm round my shoulders, said: "He'll

feel the same. I was in his position once." I stared into his deep grey eyes, in astonishment.

"You? But no-one could ever reject you."

"Well someone did, just about the same time, at university. She was two years older than me and I adored her. She dumped me after a year with a letter not even the courage to tell me to my face. Thank God she did. A shallow creature who taught me a lesson. You had courage and told Grégoire the truth face to face. That's a measure of your character and he'll remember you with affection and more important with respect. And he, being the man he is, I'm sure will find his Alix."

By the time we all arrived at the golf club to commence the celebrations I was feeling decidedly giddy, headache returned with a vengeance, weak and nauseous. I saw Grégoire immediately and he me, instinct I suppose. Our eyes met momentarily then we glanced away at anything, anyone but each other, a pain developing in the pit of my stomach. Our family closeness and the occasion demanded that we meet. We greeted each other in the time honoured French fashion with a kiss on each cheek just like old times, times of our brother and sister days at Acacia.

"Weak is the will of man, his judgement blind;
Remembrance persecutes and hope betrays;
Heavy is woe – a joy for human-kind,
A mournful thing, so transient is the blaze!"

The words of that poetic master, Wordsworth, came to mind one of his sonnets if I recall correctly written ironically at the time of the battle of Waterloo.

Grégoire's lips were cold on my flushed, almost feverish cheeks, our bodies stiff like two puppets with no-one there to even inject a semblance of life by pulling at the strings. It was indeed our Waterloo.

I hid away as much as possible taking refuge beside an aggressive variegated ivy plant, the leaves of which activated by an overhead fan seemed to attack me from time to time. A further asset to my desire to remain unnoticed was the fact that our table whether by hazard or design was situated in a corner. Fortunately I knew none of Graham's friends and so I was spared any request to dance except a duty jig with Graham, one with David and kindness itself Oncle Thierry for a waltz when he smiled sympathetically, understanding my unhappiness despite the greater misery I must have inflicted on his dearest son. Later I was to learn the word had circulated. Leave Caterine alone. And so the evening dragged on, the evening of an event but uneventful for me except for my misery until "the incident" and my misery complete.

"Caterine, may I have the pleasure of this dance" startled me out of my apathy, I looked up to see him: Gildas, the close friend of David and Alix, the highly regarded host to Papa and Maman and the imposing detached figure of his memorial service.

"Thank you but no I can't dance with you" to the combined shock and horror of my family sharing the table, I stood up, pushed back my chair and departed running rapidly. I reached the ladies loo just in time before I vomited.

It was chicken pox at 19, incredible. I woke up next morning covered in spots and sympathy.

"A bad case," the McCallum's doctor concluded when summoned. "Nasty, over the scalp and in the ears less on the body." He left a prescription, some cream for the itching and a bath balm.

The incident was forgotten, written off. David spoke to Gildas and he sent his best wishes for a speedy recovery. This was reiterated in a letter to David and Alix in which he thanked them for his inclusion in the private party and looked forward to their forthcoming visit to la Touraine. Maman showed it to me.

The family crest on the white note paper, so thick it could

have stood up unaided and unusual handwriting for a man, a style like copperplate, a distinctive no wrong a distinguished hand.

"Patronising bastard" I thought then regretted it. There was only one problem my sixth sense. "An asset" Maman had said but also "a curse". I sensed a danger in him, this man, Gildas, le Comte du Gilbert. I fell back on my pillows having eaten no breakfast, head throbbing, weak and drowsy.

It was at that point I saw him, a crooked man old and gnarled, beard weighing down his head, chin nudging his fleshless chest.

"Who are you? Why are you here?" I whispered. The man looked up and I was shocked, his eyes were shining, incandescent, youthful in a withered face.

"I'm here for you" the voice like the body was feeble, scratchy as an old gramophone record. Suddenly he stood up, larger, more youthful and the voice grew stronger as he spoke "the moving accident is not my trade. To freeze the blood I have no ready arts. It is my delight alone in summer shade to pipe a simple song for sinking hearts."

The image shrank into its former crooked shape. I awoke with a start sweating, clammy and rose staggering, legs unsteady, to the washbasin burying my face and gulping some water.

Gazing in the mirror I thought "Mon Dieu. You look awful, eyes red, spots on my hairline, my neck and as I knew from the itch all over my scalp. I applied some of the doctor's lotion to try and cool the irritation and returned to bed. Stupid dream, even crazy, it must be the chicken pox. However I tossed and turned, unable to fall asleep again, my mind trying to forget those words "the moving accident is not my trade, to freeze the blood I have no ready arts."

Chapter Five

The autumn term of that year seemed finished even before it started. One day I was enrolling with Shona and the next departing for Christmas at Marchmont with Maman, David and Alix.

"You're looking tired, Caterine. Don't work too hard over the holidays. Have some fun for God's sake!" Shona scolded me.

"I promise. The course work is ahead of schedule, but the problem is the dissertation. Donald, however, although initially against it has been exceptional in his support."

Shona put down the iron, clothes pressed for the holidays forgotten, and sat down beside me on the sofa.

"You called Professor Cameron 'an unusual man'. You were right. Not tall, certainly not handsome with an uneven gait; but he stands out, commands respect. I saw him in the cloisters yesterday as I was leaving my German tutorial. Everyone parted as he approached, like the Red Sea!"

Shona was travelling to London and Christmas with Gerald Braithwaith and his family. We kissed *au revoir* at Glasgow Royal Exchange Square and made our way to our respective trains. As mine sped through the mature Scottish landscape I was buoyed up with anticipation. The train rushed through familiar terrain worshipped by my father and grandfather alike and I became lost in their memories. Suddenly I realised we had arrived. Hauling my suitcase from the overhead rack I gathered together hastily my handbag Sinclair mohair beret and scarf. I reached the open carriage door just before a surprised porter was about to slam it shut.

"Petite" Maman shouted excitedly "I thought you'd missed the train". I laughed kissing her, the other passengers perplexed at this tall tartan clad lady speaking French.

Chattering animatedly we drove together to our Georgian family home, the Scottish Sinclair base. We had time to spend, a few days together, exchanging news, shopping, preparing Christmas Fayre prior to David and Alix's arrival on Christmas Eve. Unfortunately they phoned to inform us of a delay which meant an evening rendez-vous. I must admit when they appeared at 10pm they both looked exhausted. Alix was especially pale.

Greeting us with less then usual ebullience David apologised "Sorry Maman, Petite, it's possible Alix and I've caught some bug. We both feel rotten and nearly cancelled the visit. Do you mind if we have a hot toddy and off to bed."

"Of course not" Maman replied "on you go, have a hot shower, bath, or whatever you want and we'll prepare the whisky. Nothing else?"

"No thanks Maman, that's all tonight"

The following morning we were catapulted from a rediscovered heaven into our previously experienced hell. They told us sitting together on the sofa, hands clasped, apologising for the timing but fate had spared them no choice. Does she ever! Her hand spreading predetermination on destiny's path, usually too rapidly for us mere mortals to discover another way. It was a tumour. They had known for two weeks: behind the left ear and pressing on the brain. An operation was required in January, delicate, intricate, ten hours of surgery. Alix burst into tears, sobbing. I wanted to comfort her but felt paralysed and terrified to look at Maman. There was complete silence. Time stopped, history repeating itself.

Suddenly, piercing the silence Maman spoke. " Right David – let's look at the positive aspects. It's non-malignant and you have secured Xavier Texier for the surgery."

I was startled and now dared glance over. She was in battle mode. David saw it too and we looked at each other, tears stifled by me, although eyes watery. Alix was brave now, solemn but calm. Discussions ensued, facts re-visited, decisions re-confirmed.

To my amazement, Maman made a statement before lunch.

"I think under the circumstances we should spend Christmas as intended, despite this" she hesitated "flaw on the horizon." She poured out a glass of champagne for each of us. "My toast to the Sinclair family, this time we will win."

We struggled through Christmas mainly because of the combined mental tenacity and fortitude of Maman and David. The subject of the operation had been clinically dissected already. I attempted to speak to David alone but he forbade any discussion on his illness. Flashing that formidable smile he replied:

"Petite, it's Christmas, no more disturbances to its tradition of peace."

For the first time for me a rejection to no more communication but when I reflected, I understood.

On Boxing Day, Alix followed me into the garden leaving David and Maman in Papa's study sorting out some books for my brother.

"Caterine" she grasped my arm facing me almost distraught " he is so undeserving of this and we're so happy. I wish it had been me for David has so much more to offer," tears in her dark brown eyes which were full of sorrow, hand shaking as she attempted vainly to wipe them away.

" Alix" I said softly "either was the same, a twin problem damnable for both of you."

" Yes I suppose I know that but" she stopped, fighting to control her grief and then continued " David will no longer discuss it, switched off. Oh God what will happen to all of us if he fails to survive?"

My arms around her, I thought too, then I realised how blind I had been. Death comes to all of us at any age, any place, anytime. It is everyone's fate in life whatever colour, whatever creed, whatever conscience and whatever class.

My brother was not afraid of death. I knew that from discussions over the years. No, his anxieties lay in reaching a darker horizon, worse even than Papa's.

For Papa survived the climb but not its aftermath. David knew he might survive the operation but waken up dead, to a brainless dawn.

Slowly Alix and I walked round the garden to rejoin Maman and David in the house.

" I'm sorry Caterine, I shouldn't be burdening you with my fears. I am usually a calm person" her voice trailed away. I replied quietly "What's a sister for?"

It started to rain, I remember. The garden looked dull and lifeless. Certainly it was not the best time of year but its customary appeal even in winter had gone, its vitality lost, suddenly disappeared, new life dead.

Foreboding filled my thoughts, my mind in a nightmare of despair with visions of bleakness, surrounding my soul.

Three days later another shock struck the household.

"Christ almighty" David cried "it's not possible."

We were sitting in the morning room after breakfast attempting to read papers or periodicals before a roaring log fire, just, in fact, trying to be normal in what had become our abnormal even monstrous world.

We all snapped to attention at David's uncharacteristic

expletive. He was reading a copy of ' Le Monde' (one day old) which Maman ordered to keep herself abreast of events in France, every week.

" It's Gildas" he looked up visibly shocked.

"Isabella, she's feared dead, out riding when a freak snowstorm caused havoc in the region, cars abandoned, people missing. Her horse returned without her and a search is underway. My God, how dreadful for him. I must make contact. He phoned me just before our visit here, so concerned about me."

We gathered around to see the article but I saw only the photograph, the imposing figures of Papa's memorial service, manicured to perfection: the monochrome of a newspaper article emphasising my memory of cool, sea green eyes. It was to be many months before her remains were found.

University term re-commenced on the 8th January. David's operation was scheduled for the 15th in Paris. With some trepidation I went to see Donald Cameron and haltingly explained the circumstances. I requested five days leave of absence covering the day before, the day itself and three days after the operation.

"It is very important to me Donald. I'll make up the study lost, I promise, but I need to be with my brother and family at this time."

I knew he was totally against leaves of absence (except unavoidably funerals, 'a cold bastard' was the general consensus). I had decided however if he refused me I would take the time despite him.

He looked at me shocked. " Leave of absence, five days leave of absence, you can't be serious?"

" I am Donald and I will take the time with or without your permission," I replied defiantly. I was shaking now, my temper roused. How dare he try and deny me this compassionate request.

"You're a cruel, cold blooded tyrant" I began …

"Caterine" he interrupted, "before you continue, please let me finish. You will pack your case and return to your brother and family immediately. Do not return until you feel ready to re-start your studies: five days only, what rubbish!" I was astonished and then humbled.

"I apologise for my remarks" I said somewhat embarrassed at my outburst.

"Nonsense, I know my reputation and you're overwrought, quite understandably. Nothing in life is so important as the health of a loved one. My sincerest wishes for a successful outcome." He came over to me and we shook hands.

"Thank you" I replied and left. No 'cold bastard' then, a very unusual man.

David entered the operating theatre on 15th January at 9am. He exited it at 6.45pm. Nine and three quarter hours later. All we could do as a family was wait. Wait for fate to show her hand, wait for the aftermath – the consequences of what went before. The evening prior to surgery David asked all of us to visit him personally. Maman first, myself next and then Alix. What he said to Maman and Alix I know not, they were personal and private as were his words to me. Suffice to add what I experienced during our private talk demonstrated the courage, integrity and quality of character of an exceptional man, my dearly beloved brother, David.

The surgeon, Xavier Texier, suggested we wait in our Montparnasse apartment for the major part of the operation, returning to the hospital at 6pm when the surgery should be nearing completion. If, as he put it, there were any unforeseen developments we would receive a call. This plan was also David's personal request and we all complied with his wishes. No call was received.

At 6.46 Xavier Texier entered our private waiting room. He did not have to utter a word, his face said it all. He was smiling. "Well, that's that. David will not be seeing his unwelcome visitor again. He's in a stable condition and a fit young man. Now it depends on how long it takes for his body to recover and to heal itself." He did not, of course, refer to his mind.

On the 20th January I knocked on Donald Cameron's door and I too was smiling, grinning actually. "He's fine – 100% – obviously recuperating but no complications, mind sharp as a needle, unimpaired, no problems at all."

"Wonderful!" Cameron exclaimed "what a relief for all of you. Right, a celebration's in order. Is your flatmate, may I ask, male or female?"

"Pardon" I replied. "Oh heavens, female, Shona Carruthers. I've no time for anything else on this course. I've barely time to eat or sleep." I stopped suddenly, alarmed at another outburst, but Cameron laughed.

"Well" he said "bring your female mate and join me for dinner to-night. Meet me here at 7.30, dress casual but elegant."

I was dumbfounded, but not as much as Shona.

"My God!" She exclaimed when I told her. "What on earth should we wear?"

It was an unusual evening as befitted an unusual man. He had reserved a table (or so we thought) at an expensive restaurant near Royal Exchange Square which specialised in Scottish fayre and he was scintillating company: witty, amusing and full of hilarious anecdotes. If I was astonished, Shona fell completely under his spell and that Hollywood smile. It turned out that the table was a permanent reservation as he dined out often.

At the end of January I received a text message from David to give him a call adding 'absolutely no problems'. He and Alix were in Paris with Maman for a few days and then flying to Barbados staying at our haunt the Caribbean Club in St James. It was where they had spent their honeymoon. Alix answered my call to Montparnasse bursting with the news. She was pregnant and it was twins. Mon Dieu, I nearly dropped my mobile and started dancing round the room with joy. Shona emerging from her bedroom, study forgotten, exclaimed "Caterine, I can't hear myself think!" Somewhat irritated until sharing in my happiness.

Alix told me: "I realise now why I was so 'weepy' at Marchmont, my hormones were doing double somersaults!"

Shona spoke to her too thrilled for both of them. Then congratulations to David. I cannot remember him so emotional since Papa's demise and of course Maman; more chatter, laughter, pure joy.

Chapter Six

My dissertation subject was the history of painting from the cavemen to the present day. Part of it only would be required for my doctorate degree but all of it would be presented as a candidate for the newly instigated award now ratified. I was very blessed. The travel required was outside the bursary budget. David and Maman offered to pay for it but Donald refused. Other plans were in place. Bartholomew Gilmore opened his benevolent wallet again and would accept no reimbursement. I wrote to thank him and received a call a few days later.

"Caterine, your efforts have given me already great pleasure. To use a blunt expression you've got guts as well as great ability. Often they don't coincide. I know you'll give it your best shot. Just one warning …"

"What's that?" I asked cautiously holding the receiver.

"Make sure I'm not the bull's-eye! Good luck."

I laughed and bid him 'au revoir'.

Soon afterwards I found myself spinning like the proverbial top all over Europe. Apart from attending lectures and tutorials as usual my free time, weekends and term holidays had to be maximised to cope with the workload.

Donald in conjunction with Maman and David set up an

explicit timetable. Sometimes I felt like a puppet pulled hither and thither to everyone's tune but it was to give me an opportunity always to have a failsafe, always somewhere I could wind down especially at weekends although they were also work orientated.

What a support team they were, I nicknamed them the posse.

For my dissertation research I visited numerous galleries from the National and Tate in London to the Prado in Madrid, Royal in Brussels and Antwerp, the Uffizi in Florence and even the Sistine Chapel in the Vatican to gaze in awe at those creations of Michelangelo.

The Louvre in Paris was a second home to me overflowing with masterpieces from the incomparable Leonardo da Vinci's Mona Lisa to Mantegna's The Crucifixion interspersed with exhibits from such geniuses as Raphael, Degas, Titian and Watteau, plus hundreds more. Of course I was still absorbing and revising on antique furniture, ceramics and classic architecture for the general exams.

The "posse" as I named them ensured that during any weekend I was able to travel easily to Maman in Paris, David in Zurich and Donald in Scotland. Shona was a staunch friend and I spent time with her at KG, our beloved Kelvingrove apartment or at Marchmont for weekends when we would study for a designated period and then ride out on Jimmy Black the local farmer's two hunters. It had been decided, in consensus, that barring emergency Saturdays were sacrosanct for sports, relaxation and some form of leisure. And so with Shona a format prevailed, we walked together for miles and cycled for many more. Our chatter switched between French and English which Shona benefited from for her joint honours degree in modern languages.

In my final year, just before Christmas I lingered after one of Donald's lectures to clarify a point about Renaissance architecture.

"Come and have coffee in my rooms, Caterine," Donald grinned, "I have a new supply of your favourite chocolate!"

"Let's go," I laughed and soon we were seated together on his Chesterfield sofa munching my favourite brand of chocolate bar.

Donald's rooms were exceptionally well furnished, all cabinetmaker pieces and antiques. This had puzzled me at first. When I had ventured to comment, he had dismissed it.

"Inherited from my predecessor" he had replied casually. "It will be donated to my successor likewise". He had glanced round and continued "unless I can pack a large removal van in the cloisters one foggy winter night and spirit all away!"

I had laughed at the absurdity.

"Thanks for the coffee Donald and of course the chocolate. I'll see you on Monday," I smiled as I reached for the door handle.

"You've forgotten, Caterine, I'll see you at the University Christmas Ball on Saturday," Donald replied.

There was silence.

"No, Donald, you won't. I'm not going to this year's Ball."

"What! Why not? There's no way you should be working this weekend. Don't be ridiculous and let some boyfriend down. I expect to see you and claim at least one dance" and he smiled his Hollywood smile. I looked at him releasing the door handle.

"Donald, I'm not going to the Ball because I don't have a partner, never mind a boyfriend. No one asked me. I'm never here to meet anyone. I don't mix in the same year now, nearly everyone from my year's graduated and my lectures are so diverse, some here some in the Sorbonne and then the travel. It's just not possible."

I halted, my voice faltering, feeling somewhat foolish. There was a pause. Then Donald said:

"Well, I'm inviting you. Now do you have an appropriate dress here, if not you can...."

I stopped him, exclaiming "you can't be serious. Partner you, a Dean of the Faculty. It's unheard of, unconventional, why you are.." I hesitated.

"Not acceptable," he finished the sentence for me, now grinning.

"Of course not," I replied, "but the other students, lecturers, Deans, will be ..." I hesitated, and changed the adjective from 'shocked' to 'surprised'.

"Excellent," Donald said, "loosen some dead spiders from their cobwebbed brains!"

And so it was settled. On Saturday evening he collected me from KG and we set off for the Christmas Glasgow University Ball. Donald wore Prince Charlie regalia and I had chosen my dress Sinclair evening kilt with jabots and velvet waistcoat.

On reflection I have to admit the reaction of the other guests amused me. When we were announced by the MC, the dancing ceased and everyone stared in astonishment as the orchestra continued playing in ignorance of this 'drama'.

The evening was a memorable one. Gerald and Shona joined us first. Suddenly people seemed to flock to our table. Neither Donald nor I were short of partners. Donald knew every dance faultlessly and entertained us, other students and members of the university staff with anecdotes, humour and impersonations. These included one of the University Chancellor and in his presence.

The Chancellor's reaction: "My God, Donald, you're better at me than I am. I'll need to practise."

The evening was hilarious.

Donald took his leave at KG with the words: "Mademoiselle, c'était formidable. Bonne Nuit". Kissing my hand.

I laughed "D'accord, Monsieur, formidable. Bonne Nuit."

Gerald and Shona were staying with other friends in the west end– a diplomatic decision! After a quick shower I flopped into bed to dream of old-fashioned evenings of song and dance in the Scottish Highlands in the days of yore!

One fact was certain during the Monday morning lecture from Professor Donald Cameron. By tacit consent, no hilarity now. It was business as usual. Everyone understood: the measure of a very unusual man!

Graduation! My graduation! Now I could really call myself Dr Sinclair. It was an exciting day, a day of fulfilment. The gaining of a doctorate was somehow rather special. I now felt able to be compared with Papa and David at least on the academic ladder, although I was only on the early rungs! For me however it was a new beginning, the dawn in the distance of a different horizon and I was tingling with anticipation.

The weekend following the ceremony we held a mini celebration at Marchmont with friends and family in mid July. The weather was fine, warm, inviting good humour, good wishes and good luck.

Uncle Fergus and Aunt Bebe with our Australian cousins joined us on a special visit. The 'doublet', the nickname for Alix and David's twins, three years old now, were permitted a display of showmanship with all the other young children of our family and friends. They entertained us hilariously with their antics on the lawn. How lovely to share with them in the innocence of childhood, untainted by the sickness of our society, unimpaired for now by the growing cancers of our scientifically sophisticated modern world. And Grégoire was present too with his fiancée, loved and in love, he had found his Alix to quote David. What a party it was and a very special day. I wandered off amongst the celebrations to have some private thoughts and sat in my special place on a seat in the rose garden.

Suddenly a voice at my shoulder interrupted my reverie and I turned in surprise. It was Gildas. I knew he had received an invitation but had not expected him to attend. David,

Maman and the family had spent numerous holidays at his château in La Touraine. For some reason usually work defined I had never been able to join them. In fact I had not seen him since that ignominious incident at Graham McCallum's 21st.

"Caterine," he addressed me, "a small gift to congratulate you on a splendid achievement."

I opened the exquisitely wrapped box. It revealed a diary, leather bound, gold embossed – a ten-year diary, my name engraved on its outside cover. Inside there was a note on that white crested paper, " To Caterine Sinclair to record her future memories." It was written in that distinguished hand. I looked up to thank him but he had gone.

Some red roses from a nearby bed had already cast their petals and an unexpected breeze blew them in front of me, lifeless at my feet. I shuddered. It was as if a phantom had been standing at my shoulder threatening my very being, my future life.

I shook myself and my imagination moving forward again to meet my guests.

Donald Cameron and Bartholomew Gilmour were both there delighted to be present at this post celebration. I felt particularly honoured. From each I had received an unexpected present the day before my graduation ceremony. At a meeting in Donald Cameron's rooms at Glasgow University Bartholomew Gilmore had handed me a cheque, for £5,000. I was overwhelmed, speechless.

"You've given me so much already" I said to him "Your endorsement and the bursary have allowed me to explore and develop unlimited, obtain knowledge, travel, discover territories otherwise unbidden."

He interrupted me "It's completely justifiable this graduation gift, you've worked dedicatedly and deserve this brilliant degree, even beyond what Donald and I had expected. The ultimate summit , the Gold Medal for the Premier Fine Arts Student in Europe. Use the cheque to invest in an antiquary which gives you pleasure, pleasure throughout your life as your achievement has given me."

He walked forward to shake my hand. On impulse I kissed him on both cheeks. He flushed and replied "Best thing that's happened to me in years."

Donald and I joined in his laugher before he left.

Donald also had a present for me but quite different – a painting, my 'specialised subject.'

"I can't accept this," I stuttered recognising it, looking at it in disbelief.

"Why not?" he inquired.

"Its value: at auction this would fetch £18,000 perhaps more in to-day's market place."

"You still have some fine tuning Caterine," he responded, "over £20,000." Is that your only objection to accepting, its value?"

I was staring at it, its young beauty still maturing.

"Yes, well yes, I suppose so," I replied in stupefaction.

"Then I suggest you accept it before I change my mind at your obduracy. One day I may explain why I decided to present you with it, or I may not!"

I took the painting clasped in my arms. I left in disbelief in my old battered family car. Where on earth had he found the money? How could he afford it? Should I return it? I would consult the family. My God, he was indeed an unusual, a very unusual man!

Thereafter Donald Cameron was again in charge. Not that my family was left un-consulted but everyone agreed that I should accept his advice. To decide which way to tread, which path to follow, to climb this mountain of ambition and achieve the summit of my success.

I had been privileged to receive several offers from the great Fine Arts houses of Europe, including Dunns, Crichtons and Montague-Smythe, the latter the most prestigious.

Founded in 1765 by Sebastian Montague, it had held its first sale under his own name, an innovation at that time. That sale of an historian household effects raised a four figure sum a fortune in the mid 18th century. Recently Montague-Smythe held another auction for the contents of another house with royal connections. This sale realised many millions of pounds Sterling. Globally their offices now spread over 80 countries and they were a major force in the United States.

Consequently on Donald's advice I had chosen Montague-Smythe, one of the oldest Fine Arts valuers and auctioneers in the world and with a contract befitting its domain. As it was in this arena I had decided to pursue my ambitions, this was the house we concurred in which I could realise them.

In early August I spent two weeks with David and Alix in Zurich. For one week of this period my dear brother was still working on a special project for the mercantile bank, leaving their newly purchased traditional Swiss house early in the morning and returning about 8pm at night.

"Is David not working too hard?" I asked Alix.

"How do you think he looks?" she replied as we sat at their breakfast bar over coffee, Angus and Alexandra had been deposited at the home of nursery school friends for the morning.

"Never better, I must admit," I conceded, "but" hesitating …

"I understand only too well your concerns, Caterine, but I assure you he's thriving, loves the job. David consulted Xavier Texier for "check-ups", nothing, a clean bill of health. The uninvited guest who gate-crashed our marriage has been totally evicted, consigned to the past, never to revisit ."

Alix picked up the coffee jug and refilled our cups.

"Now as you know, David's taking a week's holiday from Friday. What would you like to do?"

"Just join in the family life", I replied.

We smiled at each other and raised our cups, "Santé"!

For that holiday week that is exactly what we did.

We took the doublet to children's holiday entertainment in Zurich, played games in the spacious garden, walks in the surrounding countryside, riding at the local stables and then some shopping.

Maman, who was staying at Uncle Thierry and Aunt Sylvie in Bergerac had given me some months ago a cheque. It was the financial realisation of an endowment policy set up by herself independent of Papa's estate. Most of the sum I had re-invested but with the balance I had retained I bought first of all an antique lamp for David and Alix's new home which I'd unearthed in a "brocante" outside Zurich plus two old-fashioned photograph albums for each of the children, which I had discovered on my European travels. As yet for Maman, I could not find an appropriate gift!

All the family kissed me *au revoir* at Zurich airport. I flew directly to Glasgow, collected the Sinclair jalopy, which started on the second attempt and drove to KG. The apartment had remained empty over the holiday period since my graduation. Depending on my career options a decision would be taken to retain it and rent it out or sell, according to market conditions.

I was pondering these options sitting in Donald Cameron's rooms at Glasgow University the morning after my arrival from Switzerland, waiting for him to appear.

The phone rang. I hesitated and then answered it. It was Donald.

"Caterine, there's been a development. I'm at Glasgow Airport and its bloody chaos. Can you collect me? I'll be in the bar at the airport hotel."

The line went dead. I was annoyed. This would take time and I was meeting some of my fellow graduates for a meal that evening including Shona. I texted her an explanation, apologising if I was late.

Donald identified amid further chaos at the hotel returned with me to his university rooms.

"What on earth is the problem?" I asked. " You've said nothing, completely silent, rude almost. Why?"

I was angry now, temper roused, ten minutes only before meeting Shona and my pals for dinner.

"I've been thinking, pondering," he muttered frustratingly. "We need time to talk. Let's go for something to eat, to my restaurant."

He always referred to it like that – the one I had dined with him and Shona after David's operation and the celebration that all was well.

I was now furious.

"What do you mean? Have you not dominated my life enough? For the last five years I've lived in your pocket exercised now and again at your control, a puppet dangling on your harness, pulling me when you wanted me to perform to your tune. I've had enough, I'm not your mistress, find someone else to satisfy your warped desires."

And I left childishly slamming, with difficulty, the heavy oak door!

The meal was not a success, not for me. I joined in the reminiscences, the anecdotes and the laughter but my contribution was shallow, hollow, an act. I was miserable. Shona recognised it of course. We returned to KG for the night and we talked.

"Caterine, I am unable to advise you on this complex subject. Suffice to say your achievements are outstanding, remarkable but perhaps for me not surprising knowing you as I have done from our early schooldays; however, even I didn't expect such academic accolades. You've won the ultimate glory; not a Scottish award nor a British one but the award encompassing every country in the E.E.C. The gold medal of Europe – the crown laureate. Is this not enough for you?

I love you as my dearest friend but I fear sometimes for your future. Your temper is one thing but it flashes and is extinguished and who's perfect? Certainly not me. No, what concerns me is a part of you I fail to understand. This man, Donald Cameron, I remember I called a slave driver. Then I met him, recognised his qualities. My final comment: you were a slave demanding to be driven, pleading for the pain of his academic whip. I think he deserves a laurel from your victory crown. Good night Caterine!"

I sat for some time. How long I cannot remember now. What I do recall is that the relentless rain which had persisted all that day ceased. As I adjusted my curtains, I saw a dark sky and surprisingly a full moon, casting is luminous light over the city: a welcome omen.

We met in the university car park. I was arriving, as he was about to depart.

"I was coming to see you," we said simultaneously and then we were 'mates' again. Two stupid, intelligent human beings with one goal in common: over coffee the discussion ensued. The development – de Veres!

It was a young house, a virgin in fine arts. Its history was its founder Albert de Vere, but with no past. De Vere had established the company only six years previously: a former director of Dunns an achievement gained in his early thirties, there had been a fall out, hence his exit. De Veres however, was growing rapidly its reputation increasing – risks were taken but had paid off: for example the Gough collection. The other houses had walked away from it as too modern for the market place and had been proven wrong – records were achieved for this type of portfolio a market recognised by Albert de Vere, targeted and won.

Donald was pacing up and down his rooms, more disturbed than I had ever seen him – a man at a crossroads, no actually, my crossroads!

"He phoned me personally," Donald told me, "with an invitation to their Paris head office all expenses paid of course. I tried to contact you, failed and just caught the flight."

" But," I replied, "we discounted them, too young, requiring to mature.

"Yes, yes I know that," Donald replied, now sounding irritated.

This time I kept my temper, refrained from my usual retort, recognising his concerns for me knowing how much I needed his advice and also what care he had taken to provide it.

He muttered, " Difficult, damnably difficult."

"Donald," I said, " I have an idea."

"What is it?" he replied absently still immersed in concentration.

"We need to talk," I continued "Let's go to your restaurant for something to eat, I have no prior engagements!" We laughed and we did.

The decision was made – DE VERES! We flew together to Paris to negotiate the contract and I signed. Albert de Vere's qualities I recognised and we established a common bond. Donald donated me from the academia of his cradle into the arms of my future parentage to be raised and to develop into what I wanted to become.

Chapter Seven

The appointment at de Veres sealed the start of my career climb: grappling with facts and information, spending numerous private hours of study to absorb knowledge, attempting to gain that elusive experience in as short a period as possible. In retrospect this was the ascent of my personal Eiger, just for Papa and to redeem myself. Every word I read, every fact I learned, every image I saw, every comment I heard – I remembered them. They were locked away in a compartment of my mind but I held the key waiting to open the door of opportunity, trap my prey of ambition and devour its success.

Of course I worked with the de Veres team based in Paris: most were young, all enthusiastic, very knowledgeable and particularly motivated.

Everyone was a high achiever, competitive for promotion opportunities but unified by one common factor: the master himself, Albert de Veres.

After my initial induction talk with him on my first day in the Paris headquarters, he had concluded:

"Most important, Caterine, we work as a team. In the general work environment we share our information and experience, assisting each other, to the benefit of all and the success of de Veres."

"Yes, M. de Veres" I had replied "I'll remember."

"And remember one other factor" he said as I turned to leave.

"What's that?" I asked anxiously, thinking for some obscure reason I might have a hole in my tights.

"I'm Albert. As I said it's a team effort, but one warning. Don't hide any mistake from me. Be honest and you'll receive my full assistance to correct it and learn from it."

He came forward and we shook hands.

"I'm delighted, as I said earlier, you accepted my offer to become a member of our team. Bravo."

As I left his rooms, I was reminded of a man of similar persuasions: Professor Donald Cameron!

Before Easter, eight months after starting with de Veres, I was bustling round the Montparnasse apartment awaiting Shona's arrival for the weekend. Justine our loyal French maid had performed one of her annual 'spring cleans' which meant complete perfection, nothing out of place but nothing 'in place' either and some of my dictaphone tapes had walked from the middle of my desk to explore the rooms of the apartment no doubt coming to rest in some unbidden corner!

Suddenly, the doorbell clanged. It had always been too loud but Maman and I had never rectified it. I hurried down the stairs and along the corridor to answer it.

"Shona" I gasped " you said you'd call me from the station to collect you and Mon Dieu you're soaking wet. Did you walk from the station in this rainstorm?"

Shona nodded. She was a sorry sight. Water streaming down her face, short brown bob plastered to her cheeks and puddles developing all round her from large drops deposited from her raincoat on the entrance tiled floor.

"My God, what a mess," I cried " you must be mad."

Immediately, I regretted my remarks. Shona's face

crumpled as she burst into sobs, teardrops and raindrops mingling indiscriminately on her wet, mournful face.

Twenty minutes later, after a hot shower, a change of clothes and a brandy and soda Shona looked better, rain drops gone but tear drops not!

"It's Gerald" she told me voice trembling " we've had a terrible row. He won't speak to me". She broke down sobbing again.

Eventually I calmed her and then Shona explained what had happened.

The Marketing Director at Masons, the textile company where she worked had invited her to lunch, emphasising it was a business proposal. Shona had smiled weakly recalling the remark.

"Mr Jackson offered me a management position in their Geneva office, to launch a new product line," Shona continued. " Initially researching and then establishing distribution in Switzerland. If that was successful, I would be given the opportunity to expand sales into Germany and France." She hesitated, but I remained silent.

"They, I mean the company, seem to be very pleased with my progress."

I knew that was an understatement by Shona, but disregarded challenging it, letting her continue.

"Mr Jackson has given me a week to make my decision, that means next Wednesday. I admit" said Shona sipping now at her brandy, " I was surprised and excited. Dad and Mum are on holiday and so I have not contacted them as yet but of course, I phoned Gerald." To stifle tears, Shona took a gulp of brandy this time.

"He was furious, Caterine, said I was betraying him and our future. I told him I was unsure and would meet him the following evening to discuss matters but he was adamant: no meeting and certainly no discussions. It was him or the job!"

Her voice broke again.

"What can I do? I've no choice. The wedding is set for September, under six months time and I've promised to marry him. We've been together for so many years and made a commitment. It was wrong of me to consider this promotion, put myself first, but I was so pleased to receive the credit for some of my ideas and I thought Gerald and I could at least discuss some options, perhaps ...."

"Shona," I interrupted her "wait here in the salon while I go and change. We're going out to dinner."

"Caterine, I can't. My mind's a mess."

"That is why we're going out," I replied refilling her brandy and soda, " to a little discreet restaurant nearby and in a taxi in this downpour. While I change put some thoughts together but no discussions over dinner. Tell me your thinking to-night when we return."

It was 2.30 in the morning before we retired for the night! What a battle. I wished Maman had been there to lend her logical mind but she was staying with friends near Avignon for ten days, with whom she'd been at university. On Saturday morning after a late breakfast of *pain de campagne*, *confiture* and coffee I sent Shona out for a walk in Parc Georges Brassens and took the opportunity to make some discreet phone calls.

In the afternoon Shona and I explored some of the Parisian markets and mesmerising melée of shops returning to Montparnasse for supper.

Over apéritifs, we talked again about her dilemma.

"I really enjoy the job Caterine and obviously would relish the opportunity to work with the Swiss sales team planning our assault on the market place. It's not as you know, a large market by volume in an European equation but lucrative and sophisticated," she sighed, "but I owe Gerald so much over the years, his devotion, his steadfastness and of course his love, plus he's worked so hard on his medical career and is still studying for us."

She finished her *kir* and looked at me somewhat shamefaced.

"Would you mind if I phoned Gerald now, before we eat. I'd feel happier if I've spoken to him. I know you think I'm weak, but I do love him. Probably I was too hasty, lacking any consideration when I told him about this job opportunity," she said fiddling with the sapphire and diamond ring on her finger.

"Of course not Shona," I replied " it's your decision. Call him now and I'll set the table. Our quiche is ready in the oven."

Ten minutes later she returned all smiles.

"That's settled. I'm staying at his flat tomorrow night after arriving at Gatwick."

My heart sank, but I served supper, without comment. After eating, we listened to some of our favourite music, reminding us of evenings at KG, when we could relax and forget study.

We played some modern classics, film music and then a few vintage favourites from Haydn, Beethoven and finally, the finale Ravel's Rhapsodie Espagnole.

Shona kissed me good night.

"You're my best friend, Caterine, always. Incredible really to consider we've been pals since kindergarten! *Incroyable!*"

"Shona," I responded " that's my word!" and we laughed.

Arrangements were made for the morning when Shona was taking a direct flight to Gatwick.

As I left her at Gare du Nord, both of us standing on the platform, I handed her a note inside an envelope. She looked at me startled.

"What's this Caterine? I don't understand."

I grinned " Well unfortunately, it's not money, Shona but the contents, I think, have even more value. Open it during your journey! Au revoir et bon voyage!"

Shona phoned me from her London apartment on Monday evening. Her decision was made. She chose Geneva. The wedding was off!

And the note? The advice I received from Maman and David during my discreet phone calls. Advice which confirmed my opinion.

The note read:

Dear Shona,

Just ask Gerald why?

1/ Why was he not prepared to sit down with you and have a discussion, look at options with you, the woman he loves?

2/ Why was he not prepared to consider your career as you considered his if you are the woman he loves?

3/ Why did Gerald create this crisis and how will he respond in the future during other crises when he is married to you, the woman he loves?

4/ Then ask yourself:

Why do I want to marry this man?

Then make your decision.

With love

Caterine, David and Aunt Véronique.

For several months after Shona's visit to Paris, I became immersed in my work: projects, travel, presentations and study, I suppose it was an insular existence, but I never noticed absorbed in a world of 'objets d'art' which were my love affair.

Naturally I went on some dates, the theatre, concerts and dinners and participated in various social activities often with Albert de Vere, his wife Céline and their two young children, whom I thought adorable.

"Caterine," Céline upbraided me often "you're working too hard. You must wind down!"

"Not yet" I replied laughing "too much to do, too much to see and far too much to learn."

Then at the end of June of that year I received two wedding invitations for the month of September, three weeks apart: one was to Grégoire's and the other to Elisée Silvère's, the younger sister of Gildas. I accepted both.

Grégoire, dear Grégoire, it was such a joyous occasion: a real family reunion.

"Mon Dieu David" I said "I can't believe Angus and Alexandra are four years old already. I'm beginning to feel an aged auntie at 24!"

My brother laughed.

"I'm shocked too, Petite. How time flies!"

"But not fast enough for me" Alix groaned. "Hurry on Christmas!"

"I think you look brilliant" I said smiling at my sister-in-law. "At least it's not twins again or are you keeping a secret?"

"Caterine. Don't dare joke about that. One more is quite enough!"

David and Alix were expecting their third child in December. Everyone was overjoyed.

"Ladies and gentlemen. Please raise your glasses: the Bride and Groom."

I turned to look at the wedding party.

Grégoire, dearest Grégoire bursting with pride – on his side his lovely serenely smiling bride. They were followed by Maman, the matron of honour, tall and striking with Marie-Thérèse, the chief bridesmaid in her elegant creation from the House of D'Aquin which she had joined as a designer.

Then the bride's parents with Oncle Thierry and Tante Sylvie. What a family occasion!

The wedding two weeks later at that beautiful château in La

Touraine was not any less memorable, perhaps that is a summation of what a wedding should mean. Being close friends of the du Gilbert family we had been invited, the Sinclair clan, to spend the weekend.

Unfortunately, I was working 'double overtime' on a project for Albert and had excused myself from the Friday dinner party arriving later that evening about 10 pm.

"Mon Dieu" Maman greeted me in the entrance hallway. "We were becoming concerned, and you're looking tired" she added reprovingly.

"Just the drive" I answered stifling a yawn.

"Come in" David put his arm round my shoulders. "You need a post aperitif and Alix's waiting."

We entered what I assumed was the grand Drawing Room. It was majestic, alive with activity, embraced by elegant guests. I was annoyed with myself for not showering and changing at the château instead of the office; my jade silk coat dress had suffered from the journey, creased and limp. Suddenly I felt ill-attired and unusual for me ill at ease.

It was at this point that the imposing double doors of the Grand Drawing Room opened to reveal the equally imposing figure of Gildas himself, surrounded by a group of guests and family members, some whom I recalled from David and Alix's wedding.

On seeing me, Gildas strode over.

"Welcome to Saint Roche Rivière, Caterine," he greeted me in his usual cool manner. "I'm sorry you've been unable to join us here before. Let me refill your glass and come and meet my family and friends."

I had no choice but to follow him. Soon I was embroiled in chatter and banter which I would have preferred to avoid.

Handing me my champagne flute now refilled, Gildas asked:

"As you haven't been able to visit Saint Roche Rivière before, what about a tour on Sunday after we've recovered from the wedding celebrations? I'd enjoy showing you my family home."

"Thank you, Gildas" I replied, adding somewhat prosaically, "it would give me much pleasure."

When I flopped into bed in my luxurious suite taking little interest in the detail of the traditional 17th century décor and my surroundings, I realised that I was tired, very tired indeed!

'When I from Hawes to Richmond did repair
It chanced that I saw standing in a dell
Three aspects and three corners of a square
And one not four yards distant near a well.

What this imported I could ill divine
And pulling now the rein my horse to stop
I saw three pillars standing in a line
The last stone pillar on a dark hilltop.'

The crooked man was standing beside me then suddenly wafted away but pointing with his riding whip into the far beyond.

I awoke startled, shaken, unaware of my surroundings when my alarm bell shrilled –7am.

Stumbling out of that unfamiliar bed, I realised where I was, shaking myself into reality. Too much work, Céline was right, I must wind down: my imagination replicated in my dreams was running riot.

I washed away the fatigue and images in a exhilarating hot and contrastingly cold shower!

The wedding ceremony on that Saturday afternoon in the family chapel was simple and moving just like the one three weeks earlier: the bride equally as beautiful and serene as her groom was proud. The setting, naturally, was of a different dimension as befitted the du Gilbert status.

As for the wedding feast, it was quite magnificent with tented awnings erected stretching from the Grand Drawing Room doors open at both entrances admitting the lazy September sun.

Aromas from the fragrant butterfly trees wafted in from the shrubbery while scents from a plethora of blossoms in the glorious gardens permeated the joyous atmosphere.

Maman joined me on the south terrace.

"Quite an occasion Caterine. Don't you agree?"

"Breathtaking" I answered looking round. "How privileged to own all this."

"Almost unfair if you haven't earned it" I thought to myself and then wondered if I was being unjust. According to David, Gildas worked assiduously to protect and enhance the family heritage.

With a sigh I wandered back to my suite to change for the evening party.

During the night time celebrations, from time to time, I observed Gildas and was surprised. Much more sociable than I had expected, he circulated constantly amongst his guests, male or female where hilarity seemed to prevail.

I danced often with members of my own family and the du Gilbert's including Gildas's cousins Jacques and Philippe whom I had met at David and Alix's engagement party: Jacques was accompanied by a well known French TV presenter and Philippe by a British supermodel!

Suddenly I discovered that I was enjoying myself. David teased me as I sat down at the family table, after a vigorous jive, hastily gulping some welcome water.

"Watch out Petite, too many suitors. You're spoilt for choice. This could be dangerous."

I laughed. "No chance, David. I've more important priorities."

Turning to Alix on my other side, I ventured.

"Gildas seems very sociable, not what I expected."

"But he's always like that, Caterine" Alix replied "an amusing, attentive and generous host and so much fun with all of the children. They adore him."

I was completely taken aback.

"I haven't seen him with any partner. Doesn't he have a personal guest?"

There was silence, then Alix giggled.

"What is it? What do you know I don't?" I asked.

"Well" Alix replied looking round, not wanting to be overheard.

"It's no secret, at least not in the family, Gildas keeps a mistress in Paris."

"Pardon? What do you mean?"

"Of course, mistress is not the right word, as he's widowed but you know" and she grinned.

"But why's she not here? Surely they'll get married."

"Don't be ridiculous, Caterine, men like Gildas don't marry their mistresses" Alix replied still grinning.

"How naïve of me" I thought. "Poor girl, probably madly in love with her Count but a dangerous liaison. He would not marry her. She was kept only for his sexual pleasure: a typical aristocratic bastard – that just about summed him up!"

Suddenly, I heard those familiar tones at my shoulder.

"Are you well enough to dance with me this time, Caterine?"

More laughter erupted from the family gathering.

"Certainly Gildas, I've outgrown the spots!"

It was a waltz, traditional Strauss: he danced well, holding me firmly and leading us expertly round the crowded floor.

"I know you like your horses and ride well David's told me.

What about a trek tomorrow afternoon with your family over the estate?"

"I'd enjoy that" I replied as the music finished and we walked to my table. For some illogical reason I felt apprehensive. Why?

As Gildas had already danced with Maman and Alix, he sat down and joined in the general banter for a few minutes and then left to attend to his guests.

Suddenly I felt chilled, although the room was still warm but the flames on the candelabra in front of me flickered and yet there was no draught.

Instinctively, I turned round: glancing over my shoulder I saw him, Gildas, standing at one of the pilasters staring at me. Immediately he registered my look he strode off moving through the melee mingling with his guests.

For some reason I felt unnerved. Turning back I heard David's voice:

"Good heavens, the candles have gone out. How bizarre. Caterine, give me your candelabra and I'll relight it from mine."

Automatically I stretched out my hand.

"Damn it, it's hot!" I exclaimed.

"Don't be ridiculous" David answered "it's solid gold, you must have touched candle grease. Leave it to me."

He walked round to my place and re-lit the candles from his own.

Everyone clapped.

"Bravo David, we're back in business."

But I still felt chilled.

On the following morning, Sunday, Gildas gave me his personal conducted tour of Saint Roche Rivière. The actual château architecture came as a surprise to me. Built at the beginning of the seventeenth century on the site of a fortified castle razed to the ground by a felonious nobleman, it enchants any visitor with a haunting medieval power and yet still encompasses the grandeur of Louis XIV's vision.

The original owners, the du Gilbert ancestors had been influential courtiers, close to royal family and the crowns of France. No one would have failed to be impressed! Gildas was very well informed about the furniture and artefacts naturally all bearing the mark of the cabinetmaker. It was ornate and majestic, walls covered with paintings of noble family figures gazing haughtily down at us as we walked below. All the tapestries which draped the walls were exquisite their sometimes faded beauty only emphasising the past proud history and continuing majesty of a magnificent member of the incomparable châteaux of France.

It was as we returned together to the entrance hallway with the rusticated pilasters passing the former guardroom that the incident occurred. Gildas and I walked over to join David, Alix and Maman who were waiting for us. The doublet were playing in the grounds with the coterie of family and friends remaining for a second stay overnight. Gildas had with his sister Elisée, a younger brother called Frédéric, aged twenty-five. The doublet had fallen in love with him and he in turn was happy to entertain them. He was fun, amusing, and had whisked them off to the stables and two adorable Shetland ponies.

Alix and I were standing at the entrance to Gildas's private sitting room the door of which was open. Gracing both sides of the entrance archway were two paintings. Alix exclaimed staring at the one on the right,

"It's so vivid. What is it Caterine?"

I turned to look. Alix obviously knew this room, I did not. It was furnished in the style of the late eighteenth century, early nineteenth century gracious but comfortable. To our amusement Alix and I saw two of Gildas's four cats, staring at us. Two of his cats were Persians, the others tabbies, a white and dark tortoiseshell. The latter two were sitting together reclining on a Louis-Philippe claret coloured sofa regarding us with disdain intruding on their regime. We both laughed and I turned to examine the painting. I glanced at it recognising it immediately proudly announcing:

"1887, Claude Monet," then I stopped knowing I was mistaken. Before I could correct my error, the cool tones of Gildas interrupted me, " You're correct Caterine on the period, but the artist was Edouard Manet, 1874."

There was a serious silence. I was furious but as his guest and before my family courtesy was paramount and breeding prevailed.

"Of course," I replied, " how careless of me," and wandered nonchalantly into the gardens.

I was seething, controlling my temper with great difficulty grateful for the fresh air. David, equally casually, followed me.

"Petite, you cannot recognise every painting especially the Impressionists which you mentioned to me recently as your weaker department."

I turned to face him. "But I did recognise it, realised my error, about to correct it when he interrupted, never gave me a chance."

Alix arrived at this point as I added, "I cannot like this man and I am not going riding this afternoon. Please make my excuses".

David had other ideas and confronted me: "Caterine you will not refuse to go riding. Firstly, he's your host, invited you to his sister's wedding. Secondly, he's a close friend to Alix and me. A man highly regarded by Papa and now, having met him, Maman and the man whose assistance was a major contribution in my standing in front of you today, healthy, happy and sound of mind, sane."

I stared at my beloved brother: "What do you mean, I don't understand."

"Gildas was the man who recommended and personally secured Xavier Texier to perform my operation. Further, despite protests from me, he paid for every penny of it, accepting no offers of reimbursement."

There was no defence!

We set off just before 3 pm. Maman, David, Gildas and me on four lovely animals for a leisurely trek through woodland and open countryside on his estate. David and Maman were saddled on two three-quarter breds, more solid and docile for a country ride. He and I were on two thoroughbreds, mine a grey named Avril and he on a dark bay, Pascal.

Over lunch he had asked us our preference. " The three quarter breds for me," replied David. "Everyone knows I'm more able round a golf course than a riding school."

"Me too," agreed Maman laughing, " I'll stay safe and respect the old bones."

It was a sunny September weekend, warm but fresh and inviting. If it had not been for the earlier incident I would have looked forward to it. As it was I felt resentful, unable under the circumstances to exercise my choice and refuse to join the party.

Then some common sense prevailed. How petty, childish and very immature I thought. We were riding along the banks of a small river, Gildas and I in front, David and Maman bringing up the rear; I imagined the river to be a tributary of the Creuse on which Saint Roche Rivière was situated, one of the many lovely French waterways. The Creuse rises near Aubusson floats quietly along, meandering her way, passing to say "Bonjour" en route to Argenton and then "Au Revoir" to Le Blanc. She pauses for a moment, embraces her sister La Vienne and together they plunge to join their mother the mighty Loire.

How ungrateful and ungracious I had been; acting like a spoilt child selfish in the extreme. I glanced at Gildas beside me; his face was difficult to describe, distinctive, with defined bone structure and it reminded me of something, someone. No it had gone!

" Avril is a lovely animal," I said suddenly. "Of all your horses, do you have a favourite?"

He turned his head, startled at my addressing him.

"No actually I love all of them."

"That's what I miss most," I replied, " my animals. We had lost two cats, very old I admit eighteen and nineteen before we set off to Paris, before Papa's accident." I stopped then continued, " and my horse is looked after by cousins in Inverness, I hope one day to enjoy the company of animals again when I have a permanent base."

He looked at me, " I hope you will," he replied adding to my surprise. " Their love is far more genuine than humans."

At this point we arrived at some woodland and we halted.

"There's a gallop track on the other side of these trees, anyone game?" Gildas asked.

"You must be joking, I'd fall off in seconds," David replied.

Maman added "Gildas you must be tired hearing this from me but "me too." We all laughed.

"Caterine, do I have your answer?"

"No problem, Monsieur, no problem."

As David and Maman dismounted letting the horses refresh themselves from the river, we rode round reaching open countryside.

Gildas pointed, "Do you see that hillock?"

"Yes," I replied in anticipation,

"That's where we halt. Are you ready?" I nodded and we were off.

It was glorious! Avril responding to my touch let fly, hooves chasing over the perfect galloping ground grey mane just brushing my cheeks, finding our rhythm my hair loose under my helmet following as fast as it could! Gildas stayed with me, although with his power and the larger animal he could have raced ahead.

We came to a halt at the hillock, I was breathless, exhilarated and then glancing up I saw it.

The crooked man whip aloft pointing in my dream.

"And pulling now the rein my horse to stop
I saw three pillars standing in a line
The last stone pillar on a dark hilltop."

Forbidding, it stood above me "that last stone pillar". My images last night in my dream, I had seen it.

The voice awoke me from the image and my thoughts.

It was Gildas "Are you all right, you're suddenly very pale."

"Sorry, I'm fine," I said, dissembling, to recover my composure. "It must be the gallop. I haven't ridden for a while."

We turned, but I looked back. The image had gone!

Dinner on our final evening at Saint Roche Rivière was very informal in the smaller dining room and a buffet. Everyone mingled, relaxed still bathing in the warm happiness of the weekend's events. I, too, recognised my good fortune; privileged to participate in such a joyous occasion against the historical backdrop of this magnificent setting.

Frédéric, Gildas's younger brother, sat down beside me.

"What did you choose?" he asked studying my plate.

"The local fish and seafood. I'm not a particular fan of meat."

"Bravo," he said, smiling at me. We had flirted a little earlier and I found him very attractive.

"How long do you remain in Paris for your internship at the hospital?" I asked.

"One year," he replied then I want to specialise, probably obstetrics. " And you, what are your ambitions?

I was about to say, " the summit, just like Papa," then realised how pompous and senseless that would sound.

"The best of my ability in the world of Fine Arts," I replied. " And after tomorrow it's back to work!"

Frédéric reached out for the bottle of fine Bordeaux and refilled our glasses.

"Caterine" he looked at me very directly "I've enjoyed your company. Would you have dinner with me sometime in Paris. We could expand this subject of our future ambitions!"

I laughed. "Delighted, I would enjoy such discussions."

We raised our glasses – "Santé!"

Gildas also spoke to me, saying how much pleasure it had given him to see the Sinclair family together at Elisée's wedding. We also discussed my work but no mention of Impressionists!

Maman and I chatted in the bedroom of her suite. As with all the bedrooms it was graciously adorned depicting a period in French history during the seventeenth and eighteenth centuries. The colour scheme was warm and inviting with a four-poster bed hung in rich velvet a classic touch to a historically traditional bedchamber. For Maman and me there had been few opportunities during the weekend for private discussion.

The antics of Angus and Alexandra, the social activities plus my late arrival meant time was limited to share together.

"Well," said Maman, " I think you enjoyed yourself."

"Yes, I did," I replied hesitating. She smiled.

"David told me about his conversation with you. I decided to leave it to him and not intervene."

"It was childish of me," I responded, "It'll not happen again."

"I noticed, we all did, the effort you made with Gildas; parents killed and then the tragic loss of his wife. To all the world he has everything: privilege, wealth, status and unlike many in his category, intelligence.

You and I know in our different ways what the loss means of a, loved one; for us nearly two. For Gildas it was three. I think, he bears it with forbearance and dignity."

My thoughts wandered as memories claimed them. Then I blurted out:

"A stone pillar on a dark hilltop. I see danger in him, Maman, my sixth sense." I struggled grappling with my thoughts.

Maman stared at me, a look of horror fastened on her face.

"God almighty Caterine, I pray you're wrong," her aquamarine eyes wide in disbelief.

So did I, pray I was wrong, but time proved I was right.

Chapter Eight

It was a boy, born in a hurry, two weeks early on the 1st of December. David and Alix named him Julian not after anyone in particular, just a name they liked.

All the family met up again on Christmas Eve at Marchmont after an earlier reunion during the first weekend in December when I flew to Switzerland from Paris to be introduced to my baby nephew.

Arthur and Jane, Alix's parents, with Graham and his girlfriend Claire joined us for Christmas dinner and then departed with the triplet, as we named them, on 27th to spend the rest of the festive season with the McCallum family in Inverness-shire. Maman and I returned to Paris, Montparnasse and for me, also de Veres.

Then, in February of that New Year there was a development. One of the senior valuers, Jonathan Miles who was English left. No one learned why; suffice to add his references were never typed! Therefore a vacancy: two obvious candidates existed in the de Veres team, one a clear favourite. Making an appointment I went to see Albert de Vere and put my case. He was a short man, round face, twinkling eyes, bald pate surrounded by a fringe of dark brown silky hair. He imbued a spirit of 'Hail-fellow, well met' which put you at ease, off your guard. I knew better!

Albert regarded me with a sceptical smile. "I admire your ambition, Caterine, as I do your dedication. You've presented me with good work here, in fact very good work."

I was taken aback, a rare compliment.

"The question of your youth is not an impediment, not in this House as it may have been in others."

So he knew, I thought to myself why Donald had finally advised me to accept de Veres.

"However," Albert continued. "You've two areas, one in particular where you are still light in knowledge and more important experience. The first can be gained by more study over time but the latter, that is a different dimension. But I'll accept your application. There is an examination and an interview as you are aware."

He came forward to shake my hand.

"Good luck."

I thanked him and made one further request. Raising an eyebrow he replied,

"If you wish. It's unusual but not without precedent."

Relieved, I left his chambers.

The problem for me was time, less than a month but I had planned for that. Also I knew someone who could help me and I contacted him.

How I worked, more and even more again. Of course, my daily de Veres commitments could not be neglected, but I was not travelling. To allow me to study, in my personal time, Albert de Vere discreetly altered my roster. This occurred now and again and caused no comments.

Then, out of the blue, I received a phone call from Frédéric du Gilbert for that dinner invitation. Apparently, he had phoned several times when Maman and I were absent. Although I explained the situation who would believe I had no free dates for nearly a month!

"I quite understand Caterine," Frédéric had said at the end

of the call closing with a polite *au revoir*.

I muttered a French expletive and applied myself again to my studies on the advice from my Impressionist tutor.

The interview was satisfactory I was sure, but the examination was another matter. For the result, each candidate was summoned to Albert de Vere's chambers individually and as befitted the House in alphabetical order. I was last!

Albert stood up greeted me with the traditional handshake and motioned me to sit down.

"Caterine, I am not a man to mince words and so I'll put you out of your misery."

My heart sank. He gathered some papers together on his desk and separated one.

"I'm sure you are aware of a successful interview, the Board agreed.

Here, however, I can show you the examination errors which you made on your paper."

I looked up. It was blank!

Albert was smiling.

"Congratulations!" he said. "You've earned this promotion."

But I did not taste victory.

"You know," I said "how I achieved it?"

"Hard work, incredible hard work, of that. I'm aware. Do you mean the other element? Of course, I suspected that when you made your unusual request" replied Albert.

"I feel ashamed now. It was underhand, unscrupulous but the only way to absorb some experience of those Impressionists." Then a thought occurred.

"Albert, my discussion and meetings did not involve any personal affair."

I must have looked shocked.

"Caterine, we all have our sexual proclivities. I'm well aware Chris has a preference for the masculine members of our society. As for your method, ingenious I would say, flattered his intellectual ego. If he was naïve enough not to deduce you might be a candidate?" Albert shrugged his shoulders.

"By the way, Chris is leaving us. Before you comment let me assure you it's not on your account. It's because he came third!"

I gasped.

"Now, we'll be organising a new roster for you. It will be ready tomorrow. Take the rest of the day off, you deserve it."

I turned to leave when Albert addressed me again.

"By the way, you surprised even me. I thought you'd be second."

He winked and we laughed.

The job was a dream and I was going to Sweden, Stockholm, and my first ever visit to Scandinavia. Albert put me in the picture.

"He is a wealthy eccentric. Lives on one of those multifarious islands somewhere and nowhere on the archipelago. His collection contains many old Masters and is to be exhibited in Stockholm for the summer season. Top security of course but you will have total clearance for your valuations for the insurance company. The current one is well out of date. If you are uncertain on any point, call me personally."

"Thank you, Albert" I smiled.

"One more matter, Caterine. Those two new trainees whom we've employed on Studentships. I understand you've spent much of your free time helping them."

I think I reddened and replied

"Not so much time, they're both very keen."

Now Albert smiled.

"Yes, Caterine, you're ruthless with and for yourself; but no-one could condemn you knowing that generous hearted nature. Enjoy your first venture overseas for de Veres! Then it is a month's leave. Not bad!" he said.

"I was going to speak to you about that. When you're so

short staffed I don't think I should be taking all that holiday."

"Caterine, you've spent hours of your personal time to help us out. Let me give you some advice. Always take your holidays. If you do not someone else will take them for you."

I laughed and departed almost skipping down the corridor. I felt I was on destiny's path.

I was sitting in the bar of the gracious Grand Hotel in Stockholm, the Venice of the North with its fine views of the islands formation on which the city was built. Opposite me stood the imposing Palace of the Swedish royal family. It had been an exciting and demanding two weeks. I had called Albert de Vere only once. He had confirmed my opinion.

"Caterine, Caterine Sinclair, I don't believe it!"

I turned in astonishment recognising the voice immediately. Donald Cameron, Professor Donald Cameron, from my alma mater, the University of Glasgow: the mentor who became my mate, the mate who became my Machiavelli working unscrupulously to pave my path to my summit of success. We greeted each other in Auld Alliance mode, a Scottish hug and a traditional French embrace. I am sure the other bar occupants were perplexed. Even if many were not Swedish, the tradition of the national decorum suffered an unconventional rupture!

"Donald," I began. He interrupted with the same question.

"What on earth are you doing here?"

Then it was laughter, exchanges of information and both being alone, dinner.

"I know a very fine restaurant," Donald started to say, more laughter.

"Not Scottish here surely," I teased him.

"No," he replied seriously, "actually Swedish."

It was as usually befits an unusual man, five star quality and secluded, off the beaten track!

Back at the Grand, over a cognac we talked. I had received a letter from him about my promotion with his congratulations.

"I tried to phone you but I was travelling on my research and your Montparnasse phone was always engaged."

Donald continued. "As you know, I hate the mobile and impersonal text messages, only use mine in a dire emergency! And so, you're taking a well-earned vacation. To where?"

"Actually Donald I'm not sure. Tomorrow I fly back via Schiphol to Scotland. Maman is collecting me at Glasgow Airport as I'm staying with her at Marchmont. After that," I laughed, "a cliché – 'the world's my oyster'! No really no plans. Frankly I'd like some fresh air and time in my Scottish countryside."

Donald was in ponderous mood for a moment.

"Caterine, what about spending a few days in Inverness-shire at my old draughty Scottish Mansion?"

He was looking at me now, hand up to stem any protest. "No strings for God's sake. Do you still like your horses?"

I smiled and nodded.

"Well, there's your answer. I keep two old nags and we can do some trekking. Spend a few days. I'd love to hear more about de Veres."

We agreed to meet in the pub in his local village.

"Without an ordnance survey map you'll never find the old house," he told me.

"Let's rendez-vous at noon for a Scottish pub lunch."

It was hilarious. The pub was called "The Stand Inn" and Donald of course, one of the locals. He received comments like,

"Donald, this is the third woman this week." Or worse "not from the cradle again Donald, we thought the last one would have taught you a lesson." And finally "Donald, you've just raised the tone of this establishment. Now get out and leave your guest!"

I loved it, typical Scottish humour, and genuine words from very genuine folk taken and given in intelligent comedy. Laugh with each other and at oneself.

The May countryside was bursting with blossom

rhododendrons abounding in multi-coloured hues of pinks, reds and violets in wild profusion set against swathes of lime and oak trees lining our rural route.

I followed Donald in my old battered Sinclair saloon, still going strong, 139,243 miles on the clock as I looked at it. It was a drive of only 15 minutes from The Stand Inn until we reached woodland and then a sudden turn right onto a private country road, which certainly alone I would have driven past. Then we arrived at Donald's draughty old mansion house, transformed overnight by a magician into a work of art; a post reformation tower house, in other words a Scottish castle. I was dumbfounded, open mouthed, staring in disbelief.

Donald, having left his car at the entrance gate was standing beside me, as I sat behind the wheel of my old jalopy, sporting his Hollywood smile!

"Donald Cameron, you're a rogue, a brigand, a," – I was lost for words for once as I followed him through the gates and up the drive still struck dumb!

The "old nags" which we exercised that afternoon had also benefited from the wand of the magician. They had been transformed into thoroughbreds, the stallion Robert (after the Bruce) and the mare Mary but a very happy namesake of Mary, Queen of Scots.

The castle was in prime condition, restorative perfection and full of artefact treasures; paintings, porcelain, furniture and furnishings, a Scottish fairy tale, treasure trove of antiquary dreams.

"But Donald what about security? It must be a nightmare, the paintings alone," my voice tailed off.

"Come with me," he commanded.

One hour later I understood. The system installed rivalled any I had seen in Europe, assisted by a natural factor, the surrounding moat.

"Of course," Donald added, "this place is relatively

unknown. Also I have " in-house" and "outhouse" assistance."
"Out house" consisted of his four beloved dogs, two Alsatians and two Weimaraners with their strategically placed kennels. " In house" the magician who waved his wand, Bruno six feet eight inches and just as broad.

"My God, where did you find him?" I asked in astonishment. Donald grinned.

"On a calm evening, just as I was enjoying an incomparable Barbados sunset on a raft in the Caribbean. By the way, he trained as a chef!"

We dined on manna and ambrosia. Incredible!

Over coffee and port he told me his story.

"My great grandfather was a street trader wheeler dealer, gambler, God knows how he put his fortune together, we never knew. My grandfather told me he was unaware of it until his father died and so never asked. Their lifestyle reflected no evidence of it. Of course grandfather was born late when his father was nearly sixty. He inherited the fortune in his mid twenties.

Grandfather must have buried in his genes his father's astuteness and made the family respected and socially acceptable; he advanced from street trader to antiques dealer with a "canny eye" on the stock market and property. My father kept his head and his cool. He gestured – hence here we are.

"Your Mum and Dad are still alive," I inquired.

"Oh yes and very well thank you. This is their Scottish base, but the maturing bones benefit better in southern France and Barbados. They have homes in each!"

I sank back against the luxurious cushions of his Louis XV sofa still in shock!

"Of course, Donald continued, "I had no need to earn a living, but I loved these beautiful treasures with which I'd been surrounded all my life. Also my father was a disciplinarian." I smiled to myself. I was not spoiled and inherited the Scottish work ethic and decided on the academic life to impart some knowledge, share my love of all the antiquaries. He smiled that bewitching smile. "Any more questions?"

"No, not really," I hesitated, "no-one, no special person to share this with you Donald. Of course it's none of my business," I added as he stood up. He walked to the old fireplace with its logs almost seeming to enjoy burning in the hearth. There was silence and I waited, my senses alert, some trepidation in my soul.

Eventually he spoke, "I was married Caterine. I was married to my childhood sweetheart, silly term really. I was married to her for one year three months and twenty-one days. Then she died. He turned to face me. "She died, Caterine, during an operation, an operation to remove a brain tumour."

The few days became nearly three weeks and the three weeks much longer than that. We became lovers. He laughed me into and then out of bed. What a lover he was – and he taught me how to be loved and how to make love to a man. The nothingness, never, no more!

Chapter Nine

I returned to de Veres with a song in my heart, a very happy human being.

We were further blessed. Donald was researching for his book and was on a year's sabbatical. It was not being written on the Fine Arts on which he had several to his credit but a novel, a thriller. That was all he would tell me, my lover, my true mate, my not so unusual man.

That meant of course, no restrictions to our rendez-vous throughout Europe. For Donald, funding was not a consideration. Therefore, over a period of more than eighteen months, we travelled together or met in Copenhagen. Madrid, Florence, Brussels, Amsterdam, London, even Helsinki, there for a weekend to suit Donald's research not my work!

Of course, also in Scotland and France our beloved countries of the Auld Alliance. We spent a holiday also, at his parent's house in Barbados on the west coast not far from my family's favourite Caribbean Club in St James. I liked them very much and I think they liked me.

As for Maman, David and Alix they were at first surprised and then very happy for me. Many family rendez-vous ensued. I recall one evening in particular after dinner in Montparnasse;

Maman imparting tears of mirth still in her eyes as we cleared the dishes:

"He's the most amusing man I've ever met in my life!"

We spent our first Christmas together with Maman, David, Alix and the triplet at Marchmont, joined by Arthur, Jane, Graham and Claire. It was riotous! Donald performed one of his masterpieces, arriving at the door on Christmas Eve morning kitted out in the most authentic Santa Claus costume I have ever seen accompanied by incredibly a sleigh and one reindeer (on loan from the local deer farm). It was not only the children who were speechless! I knew no details of this stunt and was as astonished as anyone. Earlier, after breakfast, Donald had announced somewhat irritated,

"My car isn't running well, darling. I'm sure it's the carburettors again, always temperamental. I think I'll take it to that mechanic in the village. Last time, he retuned them expertly."

I had looked at him surprised.

"I noticed no problem on the drive from Cameron Castle," I replied.

"Anyway it's Christmas Eve. He'll be busy with emergencies."

"I know," Donald sighed, "But I'll try anyway. I won't be long."

Minutes later the twin exhausts exited the driveway with Donald at the helm!

"Where's Donald off to?" David had asked me, Angus tugging at his hand to complete the snowman in the garden. It was our first white Christmas for several years.

"Oh," I replied, "some problem, imaginary I'm sure with his beloved car. Anyway, I'm off to the kitchen to help Maman with tomorrow's dinner. A superb excuse to sample a few morsels," and I had headed in that direction smelling some spices emanating from there on route. Consequently, Donald's Santa Claus had been as great a shock to me as anyone.

The children were enraptured, albeit the doublet we suspected knew the truth but were far too clever to admit it! Each child was given a present (but only after promising Santa to go to bed when told to do so by Mum and Dad, put up their stockings and not to dare come downstairs on Christmas morning before given permission).

I turned away, hiding a smile. The voice was brilliantly disguised, unrecognisable. If Donald had not decided on an academic career and the antiquities he could have found an equally successful path to fame in that other artistic arena, the stage.

Maman of course, was very well organised just putting finishing touches to the turkey and adding the cream to her very drunk trifle when I had joined her in the kitchen.

"What happened about your London flights?" she inquired. " Times rearranged?"

"Yes," I had replied changing my mind about a 'finger dip' and using a teaspoon to taste the bread sauce to avoid earning Maman's displeasure.

"British Airways were most helpful as always. Our Concorde connection is now confirmed."

As a surprise Donald had decided that we should spend New Year with his family in Barbados and not at Cameron Castle. Maman was going to Zurich with David and Alix. Donald and I had to reorganise our connecting flights from Glasgow to Gatwick because of a presentation to which Donald had been invited in central London. It was an award dinner for one of his books on the antiquities, which was quite an honour.

We were leaving now on the 28th of December and would spend our Hogmanay in the Caribbean. Hence, it was a memorable family Christmas with snowball fights, songs round the log fire, fine wine and unsurpassable Scottish fayre.

On the 27th Donald and I kissed everyone *au revoir*, then to

London for an exceptional evening for his award dinner. Next morning it was Concorde to the Caribbean.

What a unique experience – supersonic flight! It is the British and French " Entente Cordiale." Donald's father met us at Grantley Adams airport to drive us to St James. Even although I had never met him, I recognised Donald's father immediately, he was his double except older! I received a very warm welcome and a duplicate Hollywood smile.

"Where's the old girl?" Donald inquired.

"Mum will be at the house when we arrive," Duncan Cameron replied as he and Donald collected our luggage and loaded it into the car amidst the constant bustle at the airport. Her apologies for not meeting you, but Anna's mother is not well and she's visiting her this afternoon."

Anna, I discovered was the Cameron home help. We drove to the west coast passing many familiar scenes for me from past holidays spent in this favourite family destination.

After just over an hour and a half, we turned into the driveway, through the lush tropical garden drawing up in front of the main entrance to be greeted by Donald's mum descending from the elevated porch. I stared in utter disbelief as Donald opened the car door for me and I recognised her. Iona Dunn MacDonald, Scottish supermodel, international celebrity married into the British aristocracy becoming a Duchess and then left the Duke, causing a major scandal to live with the father of her unborn child. It had been banner headlines worldwide. The Duke refusing to divorce her for some years and her son, Donald, obviously born out of wedlock.

She kissed me on both cheeks in French mode, chattering animatedly, still very beautiful, the grey mane of hair a trademark in her early twenties, so striking, her classic sculptured features timeless.

"I can see my earlier notoriety still precedes me from your expression," she smiled.

"My apologies Mrs Cameron but I could not fail to recognise you," I replied. Donald said nothing.

"My Dear it's Iona, as for Donald you'll know by now that he enjoys his fun. From what he's told me you're more than his match. Now come inside and I'll show you to your suite. Then I'm sure you are looking forward to a refreshing dip in the sea."

"Donald Cameron," I upbraided him, you might have given me some warning." We were sitting on the raft in the bay in front of the Cameron residence, about 100 metres from the shore.

"No way," said Donald grinning. " I wish I could have captured your expression when you recognised Mum. Quite a girl isn't she? Now if I had inherited her looks and not Dad's, I could have been a male supermodel," he said standing up arms on hips in fashion mode.

Of course, he ended up in the Caribbean waters with a helpful hand from me. That dip was certainly no punishment!

Iona and I were sitting together at one of the beachside tables under the welcome kaleidoscope patterned umbrellas enjoying a rum punch before lunch. Donald and Duncan had set off early when it was cooler, to play a round of golf on a new course near Bathsheba on the Atlantic coast of the island.

"May I ask you a question, a personal one, even an impertinent one?" I said turning away from my view out to sea of the catamarans and in the distance some cruise liner I had espied heading, no doubt, for Bridgetown.

"Certainly," she replied. "And then I may decide to answer it or not," smiling at me.

"Did you resent the Duke refusing you that divorce for all those years?"

Her response was like a whiplash.

"No, absolutely not, for two reasons. One, I had married him under false pretences, although I can honestly say I was unaware of them at the time. I was young, immature and fêted to a ludicrous level; my parents tried to advise me of the possible consequences, but I listened with deaf ears. Secondly, I had betrayed him and myself."

She stood up, a still classic figure taking a few steps from the flagged patio onto the sand. There was silence, I feared too much intrusion but I awaited her response.

"Caterine," she turned back to address me again. "What I'm about to say to you is known only, to Duncan, Donald, and the Duke. When I realised I was pregnant, I panicked. The child growing in my womb was not I knew the Duke's."

She answered my unasked question.

"The timing wasn't possible, first let me confirm that, not any," she hesitated, "failure on the part of Arthur. However, in my state of fear of the consequences I led him to believe that the pregnancy was ours. I let him believe that for almost one week, six days of joy and happiness for him; of despair for me. It was an unforgivable lie, almost a satanic sin. On the seventh day I told him the truth hardly a Biblical gesture. Arthur deserved his revenge."

Iona continued, "I should have been punished more, if Duncan had abandoned me because I was so much in love with him but he stayed by my side, acknowledging the child was his and shrugging his shoulders at all the scandal. That's when we bought this property, selected, secluded, safe from the gory glare of international publicity."

We both heard the car arriving.

"Now," she took my arm, "let's join our very lucky lovers!"

Laughing together we walked towards the house.

On the third of January, reluctantly we took our leave to return to our respective work commitments. It was a fond farewell at Grantley Adams with open invitations for return visits. I liked Donald's parents very much and I think they liked me.

Donald and I spent many weekends also at Cameron Castle. I can recall one in particular. It was in the month of May almost exactly one year after we became lovers. And some redecorating was in order.

"I'll move my clothes from the dressing room into one of the guest bedrooms." Donald told me in organised mode.

"It will give me the opportunity to clear out items of clothing I no longer wear which I'll pack into a suitcase for the local charity."

A busy afternoon ensued, the charity van arrived as arranged, very grateful for the contributions to their stocks.

We rode out on Bruce and Mary savouring the May countryside with its awakening from its earlier spring surprise to develop into the future summer splendour.

As I was changing for dinner Donald called from the hall.

"Darling, where's the blue suitcase?"

I emerged from our bedroom already dressed for dinner anticipating one of Bruno's speciality cocktails. Bending down to adjust my shoe I replied:

"Why with the brown one, of course. The charity took them away as you instructed."

"Caterine," Donald looked aghast, " I said only one was to go, the brown one, the other contains my best kilt and my Prince Charlie; sporran, everything!"

I stared at him appalled.

"Oh my God!" I looked at my watch, "they'll be closed. You won't be able to contact them until Monday. "And we've the wedding tomorrow. No time even to hire!" I gasped.

Donald looked at me.

"I'm not amused, not at all amused," he said tersely.

Crestfallen I walked with him to the drawing room for our pre-dinner drinks.

"Caterine, Caterine Sinclair, you're a rogue, a brigand!" Donald declared.

I laughed. The blue suitcase sat smiling at him in the middle of the room adorned by a massive tartan bow!

"You're wicked," he grinned. I was completely convinced it had disappeared in the charity van. Our glasses touched in the traditional Scottish toast "Slainthe."

In the September of our second year together I received an invitation. It was to the christening of Elisée Silvère's first child, a daughter to be named, Félicité. To my surprise, Donald was included.

I phoned David still in Zurich although now promoted to the board of the Mercantile Bank.

"Has he?" he replied. "How typical and thoughtful of Gildas I mentioned Donald to him last time he asked about you. Said we were delighted you had found a hobby outside work!"

"David Sinclair," I began.

"Sorry, favourite sis, the triplet beckons. Love from all of us. See you and Donald at the Christening."

Donald arrived at Montparnasse having taken a taxi from Charles de Gaulle on the Friday evening before the weekend of the celebrations. We were departing on Saturday morning to drive to La Touraine the christening taking place in the family chapel at Saint Roche Rivière.

I had been packing, muttering, uncertain what to take. Ridiculous really as I travelled all my life. Donald, perfectly prepared was sitting back no doubt eyes closed now, absorbed by Dvorak's 9th Symphony, in the salon.

To my further frustration, the new sandals, the ones I had bought hurriedly yesterday to match the emerald outfit I was wearing for the ceremony did not fit, too small. If I wore them, I would be walking like a poor cripple. *Merde*!

Donald appeared suddenly, head round the bedroom door.

"You're taking a long time, darling, problems?" he inquired looking the essence of decorum.

By now, I was becoming ill tempered, irritated.

"Oh, you wouldn't understand," I almost snapped, "and look at me!"

I was standing just emerged from the shower and glancing at my reflection in the antique swivel full length mirror.

"I'm completely out of proportion!"

"Caterine, put on a dressing gown or something and come down to the salon," Donald replied, "We need to talk."

Taken aback I complied and joined him on the sofa a few minutes later, the strains of Dvorak still melodious in the background.

Donald looked at me, shaking his head.

"One factor that puzzles me about you is your unawareness of your beauty."

"Pardon!" I stared in turn at him.

"Caterine, you look in mirrors but fail to see. Let me describe you to yourself.

Height 5 foot 10 inches, about right?" I nodded still confused.

Donald continued. "Long, strawberry blonde hair, thick glossy hair, broad breasted, slim waist and hips and legs that should be advertising designer tights. And your face, the most remarkable I think I have ever seen with large violet blue eyes which change colour like a chameleon according to your mood. I think every male student in your university year was in love with you or certainly your looks, not to mention the lecturers! Now your response!"

I was dumbfounded.

"But I'm not pretty," I began.

"No not pretty," replied Donald, "stunning, top of any league, the loveliest creature I have ever seen."

I was thunderstruck. I still am!

The christening on the following day at Saint Roche Rivière, I found particularly poignant. Of course, this little lady was the first addition to the du Gilbert family for many years. Perhaps that was part of it.

The rain had thundered down on Friday night, literally, a

typical electric storm, but on Saturday the gods smiled, the oppressive atmosphere washed away and a watery sun struggled out before the late morning ceremony. It was a gathering of family and close friends almost identical to the group who stayed for the second night of Elisée's wedding.

As Donald and I entered the grand drawing room for pre-luncheon aperitifs, I recalled that earlier du Gilbert's celebration in this majestic venue.

Suddenly I heard my name hailed from a group of guests I knew well.

"Come on Donald and I'll introduce you to Gildas's cousins. They're friends of Alix."

Together we walked over to join them. It amused me to see that this time Jacques was escorting a rising star in the French music industry and Philippe a very beautiful and internationally renowned British stage and film actress.

Much banter was exchanged in English and French which generated hilarity; comments about differences in accents, with Donald concluding with a rendition of various Rabbie Burns verses, the ones only quoted at private parties. Thank God no-one fully understood them!

Suddenly Donald exclaimed: "Ah there's David waving. Let's join him and Alix."

He smiled to the group: "Please excuse us. We'll meet again this evening, I'm sure" and he whisked me away.

I looked round surprised: "Where's David? I can't see him or Alix."

Donald replied. "Neither can I, but I had to rescue you from this lions'den. Both of them were ready to pounce!"

I burst out laughing. "Donald Cameron, have you no faith in me?"

"Not in that jungle even with cognizance of your survival techniques!"

Looking at his set expression and still chortling, I thought what a very special man he was and how lucky for me to have found this love affair. Hand in hand we moved forward to find the family.

After an afternoon spent exploring the estate, walking for miles over moor land and through forest paths entranced by the expansive tracts of splendour and tranquillity, Donald and I retired to change for the evening buffet. We had been allocated separate suites as etiquette demanded but discreetly linked by adjacent sitting rooms!

"Very considerate of Gildas," Donald announced. "I'll thank him at dinner!"

I was still giggling as he turned on our shower!

Coming in the reception hall prior to dinner, we were greeted by Rodrigue and Elisée and then mingled with the other guests.

Frédéric was there of course, his arm decorated by a classic blonde.

"Not bad," Donald commented, "very sexy."

We joined up over aperitifs and Donald soon had Frédéric and his girlfriend in stitches with an impression of Jacques Chirac.

I wandered over to talk to many other family members I knew, friends like Albert and Céline (I had discovered that Albert's father had been friendly with du Gilbert cousins) and then joined Maman.

"Where's Donald?" she inquired after several minutes.

"No idea," I replied, then saw him in earnest conversation with Gildas.

The buffet reminded me of the ones in Barbados at the Caribbean Club, which had served classic French cuisine flavoured with exquisite West Indian overtures.

The choice was expansive: pâtés, ratatouille, consommé, roast pork, venison, pheasant, turbot and seafood, a range of delectable vegetarian and pasta dishes, salads galore, a mouth watering collection of cheeses and fruit plus puddings 'to die for'!

What struck me were the flavourings inclined to discreet spices, different from the traditional French herbs. Then I discovered from Donald that Gildas's new chef had been born in Martinique.

"You chatted to Gildas for a long time," I remarked. "What were you discussing?"

"Oh, this and that," replied Donald airily. "Plus, I disclosed 'whodunnit' in my book!"

I laughed at the absurdity.

"Actually," Donald was serious for a moment. "He's an intelligent man, a highly intelligent man. I liked him."

On Sunday morning after breakfast, prior to our departure, Donald, David and Gildas became embroiled in a debate about the respective electoral systems of Britain and France. As Maman and Alix had disappeared, I went for a stroll.

The weather had been very changeable over the previous few days: the sky was now overcast, the morning sun just a memory and a cool north easterly wind imposed its unseasonal characteristics, but it remained dry.

Pulling on my angora jacket I set off in the direction of the stables. I had been walking for only a few minutes when I heard a male voice hailing me.

"Caterine! May I join you?"

I turned smiling, it was one of Gildas's cousins, Philippe.

He greeted me in traditional French mode albeit taking a little longer than necessary!

"Of course," I replied "everyone seems to have deserted me!"

"How could anyone with eyes and intelligence abandon such a gorgeous creature as you." Philippe said with a sweeping bow.

I laughed, he really was a charmer.

We exchanged some friendly banter and then Philippe pointed:

"There's the ruin of the old hunting lodge, come on it's quite interesting."

I gazed at the remains of the fallen building curiously.

"What happened!" I asked. "Do you know?"

"Oh, something about a doomed love affair. An adulteress wife found 'in flagrante delicto' by her husband. Folklore claims he trapped the lovers inside and burned it down."

My mind stirred and so did that figure of the crooked man.

"You see these lifeless stumps of aspen weed
Some say that these are beeches others elms
These were the bower and here a mansion stood
The finest palace of a hundred realms.

The arbour does its own condition tell
You see the stones the fountain and the stream
But as the great lodge you might as well
Hunt half a day for a forgotten dream."

"Caterine, darling, you're on another planet!" It was Donald's voice.

Returning to reality, I said shakily "I'm sorry. I thought I saw something."

"It must have been my gruesome tale of days of yore" Philippe laughed.

"Well, it's turning cold and time for us to return to Paris" Donald said taking my arm.

"See you soon" Philippe called as he walked onwards.

"I hope so" I replied, still distracted.

"Not bloody likely, ready to pounce" Donald muttered under his breath.

I attempted a laugh, but is was a hollow sound because as I looked up I saw the jagged branch of a dead elm tree tortured in its lifeless frame.

I felt suddenly chilled, very chilled indeed.

It was Christmas and he asked me to marry him in the drawing room of Cameron Castle. Before I could answer, he held up his hand.

"Please, let me continue. My feelings for you I have re-iterated many times. God knows what you see in me, certainly not my looks, although I can be amusing!"

"Donald," I began, "you're being flippant and," he interrupted.

"Caterine, darling, no, very serious. I flatter myself when I say to you I'm confident that you love me. I know, also, that you're not in love with me, but we share that sexual equation which we both require in a long-term relationship.

The fact that you are not in love with me poses me no problem because I am sure I can make you happy, but it may pose you one. That's why I ask you to postpone your response. Take time to think."

And, I did.

I returned to Marchmont and Maman. She guessed but said nothing. The decision was mine alone. I walked for miles in my beloved Scottish countryside; rode out on one of farmer Jimmy Black's hunters, which I exercised for him from time to time. I thought, I reflected, I pondered.

On the fourth day I returned to Cameron Castle with my decision. We kissed, not 'Au Revoir' but 'Goodbye.'

I returned to de Veres, the song in my heart lost in a tuneless chorus praying I had made the right decision. This time a very unhappy human being.

I immersed myself in my work and I missed him. I missed him dreadfully. Several, no many times I picked up the phone to call him and then replaced it, knowing it was selfish, unfair.

He deserved his freedom to find, if possible someone else to love him and be in love with him. What I would have given him was not enough.

Of course, eventually I went out on dates but they were literally that, fleeting dinners or concerts, theatre, sporting events, outings, short term social activities, long term longing and love, a void unfulfilled.

Eventually, I found some stables to the south west of Paris near Versailles and spent many happy hours there with the owners at weekends; mucking out, grooming and exercising the horses. It was a family complex with three young children and we became friends.

My work and career progressed. I was now Senior Manager of the valuations department and taking auctions, which I loved.

Albert became my mentor now, guiding me like Donald but more gently with his milder majestic whip. Our love affair was purely an academic one, completely divorced from his devotion to his lovely wife and two children – a love affair of the arts.

The next Christmas, I returned to Marchmont and the first family reunion for almost twelve months. After the celebrations, I stayed with Maman alone for a few days.

Looking through the local paper, an announcement caught my eye.

"*Mon Dieu*, Maman. Is that castle on the Benderloch now open to the public? What a surprise!"

"Yes," replied Maman. "I heard of it in the village last week. The owner, the old recluse died at nearly ninety and the grandchildren in their twenties have inherited. As I understand, they want to restore it and have opened it up as a start to raising funds. Heavens knows what it will cost."

"Have you seen it?" I asked.

"No, petite. Why?"

"Lets visit it this afternoon. It has always fascinated me. The building dates from the Reformation period, like," I hesitated, "like Donald's."

We wandered round. It was not in such poor condition as I feared, but restoration would still cost a six-figure sum.

"About £200,000," confirmed Malcolm Douglas, " according to the estimate.

Of course, we don't have that kind of money and to raise it, well, that's a full time commitment and you need contacts. As for grants, my sister and I have done some homework. The irony is that Douglas Castle isn't in such a dilapidated condition. Having received an earlier financial package, it no longer merits an additional one. Sadly, Gillian and I will have to sell." They both looked utterly dejected.

Maman and I were sharing a cup of tea with them. It was now after 5 pm and any other visitors had left.

Sitting in the morning room after dinner, soothed by Greig's Peer Gynt, I was reflecting on my meander round the castle. Something had been troubling me; the way the cloth fell and a hidden energy, but it was dirty, covered in years of grime. Turning back to my book, I dismissed it.

It was in the shower next morning when an image hovered in my mind, dangling out of reach. I concentrated but it was gone. Suddenly, at breakfast I cried out,

"Christ Almighty," spilling my tea.

"Maman looked up shocked at my expletive but before she could remonstrate, I had grabbed her arm, boiled egg and warm toast forgotten.

"Quick, back to the castle. I'll get your car keys."

"What on earth are you talking about, Caterine? Have you lost your senses?"

"It's a holiday today, Maman, they should still be there. I'll explain on the way."

Malcolm and Gillian Douglas also thought I was mad. At

my request however, Malcolm removed the painting from above the fireplace. Turning it over in trepidation, I saw what I had hoped. It was Poplar. I stared at the painting again. The fall of that cloth, the naturalness of the figures and that distinctive energy; but the scene was so obscure. I could not be sure but instinct was talking to me and I made my decision.

"Malcolm, Gillian, I don't wish to raise false hopes but this painting might, just might be of some value. I would like your permission to take it back with me to Paris and de Veres. The intention would be to have it professionally cleaned, examined and if justified evaluated.

"You'll receive an official de Veres receipt, naturally and I will as a contribution of what I hope will be a successful restoration, pay for the cost.

Being Scottish and fiercely independent Malcolm and Gillian refused to accept my offer of paying de Vere's fee. Discussions ensued. After some bartering it was agreed; costs were to be split, 25% payment by me and 75% by Malcolm and Gillian. We shook hands in turn. Agreed!

Next day, I arrived in Paris the painting wrapped and boxed carefully by Maman and me. It was carried as hand luggage, fortunately not being too large. I said nothing to Albert de Vere but took it directly to the expert, Professor Bertrand, we consulted for any authentication or restorative work. Then I awaited his verdict.

Five days later he appeared at my office, the painting artistically boxed, I knew by his expression.

"Caterine, we may be approaching the dawn of a new century, but I'll stake my reputation that this is the find." And he opened up the box.

Tears filled my eyes. Fate had pointed her finger to show me my destiny.

It was a devotional scene with the Angel Gabriel painted by Masaccio, a youthful genius, during the Italian renaissance, he died young in 1428, only 28 years old, but he inspired so many later artists, Lippi, Castagno, Botticelli.

He was rare, only a few paintings by his hand. It was priceless!

I picked up the house phone, my hand trembling, and called Albert de Vere.

"Caterine, I am about to enter the Boardroom. It will have to wait."

"Albert de Vere, "I said with authority, " this cannot wait!"

I knew he was annoyed by his tone of command as we entered his rooms. Then he saw Jules Bertrand and then the Masaccio, unveiled a second time. His expletive language I will omit.

Then I told him my story.

Several phone calls later I finally located Malcolm Douglas. The following day Albert de Vere and I were in Scotland at the castle. The deal was sealed. Of course, Albert and I stayed overnight with Maman at Marchmont.

Over dinner at one of Argyll's most exclusive restaurants, courtesy of de Veres we talked, just Maman, Albert and me. We were all very excited. A later celebration was planned with Malcolm and Gillian.

"Unreal, found in a Scottish reformation castle. No one had any idea of its value and even how it arrived on the wall!"

Albert looked at me. "Bloody brilliant Caterine, you have a unique talent, your hard work, your dedication, that was a major part of it, but to recognise that Master," he shook his head. "Jules showed me the photograph which he took before the painting was cleaned; unrecognisable, to almost any expert! That is a gift, which cannot be bought or developed through teaching or learning. You deserve your triumph."

Then Albert said something, which astonished me.

"You must somehow have foreseen the hand of fate for your future and honed your studies to determine that vision.

Champagne glasses raised, he and Maman toasted me.

"Congratulations and santé!"

I felt embarrassed, humbled even, and to change the subject I asked,

"Any idea of its value Albert? What price it will achieve at auction?"

"No." Albert replied, now regarding with anticipation his 'salmon en croûte, " but I can confirm it's starting in the millions and I don't mean that value in French Francs, I mean Sterling!"

Maman gasped, nearly choking on her first mouthful of turbot.

The painting set a record for early Italian Renaissance, and my reward; a handsome commission but more important, a special birthday present, a seat on de Veres Board of Directors at 28, the youngest ever in the art world.

I looked up and saw Papa's face smiling down at me. We had won!

Malcolm and Gillian attended the auction of course. And we indulged in another dinner in Paris with the de Veres Board. Although Albert had advised them of the painting's price potential at the auction, they were speechless at the outcome.

I had joined them in their hotel suite for a private aperitif prior to the dinner.

"Caterine, what can Gillian and I say. Words are inadequate. Not only have you saved our beloved castle, but" Malcolm grinned now, Scottish humour in vogue,' "the change has made us multimillionaires!"

"Please reconsider our offer on the pact we agreed at the castle, 25%/75% split, this time based on the painting's sale price."

Gillian added, "Caterine you must understand how important this principle is to both of us. Without your recognition of the Masaccio we would have lost our inheritance from Grandpa Douglas all our future plans in ruins, the castle would have been sold to a stranger, lost to the Douglas family and what we dreamt of as our destiny."

I pondered before my reply and then I told them about Papa.

Five weeks later, I remember I received a package, delivered by courier to my office in Paris. Inside the silk lined velvet box was an exquisite brooch, in the form of a painting, a replica of the Masaccio. The brooch was in gold Filigree, studded in diamonds, figures designated in multi-coloured gemstones set on a canvas of platinum. It was a jewellery masterpiece.

On removing it from the box, I found in a small pocket, a gold chain and realised on turning the brooch over that it had been designed with a folding gold clip to be worn also as a pendant. The enclosed card read simply:

To Caterine,

For realising all our Destinies.

Let us present you with your Masaccio.

Congratulations!

With our Love

Malcolm and Gillian

At Douglas castle,

Benderloch

Argyll

I sat motionless at my desk, the unique brooch resting in the palm of my hand knowing that it was of much more value to me than the money I had refused to take from the proceeds of the de Vere auction.

Why? The painting belonged to the Douglas family, their heirloom; my contribution had been my professional expertise, a donation from the opportunity offered to me by my Sinclair heritage.

From our Scottish connection a mutually satisfying outcome and for all the parties concerned – justice.

Chapter Ten

During the five weeks prior to receiving my unique present, much excitement was generated in the art world. To my horror, I became something of an instant celebrity with the attendant publicity followed by newspaper and television interviews. I hated it but could not refuse as it was free advertising for de Veres.

Absurdly I also received a call from Première Classe, the top French model agency offering me a job. Albert, on hearing about it, arrived breathless at my office having taken the stairs two at a time, lift forgotten, panic stricken lest I accept.

"Don't be ridiculous," I reassured him. "It's not my style, if you excuse the pun and anyway at 28 I am too old."

Donald called me from Cameron Castle with his hearty congratulations creating a few tears in my eyes as we said, 'au revoir'. In fact I took many calls from well wishers and was sent an avalanche of letters including one from Gildas on that thick starched white monogrammed notepaper.

Maman and I flew to Zurich for another celebration with David, Alix and the triplet. They were thrilled for me. Before I left David spoke to me.

"Petite, don't stop looking. There is more to life than work. I wish it could have worked with you and Donald but worse to have made a mistake."

"Yes," I answered quietly grateful for his brotherly bear hug.

After Zurich, it was a visit to Shona in Geneva, for the weekend, one of our many rendez-vous when work commitments permitted. My train was on time but she was not there to meet me. This was out of character as she was punctilious. Then a tap on my shoulder, I turned round, who on earth was this?

"Shona, Mon Dieu, I didn't recognise you." I said in astonishment.

"No," she grinned, "you walked past me just like Dad and Mum last month!"

I stared at her.

"How much weight have you lost and your hair, make-up, well everything!"

"Come on," she said. " Let's have lunch and I will tell you my story."

At last Shona had taken her weight problem in hand and on an approved medical diet had lost over two stones.

"Then I decided to have a complete 'make over'. My hair had grown from my old thick brown bob, I had it trimmed to shoulder level and blonde streaks. And here we are!"

We were sitting in a little fish restaurant with a glass of Chablis and some gourmet sea food.

"A new man?" I inquired.

"Perhaps but not the marrying type! Anyway after all these years with Gerald, I'm enjoying my freedom."

"Heard about him recently?"

"Yes, Dad met his uncle in a Medal on the golf course. He is with Médecins sans Frontières in darkest Africa. Can you imagine me in the jungle? No, marriage for both of us would have been a mistake."

"Well," I replied. "You look fabulous."

"Caterine, I would return the compliment but that's not new you always do!"

It was a most entertaining weekend.

A few weeks later in early April I was sitting at my desk when I heard a knock on my door. It was Albert.

"Caterine, "he frowned, "I need a favour."

He walked over to my window, which looked over Parc Monceau in the 8th Arrondissement.

This was my new office as befitted my Director status. I had been given 'Carte Blanche' to decorate and furnish it as I wished.

"Bloody hell Caterine," Albert looked round. "This resembles a salon not an office."

Alarmed I replied, "Albert, I was well within the budget."

"What? Yes, yes, I know that Caterine. I passed it. No, it's so relaxing, comfortable, would you like to redesign mine?"

I laughed. "Delighted, if you wish!"

"The favour. I realise how busy you are but let me explain. A friend of my father's just died. He had no children so the château and estate have passed to other family members, cousins, I am not sure exactly. But I received a call for our assistance, evaluations and restorative work. It's a major job and apparently lots of paintings not only in the château on the walls but stuffed in a cellar.

With the family connections, I'd like you to take it on, put a team together. Are you still working on the Bryand dossier?"

"Yes," I replied, "but almost finished. The English section completed and only some finer points on the French property."

"OK," said Albert. " Pass it to me and visit this château, it's on the Cher."

"What a coincidence," I explained, "that's where my 18th century farmhouse is situated, the one I told you I'd bought. I'm still looking for furniture and furnishings."

Albert looked up from his notes, smiling.

"Perfect, that means you can spend time there on route.

Now what's the new owner's name? Ah, here we are and the directions. The proprietor is Professor Martine."

"And the château, what's it called?" I inquired.

Albert replied glancing again at his notes, "BeauRobert."

My appointment with Professor Martine was arranged for 11am on the Tuesday of the following week. I drove from Paris after work on Monday and spent the night at my farmhouse named 'Delphinium.' It was my intention over the coming months to spend time decorating it in its original style and to hunt around in the antique shops and the 'brocante' for furniture to complement its traditional early 18th century history.

BeauRobert was well hidden off the beaten track but only 30 minutes drive from Delphinium. I had received a map with directions and followed the designated route turning into woodland and a long meandering track in the forest, with a multifarious variety of trees and shrubbery.

Suddenly I emerged into a different terrain. It was breathtaking.

The gates were unlocked as I had been advised and I drove up the imposing driveway enchanted. It was lined with the King and Queen of trees, oak and acacia greeting me in regal fashion. BeauRobert stood boldly before me built in classic renaissance architectural mode, like Chenonceaux, Azay-Le-Rideau or Chambord. But for me, a lover of all the others, this Château was unique, mesmerising just like the Masaccio and it was situated in the middle of a lake or so it seemed as you approached.

As I arrived, skirting the lake to reach the main entrance some black swans on the shimmering water regarded me with distaste and then turned away in disdain taking off suddenly, flying low but gracefully over my car as if to indicate what an ugly and inferior means of transport it was. I smiled at their wisdom and pulled at the external bell.

Professor Martine entered the salon library into which I had been shown and I stared at him in shocked recognition.

"Caterine, what a fortunate surprise. I couldn't believe it when I saw your name on my appointment list."

"Philippe!" I stared at Gildas's cousin "I'm sorry, I'd no idea …. " I hesitated

Philippe smiled. "I do work as well, Caterine. You've only seen me on social occasions. I'm a medical professor, with practices in Switzerland. Come on I'll show you round the château. The owner was my uncle. Then you can tell me what you think."

"It's exquisite." I commented, "and really in quite good condition."

"Yes," Philippe said. "But valuations are quite out of date. Oncle Arnaud was not interested in renewing them. Fortunately, his notaire handled all his paper work and so essentials were paid, household bills attended to and insurance premiums but not current values. Now let's have a glass of wine to celebrate our unexpected rendez-vous."

Philippe was at least David's height, handsome, tanned and broadly build. I knew that he had played rugby at international level. I was not surprised.

We discussed details.

"You have carte blanche," he informed me. "The costs are not a consideration."

"Thank you, Philippe. I'll send you the contract and put a team together. If you approve the paperwork, we should be able to start immediately."

"That's fine. Our family look forward to working with you."

We shook hands with him smiling, holding mine a little longer than necessary. I returned to my farmhouse made a few calls and then drove to St Pierre des Corps, left my car in the de Vere parking area and caught the Montparnasse TGV to Paris, a handsome face a little in my mind.

I chose my team. Two senior valuers Christophe and Christian plus one of the two studentships, Sabine. First of all, I cleared my third member with Albert as it would be seen as a promotion for her plus warranted a salary increase.

"She's progressing very well, Albert, but I'll watch her closely. I think she deserves this opportunity albeit still young."

Albert cleared his throat.

"Agreed Caterine. Youth is not an impediment in this house as it may have been in others." He was grinning and we laughed. I recalled his words to me when I made the application for the senior valuer position.

I called Sabine to my office to break the news. She was astonished but thrilled.

"I don't believe it, thank you, Dr Sinclair."

"Sabine, it's Caterine."

The work was soon underway.

During the week I based myself at Delphinium and most weekends now. I loved it.

Built at the beginning of the 18th century, it consisted of a study, dining room, sitting room and an oak finished modernised cuisine with a pantry adjacent.

Magnificent beams were a feature of the property particularly in the main reception room which led to four bedrooms, two en-suite with a further family bathroom. It was in very good condition.

The team were staying during the week in an auberge in the village near BeauRobert returning to Paris each weekend.

Philippe Martine was not present everyday at BeauRobert, of course, and had left me a mobile number where he could be contacted if we encountered any problems. A few members of staff living in, Félix and Yvette, who were husband and wife plus the cook, Agathe were very knowledgeable on a general basis having worked at BeauRobert over a number of years. Any daily queries could be answered by them.

A week after our work commenced, on a Tuesday, Philippe appeared before lunch.

"Well, Caterine, I received no call so I assumed all was well," he said finding me in the larger hall. He was immaculately dressed, pale blue linen suit, jacket double breasted, shirt with a white colour and monogrammed silk tie.

"Everything's fine, thanks," I replied as I put aside my clipboard thinking how attractive he looked.

Philippe smiled. "I asked Agathe to rustle up some lunch, please join me and we can discuss developments."

I enjoyed the following hour. He was amusing sophisticated naturally, well travelled and he loved BeauRobert.

To my surprise without warning he returned on Thursday of the same week about 5pm. I was studying some of the paintings which had been stuffed haphazardly in a room in the basement. Most would have to be cleaned but no Masaccio, I was sure of that. The team and I had moved them to the gallery on the first floor where the light was better and where we had space to evaluate them. Philippe examined some with me. Most were by French artists but not of any significant value. There were two others, minor artists from the Utrecht school which at auction might fetch in total 200,000 Euros. Philippe was surprised.

"*Mon Dieu*, I wouldn't hang them in my bathroom," he exclaimed and we laughed.

"Your Oncle Arnaud knew his paintings Philippe the ones of value grace the château walls."

"Caterine, have you time for an aperitif before you leave?" he inquired.

"Of course, delighted" I replied.

We sat in the salon library with our drinks. Agathe, I assumed at Philippe's request had prepared a few canapés, smoked salmon and pâté de campagne. I realised with a flutter of anticipation that this had been planned.

We discussed the château's contents for a few minutes and a few surprises the team and I had discovered: some Sèvres Porcelain items and a dinner service plus three pieces of furniture that were absent from the out dated valuations.

"Of course, you may decide not to sell although I hope de Veres will be offered the option if you do. These are major omissions. It will be next week before I can confirm the valuations."

Philippe did not reply at first, appearing distracted. I thought to myself surely he would not give the sale to another auction House. We never stipulated this in our Contract although other auctioneers and valuers did. Albert found this condition distasteful, 'beneath this house' he had told me for all his ruthlessness.

Philippe emerged from his reverie. "Sorry, Caterine, my thoughts were elsewhere, no, absolutely not. De Veres would be granted the option rights if it was decided to sell."

He was looking at me directly and I returned his gaze smiling.

"Caterine, my thoughts were not exactly elsewhere but about you. I've enjoyed your company but the time for me has been far too brief. Please join me for dinner one evening in Paris. It would give me great pleasure."

Still smiling, I answered, "Me too, Philippe, thank you."

He called for me at the Montparnasse apartment at 8pm a week later. We dined at Soirée, a restaurant established only two years ago but rivalling the best in Paris.

It was a gourmet meal. From the staff's attentiveness Philippe was obviously a regular patron, no doubt accompanied selectively by a coterie of companions. I liked that. The thought amused me, measured my mood.

As the taxi slowed down in the Montparnasse traffic, still in midnight mode, he took my hand.

"Would it be an imposition to ask you to meet me tomorrow

at BeauRobert I know it is a Friday jour de fête but I leave for Berne on Saturday and would like to examine that porcelain and furniture again."

His hand was warm and inviting in mine. My senses quickened as I looked into those dark and bewitching brown eyes.

"Of course not, Philippe."

We were to meet at noon.

I arrived at 11.45 on the following morning. As I entered the reception hall my mobile rang. It was Philippe.

"Caterine, my apologies, I'm so sorry. I tried to contact you in Paris but was too late. I must fly back to Berne, medical demands I'm afraid, one of my patients. I'm calling you from the airport. Can we meet instead at BeauRobert on Tuesday?"

"I'm sorry Philippe but I shall be in Paris again on Tuesday for a meeting. I return to BeauRobert on Monday just for the day and then again on Wednesday afternoon."

"Damn it," he exclaimed.

I, too was disappointed. There had been no one of meaning in my life since Donald and I found Philippe a very attractive man.

"OK, what about next weekend. I'll call you. Please confirm where you'll be."

I did and we said *au revoir*.

On the Monday following, after discussions with the team, I was wandering around the grounds breathing in the floral shrubbery scents and assessing the structural work required which would be handled by an associate company in which Albert de Vere had an investment. I came upon a gate to the walled garden, which as yet I had only viewed, from an interior access door onto a terrace, always locked. This gate I had never seen before but a key was visible and turning the handle I entered.

The garden was somewhat overgrown but quite

extraordinary, thoughtfully planted with a horticulturist's care. I could identify lilac and hydrangea bushes a chorus of colour embracing the grassy path. As I meandered onwards a rose garden came into view, with such a profusion of plants old garden and modern mixed with some climbing species clambering up and caressing the greying stone of the ancient boundary wall and transforming it into a floral canvass.

I knew a swimming pool existed in the further corner on a slightly elevated site facing south as did BeauRobert. Making my way through some undergrowth I emerged from the shrubbery and halted in shocked surprise.

Facing me with an identical expression on his face was Gildas! He was soaking wet hair plastered back not his usual sartorial elegance, in shorts no less. Obviously he had been in the pool. I was taken aback and for the first time he looked semi-detached.

"Mon Dieu," I exclaimed. "What are you doing here? Did Philippe invite you?" Gildas looked perplexed.

"Pardon," he responded.

"The new owner, Philippe Martine, your cousin, are you his guest?"

"Philippe?" he answered. There must be some misunderstanding. Did he not tell you? He is not the owner of BeauRobert, I am. I inherited it from Oncle Arnaud."

I was flabbergasted, felt a fool.

We met again in the smaller salon for coffee. The staff had laid out a tray on which rested a silver pot, two cups and saucers, napkins and a plate of petits fours. Gildas appeared, hair still wet and for him casually dressed in tan coloured chinos, a cream open neck shirt and a striped lemon and maroon pullover.

"Well, this is a surprise," he said smiling at me. "I knew we had engaged de Veres but hadn't expected a member of the Board. Please pour out our coffee."

Then he explained his plans.

"Saint Roche Rivière is too large these days for my home and I am lacking privacy. So many weddings, conferences and now we've been approached by a film company.

BeauRobert I have always found special and very private, quite unknown. I played here as a child with Elisée, Philippe and Jacques before Frédéric was born. So," he turned from the window with its view of the lake, "so I've decided to renovate it and live here. I've already installed myself at the weekend in the suite adjacent in the west wing, which leads out to the walled garden. Now tell me how are you progressing?"

Forty eight hours later it happened. I arrived just after 3pm on Wednesday after a long meeting with Charles Damion, a fellow board member over a disputed valuation. Sabine was upset I saw it immediately. Eyes reddish and swollen despite attempts to disguise it by bathing them.

"What's wrong Sabine? Are you unwell?"

Bad time of the month I had thought. I will recommend Maman's remedy. I was wrong. Sobbing Sabine poured out the story.

I was furious, how dare Gildas criticise our work and to my staff, not even the courage to address me personally.

"Where is he?" I demanded of Sabine.

"Please Caterine, don't tell him, he's so forbidding and he'll be even more angry."

At last I calmed her down. I knew she must have been very upset to react like this, she was what the Scots would call a 'toughie'. She came from no privileged background. Her parents were born in French Cameroon, moving to Paris to work hard for their family unfortunately her father had taken ill and fallen into alcoholism, now in and out of jail for petty crime. Her mother, Mathilde, whom I had met was the backbone of the family proud of her daughter's as she put it 'aristocratic taste'.

"He's gone Caterine. I have no idea when he'll be back."

"Right," I said seething, "return to the auberge and take the rest of the afternoon off. Walk round the village enjoy some fresh air and leave this problem with me."

She protested saying it was unthinkable, time off. She looked shocked.

"Sabine," I repeated, "that is an order from a member of the de Veres Board, a 28 year old female director." I was smiling. She relented then and said something very touching.

"You're the best thing that has ever happened to me. Maman agreed. "A lady," she told me, true breeding, no airs or graces." Then Sabine departed for the auberge. Now I was shocked!

Gildas returned just before 8pm, I was waiting. Built up tension was now at boiling point. Christiane and Christophe when questioned reluctantly admitted similar innuendos but had refrained from telling me, knowing his criticism unwarranted and both more experienced. How cowardly of Gildas to pick on Sabine the most vulnerable. He would recognise her background certainly, see her as a peasant trifling with, aspiring to, God forbid, his aristocratic clothes. I had been right all those years ago a sanctimonious bastard, no, a snobbish sanctimonious bastard!

Naturally, he was surprised to see me standing at the window of the smaller salon. I had watched until I saw his car appearing in the diminishing light advancing up the imposing but enchanting driveway, skirting the lake to arrive at the door. By custom Felix would drive it round to the garages.

"Are you working late? Is there a problem?" He asked immediately he opened the door.

"No, I am not working late but there is a problem. What you have done merits a tirade from me but I'll not give you the pleasure of delivering it. Suffice to say you have criticised my staff behind my back, and a further insult, raised a subject which has never been discussed: an act of cowardice not even the courage to question me to my face!"

"What are you talking about? I don't understand."

"Your words to Sabine today and earlier innuendos to Christophe and Christiane, especially yesterday, that the work was taking too long. That's preposterous. We are well within the time scale allocated." I was glaring at him, now, I knew he had no defence.

"Today, to Sabine?" Gildas looked bewildered but I wasn't here today or yesterday I was visiting Elisée and the family, staying overnight. I've just driven back."

Horror stricken suddenly I knew. It was Philippe and entirely my fault the true ownership of BeauRobert was unknown to my staff. They saw the proprietor as Professor Philippe Martine to whom they had been originally introduced.

On Monday after my sudden encounter with Gildas in the walled garden and then coffee I had not informed my team of his status. They had been in ignorance compounded by my absence on Tuesday.

Staring now, still horrified, I realised he had come to the same conclusion. I stuttered an apology trying in some way to justify my accusations but Gildas waved away my attempts.

"That in itself is not important an error. What is more disturbing is the fact that after all the years we've known each other, the closeness of our families that you consider me capable of such conduct. I know you dislike me but am unaware at any time of offending you or earning your displeasure. Am I wrong?"

I was rendered speechless, still trying to recover and come to terms of what I had accused him. Then Papa's words echoed from the past – 'be honest'.

Looking at Gildas I answered.

"If I gave you the impression I disliked you, I apologise. That was wrong of me, quite wrong, a mistake. As for my remarks they were uttered without any consideration I'm afraid I have a temper, my worst fault. Sometimes I speak first and think afterwards."

"Well," came his reply, "it appears we have both been mistaken. Please join me in a glass of wine and let's call a truce."

And so a pattern was established. When Gildas was at BeauRobert during the week, we shared as time permitted coffee, a light salad lunch, or an aperitif, the latter usually on Friday evenings before my weekend departure. We discussed the team's progress, examined artefacts and generally he was appraised of developments. Family connections were touched upon naturally but it was mainly business.

Professor Philippe Martine was no longer in the picture, Gildas was as shocked as I at his comments to my staff and at my request relayed my sentiments.

"My cousin offered his assistance knowing I was unable to be present in the early valuation stages." Gildas informed me. "He's returned now to his home and work based in Switzerland."

"So," I inquired, "he has a general practice in Zurich and Berne."

"Not quite," said Gildas, somewhat amused, "he's probably the finest plastic surgeon in Switzerland!"

Exactly one week later, I was sitting in the walled garden munching an apple after lunch: it was a dismal day, sky overcast threatening rain. Suddenly I heard the click of a door closing and then voices emanating from the open window of Gildas's study.

"I can't credit this Gildas. All those funds missing from that Maintenance Account. I'm speechless."

It was Bernard Thevot's voice, the senior accountant with whom I had discussed the de Veres budget. He seemed very agitated.

"You're not alone" I heard Gildas replying, voice terse.

"But how can you be sure Victor's guilty?"

"The evidence is indisputable. And to think I paid for his accountancy training – some thanks!" Gildas replied voice raised in anger.

"My God!" Bernard exclaimed "I trusted him: so bright, even gifted, thriving on additional responsibility and I gave it to him! He's turned out a thief, an embezzler. I'm shocked, appalled. What happens now? Criminal proceedings I suppose."

"Of course" Gildas replied. "The police are waiting in the entrance hallway with Victor."

"Already *mon Dieu*. But waiting for what Gildas?"

"For you, Bernard, the real culprit. I've suspected you for some time and set a trap with Victor's co-operation. As you said, he's exceptionally bright. You made an error in your calculations Bernard: an omission which was a fatal flaw: you underestimated a du Gilbert!"

I turned away apple core in my hand, as Bernard's beseeches for mercy rang on deaf ears. How fortunate I had been seven days ago after my accusation to Gildas to escape a more serious fate.

I had learned a lesson – never underestimate a du Gilbert!

Christophe, Christian and Sabine had worked exceptionally well together as a team. Midway through the project after about six weeks I invited them for dinner at my farmhouse. Our meals together had been in the local auberge for business. This was social and on a Thursday evening. Christophe and Christian were embarrassed and I realised why.

"A prior engagement?" I inquired.

"Do you mind Caterine? You see there are two girls in the village and …."

"Enough, another time. Enjoy yourselves!"

"What about you, Sabine?"

"I'd love to," she replied shyly.

She found Delphinium idyllic.

"It's just magical she told me. And the gardens! Of course as you said they need attention, a lot of work but to inherit such maturity and beauty. I've always lived in an apartment" she sighed.

Sabine was sitting at the antique oak dining table, which I had unearthed after much searching in a back street in a derelict shop on the outskirts of Tours. It had now been restored to its late 18th century handsome glory.

I was concentrating on preparing the meal, which was simple enough: melon au porto, prawns Provençal with fresh spinach and the salad course with its traditional cheese selection. Pudding was very drunk 'rhum babas' courtesy of the local patisserie washed down with a bottle of 'Méthode Traditionelle' Touraine rosé.

"I am so glad that Professor Martine's not the owner of BeauRobert." Sabine muttered, "a nasty nasty man and it's Le Comte, he's so very handsome."

"Pardon, handsome, yes, he is, albeit we don't like him. Philippe Martine is a very attractive looking man." I responded, preparing to strain the spinach.

"Catherine, not him Le Comte, he's gorgeous."

I turned to look at. her. "What did you say?"

"Gildas du Gilbert, I was saying he's gorgeous, drop dead gorgeous. Six foot four and what a body, whew!"

I was now staring at. Sabine, the spinach stock over spilling into the sink.

"Body, when did you see his body and what do you mean 'gorgeous'."

"Caterine, are you blind? You've told me you've known him for years. That day he appeared at the Château. I was in the kitchens with the staff when he arrived requesting some coffee, remember you said you joined him in the smaller salon. Of course I was unaware he was the owner then, he was in his swim shorts, towel round his neck. Mon Dieu with his looks, stature, wealth, women must fall at his feet!"

"Put like that, I suppose they must." I said thoughtfully.

"Of course the staff think the world of him, Agathe worked for his late father and she told me they are rather alike, considerate, thoughtful, even generous. Le Comte paid for her daughter's orthodontic treatment. They didn't like his late wife, I know it's wrong to say this because of her being dead but Felix and Yvette also worked at Saint Roche Rivière. Apparently she treated all the staff like dirt and used her title all the time. No-none could understand why he married her. But he doesn't take prisoners, they told me. Gives and expects absolute commitment and loyalty. Cross him at you peril!"

I looked at Sabine flabbergasted, meal temporarily forgotten.

"My God, Sabine. Where did you find all this information?"

"Why, Caterine, I told you the staff. They talk to me. You see they know I'm like them" and she was smiling "I'm from their class!"

Chapter Eleven

On the Friday following that weekend when Sabine dined at Delphinium I sent the team packing after breakfast. Monday was a 'jour de fête' and they deserved a break, it meant for them a snack on the TGV and arrival in Paris for the start to their holiday from Friday lunchtime.

I worked on my own for the rest of the afternoon encountering Gildas as I was walking through the smaller hall.

"Caterine, I must excuse myself from our Friday evening aperitif. I am dining in Orléans and staying overnight. As it's a 'jour de fête' on Monday shall we rendez-vous on Tuesday?"

"Yes, of course." I replied.

It was ridiculous but I was disappointed not to share our Friday evening aperitif before my return to Delphinium or to Montparnasse. Over the last few weeks it had become a welcome habit.

Suddenly, screams erupted from the kitchen. Together we raced to the stairs, Gildas first with me close behind.

We were greeted by a ghastly sight. Agathe staring in horror at one of Gildas's tortoiseshell tabbies, Leah, blood pouring from a gaping wound in her side, tottering and then collapsing on the kitchen floor.

Gildas moved swiftly.

"Caterine, blood a problem?"

I shook my head still shocked by the extent of the wound.

"Right," he said, "hold the ripped skin together like this as tight as possible to stem the bleeding. I'll only be seconds."

The poor animal body in spasms was crying out in pain. No hope, I thought, a vet would have to materialise out of thin air, and too far to the village I felt helpless.

But the vet did. Gildas, medical bag in hand worked fast. Anaesthetising, cleansing and suturing, me assisting when he asked.

It was over.

"Gildas," I stared at him astonished.

"This was my chosen career," he answered, " but fate dictated another path earlier than I had anticipated."

He was frowning now. "The next few hours are critical."

He bent down and kissed Leah still under anaesthetic on the head.

"Mignonne," he whispered, " keep fighting. And I have this dinner guest speaker."

He glanced at his watch. "Too late to cancel now."

"I'll stay and look after her," I said, "anything to help."

"Will you Caterine. Mon Dieu, you've blood on your clothes!"

"We both have," I replied." But they can be cleaned and anyway, I've a change in my car. A habit from travelling."

So the arrangements were made. Gildas phoned the local vet whom he knew. That was my contact if there was any change in Leah's condition: signs of shock, trauma, an increased heartbeat. Having helped in the local veterinary surgery in Oban for a summer job I had some basic knowledge. Gildas instructed me reminding me how to check for any deterioration in her general condition.

He waited with Leah while I collected my clothes from the

car, showered and changed. Yvette had shown me to one of the guest suites for the night.

This extra set of clothes with my overnight case and toilet bag was a long term habit. My working hours were irregular and an evening commitment, business or social often meant no return to home base when using my car; hence the precaution. It had saved time and trouble on numerous occasions.

My change of clothes tonight amused me: Silk black and white striped shirt and black velvet breeches with underwear sown into the lining. Perhaps a little too couture driven for cat sitting. Then I reflected as I descended the stairs Leah deserved the best!

At 6pm Gildas left, his overnight stay with friends cancelled.

"It will be nearly 2am" he told me "before I return. If Leah stays peaceful, take some rest yourself."

Leah remained still, her general condition, after the shock of her injury and the surgery returning closer to normal drifting out of the anaesthetic and into, I hoped, a normal pattern of sleep.

It was now 11.45 pm but although I felt she was restful I could not leave her. She was on a cushioned bed in the kitchen and after stroking her little dappled coloured head again, I rose to refill my glass of water.

Yvette appeared in her night clothes.

"How is the little cat, Madam? We're all so fond of her."

"I don't know, Yvette, but she seems quite peaceful."

Then Yvette exclaimed : "Madam you've not eaten. Agathe's tray's untouched."

"Apologies to Agathe, Yvette, but I have no appetite."

We said good night.

When Gildas reappeared in the kitchen it was ten minutes before two in the morning.

"You never left here all this time." He asked.

I smiled anxiously.

Gildas threw his dinner jacket and black tie onto the oak dining chair kneeling down to examine Leah thoroughly.

"She will make it." He announced. "More rest and good care."

He gave her another injection to maintain her sleep pattern. Collecting his jacket from the chair, he took my arm.

"Come on," he said. "Brandy's for both of us, veterinary orders!" and we retired to the smaller salon.

I watched him as he poured out the cognac, noting how his burnished copper hair curved down the back of his neck as of many years ago.

Taking the brandy goblets from the Louis XIV table, he then raised his, after handing me mine.

"*Santé et merci,*" he toasted me.

I took a sip enjoying the warm quality glow of the cognac. Gildas was sitting back eyes closed for a moment obviously tired from the driving. I looked at his face and its profile. Suddenly, I knew. That was it! A Renaissance face – Renaissance man.

Mon Dieu how blind I had been. It reminded me of a painting 'Doge Leonardo Leredano' by Giovanni Bellini right at the beginning of the 16th century. It was a painting depicting the head of the Venetian Republic encompassing the dignity of the sitters rank yet the face vibrant, alive with individual character.

Then an intake of breath as my eyes saw where my mind had failed.

I was in love with this man, Gildas, Le Comte du Gilbert, the close friend to David and Alix, the highly regarded host to Papa, the man for whom Maman entertained great respect, the detached figure of my imagination – not detached at all!

Gildas must have heard me because he opened his eyes and returned my gaze: He saw it of course my look revealing all.

Bending his head, he brushed my lips with his. The shock was palpable!

"This must stop." I heard myself saying as I stood up. "It must stop now," I found myself repeating struggling for words.

"It's not a good idea," and I turned to face him. He was also standing now.

"Actually," he replied taking two paces towards me, "I think it's a very good idea." Hand now in the small of my back, he pulled me gently towards him and placed his mouth firmly on mine. A dangerous kiss, positive but not yet too passionate, inviting a response.

I made the fatal mistake, lips parted now, I kissed him back my arms around his neck, fingers tangling in the longish hair and then complete abandon. The electric sexual equation had begun to culminate in its eventual logical conclusion.

His hands were now gently massaging my buttocks, dropped from my back and moved then slowly achingly slowly up and round to my breasts, thumbs caressing my nipples through my striped silk shirt. Still kissing me pulling provocatively at my upper and lower lip as yet no tongue in play.

That is when I lost my head, the possibility to retain a measure of control.

I remember every second of it my hands moved down top button undone trousers unzipped, hand grasping his erection and worse much worse, down on my knees tasting him.

He allowed me to pleasure him for several moments and then picked me up through the salon, his adjacent study, to his private suite kissing me all the time tongues now in play.

He placed me against the decorative cushions on his bed pulling them at right angles to the floor. Unzipping my striped silk shirt, he then unbuttoned his starched white one so that he was standing facing me wearing only his shorts.

He looked at me, sea green eyes locking me in. I felt hypnotised.

It became the most erotic night of my life.

I remember him stepping back studying me.

"Pull down the right strap of your brassiere he told me, "I want to look at your breast. Pull it down slowly."

I did so my body now trembling completely under his spell.

"Now stand up and unhook the brassiere so that it falls to the floor" was his next command.

"*Magnifique*," he murmured as he approached me. He took each of my breasts into his hands and made love to them, kissing, licking, teasing them, my nipples flushed and hard aching for his touch.

Gildas stepped back again.

"Now remove your breeches," he ordered me.

"I want to see you standing opposite me naked."

I did as he asked my body now throbbing, the sexual electricity rising in temperature dictating the actions.

He gazed at me for several seconds.

"*Complètement magnifique*, sit down against the cushions on my bed." He motioned.

Stepping out of his shorts he walked towards me, I attempted to caress him again but he murmured.

"Later it's your turn first" starting to stroke me watching my face his fingers moving at first slowly then more intimately urgently, the sea green eyes mesmerising me holding my gaze.

"You know what I am going to do, don't you?" he asked. "Would you like that?"

I nodded, "but I want to touch you too" I remember saying breathless now.

"Very soon," he murmured his mouth moving over my body again accepting my offer to him of my breasts, my hands underneath each as he sucked the nipples again and then his mouth exploring down over my navel one side to the other my hands now behind his head guiding him although I knew he needed none. I heard myself moaning.

My body was now pulsating and starting to arch. I could feel it, the sound beginning deep in my throat.

He moved us swiftly and expertly into that classic unorthodox position.

We lay locked together in the after glow.

I woke up just before 7am in ecstasy and excrucuation as the memories of the night and our love making came tumbling back. I was horrified, my conduct unforgivable even deplorable. My god, we'd never actually been on a date!

I recalled every second of the night and not even too much wine: one sip only of the cognac. And worse, I had made the first move! What must he think of me? Cheap, certainly at best, at worst, a whore but without paying the fees!

Then I thought of the family, the connections, more embarrassment, mortification. Sadly, I knew one fact, I was completely and utterly in love with him. That was why for the first time in my life, I had lost my head. The explosion of that sexual chemistry had resulted in absolute abandonment. I had literally lost my head.

With Donald, it had been a gradual process, the development of our love making and I knew he loved me. Last night had gone from, well nothing, to everything. Bloody Hell!

I stumbled out of the bed and then saw on the Louis XIV tulip wood dressing table a tray. On it sat a jug of freshly squeezed orange juice, croissants, and a thermos of coffee plus a note. A note written in that distinctive no distinguished hand on white starched monogrammed notepaper. It confirmed what Gildas had said before I slept. On his return, dinner tonight. He was collecting me from Delphinium at 8pm. Probably this was my fee!

That was when my decision was made.

He was on time, punctilious to the minute, surprised I saw he was driving his beloved classic car, which had belonged to his late father.

I was trembling with tension, but resolute. No revelations of my feelings for in the end it would be rejection for me. His stature, his looks, his wealth meant he would enjoy the pleasures of many female companions, Sabine's words echoed in my mind, 'women must fall at his feet'. Well, I had managed that once already and made a fool of myself last night, never again! On reflection Sabine's words had not been entirely accurate. Knowing Gildas as I did now as a lover, women would not just fall at his feet, they would grovel at them

As I opened the door he stepped forward to embrace me but I stepped back avoiding him and turned from the entrée into the séjour.

"Ma Chérie what's wrong?" he inquired anxiously.

It took all my resolve to face him, this man I knew I loved, and betray those emotions.

With my carefully rehearsed speech I addressed him.

"I wish to speak to you. Firstly, to apologise for my conduct last night. It was quite out of character, in fact, completely out of character; for some illogical reason, I lost my control. It will never happen again." Forcing myself to look at him.

He was staring at me in utter disbelief at first and then some realisation crept in.

"By those statements am I to understand that last night meant nothing to you, nothing at all but, what did you say, 'a loss of control'?"

I had anticipated a response like this and my prepared reply was ready.

"Well, I cannot deny some pleasure of course, albeit somewhat unorthodox for me, out of my usual norm."

I had said it: cold blooded words in a tone as cool as cucumber, completely under control.

He looked at me with utter contempt, in disgust. I wanted to admit that what I had said was a lie, an act, but my pride was crucial and I returned his gaze.

"Christ Almighty," he exploded, "you're like stone, inanimate, hard and heartless, so divorced from the other members of your family. I was completely deceived by you, more fool me. I thought we made love last night. Obviously, you saw it as sex, a passing interlude. What was it? 'some pleasure but unorthodox'. Is this how you amuse yourself on your European travels. One man here another there, trifling with each individual's feelings and affections until you've found your 'norm!' You're a disgrace to your family and unworthy to bear their name!"

And he was gone.

My resolve and my knees shaking uncontrollably now gave way, I sank onto the sofa, his words reverberating like a horrendous headache. His final remarks the most insulting ever addressed to me, ever by anyone, but deserved.

When I looked next at my watch it was 8.35pm and I had made my decision.

The summer evening was warm and balmy, the variegated varieties of shrubbery scents almost tangible to the touch. Ironically a time of tranquillity.

I found him in the walled garden which he loved so much standing beside the old well now out of use, its water contaminated not even pumped up for the benefit of the shrubs. He turned as I approached him the sea green eyes in iceberg mode and I knew this would be far from easy for both of us.

"I have come to apologise," I began.

"For what," he retorted. "That during our sex last night, you failed to inform me of your traditional norm?"

"Gildas," I was desperate now to try and make him understand. "What do you want me to do? Go down on my knees?"

He stared at me coldly, very coldly and then smiled, a sardonic smile.

"I believe, Madame you've already performed that particular act."

I turned away sick in my stomach, tears in my eyes realising I had lost him and ran stumbling now for the gate. But he caught me.

He saw my tears.

"Caterine, I just want the truth, the truth about last night."

I looked at him, this Renaissance man and I replied, "I never told you the truth, because I've fallen for you, completely and utterly in love with you. Now just let me go."

But he kept holding me, pulling me against him and his next words:

"Thank God, *Mon Dieu*, thank God!"

I looked up at him in astonishment, what did he mean?

"Caterine, Chérie, I've been in love with you for years!"

We never made the dinner but we did make the bed. This time we made love slowly and evocatively, my gazing down at him as his delicious strokes made me come, again and again and again.

Afterwards we talked, his arms round me, my head on his chest.

"Chérie, why all that deception, God, I was so angry at what you told me. You were so cold, frigid and I was so hurt, could not understand that I'd been mistaken."

"Darling, I was embarrassed, ashamed almost at the speed of our intimacy, I was shocked at my complete abandonment. After all, I hardly knew you as a man and then the family connections. I thought," hesitating, "that you might think less of me. I'd lose your respect."

"Caterine, we made love to each other. That's what was important. We made love," and he kissed me on the forehead.

"I also made the first move," I added.

"Yes," Gildas replied. "Superb, quite delicious actually, it gave me the signal." He smiled at me a very sexy smile and leaned forward kissing me again gently on my lips.

"You know," he continued," I was rather pleased with my performance last night". He was looking almost smug.

"Pardon," I replied.

"Yes, rather pleased: an expert manoeuvre into that unorthodox position considering I was out of practice."

I looked at him wide eyed. He was now grinning.

"Gildas du Gilbert," I cried, "you're a conceited, arrogant …."

He finished the sentence for me. To my horror he repeated the words I had used to describe him all those years ago,

"….. sanctimonious bastard."

I gasped, "you overheard me?"

"Yes, I had turned back. I've never forgotten those words." He was still grinning.

"And now Madame, I'm at last in the perfect position to make you pay for ever daring to utter them."

And I did. I am delighted to say I did.

Chapter Twelve

On Sunday, at last, we were able to sit down and find out about each other, fill in all the gaps. There was so much missing over the years. Gildas was 25 months younger than David, 35 now to my 28. Just perfect.

I loved him, was absolutely in love with him. And I knew he felt the same about me.

We were sitting in the smaller salon after breakfast, Leah on my lap. Despite her stitches she had abandoned her cosy cushioned bed which we had brought from the kitchen and miaowed for more attention. Consequently she was placed carefully by Gildas on my lap.

"When Gildas did you realise about your feelings for me? I'd no idea, no idea at all!"

He hesitated, "I hope what I'm about to say will not upset you too much but it was actually at your father's memorial service at the reception in the British Embassy in Paris. I suppose it was 'un coup de foudre'! I never believed it could happen and certainly not to me."

I stared at him shocked, incredulous.

"But I was what just 18 and so gauche. It's not possible."

"No, Chérie not gauche even then at 18 a stunning looking young lady."

"But," I stumbled on the words, "you were married, your wife."

"Yes," Gildas sighed, a pained look in his eyes. "My wife, Isabella. It's a long story, a very long story." And he began.

"Our marriage was a sham almost from day one. A mistake on both our parts. She despised me and to her I became indifferent; also I learned later she was in love with another man. Whom I know not and never cared enough to find out."

He shook his head. "Why she married me, I'll never understand."

I now felt sad for Gildas and I suppose for Isabella too in a way. What a mess!

"But you must have realised during your engagement." I began.

Gildas stood up. He had been sitting on one of the Louis Philippe sofas in the smaller salon with its view of that shimmering lake. He walked over to the window touching almost absently the cerise velour drapes.

"No," he replied softly. "There were exceptional circumstances. Isabella and I had been boyfriend and girlfriend as teenagers and then drifted apart. Isabella preferred a faster life style, to use a cliché 'the jet set.' It was a style distasteful to me, shallow, hollow, oddly what our marriage became, a sham.

Our parents, Papa and Maman, Oncle Matthias and Tante Eugénie as I had addressed them from childhood were close friends from school days. They were travelling together in early summer to the wedding of the son of mutual friends.

Independently, Isabella and I had taken them to the airport at Tours where Papa kept his small private jet. He was a first class pilot, a member originally of the French 'Armée de l'Air.' Naturally, we sat together in the airport executive lounge exchanging news not having seen each other for some years. We waited to see them take off."

He stopped for a moment and I knew.

"They never did. A landing aircraft took a wrong turning on the runway and collided with Papa's plane. It exploded."

Gildas turned towards me his face filled with sorrow.

"Maman survived a few hours, brutally burned."

I ran to him the tears streaming down my face and he caught me in his arms, together in the agony of our abyss.

Lunch was cancelled. We went for a long walk through the woodlands, hands clasped in memories, our tribute to shared sorrows.

Over a light supper he told me the rest.

"So, in our twin torture and torment consolation for Isabella and me became a commitment and from a fatal accident we created a further fatal error, ironically just like the pilot of that other plane, to another Hell, a lifeless life. And then Isabella's own accident. God forbid I never wished her dead."

Gildas looked at me the pain mirrored in his eyes.

"I blame myself for what happened."

"What do you mean? I don't understand," I replied anxiously.

"That morning, we'd argued violently something we never did: we led unofficially separate lives not even enough passion to quarrel. I wanted a divorce. Isabella refused. I failed to understand why."

"But you're in love with another man," I had said to her.

"Yes," she had replied, "but he can't make me La Comtesse du Gilbert, this way I keep both."

I was shocked and saw Gildas's distress.

He continued: "I lost my temper, rare for me and told her I'd proceed anyway. Consult my solicitor, have her followed if necessary to obtain grounds. She was furious. That was wrong of me, knowing how highly strung she was I should have kept my composure, awaited another opportunity. Anyway, I left for the day and my appointments arriving back late. By this time her horse returning alone, a search was underway and then that freak snowstorm, unique in La Touraine.

We would have found her earlier but she'd ridden out on an unusual route for her, completely the opposite direction on poor riding terrain: rocky underfoot, and heavily wooded."

"Well," he sighed, "you know the rest. Eventually more than eight months later we found her helmet, her whip, that flawed stirrup leather, her mobile phone, and her remains."

For the following few weeks, we kept our love affair a secret. Not from the staff of course. That was not possible as I was spending most weekends at BeauRobert. However, Gildas and I also stayed at Delphinium. He fell in love with the old farmhouse too, working in the garden, helping me to choose furniture even turning his hand to decorating to my amazement.

"I'm no Masaccio," he laughed, "but I can paint walls."

The project at BeauRobert now finished, apart from some restorative work, I received a further surprise and this time from my team.

Two gifts: a mature three feet tall variegated ivy plant for a corner of the séjour and an exquisite blue and gold Limoges porcelain vase which I had admired in a local second hand shop. I was astonished and very touched.

Christian made a little speech. We were all dining at Delphinium. He finished with these sentiments.

"Sabine found the words for me. We've all learned so much from this project and you Caterine, have made it so pleasurable. The best thing that's happened to each of us – a leader, a lady, and we'd be honoured if you allowed us to call you our friend."

I was almost in tears as each member of my team came to embrace me in the traditional French style.

Sabine was last whispering, "I'm so pleased I opened your eyes – drop dead gorgeous." And she winked.

We were to be married, Gildas and me. He proposed in traditional fashion, in our favourite place, the walled garden, down on one knee; red rose in one hand and ring box in the other, hidden from me in the pocket of his towelling robe all morning.

It was the middle of summer, July, and 35 degrees centigrade. We'd emerged from the pool, Gildas's hair plastered back, burnished copper, wet and sexy. I recalled the first time I'd seen it like that and smiled to myself.

"You were very confident of my reply," I teased him as he produced a bottle of vintage champagne already prepared in the ice box.

"But naturally, Madame," he responded making a bowing gesture. "I knew you wouldn't fail to recognise an aristocratic antiquary with your academic good taste!"

The ring, appropriately, was in an antique setting: a square cut magnificent emerald, the stone he knew was my favourite, surrounded by diamonds. Completely perfect!

We laughed as he placed it on my finger. It fitted but just a little tight and so would have to be adjusted.

"Now," Gildas said, "if it had been a question of judging the size of your left boob, the fit would have been perfection."

His smug expression disappeared as I pushed him into the pool, towelling robe included: what simply happy days.

Of course, our respective families were totally unaware of these developments and we decided to have some fun. Eventually after various e-mails, faxes, and phone calls, a week-end rendez-vous was confirmed for all to visit BeauRobert. Rodrigue, Elisée, Félicité, Frédéric, Maman, David, and Alix with the triplet. It was a brilliant plan.

Maman phoned me at Delphinium.

"Petite," using the family endearment for me "Gildas has invited us to his château for a weekend at the end of the French holidays in August. I hope you can come."

"Oh yes," I replied, "but not the Friday evening unfortunately, I'll arrive on the Saturday before lunch."

"Oh very well," sighed Maman, "I assume work prevails, as usual, I'll tell David."

As I replaced the receiver and put on Mendelssohn's Hebridean Overture, I felt like the cat which had stolen the cream. With a Cheshire grin spreading over my face, I phoned Gildas. The plan was now in place.

I watched from Gildas' study, behind the blinds. It faced west to the walled garden but also south like the smaller salon from the west wing onto the lake.

The vehicles appeared one by one in the driveway, everyone arriving within the hour in time to freshen up before dinner. The triplet and Félicité, familiar friends jumped from the cars anxious to escape from their seat belt restrictions and explore the grounds.

Everyone gathered in the grand salon for aperitifs at 8pm. The stage was set for a planned performance. I could hear Gildas addressing everyone from my hideout under the archway in the larger hall. I was trembling with anticipation.

"My family and dear friends I invited you all here to introduce you to my future home BeauRobert. I'd like also to take the opportunity of introducing you to my future wife."

There were cries of shock and exclamations.

"My God, Gildas," David's voice, "who is she?"

Next Elisée: "I can't believe it, you've said nothing!"

Then Frédéric "Come on Gildas, it's one of your jokes. We're not fooled this time!"

Then Gildas' response, "please wait a moment and I'll bring her to meet you," amid murmurings of speculation.

He appeared in the hall grinning, coming towards my hideout, kissing me on the forehead.

"Now let's step onto the stage and have our fun!"

I could hardly contain my excitement. With Gildas' arm around my shoulder, we entered the room.

Silence prevailed. No one moved. Shock and utter disbelief registered on everyone's face stretching from Rodrigue and Elisée, past Frédéric to Maman, David and Alix. The silence was broken by my dear sister.

"But Caterine dislikes you so much!" Then in horror clamping her hand over her mouth.

Gildas and I burst out laughing and then bedlam but happy bedlam with shouts of delight, congratulations, hugs and kisses galore. What a joyous occasion.

"Maman," I asked when eventually finding her on my own. "You're not too upset I didn't let you into the secret first?"

She looked surprised and then smiled.

"Petite, I can't imagine a lovelier way of learning this news, 'with the family' and she kissed me again.

Gildas joined us, "Véronique, you've just given me permission to marry your beloved daughter. May I make another request?"

"Certainly, Gildas. What is it?"

"May I be allowed to call you Maman?"

We were both very touched. Our glances saying it all.

"Gildas, I'd be honoured."

David and Alix came over to join the three of us. After the initial congratulations earlier, they still looked shell-shocked.

"Well, David, Alix," said Gildas. "I've won my bet."

"Yes, you have," replied David, as he and Alix hugged me again.

"What bet?" I asked bewildered.

Gildas was smiling and put his arm around my shoulder.

"Oh," replied Gildas, "during my phone call to David inviting the family to BeauRobert I mentioned I was going to introduce him to a new occupant at the château whom I bet him he'd be delighted to take for a stroll."

"New occupant," I stared at everyone. "but I was never mentioned. It was to be a surprise."

David answered. "Gildas was a cunning devil. He described the occupant to me and I informed him there'd be no stroll. Impossible."

I turned to Gildas, perplexed.

"I don't understand. This is ridiculous. Who's this new occupant I've never met," sounding irritated.

He looked surprised.

"*Mon Dieu*, Caterine. Calm yourself. She's my new thoroughbred filly. You!"

I joined the merriment as everyone collapsed in laughter at my expense.

I phoned Donald as I'd promised him I would.

"Don't let me see it in a newspaper announcement, Caterine." Were his final words to me before I left Cameron Castle and our 'goodbye'.

He had news too! Whispering to Gildas I passed him the phone – more laughter and a suggestion from Gildas. It was arranged. Dinner in Paris, date to be confirmed with Donald's last words echoing in our minds.

"I've found an exceptional restaurant!"

Gildas and I had decided to announce our engagement formally the following weekend, the day after the annual château ball held in Paris every September. We had been discussing the invitation during the weekend he had proposed to me in July. I smiled as I recalled our conversation.

"You'll be my honoured guest," Gildas had said making a formal bow.

"And if I'm otherwise engaged?" I had commented.

"You can't refuse. As chairman of the committee, I command your attendance!"

"Delighted, M le Comte. May I request a new gown for this auspicious occasion?"

"Of course Chérie, whatever you wish on my account."

"Gildas," I had replied somewhat embarrassed. "That was my banter. I've numerous evening gowns from which to choose. A new one is extravagance."

We had been sitting in the smaller salon on a Sunday, late afternoon, having ridden out on Pascal and Avril, Leah as usual curled up, paw over her nose, on my lap. Since her operation she had followed me like the proverbial shadow.

"It's her way of thanking you" Gildas had told me.

"I insist," Gildas had turned towards me having risen to look out of the window with its view of the lake, the sun shimmering over the water highlighting the ebony elegance of our beloved black swans.

"Have a gown designed especially for the château ball as a present from me. There is one condition."

I had looked at him inquiringly.

"Please ensure there aren't too many buttons so that I can remove it rapidly afterwards!"

He had walked over bending his head to kiss me on the forehead. Leah had woken up and meowed at being disturbed. We had laughed and Gildas kissed her too. She stretched herself and then started to purr.

"She also approves of your kisses," I had said smiling.

"I'm sure I can improve on that effort," Gildas had replied holding my gaze.

Leah was retired to her cushion, Gildas and I to partake of an early pre-dinner aperitif!

The week following I made an appointment with Marie-Françoise at D'Aquin. It was a well established couture house but suffered now from a somewhat dotary image, patronised mainly by elderly chatelaines. Marie-Françoise, with the newly installed management team, was hungry to attract younger blood.

I remember our conversation verbatim.

"It's the château ball," I explained, "and I would like something special, different."

"A new beau?" she smiled.

"Perhaps," I replied unable to reveal my news.

"What do you suggest? You know green's my favourite I thought jade."

Marie-Françoise frowned. "not green, it's in vogue. Everyone will be wearing it."

"Black then." I suggested, another favourite.

"Too obvious," Marie-Françoise responded, looking at me thoughtfully.

"I've an idea. Come with me."

It was incredible. The performance lasted over an hour, my lunchtime, although I rarely used the allocated period. Neither did any of the directors of de Veres. Lavish lunches were not countenanced unless by client appointment and only after a major transaction had been sealed. Time was too precious. Usually, I walked in the nearby park, then joined Sabine for a salad and coffee in my office.

At last, she was satisfied. I phoned Sabine explaining I had been delayed and hurried back to de Veres. Over the following weeks there were many visits to the inner sanctum!

On the day of the ball, Gildas met me as arranged at 5pm in my office. As I was still 'en rendez-vous' he spent time with Albert and then they both joined me.

I introduced Gildas to my client, the heir to a British Dukedom: not just a title, a wealthy title, Johnny, Marquis of Roxford.

He was my age, late twenties, about 5'10" with dark brown wavy hair and not handsome; but he had a rugged appearance, a striking personality plus a droll humour. He was a rogue and a magnet for the ladies, being one of Britain's if not Europe's most eligible bachelors.

Further, he was no fool. He had a profound knowledge of

the fine arts, paintings, porcelain and antiquities, investing wisely to augment the family coffers. We enjoyed a mutual rapport. I liked him.

It had amused me to encounter Johnny several months earlier through de Veres. Johnny, Marquis of Roxford was the heir to Arthur's Dukedom, by his second marriage, Arthur being the first husband of Iona Dunn MacDonald, the mother of Donald, Professor Donald Cameron!

Having taken coffee with Gildas and Albert, Johnny rose to take his leave.

"Caterine, I always enjoy the company of a beautiful woman, especially one with a brain. I arrive with my set budget, listen to your advice and leave enhanced by my purchases no doubt, but my budget in tatters, my credit exhausted, an impoverished man!"

We all laughed at Johnny's crestfallen expression. He continued,

"One factor disappoints me about you, however Caterine."

There was silence and I looked at Johnny perplexed.

"Yes, a great disappointment. You'll be accompanying Gildas to the château ball to-night and not me! *A bientôt*"

Laughter prevailed.

Gildas and I departed together a few minutes later. As we arrived at Gildas's car he asked.

"When did Johnny invite you out?"

Surprised I turned to face him.

"How did you know?"

"I knew. Just call it male intuition," and he grinned.

"Oh, several weeks ago. I explained I was otherwise engaged!"

"My God" Gildas replied, "I arrived just in time. You might have become a duchess!"

"Don't be ridiculous, darling and anyway it's my Count I want."

Before he opened the car door, Gildas made an unusual gesture in public. He bent his head and kissed my lips.

We were staying in the Montparnasse apartment and I used Maman's bedroom to change into my evening wear, Maman now returned to Marchmont. I stared at my reflection in her antique swivel full length mirror.

The gown's fabric was a specially woven gossamer silk and sculptured to my body like a second skin. It was high-necked not in the current mode of deep décolleté which I disliked, an opinion I knew shared by Gildas.

The skirt was split at one side to just above the knee, revealing and then not revealing.

The colour I could barely describe. It appeared to be violet, an unusual violet spreading to hues of lilac as light pervaded it with my natural body colour seemingly contributing to the transformation. The collar at my throat was studded with rhinestones, in variants of blues and violets, reflecting the colours of my eyes.

Again I looked at the colour of the gown, a unique colour, from a special dye developed by D'Aquin's master of materials, Marcel, a true master of his art.

My hair I had left undressed, loose, and contrary to the mode for chignon or French plait, caught back from my forehead by a silk ribbon matching the gown.

As I opened the door to the Montparnasse salon, Gildas was standing at the window looking out for our car. He turned as I entered.

"What do you think? Do you approve?" I asked turning round slowly to reveal the gown.

There was silence.

Alarmed, I looked at him.

"Don't you like it? I know it's not the current fashion, but Marie-Françoise and I thought …."

Gildas interrupted me, saying softly.

"It's breathtaking: the fabric clings to the contours of your body and the colours are your eyes. And you've left your hair, wild, undressed as I first saw you. I've never seen any woman as beautiful. *Mon Dieu*, you'll cause a sensation, but then you always would!"

The phone rang. It was the porter. Gildas placed my matching silk cloak round my shoulders and hand in hand we walked to our waiting car.

Our announcement by the M.C. certainly caused a reaction. It had been Gildas' suggestion and I concurred. " Le Comte du Gilbert and Mademoiselle le Docteur Sinclair, his fiancée."

The grand ballroom activity ceased. Faces, shocked and astonished stared at us as we descended the marble staircase. I felt so proud to be on the arm of this exceptional man, our love affair now declared in public, honoured to have been asked to be his wife. Gildas whispered to me. It was a private remark, jocular but with a 'double entendre' and I had to stifle a giggle.

Ecstatic, I walked with him to join our families and friends.

Towards the end of a memorable evening, I was escorted from the dance floor by Jérome, Rodrigue's younger brother to join Gildas, Frédéric and Rodrigue himself.

The ladies from this group absent, sharing some female gossip, I surmised. Jérome was quite a character with a caustic humour.

"You know Caterine, you ought to reconsider this marriage to Gildas. He's past his prime now; you need someone younger, under 30, like me, a fine prospect" and he kissed my hand.

This caused much amusement.

"Jérome, regretfully, that's not possible," I replied, sighing. "You see I've promised Gildas I'll take care of him in his dotage: wheel him round the grounds in his chair, help him with the stairs, although we'll probably install a lift and perform general nursing duties."

These remarks generated hilarity from the men.

I glanced at Gildas. His expression was impassive, although one eyebrow was raised!

"Bravo Caterine," exclaimed Frédéric.

"Well, 'elderly brother', there's no answer to that!"

Gildas glanced round the company, his eyes looking finally at me.

"But I do have a reply and Caterine shall receive it."

There was silence and I smelt danger.

Gildas continued. "She shall receive it from me later."

He paused. "She shall receive it from me in private."

He paused again. "And she shall receive it in person!"

The meaning was obvious. Whistles erupted and hoots of laughter and I knew I was blushing.

"Chérie, it's time to dance."

"Gildas," I said shocked," that was a very risqué remark. I don't think ….."

He interrupted me.

"You deserved it and it was said amongst family with no ladies present."

"What do you mean?" I retorted annoyed, "don't you consider me a lady?"

Moving us deftly between two advancing couples, Gildas replied.

"Oh you are a lady by birth, breeding and general behaviour certainly, but in one area you aren't one."

"Pardon! This is making me angry, Gildas. What exactly do you mean?"

"I mean that you do not behave like a lady in my bed and that is exactly how I want it and he swung me into a spin."

There was no answer to that and he received none!

On the following morning we were besieged. Media forces

were battling for position outside our apartment; the pavement area and entrance to Parc Georges Brassens, covered by a moving mass of mayhem juggling technical and photographic equipment including what appeared to be a television crew which we espied from behind the balcony blinds of the salon.

We had been alerted by the night porter just after 6am!

Gildas and I were bewildered until we received a call from Albert on my mobile.

"*Merde!* Gildas exploded, "We must get out of here."

Albert supplied the solution sending an unmarked de Veres van used for certain clients and admitted to the private underground car park by a very concerned porter.

We had packed hurriedly and clambered into the rear of the van with our suitcases for a rocky ride arriving at Albert's house south west of Paris, on the outskirts of Versailles at 7.30am. Gildas's car remained in the Montparnasse car park as 'proof' for the porter to assure the attendant media we were still in residence.

Albert greeted us grinning, accompanied by a sympathetic Céline. He spread out the front pages of France's most popular daily paper. Gildas and I stared in shocked horror. The headline read:

"Comte du Gilbert to marry de Veres director."

Underneath the article referred to Gildas as: "the handsome count, one of France's most eligible bachelors, widowed tragically ten years ago, is also an astute businessman. He controls the du Gilbert enterprises from his headquarters at Saint Roche Rivière, the magnificent château on the Creuse which has belonged to his family for generations."

I was described as: "the Franco-Scot, only female director of de Veres, the premier Fine Arts Auction House in France (Albert would be preening his feathers at that accolade I thought) was a graduate of Glasgow University and the Sorbonne. She was the first recipient of the prestigious Gold

Medal of Europe as the top Fine Arts scholar. Mademoiselle le Docteur Sinclair caused a sensation at the Château Ball in Paris last night wearing an exquisite D'Aquin gown moulded to her voluptuous body like a silken glove."

Beside the article, marked 'exclusive' was the photograph.

That kiss from Gildas outside de Veres before opening the door of his car. Some errant photographer had struck lucky!

Over breakfast Albert commented:

"I tried to warn you. I know, Gildas, you maintain a low profile but that only enhances the enigma. So this announcement had to be news."

"As for you, Caterine," Albert sighed, "you can't expect to turn up on the arm of your celebrated fiancé at the Château Ball dressed in that gown and think you'll be ignored."

Céline added, smiling.

"You brought the house down. Both of you the main topic of conversation all evening: the talk of Paris."

"Frankly," Albert continued, "considering your combined intelligence, I think you've been extremely naïve. After all no-one had any inkling of your love affair: never seen together anywhere and certainly not on the social circuit, spending your time at BeauRobert or Delphinium. You've to be congratulated on maintaining your privacy but you can't be surprised at the public and media interest. Your own families only learned of your engagement last week-end and us with other of your closest friends during the following week."

Albert shook his head replacing his coffee cup in its Limoges saucer.

"By the way," he added "Saint Roche Rivière is also besieged. I phoned Dominique to check. She was frantic. She told me she'd attempted to contact you at Montparnasse but you must have just left. She tried your mobiles and BeauRobert. No response."

Gildas and I looked at each other feeling very foolish, non-plussed.

"After your call, Albert, we switched off our mobiles." Gildas replied. "The BeauRobert staff are on special leave to celebrate our engagement which they knew would be announced formally in the press this morning."

There was silence.

"I apologise, Albert, not one of my better strategies, introducing Caterine as my fiancée last evening. It just seemed appropriate and, frankly I was so proud to show to the assembled company this exceptional lady who'd honoured me by agreeing to become my wife. Thank you on behalf of both of us for your prompt rescue."

I was startled. It was uncharacteristic for Gildas to offer such comments outside the family.

He glanced at me and our eyes locked. I felt that incredible energy flow between us, even at this distance. Gildas continued, picking up the newspaper article with the accompanying photograph.

"Last night at the Château Ball, I received jocular remarks from male members of my family: that I was now over 30, of advancing years, past my prime. On examining this photograph today, those members of my family will observe that I have their advantage as you have too Albert."

Looking surprised, Albert replied, "Pardon why?"

"Because our years are not advancing but maturing. We've found our partners in ladies of beauty and wit, of sophistication and intelligence. Ladies of fine taste who appreciate us, their antiquaries as rare and valuable assets, always in their prime!"

We all laughed uproariously as Gildas raised his cup of coffee.

"*Santé!*"

After an hour spent with Albert, Céline and their two

children, Gildas and I submitted to the final part of his plan.

A de Veres limousine ferried us to our sanctuary, our beloved BeauRobert known only to our family and close friends. Saint Roche Rivière was still Gildas's official residence and the Montparnasse apartment mine.

Albert, of course, was in his element. On the Monday morning of the following week he invited the assembled media into his offices at de Veres and acted as our official spokesman.

"Gildas and Caterine have taken a few days holiday and would like to thank all concerned for their congratulations and best wishes. As yet no date for the wedding has been set."

It was free publicity for de Veres plus also D'Aquin. Marie-Françoise phoned me at BeauRobert to tell me they had been inundated with inquiries for couture garments.

It had transformed their dotary image overnight, opening up a younger market place. Marie-Françoise and her management team were ecstatic.

From them, I received a magnanimous gesture – a wedding dress as a wedding present. Further free publicity for them and no cost to me, plus my 'exquisite gown' for the Château Ball was prepared for me as a sample 'on approval', no payment required.

"No way," I protested, "it's an engagement present from Gildas."

"Caterine," Marie-Françoise replied, "choose an outfit instead from us for your trousseau as a present from Le Comte."

"Marie-Françoise," I interrupted, "it's Gildas."

"D'accord," I could hear the smile in her voice, "Gildas."

"Mon Dieu! What a shock when I heard from Maman in a phone call last week of your engagement to be announced in the Saturday press, knowing you were wearing our gown at the Château Ball accompanied by your 'new beau' as you'd confirmed to me in the summer, with such nonchalance."

Le Comte du Gilbert, Gildas, the enigmatic dream of all my contemporaries. Caterine, hearts are broken all over France."

We laughed together.

"See you soon!"

Gildas and I spent the following week working together on our diverse projects at BeauRobert grateful for our very loyal friends. Eventually, tentatively we dined out together in Paris. We received attention, whispered remarks plus overt congratulations from mutual friends but no photographers. The media had moved on. By their standards we were old news and we courted no revival!

Our next dinner date was arranged for the first weekend in October, also in Paris: a rendez-vous with mutual friends.

What a reunion. Gildas and me Donald and his fiancée Shona Carruthers, my school, university and 'after' best friend. Incredible. They had met again at some charity dinner in Invernesshire. Shona and I repaired to the 'loo', more an excuse for a chat.

"I nearly dropped the phone when Donald told me," I said. "You're obviously very happy. How strange life is."

"Yes, Caterine, I can hardly belief it. As for Gildas, I can honestly say he's a magnificent specimen of male humanity. But I wouldn't change him for my Donald!"

"Shona," I said taking her arm, "I wouldn't give you the chance!"

Two happy laughing human beings returned to join their lovers and a gourmet dinner.

"Just one cautionary remark, Donald" said Gildas as we studied the menus.

Three pairs of eyes regarded him inquiringly.

"For Heavens sake let's arrange the weddings on different days."

"You're right," exclaimed Donald "diaries out, now who's first?"

We spent the night with Maman in Montparnasse at her invitation. One practicality concerned me, Gildas certainly to his discomfort offered a solution. Over port or cognac he turned to Maman.

"Véronique, pardon, Maman." he smiled. "Caterine explained about the four bedrooms. As there are five of us I'm quite happy to use our camp bed, it's in the car."

Maman looked surprised, even bemused. She stood up, from the coffee table and walked to the window. No one spoke.

Turning around she answered him.

"Gildas du Gilbert, did I or did I not give you permission to marry my daughter?"

For once Gildas looked taken aback.

"Yes, you did," he replied.

"I should never have given that permission if I'd thought that the Scottish and French bloodlines had not been intelligent enough to have the pleasure of sharing each other's beds! Further," she addressed Donald and Shona, "I assumed also you'd not been equally ignorant."

And so we all said, "Good Night!"

After breakfast on the following morning Maman and I sat down over another cup of coffee. Gildas. Donald, and Shona left us some time together and walked around Montparnasse via Parc Georges Brassens.

"Petite," said Maman kissing me in one of her spontaneous gestures. " You've made me a very happy woman. I never expected a feeling quite like this again. As for David and Alix I think they're still shell shocked. I thought there was someone, fewer visits from you, although I knew you were working on 'Delphinium', plus your voice lighter on the phone and more laughter."

"Maman I've neglected you."

"Nonsense," she smiled. "You have your life to live and I've found I must also live mine. You're engagement is a blessing for all the family and to such an exceptional man. It's obvious how much in love you both are."

"Now tell me" she held up her hand, "not the details of course, but when did you realise your feelings for Gildas?"

I told her about our talks at BeauRobert, the discussions over the artefacts, our evening aperitifs and then Leah's accident. However, it was an edited version but Maman would have filled in the details!

"And so," she continued, "I was right about that premonition of yours. The connection, the danger, was the attraction you felt unknowingly for him, not a threat."

"Obviously, " I replied. " I was blind."

Tragically, we were both proved wrong.

Chapter Thirteen

During the months before our wedding I experienced strange images in my mind. Sometimes during the day I sensed someone was following me like a phantom on my shoulder and I would turn round: but no-one was there.

Since my teenage years I had lived with these fearful spectres but had been less aware of them, too immature to recognise any significance in their messages.

Occasionally these apparitions invaded my sleep, dreams turned to nightmares when Gildas would hold me, my body trembling, not from the afterglow of loving but from the early advent of fear.

"Chérie, what is it? Can I help?" were his entreaties.

"I'm sorry, Darling, just memories about Papa and David, morbid memories best forgotten."

So elusive and tenuous were these images, infrequent shadows that I dismissed them, fool that I was.

These words and messages accompanied often by Wordsworth's poetic imagery from his sonnets of the imagination.

"There's neither dog nor heifer, horse nor sheep,
Will wet his lips within that cup of stone;

And often times, when all are fast asleep
The water doth send forth a dolorous groan."

When I reflect now, how naïve I was not to recognise the threat he posed, too immersed in my happiness, too ignorant in my ideology. I was blind to his threat. Perhaps I was also petrified by the perfection of those months when my career and my love affair seemed to be blessed by a Midas touch which rendered me unable and even unwilling to read the signs from that legend. Instead I dallied down the driveway to the destruction of my dreams

Our wedding date proved more complex than we imagined, not only regarding our dual commitments but to ensure the day and date was an acceptable one for all we wished to attend. We discussed it at length.

"Caterine," Gildas told me, "it's your day, your choice. We can have Saint Roche Rivière decked out as you wish even grander than Elisée Silvière's wedding."

"Gildas, it's our day and I'd prefer to be married from BeauRobert."

I was standing in Gildas' study, Leah perched on my shoulder, my stroking her little dappled head as I looked out at the black swans on the lake.

I turned to receive his response. He was smiling and walked over to put his arms round me and Leah. She licked his face but did not move. We laughed together at her feline determination.

"I'd hoped you would want our wedding to take place here," he replied, kissing me in that very loving fashion on the forehead, bending his head to reach mine. Leah received a kiss too, what a lucky pussycat!

At dinner with a starter of asparagus in a butter sauce followed by one of Agathe's superb seafood dishes we discussed the wedding preparations again.

Gildas and I had been very touched by the staff's response. After our engagement had been formally announced, we had received from them a floral bouquet encompassing duplications of many of the flowering shrubs from the walled garden. In addition to this gift was a large box about four feet in height. The card attached to it was inscribed: 'to Monsieur Le Comte and Madame his fiancée from the staff at BeauRobert. May our gift grow with your prosperity and happiness.'

The box contained two rhododendron bushes erupting wild in Scotland but also nurtured in many domestic gardens there. These were shrubs I loved but missing in the walled garden or even anywhere on the BeauRobert estate.

I had spoken to Félix about my affection for the rhododendron and he must have taken personal note. More incredibly, the name of the red flowered plants, which they had chosen, was 'Lord Robert'! Gildas and I were overwhelmed by such a thoughtful gesture.

After dinner we walked in the grounds, the late September air still caressing, hands clasped; no need to speak, our thoughts in tune, with many mutual memories.

Over coffee I said to Gildas.

"BeauRobert is where I realised I was in love with you. Frankly I'd prefer a more private celebration here with just our families and close friends.

"I agree," he replied "exactly what I wanted too!"

It was arranged for the 5th March of the following year, my birthday celebrations on the 19th during our honeymoon.

Towards the end of October, in Paris, I had a long meeting with Albert de Vere, fate as I thought, smiling on me again.

"That's unbelievable, Albert! What a coup for de Veres!"

"I must admit I'm delighted, Caterine. I worked on it for over a year. In fact that was the crucial meeting I was about to chair in the Board Room when you interrupted with your Masaccio!"

I gasped. "Albert, I'd no idea."

"Caterine, it was more than worth it. That discovery of the Masterpiece, the auction and the publicity brought us recognition as serious players. This contract establishes our maturity at a very young age."

Against formidable odds, Albert had secured a contract. A contract for the updated valuations plus any restorative artefact work for the premiere Loire Valley châteaux. It included furniture, furnishings, paintings and the buildings themselves. It was worth millions!

"My offer to you, Caterine, is to take overall responsibility for the planning of the project with regard to the logistics. Obviously, you'll be assigned command control of the paintings; assessment, valuation and restorative work where required.

The other directors will be responsible for their particular specialised genre, but you will be Operations Director. I will control the financial structure, as well as maintaining my role as M.D. Of course there is a disadvantage for you – no travel in Europe and very boring, based between Paris and BeauRobert, near your future husband. What do you think?"

"Albert" I cried, running over to throw my arms round him, kissing him on both cheeks, "it's a dream come true!"

"But not for me "Albert sighed.

"What do you mean" I stared at him incomprehensibly "I don't understand."

Turning to look out from his penthouse suite over the unique images of Paris, he replied:

"You will when you receive your salary increase!"

He turned back to face me as he winked.

When I drove through the woods surrounding BeauRobert I found myself ambivalent where my priorities should be focussed. In fact on reflection should I be working at all? Emerging from that verdant landscape I stopped my car gazing at the breathtaking beauty of our château in the full moonlight. The oaks and the acacias were waving to me in the light breeze standing tall and elegant against the background of the autumnal tapestry welcoming me home.

Through my open car window, I breathed in the scents from the shrubbery still tastefully tangible to my senses and pondered yet again if my original decision was the right one. Starting the engine I drove on skirting the lake to arrive at the château's main door.

Félix would drive my car to the garages. He considered it his duty but in fact I knew it was his treat! He opened the massive oak door even before I had inserted the key.

"I was in the larger hall, Madame," he greeted me "and heard your car; lovely evening, still warm for this time of year."

"Yes, Félix, how fortunate we are. Has Monsieur returned?" I inquired.

"Yes Madame, Monsieur le Comte awaits you in the salon library."

I smiled to myself at Félix's formal tone and title for Gildas. Despite numerous requests Félix remained immersed in the 'old school', Gildas could never be referred to as only Monsieur, he was Monsieur le Comte!

"Thank you Félix, tell him I'll join him in ten minutes."

I was showered and changed in nine as I glanced at my watch. My petrol blue angora business suit replaced by one of my many pairs of knee breeches, Gildas's favourite outfit for me. This time the breeches were emerald green cashmere with a matching sweater striped in black. On my entering the salon library Gildas jumped up to greet me, laying aside the local newspaper delivered on Fridays.

"You look lovelier than ever," he said with his usual kiss of welcome. "And later than expected. Any problems?"

"The opposite," I replied smiling broadly and relayed Albert's news.

"What an extraordinary achievement!" Gildas exclaimed.

"A celebration's in order and he disappeared to return with an opened bottle of vintage champagne.

"Chilled already? How?" I asked bewildered.

"I've news too?" Gildas was wearing his special smile, which I always found so sexy.

"What is it? Come on you're teasing me!" Gildas, still grinning filled the crystal goblets and handed mine to me.

"The British film company have confirmed their request to locate the historical saga at Saint Roche Rivière. The film and television rights are to be negotiated next year. It's worth a lot of money and prestige for the château, for France and for us, plus the attendant exposure and publicity for the local tourist industry."

"Mon Dieu!" I exclaimed, "but I thought you were going to refuse."

"I reconsidered. Madness to refuse when it was not what I would consider an immoral exposure. The book is a classic but not yet filmed. If they had requested BeauRobert the answer would have been negative but Saint Roche Rivière is already a commercial enterprise and will benefit from further fame."

"You were right Caterine, when you urged me to accept."

We raised our champagne goblets, 'Santé!'

Gildas continued. "What about inviting Albert and Céline to a family weekend here; try and find a date to suit Rodrigue and Elisée to join us. They struck up a rapport at that château restoration dinner at Saint Roche Rivière."

"A great idea. I'll phone them tomorrow." I agreed, thinking it was such a thoughtful gesture.

As we sat in the salon library its walls glowing with warm cherry wood bookcases, my thoughts wandered as I sipped at my champagne. I looked at the multifarious early editions lining the walls. They returned my gaze as did all the volumes as if personified, their titles conjuring up their characters; the autobiographies, biographies, travelogues and fiction, proudly proclaiming their heritage to posterity.

On hearing Gildas voice, I roused myself from my reverie.

"Chérie, where were you, reflecting on that meeting with Albert in Paris?"

I stood up and walked to the fireplace admiring yet again the Renoir, which graced the alcove wall. The slowly tumbling logs burning in the fireplace reminded me of Marchmont and family gatherings, warm evenings after similar autumn days.

"Actually, no, darling." I replied. "I was looking at the bookcases and their contents, reflecting I suppose on their history." Standing still at the fireplace, I told Gildas of my misgivings about continuing to work if perhaps my priorities were out of order and that I should be playing another role in his life, my job set aside.

"You gave up your career for your responsibilities. Shouldn't I relinquish mine?"

Gildas put down his champagne goblet with its protective coaster on the walnut bureau bookcase and came to join me standing at the fireplace.

"Caterine, we've discussed our future plans and the circumstances are totally different. I'd no choice. You have," he replied.

"And remember, I was proud of my ancestry born the heir to that inheritance. I owed it to those forebears, to Papa and Maman, to the future generations Elisée, Frédéric and their families to take on this mantle, of and for my beloved France."

"Gildas, I do understand the different circumstances. Your parents were only in their early fifties when that tragic accident happened. But I want you to know that you're more important to me than my job or any career. On one of my visits to Zurich, David said to me: "Petite, keep looking. There's more to life than work." My brother was right."

"Agreed," Gildas replied, "but you're forgetting an important factor."

"What's that?" I asked looking up at him."

"You also have your inheritance: outstanding talent and dedication which has seen you rightly recognised from the student Gold Medal of Europe to the Masaccio triumph and onwards to the Board of de Veres at 28. Incredible! Innate ambition honed and spurred on by your Papa's untimely death, David's love and Véronique's battle to recovery."

He paused. "I hate waste, talent neglected, academic ability uneducated, individuals gifted in some dimension but left undeveloped. Both of us were offered the opportunities to achieve our goals and seized them. We were the fortunate ones. I'm enjoying my second career. Don't abandon your first."

I bent down to remove the poker from its wrought iron stand, deep in thought, adjusting the logs in the fireplace generating a flurry of flames. Standing up again, I put my arms around his neck, fingers tangling in the longish hair and kissed him.

"Thank you, darling I have my answer."

His eyes held my gaze.

"Caterine, we share many things but the most important are our love for each other and our integrity. I know that neither of us will betray those."

With the development of events and in hindsight, I can only reflect what a capital statement of irony that was.

Chapter Fourteen

Donald and Shona were married first nearly two weeks before Gildas and me. The ceremony took place in the local village church with a reception of course at that unique Reformation tower house Cameron Castle. It was a memorable day.

Donald's speech was a masterpiece! With Maman's permission, he referred to that evening we all spent at Montparnasse when she made it clear to Gildas, Shona, Donald and me that she assumed each engaged couple shared the same bedroom. Donald concluded his hilarious speech in sombre mood.

"We were all shocked. It was very embarrassing albeit Madame Sinclair is French," he continued.

At this point there were titters of laughter from the younger crowd.

"Of course," Donald paused, "we'd no option but to comply. Looked fools if we didn't."

There were gasps from the younger crowd and expressions of horror on the older. The minister's face had turned an unhealthy shade of pink and he was tugging at his white starched collar.

Donald shuffled his feet embarrassment written all over his face.

"I can tell you," he said, "all four of us agreed the next morning, that it was very uncomfortable. Wasn't it darling?" turning to his bride.

Shona could only nod, in convulsions, knowing Donald as we all did and guessing the punch line.

There was a stunned silence. Gildas and I exchanged glances.

Donald paused again looking pained.

"Yes, it was very uncomfortable indeed lying together in that double bed with Paris temperatures of 28°, fully clothed!"

The room erupted including the minister: a hilariously happy day.

What about our wedding: the day Gildas and I were married and I became his wife, la Comtesse du Gilbert? We were among our family and close friends at our beloved BeauRobert. It was a day of dreams, utterly unforgettable.

Gildas and I had given ourselves a present: five and a half weeks of vacation.

The first two were particularly for ourselves, spent in Martinique. After some searching, Gildas had found a hotel with the accommodation housed in individual cottages, strewn discreetly around six acres of grounds. Each was surrounded by fragrant shrubbery totally secluded with a private swimming pool installed in every individual garden. Our cottage was only a few sandy steps from our favourite water, the incomparable Caribbean.

There were two restaurants, dancing in the evening to those exceptional West Indian steel bands plus a nightclub; this we visited once. It was faultless in its entertainment, but for us too sophisticated not to our taste.

We spent our daytime in the enticing Caribbean either swimming, snorkelling, water skiing or kayaking. In the evenings, we were spoiled with delicious dinners, dallying in dance, soaking up the sunsets and luxuriating in our love affair.

Afterwards, we completed the Master Plan!

Donald and Shona had spent part of their honeymoon at Donald's parents' home on the Côte d'Azur. It was very easy travel from there to be guests at our wedding at BeauRobert.

We returned the compliment spending a weekend with them at the Cameron holiday retreat just north of St James in Barbados, where, ironically, I had first met Duncan and Iona Cameron. We emerged from the taxi, which we had taken from Grantley Adams Airport with one thought on our minds. As Donald and Shona opened the door to welcome us, Gildas and I said in unison.

"We've discovered a very fine restaurant."

As always hilarity prevailed throughout that weekend.

We were sitting together bound for Gatwick, spoiled in the first class section of the British Airways 777. Gildas had insisted on this luxury despite my protests. The aircraft with its massive majestic two engines paused in anticipation. The captain, thrust levers forward, pressed the toga switches. Responding proud in her power, the aircraft accelerated her pace, raced down the runway and roared into the rays of the setting sun.

I gazed down from my window seat at the dwindling daylight, Gildas's hand on the armrest over mine.

"I'm so happy for them," I said. "They obviously love each other."

"Yes," replied Gildas "but there's an element missing."

I turned in surprise to stare at him.

"Donald may indeed love Shona but unfortunately for him he's still in love with you."

Our eyes locked together. I made no reply. The subject was never raised again.

There followed a week spent alone together at Marchmont. I was able to explore with Gildas my beloved Scottish countryside, my inheritance from my ancestors.

The weather was cool but dry with spring promise;

daffodils and crocus lacing the landscape and the garden at Marchmont waking up from winter slumber. Gildas and I wandered round anticipating the future blossom from the budding forsythia and magnolia bushes, a display of camellias welcomed us in profusion benefiting from their sheltered bed and frost hardy.

The trees lining the periphery were varied: limes, silver birches, beeches and several conifers, guarding their kingdom like sentinels ever protective of its parameters and the conifers evergreen.

Gildas and I discussed the love of our respective families for Scotland and for France. On researching family records, we had discovered a marriage between a Scottish nobleman's daughter with a du Gilbert in the 17th century.

"Rogues and brigands together," I said and we laughed.

"Papa and Maman loved Scotland too," Gildas said, "as I told you from their many visits here."

"Yes," I reflected, "how sad that they and my Papa and Maman can't see us today."

I stopped voice faltering. Gildas took my hand again and we walked forward. There could be no point in looking back.

We rode out on my friend Farmer Black's two hunters admiring the peculiar majesty of the Scottish landscape. Hopefully, we dined well on my cuisine; normally locally caught fish or fresh pasta plus quality vegetables from our 'fruit and veg' man in the village. Gildas prepared a surprise one evening consulting one of Maman's cookery books lined up like soldiers, a library selection on numerous shelves in the pine finished kitchen. We laughed at the result the temperature too high, the skin broken, but certainly still edible, it was haggis!

A week later we took off from Glasgow Airport via Schiphol to Zurich. We were greeted by a traditional avalanche of a welcome, from my and now Gildas's family, David, Alix, the triplet and Maman, who was staying there for our family reunion. It seemed perfect.

Late on the Saturday morning Gildas and I wandered down the Bahnhof Strasse, one of the most famous streets in Europe to be compared with Bond Street and the Champs Elysées. He had wanted to buy me a hat which I had admired in one of the exclusive boutiques and I was resisting.

"Gildas, no way, you've spent a fortune on me already in the past few weeks." I exclaimed.

"That's my pleasure for the very beautiful creature who is now my wife. Come and let's discuss the hat over an aperitif."

Taking my hand, he led me round the corner towards a typically Swiss café-bar where we found a seat outside, at a corner table.

After our drinks arrived, I sat back to absorb the ambiance of the environment and the mellow temperature.

Suddenly I felt chilled as a shadowy image brushed my mind. Raising my hand to push it away, I knocked over my glass of vermouth which fell to the floor, shattered, the red wine trickling across the pavement like rivulets of blood.

"Chérie, what happened. Are you alright?" Gildas exclaimed jumping up and kneeling at my side as the waiter appeared to mop up the mess.

"Yes, darling, sorry so careless of me. I was trying to clear something," I hesitated, "something in my eye."

Pushing the images to the back of my mind, I smiled. "Now what about that hat?"

The incident bothered me because it reminded me of a similar one in the past. I still felt chilled.

Chapter Fifteen

BeauRobert! We're home! How exciting to return from the celebrations of our love affair to rejoice in the château where it began.

It was now early April, a Sunday, and we sat down in the smaller salon after lunch, Leah as usual on my lap, to reminisce over the years and recent months.

"You know," Gildas began, "it was quite a shock when I first met you, not at all what I'd expected."

"What did you imagine, a monster?"

Gildas paused, standing up to walk over to the window overlooking the lake.

"Certainly not, but then I was unaware of your temper."

"Mon Dieu, I know, so unpredictable!"

"Chérie, it flares and is extinguished. It's not a moody, selfish temper and often to defend the conduct of others. It's one of your attractions. Who am I or any human being to claim the arrogance of some perfection?"

He continued, "your Papa had described you to me. He told me you resembled Véronique in looks and stature, but his description of you still gave me an impression of his 'little girl'. Natural of course, how most fathers would envisage a teenage daughter.

"Remember, also, I'd never met Maman. Ironically my earlier planned visits to your family in Scotland cancelled. At first, due to Frédéric's rugby accident and the second after those serious floods in La Touraine which threatened damage to Saint Roche Rivière."

"I remember," I replied "the family were very disappointed."

"Hence my shock," Gildas smiled at me "on meeting you. Standing staring at me was a young lady, statuesque with long strawberry blonde hair, wild, undressed hair and a remarkable face, incredible, with large violet eyes unusual enough; but after my remarks to you seemed to change colour to a steel blue."

Gildas laughed. "That is why I turned back with an excuse to readdress David. It was to look at you again."

"And my comments halted you?"

"Yes, but couldn't change my recognition of the 'coup de foudre'! I didn't believe such phenomenon existed and certainly not for me. Many times your image appeared in front of me, even at business meetings. I think actually that's when I made my best decisions."

He walked over and kissed my forehead.

I stared at him I was dumbfounded.

"But why no indication or gesture of your feelings for me after," I hesitated "after Isabella's death?"

"Well, I saw you on very few occasions which complicated any approach and anyway you were just starting out on your career. Next time we met after I was widowed was at Graham McCallum's 21st and you turned down my dance invitation!" Gildas reminded me. "I must have been quite repugnant. No-one else had refused me that evening!"

I laughed. "You know I had chickenpox. Heavens, just made the loo to vomit. What a ghastly seven days."

"Then I came to Scotland for your graduation celebrations at Marchmont."

"And gave me the diary," I said "but you left before I could thank you. Why?"

Gildas walked to the fireplace looking up at the painting which we both loved ,the Renoir. He turned to face me.

"Because I was in tears in my soul: wanting to declare my feelings for you but knowing you'd find the idea ridiculous, preposterous even laughable. The only reaction would be rejection by you."

I lifted Leah up placed her on my cushion and walked over putting my arms round him my head on his chest.

"How ironic," I said thoughtfully. "Just as I felt sure you would eventually reject me after that first night we made love here at BeauRobert. How strange life is."

We spent the rest of our final holiday week together in the same mode. Each morning we checked for any urgent mail. During our absence correspondence had been attended to by Sabine for me, promoted to my assistant at de Veres and for Gildas by his two deputy managers Roger and Dominique at Saint Roche Rivière.

Then we would ride out together, saddled up usually on Pascal and Avril for a trek over the estate, finishing with a gallop over that rich riding terrain. Lunch was taken on the terrace overlooking the walled garden a little too cool as yet to sit at the pool. Our food was chosen from a buffet, prepared by Agathe, light and simple consisting of cold cuts, fresh fish or some pasta dishes with plenty of fruit and cheese. During the week it was accompanied by a glass of water and at weekends some Chablis or Bordeaux.

On the Tuesday of that week, after lunch, sitting in the salon library I said to Gildas.

"Close your eyes I've a present for you." And I placed it on his lap.

He looked down with curiosity and then smiled gazing at me.

I said quietly, "Please open it at the bookmarker."

On that page, the 5th March of the current year, I had written.

'At Beau Robert the château of dreams,

To my husband from his wife.

Thank you for a day utterly unforgettable.

I shall love you always for the rest of my life.

   Caterine'

Gildas looked up at me. He looked up at me from the pages of the diary he had given to me at Marchmont. The diary I had used, felt compelled to use since I had received it from him almost seven years ago, every day of my life.

I knew that look of his. We retired hand in hand for further discussions of a more intimate kind!

Afterwards, we walked in the grounds emerging to sit beside the lake watching the black swans, Papa and Maman fiercely proud of their cygnets. They regarded us with an arrogant air for daring to disturb their domain. It amused us.

"What unique creatures and how graceful in flight." I said, throwing them some pieces of bread brought from lunch.

"I was remembering," I mused "about our next meeting. It was at Elisée Silvière's wedding to Rodrigue and I was very badly behaved over that painting, David gave me a real dressing down!"

"Did he? But that was my fault," Gildas replied. "I blurted out the artist without thinking. I'd been revising on the various château paintings, aware of your knowledge and not wanting to appear ignorant."

We looked at each other and burst out laughing. What fools we had been.

"Then," added Gildas "the worst news. Frédéric told me he'd asked you out for dinner and you'd accepted."

I gasped, "You're right I'd forgotten!"

Gildas smiled eyebrows raised.

"I can tell you, if he'd not been my brother I would have knocked him cold. Especially as I was planning a trip to Paris intending to phone you in advance and casually suggest lunch."

I was giggling. "Frédéric is very attractive you know and of course, nearer my age."

The sea green eyes observed me and the reply came unanswerable.

"With apologies to my brother in his absence he couldn't handle you in or out of bed."

Gildas caught my arm before my mock punch landed, kissing my hand, my forehead and then gently brushing my lips with his.

It was a week full of memories just as Gildas had invited me to record all those years ago in my diary – a memorable week.

On Thursday evening after an earlier dinner we were packed and ready for our drive the following morning for an overnight stay with Rodrigue and Elisée. She was expecting her second child in July just three months distant.

I was looking forward to seeing them again in their 18th century manor house south of BeauRobert in the Auvergne.

I watched as Gildas poured out the cognacs in a gesture very reminiscent to me, the burnished copper hair still curling down his neck as of many years ago. I teased him.

" This brings back memories."

"Yes, it does" he smiled. "Merci, cheers and santé. To us, our families and BeauRobert."

Then we heard the sound, 'miaow.'

"Pardon Leah and to you" Gildas and I laughed at her intuition. What a clever pussycat!

We were playing one of Vivaldi's violin concertos, Number 2, when I heard the hall bell ringing.

"Gildas," I said "I think someone's at the gate," jumping up I opened the salon door to the smaller hall lifting the receiver.

We had inherited a system from Oncle Arnaud, installed in the late 1970s. It consisted of a camera security system between the main gate and the château with a telephone link. I called into the receiver looking at the camera image.

"Good evening, who's calling?"

The image wavered in front of me, but no response. Gildas arrived at my side.

"Who is it?" he asked " one of the estate staff?"

I handed him the receiver, "I don't know, the camera image is poor and I've had no answer."

Gildas repeated my efforts but to no avail.

"This is ridiculous. It can't continue. We must upgrade the system, it's quite archaic. I'll walk to the gate and find out who it is."

It was a warm evening and Gildas was wearing his customary chinos, this time in a burgundy colour quite striking with a pale lemon coloured shirt, sporting buttoned down pockets and his striped alma mater tie. I was amused. The return walk to that BeauRobert gate was nearly a mile!

Gildas appeared some time later accompanied by our visitor. By this time I could not contain my laughter.

"Caterine du Gilbert you'll pay for this and you'll pay dearly!

However, already I had taken the photograph. Gildas with mop head in hand its top covered by a plasticated rubber face we had used in Scotland for Halloween parties, was filmed for posterity. In his other hand Gildas held the wig, the toupee, which completed the picture and over his arm the small steps into which I had inserted and supported the image.

"You've a wicked sense of humour," he said grinning. "But I love you for it. It reminds me of Maman with whom we had such fun and laughter in our family as we were growing up."

The Vivaldi was finished. We waited for the following CD which was one of Mahler's symphonies. As we sat sipping our cognacs my head on his shoulder a thought occurred to me.

"Gildas, one fact puzzles me. Why did you give Donald and me that adjacent bedroom suite at Félicité's christening if you were in love with me?"

"Ah, an interesting observation," Gildas replied. Lifting his brandy goblet he stood up and walked to look out on the lake. It was a habit we shared. The water was dark now but still shimmering in the light of the, as yet, imperfect face of the three quarter moon.

"It seems an ironical answer, paradoxical, but it would have been dishonourable not to. David was very happy that you'd found someone to complement your life. All your family were. It would have been unusual, unnatural, after the period of your romance if you weren't sharing his bed."

"Could he not have been sharing mine?" I teased.

Gildas shrugged his shoulders: "Whichever way you want to describe it."

"The option was open and I gave it to you although I admit I was unable to sleep that night, disturbed with images of you in my mind. A further frustrating factor was that I liked Donald from our first meeting. A highly intelligent man, in fact I thought you'd marry him."

Startled I stared at Gildas.

"That's what he said about you. Donald told me , 'I like Gildas, a highly intelligent man.' How bizarre. As for marrying him, I very nearly did."

We returned from the Auvergne on Saturday in time for a light supper. It had been a joyful reunion. Elisée glowing in this second pregnancy with earlier problems only a memory.

"I was very frightened Caterine after that bleeding on the

3rd month but I received immediate medical assistance, one week's rest in the local hospital and then reassured." She smiled and kissed me.

"Thank you for giving Gildas back his life. He's been an exceptional brother to Frédéric and me, shouldering all the responsibilities. We love him so much and now we've you to love too." I felt very touched.

Frédéric was staying for the weekend with his girlfriend Charlotte, who was a lawyer. We all liked her. Later Gildas said to me.

"Thank God, he ditched the blonde, all body and no head. This one appears to have both."

Rodrigue was so pleased to see us fussing round to make sure we were comfortable. Félicité? She was just a darling.

"I hope the baby will be a brother," she declared.

"Why, mignonne?" I inquired as she sat on my lap.

"Oh, because Maman always tells Papa that ladies are much more intelligent."

At first silence and then we all collapsed in laughter at the wisdom from the innocent mind of a child.

On Sunday morning it occurred and life returned to its normality, the honeymoon was over!

"Caterine," Gildas called from his study, "have you moved that e-mail I received from the film company?"

"No," I replied emerging from Gildas's bathroom cleaning sponge in my hand. "It was beside the paper weight the last time I saw it."

"Well, it's not there now," Gildas called back sounding irritated.

In one area Gildas and I were complete opposites. My clothes were hung in colour selection and by season. He, although immaculately turned out was always searching for a missing sweater, jacket or tie. This stemmed from being reared with a valet.

However regarding paperwork, Gildas was meticulous and I, untidy!

Entering his study I suggested he might have put it in his briefcase.

"Certainly not," he replied emphatically. "After I read it for the second time I placed it where you said you saw it, next to the paperweight."

I knew by his expression he was annoyed.

"You must have lifted it." Then Gildas added a trifle sarcastically "unless Leah ate it, being short of breakfast."

Now I was angry. Words ensued ending with my marching out of his study and in temper childishly slamming with difficulty the heavy oak door. I felt miserable; our first married quarrel and I went for a walk. Gildas did not follow.

When I returned just before lunch I heard him on the phone as I walked past his study, now contained in our private apartment. Before, we were married, Gildas and I had rearranged his suite in the west wing. It already included the smaller salon and this became our sitting room. Beyond that and self contained on the ground floor was a spacious set of rooms. Gildas and I sharing ideas converted them, retaining his study, dressing room and bathroom, redecorating the master bedroom and installing a wedding present to ourselves, a luxury four poster bed.

The other rooms were redesigned to give me my own bathroom, adjacent to our bedroom plus like Gildas a dressing room and study.

The smaller salon faced south with access from French windows onto the lake side as well as adjoining the smaller hall. Gildas's study faced south and west to the walled garden. One window was replaced by patio doors to give access to the garden and this change replicated in my study which faced due west. We installed also for our convenience a dining kitchen. When renovations were completed we were more than satisfied. It was private very comfortable providing us with a self contained apartment within BeauRobert yet affording direct access to our beloved walled garden but retaining outstanding views of that enchanting driveway and the shimmering waters of the lake. All the restorative work had been sympathetic to the Renaissance period of architecture.

The slight headache which had developed after my walk now started throbbing. I walked through the arched hallway heading for my bathroom hoping to find some aspirin.

Suddenly I noticed my weekend mail in its large paper clip waiting for the Monday morning transportation to Paris and de Veres. It was sitting on the walnut cabinet beside my attaché case.

A thought occurred and anxiously I turned the sheaf of papers over. At the back, smiling smugly up at me was the missing e-mail.

Mon Dieu! In gathering up my correspondence I had inadvertently included the film companies' communiqué. Gildas had been right. He would be furious.

I swallowed a couple of times and taking a deep breath walked back to Gildas's study. He was off the phone. No sound now but the computer keyboard.

I entered meekly holding the e-mail in front of me. Gildas was frowning at the screen. He had designed its installation in such a way that it could be stored out of sight behind a half oak door in his bookcase.

"So," he commented, "you've found it with your mail no doubt!"

I was astonished. He turned regarding me, eyebrows raised.

"You'd have saved time and a puerile dispute if you'd checked earlier."

"I apologise, darling I was wrong."

Gildas switched off the machine and came over to put his arm around me kissing me on the forehead.

"Caterine, if this is the only problem in our married life we'll be blessed indeed. On second thoughts" he said "perhaps we should create more of them."

"Pardon. Why?" I was bemused.

"Ah," he replied "it'll give us both great pleasure in making up!"

Monday morning and it was Paris and de Veres. I commuted by TGV that incomparable French rail system leaving my car, as in the past at Saint Pierre des Corps station at Tours. It was under an hour to Montparnasse and I could work en route.

With the new contract conditions I would be able to drive to the locations, which were mostly on the Loire and base my office between Paris and BeauRobert.

I had a meeting with Sabine to update me on developments in my absence, although the last week she had provided me with copies of correspondence at BeauRobert. Afterwards, I dictated some letters with Flora, my secretary. There was a Board Meeting at 2.30pm but before that a celebration lunch.

Sabine had passed her Intermediate exams with flying colours, gaining an overall B++. She was overjoyed.

We met again in the foyer of the de Vere new offices, which were palatial in the 7th Arrondissement. This is not the traditional commercial sector of the city, which is situated on the Right Bank in the 8th Arrondissement along side the banking media. This sector looked to her neighbour the Louvre to endow her commercial elements with artistic grace.

Albert had found this building on the left bank of the Seine, a former gallery, unable to be sold for a period of years as a result of some legal dispute. He waited his opportunity and pounced when the premises became available and the price had hit the commercial floor. We nodded a 'bonjour' daily to prestigious neighbours including the various embassies, the parliament, les Invalides and la Tour Eiffel. Bravo Albert!

As I chatted to other staff members, I saw Gaston, one of the porters and asked him about his son's recuperation after breaking a leg at rugby. We communicated in sign language as he was deaf.

Sabine and I were seated now in our favourite local seafood restaurant only five minutes walk from our new premises.

"Caterine," Sabine inquired "where did you learn sign language? Gaston asked me to find out, too shy to ask you himself."

"That was remiss of me, Sabine. I'll put it right next time I speak to him." I replied.

"Actually, it was when I was at school in Paris. The director's daughter was deaf and he taught me how to communicate with her. We became friends. After an operation a few years ago as a result of advanced medical technology, she phoned, very excited, to tell me she hears perfectly. Her only problem was the tick of her clockwork alarm, it keeps her awake!" Sabine laughed.

"Now your plans?" I asked her.

"Well," Sabine hesitated. "I want to specialise in paintings. I'm sure you suspected that already. What do you think?"

"Fine, Sabine but you must obtain A+ to progress on any high level career strategy."

She looked at me shocked.

"Caterine, I can never aspire to that. Your grades I know were phenomenal, S level, the highest possible but I'll be content if I can maintain my B++."

I put down my fork from my excellent garlic butter escargots with a clatter. Other diners looked round but I ignored them.

"Sabine Dépont, that is not the attitude I expect from my assistant (and I realised now my protégée). You've the ability to perform better but in the paintings section you've got a weakness, the Impressionists."

"I know, Caterine" she sighed, "I can't come to terms with Monet, Manet, etc."

"Then I'm able to help you. I too suffered a lack of vision over that period."

Sabine, final escargot en route to mouth now dropped her fork with a louder clatter than mine. Even more diners turned round this time.

"I can't believe you had any problems," she said in disbelief.

"Well, I did. Now, do you want your 'A' with plusses? It will mean some weekends at BeauRobert plus additional work."

Sabine responded immediately. "The time's no problem, Caterine, I'll work harder than ever."

It was agreed.

Over dessert, we arranged her first weekend stay at BeauRobert; the first week in May. I teased her saying that she could reacquaint herself with the staff confirming when they had told her that Gildas and I had become lovers.

Sabine looked at me in shocked silence for several moments.

"You're mistaken," she addressed me dark eyes solemn. "The staff said nothing to me on that subject. Your relationship with the Count was sacrosanct, any disclosure outside the household, a betrayal."

"As loyal as that." I murmured.

"No Caterine, it was you who told me."

I looked at Sabine in disbelief.

"How? What do you mean?"

"After the Monday, jour de fête: that weekend you sent us home to Paris early on the Friday. Remember? I surprised you at Tuesday lunchtime with the Count on the terrace in the walled garden. I saw the look that passed between you. It was not a working lunch as you'd shared in the past."

"I told you, drop dead gorgeous!" She grinned.

There was no answer to that.

Sabine arrived as planned that weekend in May. We travelled together from 'Maison de Vere' on the TGV and by my car to BeauRobert.

After unpacking in her suite in the upper east wing, Sabine was joining us for our evening aperitif in the salon library. I knew she was very nervous.

"I'd rather not, Caterine, not with the Count and as for dinner, whew, it's not possible the staff serving me."

"Don't be ridiculous. Gildas hasn't turned into an ogre since your last visit. As for the staff, you told me you understand each other" and this time I winked.

As we entered the salon library Gildas strode over to greet Sabine traditionally kissing her on both cheeks.

"Welcome, Sabine. I'm delighted you'll be spending some weekends with us at BeauRobert. Now what's your preference for an aperitif?" he asked.

I smiled to myself as I recognised the look of embarrassment on Sabine's face.

"*Merci*, monsieur le Comte," she stuttered forgetting to confirm what she wanted to drink.

"Mon Dieu, Sabine, it's Gildas. If you use that address to me, I'll think I've turned into my late grandfather and I'd prefer not to be buried in the family vault just yet!"

The ice was broken Sabine giggled and then relaxed.

Over dinner we discovered that Sabine's brother was determined to study veterinary medicine. Gildas and I exchanged glances.

"Antoine's much cleverer than I am" she continued, "the family brains, straight A grades.

He leaves school in July and has been working in a shop and a restaurant during weekdays and weekends to earn some money. That's why I must progress to help him achieve his ambition. Maman's equally determined to play her part although she's worked so hard for both of us already."

"Unfortunately, it's a long university course and expensive." She sighed.

There was silence.

Suddenly, Sabine looked at us across the oak dining table, aghast.

"I'm sorry. I've been blabbering on forgetting where I am."

"Nonsense, Sabine" Gildas interrupted. "Caterine and I admire your intentions and you're with friends."

Over the weekend I shared my knowledge of the Impressionists with my protegée. From Realism and Impressionism with studies of Courbet, Manet, Monet and Renoir, we moved onto the Post Impressionists of Cézanne, Van Gogh, Toulouse-Lautrec and Rousseau.

That weekend was only an introduction and an opportunity for general discussion so that I could find out if possible where the 'block' was in Sabine's mind. The impediment that was causing her failure to understand the language of these great artists.

I had prepared two timetables: one for the study at BeauRobert and one for Sabine at her family's apartment in Paris. Further I had planned a programme of visits to view as many of the original Impressionist paintings as possible.

"A photograph can never 'live' like the strokes of the artists brush." I told her, "the language is lost."

Fresh air was a necessary requirement and she and I walked through the grounds before and after lunch and dinner. Breakfast was served in our respective suites. Gildas was absent only for Saturday lunch as he was visiting Saint Roche Rivière. By the end of the weekend, Sabine was completely at home in his company.

As I drove her to Saint Pierre des Corps on Sunday, she said, "Caterine how can I thank you. I feel better already about this subject although I know it's a formidable task ahead of me to gain an A or better but I won't fail through a lack of effort."

"You won't fail at all, Sabine" I smiled. "You just need to gain confidence."

We embraced on platform 2 at *'repère C'* where her TGV carriage, no 15, was designated to stop.

"It's been an enchanted weekend Caterine. You opened the box of tricks and as for Gildas," she rolled her eyes, "he's just the drop dead gorgeous magician."

I burst out laughing, saying *'au revoir'* as she left in hope and the Paris TGV.

On Monday morning I set out from BeauRobert for the direction of Chenonceau but not to visit that favourite château of mine (after my beloved Beau Robert and Saint Roche Rivière of course).

The destination was a small château called Luçay-Christian sur Loire in a village of the same name. Although not as grand as its famous neighbour, it had developed over the years a specialised fame for its history of ghosts, not just one but several claimed to be seen by numerous visitors. This feature had attracted record numbers of tourists and large amounts of revenue!

Albert and I had chosen this building as our 'test' case. A formula was to be developed here, honed and perfected and then applied to her larger more prestigious siblings. Luçay-Christian contained many features of the other members of her family: classic Renaissance architecture, an outstanding tower, an arcaded gallery, coffered ceilings and a private chapel. The château was also a treasure trove of 16th century and 17th century tapestries and paintings plus Louis XIV furniture. As I had never visited it, I was intrigued and excited.

I was greeted by a male member of staff and shown into an anteroom to await the owner, Monsieur Lundberg. From what I had seen to date little restorative work was required, pity for

Albert I thought to myself. The building was flawless, the grounds and gardens viewed from the drive to the entrance immaculate.

The owner appeared, looking decidedly disturbed. He was a small man about 5 feet 7 inches, portly, dark skinned but expensively dressed in a silver grey three piece suit, white monogrammed shirt, designer matched striped silk tie and sported (to my animal loving horror) grey snake-skinned shoes.

He would be in his mid forties I thought and from the records I knew he was from Switzerland. He addressed me in English with few traces of any accent.

"Dr Sinclair, there's been an error. Your appointment was for this time tomorrow."

He actually looked agitated. I was taken aback.

"No Mr Lundberg, I have the date here confirmed by my assistant for Monday."

He interrupted me, "Then your assistant was wrong. The appointment was for tomorrow, Tuesday."

Normally I would have protested but I was representing de Veres.

"How unfortunate," I replied, adding for the satisfaction of Sabine, "unique in fact."

"Since I'm here is it not possible for me to look round, make a few observations?"

I smiled politely with great difficulty!

"I'm afraid not. It must be tomorrow," he replied almost ushering me from the room.

I was very angry as I climbed into my car. Sabine had made no mistake I knew that. The confirmation of this date was beside me in my briefcase but I had decided not to have a confrontation.

From a business angle it would be poor judgement and a possible loss of the Contract if for example a complaint by

Lundberg was lodged. There was however another reason. My instincts told me it would be to no avail. He would have claimed another error, in computer input perhaps. Monsieur Lundberg wanted me out of the way, out of sight, out of Luçay Christian sur Loire.

Before switching on the ignition I turned my head to admire the château again. After all she had not offended me.

As I looked up I saw a figure at the window just above my car. A male figure in the shadow, very tall but hidden in the shade, pulling at the curtain as if to avoid being seen or alternatively, to ensure I was leaving. I started the engine and slowly moved off.

With curiosity I glanced back. Now I was just out of the shade, the sun struck the open window and I saw it.

A hand, adjusting the curtain was gloved, an unusual glove in colours of blue, white and red, colours of France, the cuff trim in gold. It was a distinctive glove, exclusive, belonging to Gildas, le Comte du Gilbert.

As I stared in utter disbelief, suddenly the glove disappeared. In shock, I accelerated down the driveway and out of the gates. Although I found it incredible, I knew I had just seen one of Luçay Christian sur Loire's ghosts, one of her numerous, notorious ghosts.

That was the only logical and illogical explanation.

Arriving back at BeauRobert, I went to find Gildas. Félix met me as I was crossing the larger hall.

"Monsieur Le Comte phoned Madame, he's been delayed, but will return for dinner."

A chill overtook me but I shook it off as ridiculous, my vivid imagination.

"Thank you Félix please tell Agathe not to prepare any lunch although I've returned early – a change of plan."

He nodded, almost a bow.

"Yes Madame, I'll arrange for dinner as usual" and he left.

My mind in turmoil I walked rapidly to the west wing and our apartment. After making a pot of coffee, strong black coffee, I sat on my 19th century leather sofa in my study, gazing out at the walled garden through my patio doors. Gildas had left before me this morning, early to assist the local vet in a complicated operation on a tenant farmer's mare. He had made a practice of keeping up to date with veterinary developments and worked with the village vet when time permitted. Gildas had told me he would be working from BeauRobert all day, after the operation was finished.

I thought again. Gildas knew I was starting work on the Loire Châteaux today but not which one. With Sabine's visit, his absence on Saturday plus family phone calls on Sunday evening to catch up on news no details were discussed. He knew I would not be returning until just before dinner.

Suddenly I was appalled. These thoughts were unthinkable how could I doubt this man I loved. I glanced at my watch. It was now 1.30pm. I was shocked! A morning gone and I'd been indolent. Certainly I had spent two hours after breakfast this morning with a call to de Veres at 8am, some e-mail replies and had studied a dossier again on Luçay Christian sur Loire. Further, I had typed up on my laptop part of my report to Albert on the planning strategy for the de Vere contract.

Shaking my mind out of my imagination, common sense prevailed and I returned to my desk. Opening my briefcase I set to work.

Gildas arrived back at 7.10pm.

"What a day!" he said smiling, brushing my lips with his. I could feel the energy flow from his body to mine and also my anxiety. I put my arms round his neck and kissed him intimately.

"Mon Dieu, Madame before dinner?"

He looked tired, unusual for Gildas and I felt guilty.

"Chérie, you're looking pale. Are you all right?"

"Nothing important. You look as if a drink would be welcome," I replied taking his hand as we walked into the smaller salon.

Gildas handed me my glass.

"Edmund and I nearly lost the mare, severe haemorrhaging, but we managed to stabilise her. I'm phoning him after dinner to check her condition."

"But you didn't return here as planned?" I asked looking out on the lake and sipping slowly at my drink.

"No," Gildas sighed "I received a call from Roger at Saint Roche Rivière. Those two tenant farmers are at loggerheads again so I drove there, saw both of them and then brought forward my weekly meeting with Roger and Dominique."

Felix knocked and entered. Dinner was served.

Over coffee I recounted the incident at the château – unwelcome reception, wrong date and then tentatively, the gloved hand.

Gildas burst out laughing.

"Caterine really, what an imagination!" He halted.

"But this gloved hand," I began

Gildas interrupted me sea green eyes mesmerising.

"Another figment of your very vivid imagination."

That night after we made love, I slept in his arms at peace: until I awoke crying out, seeing ill-defined dark images strange countenances and a magician with a multi-coloured hand!

Chapter Sixteen

The following few weeks were frenzied for me, for Gildas and for de Veres. The contract Albert had secured was even vaster than anyone could have contemplated and the planned increase of staff was not sufficient. The appointment of two further senior valuers, posed a problem, not from a lack of applicants but a surfeit! We were being inundated from all over Europe.

Inwardly I knew Albert was overjoyed. Everything he had worked for was now justified: the gamble to desert as director of Dunns, establish his individual identity by setting up de Veres, the financial risks, calculated decisions to accept rare portfolios while training and fine tuning his team. Just like Professor Donald Cameron, Albert had won.

The strategy for the Château Contract had been discussed and dissected by the de Vere directors at earlier meetings and was of course, theoretically in place. However, the practical element was crucial, hence the test at Luçay Christian sur Loire of which I had been allocated personal responsibility.

Strangely, after the initial hostility, the visits, the inspections, valuations and assessment passed remarkably smoothly. Even Klaus Lundberg albeit present rarely was courteous cooperative and obviously very proud of the château. It was bizarre! I began to wonder if I had suffered some mental aberration on that particular Monday.

"I admit he's formal, failing in humour but he's ensured his staff have been helpful" Albert conceded as he sat in my new suite of offices.

He had arrived ostensibly to examine a piece of treasured porcelain from a collection we were valuing. Secretly, I knew he was also looking forward to a cup of my special coffee.

He looked round.

"Gracious, welcoming, artistic, and comfortable, as always" Albert observed. "Thanks for your contribution to mine, Caterine. Céline commented on her first visit that the 'du Gilbert' touch was much in evidence"

I laughed, "coffee?"

"Now what a surprise! *Merci.*"

I went to the small kitchen to prepare it.

Apart from my personal office/study, incorporating a small salon area on a lower level which was divided by an archway, I had at my disposal, a meeting room for clients, an office for Sabine and an anteroom for Flora my secretary. I was also endowed with a bathroom including shower and changing facilities plus this kitchenette. Behind an oak door 'cupboard' in the archway wall was concealed a fold up double bed for overnight sojourns. Palatial indeed!

I placed our coffee cups on the table in the salon area and went to collect the Ming, in this case early 15th century, from the cabinet. The value of the collection was surprising all of us.

As I stepped down to the salon area, the vase in my right hand I tripped, my hand instinctively shot out to prevent my falling and the vase shattered against the archway wall.

There was silence.

"*Merde* Caterine. How bloody careless. You know the rules when handling glass or porcelain. You've just broken them and the Ming. Christ Almighty the insurance company will have an apoplectic fit!"

Keeping my composure I replied.

"I don't see a problem with the insurance company Albert. We have an exceptional record."

"Not after this we won't." Albert stormed, coffee forgotten, pacing up and down.

"I don't see why Albert," I replied still remaining calm.

He halted his pacing and stared at me. "What are you talking about? Have you lost your senses?"

"No," I said, opening the cabinet and producing an object.

"The other one was Delft" and I grinned.

Gildas laughed hilariously when I recounted the incident.

"Caterine Chérie, you took a chance on that one. I know how highly Albert regards you but he doesn't take prisoners and he's the Managing Director. How did he react?"

"Drank three cups of coffee and made me promise never to play that trick again."

I smiled, "He added a comment."

"What was that?" Gildas inquired standing at the archway in the salon library admiring the Cézanne which complemented the Renoir on the opposite wall.

I waited and he turned towards me.

"OK, I'm listening," he grinned walking towards me.

"His remark was 'God knows you need someone like Gildas to handle you, no-one else could!'"

Highly amused, Gildas's arm around my shoulder, we retired for the night.

At the beginning of the first week in June Sabine and I were finalising some reports on porcelain valuations. This was Charles Damion's speciality but he was on vacation.

"This looks acceptable Sabine, however check the figures and notations. If you have any reservations, consult me again. Otherwise pass them to Charles's assistant."

"OK," Sabine replied, "unless there are any inaccuracies they'll be ready before lunch."

"Oh, by the way, for your visit to BeauRobert this weekend would you be kind enough to ask your Maman and Antoine to join you. Gildas would like to meet them. I hope they will be free."

Sabine's hand was on the doorknob, about to leave, but it remained unturned. She looked back at me shocked.

"Caterine, is this one of your jokes? Maman and my brother at BeauRobert. *Mon Dieu*, it's not possible."

"Why?" I inquired, "Don't you think they'd like us?"

"Pardon," Sabine replied, "of course they would. You know how highly Maman and Antoine regard you. I just," she paused, "well they'd be embarrassed, out of their depth even what to wear, whew."

"Sabine, may I ask you a question?"

She nodded.

"During your first visit to Gildas and me at BeauRobert a month ago did you find yourself embarrassed or out of your depth?"

"Well no," she conceded thoughtfully.

"In that case your family will be no different. As for the dress code, you know the score, casual. For dinner, tell Maman a dress, informal and Antoine, collar and tie, jacket optional. Just confirm with me the date is convenient. I'll meet you at Saint Pierre, usual train."

I bent my head to my current task smiling to myself at Sabine's muttered 'Merde' as she closed the door to my office.

The journey from Saint Pierre des Corps to BeauRobert took just over half and hour. Sabine, Mathilde and Antoine were chattering nervously on subjects of which I have no idea. I was concentrating on the road and the other occupants. Apologies to my many friends in France but French driving habits resemble Formula 1 tactics at Saint Magny Cours.

On reaching BeauRobert, silence struck. It happened to everyone as you emerged from the drive through the woodlands: the paralysing shock of its breathtaking beauty. The oaks and acacias in royal formation waving a welcome even without any breeze. The lake over which the château looked graced any arrival with its shimmering shadows between sunrise and sunset.

I showed everyone to their suites in the east wing and left them to settle in, have a chat together, coffee and a petit four perhaps, just relax prior to changing for dinner.

Mathilde had spoken to me about Sabine.

"Doctor Sinclair, I cannot thank you enough. The time you are taking with her and now this invitation here. Antoine and I are overwhelmed and we won't let her down although," she looked round her suite "this is another world for us."

She sat down suddenly on the Chintz bed cover.

"Mon Dieu" she cried " It'll be creased" standing up in panic.

I had put my arm around her. "Mathilde, firstly my name's Caterine, secondly if the bed cover remains un-creased and the bed sheets, it means you've slept in a chair."

We laughed together and I knew she felt more at home.

During aperitifs and at dinner Gildas was just Gildas. He recounted family anecdotes as a child, stimulating conversation with Antoine about their shared love of animals and asking Mathilde how she coped living in Paris. Everyone relaxed. What a magician he was, I thought, dismissing that nightmare and any morbid memories.

The meal was simple: hors d'oeuvres, consommé julienne, roast pork or baked salmon plus the traditional French course of salads and cheese with a choice of desserts.

Mathilde was a vegetarian, this posed no problem as the consommé was made from vegetarian stock and Agathe had baked a 'tarte à la citrouille', pumpkin pie.

Over coffee, Gildas handed Antoine a white sealed envelope.

"It gives me great personal pleasure to present this to you," he said smiling.

Looking perplexed Antoine opened it up and read the contents – twice!

Then he addressed Gildas.

"This is a magnanimous gesture, but regretfully I can't accept it."

"Why not?" Gildas inquired.

"Because it's not been won on merit," was Antoine's response.

"Is that your only objection?" asked Gildas.

Antoine hesitated. "Well, yes."

I looked over at Mathilde and Sabine sitting together on the Louis XVI gilt canapé, nonplussed.

"In that case you've no choice but to accept. I visited my alma mater last month and explained my intentions to the faculty professor, an action long overdue. He set up an independent committee to decide the winning candidate. It was close but your outstanding biology marks were the deciding factor and so yours was the name I received, much as I said earlier, to my personal pleasure.

Gildas walked over, Antoine stood up an expression of shock on his face. They shook hands.

"Congratulations, Antoine Dépont, you are the first recipient of the du Gilbert bursary for Veterinary Medicine at the University of Toulouse."

It was a generous bursary: university fees paid including all books and ancillary literature, a life membership of the sports complex, free accommodation plus an annual living costs allowance for the duration of the degree.

When all was explained to Mathilde and Sabine by a now very excited Antoine they were incredulous: tears started to roll down both their faces.

"Mon Dieu" exclaimed Gildas "this is supposed to be a celebration!," as he opened the champagne.

"Gildas, what can we say? How can we thank you? It's a dream come true!" stuttered Mathilde.

"Your thanks are due only to Antoine for his outstanding academic ability, I'm due nothing. This bursary was originally an idea from my father. I have been somewhat dilatory in instigating it. By the way," he turned to Antoine, "there is one area where you disappointed me."

Antoine still holding the bursary confirmation letter turned looking concerned.

"Yes, one disappointment," Gildas confirmed.

"Your biology marks were higher than mine." And he grinned.

Everyone burst out laughing. Champagne goblets raised, four words were uttered unanimously.

"Antoine, Félicitations and Santé!"

Chapter Seventeen

June continued at the same pace as May but if I was fully occupied, Gildas was even busier. Saint Roche Rivière was hostess that month to several weddings and two major sales conferences, one for Lejaen, the French car manufacturer, the other to Banque Centrale de France an annual contract which had been established, Gildas had informed me, more than seven years previously.

The itinerary for his US visit was also being planned. It was taking place at the end of June. A British film company's executives had already visited Saint Roche Rivière on two occasions after the venue had been confirmed. The major funding however was being supplied by US investment: hence the trip.

Gildas was travelling with the film company executives to show a presentation package of the château. Further he was taking advantage of his visit for the promotion of Saint Roche Rivière to the American tourist industry.

"Caterine, I intend to leave on the last Sunday of June and return the following Friday. How does that suit your plans?" Gildas asked me at breakfast one morning.

"Fine, darling. I'll still be here" I replied stoically, "working hard while you're travelling in glamorous mode and dining out on the other side of the Atlantic."

"Chérie you know I'll hate being without you and I'm flying on Concorde solely for expediency."

I looked at him, feigning surprise.

"Oh all right," he grinned "you know it's my favourite airplane."

"And mine." I replied. "I'm quite envious. I have flown in her only twice."

"I promise a trip together later this year. Choose your destination and we'll make the reservations. My birthday present to ourselves!"

I stretched over the breakfast table and kissed him.

It had been Gildas's idea to create this dining alcove adjacent to the oak kitchen. It allowed us to enjoy meals in our apartment when we wished, to dine informally, and privately. We always took breakfast here. The only problem was for poor Agathe as often I stole some of her provisions, although I always left her a note. On reflection she was very tolerant.

As it was Saturday we walked from BeauRobert to the weekly market in the village. Our bread was supplied by the local boulangerie and most fresh fruit and vegetables from estate produce; but we always bought fish from the visiting fishmonger or treated ourselves to some other foodstuffs not grown on the estate; plus the market was such a magnet of mouth watering delicacies and multifarious other attractions: from clothes to cutlery, buttons to candles and batteries to bangles that we always returned fully laden.

I looked forward to market days wandering around with Gildas, stopping frequently to chat to all the people he knew and who now knew me. It was a unique atmosphere, animated, lively, warm and uplifting.

It demonstrated yet again how popular Gildas was in the local region: not his stature and his status as the Count that was not his style and rightly so, but as the leader of the community to whom people could turn for assistance or advice. It seems a contradiction in terms, especially with cognisance of class systems, which have caused such misery and havoc throughout history.

We returned refreshed looking forward to lunch. The phone rang as we were walking from the salon library to the dining room. It was Rodrigue: Félicité's wish was granted she had a brother, to be called Yves and all was well.

Gildas and I changed our plans for a quiet Sunday at BeauRobert and instead we arranged a visit to meet the latest addition to the du Gilbert family. We were both overjoyed. I phoned Maman and David with the news and Gildas contacted Frédéric. Tentative dates were tossed around for a future family gathering at BeauRobert similar to last year in September. How happy we were.

It was the middle of June, a Thursday. I was sitting in Albert's study adjacent to his suite of offices in the penthouse apartment situated on the top floor of Maison de Vere. We were about to enter the boardroom for what for me was a crucial meeting; a judgement for the first time as a director on a major project. Every Board member had received and perused a copy of my proposals for the implementation of the practical plan of operation for C.C. – the Château Contract.

"I'll just go and prepare the coffee, Albert," I said as I rose to walk to the kitchen.

Once in the past our new sophisticated machine broke down and I had produced an alternative from my office. It was agreed by everyone that my product was superior! Henceforth, I had performed this minor task. Albert forestalled me this time, looking unusually embarrassed.

"Caterine lets proceed immediately to the boardroom."

I became alarmed. He had been quiet while we were in his study, almost ill at ease. I had assumed the reason was personal and had said nothing. I realised now it was very personal. It was my proposals, me!

After the usual reading of minutes and adoption procedures, Albert rose clearing his throat. "Caterine would you please absent yourself while we vote on your proposals."

Every Director failed to look at me shuffling papers or examining an attaché case. I nodded and departed the Boardroom. His request for my withdrawal indicated disaster. I was doomed.

Many minutes later Charles Damion face solemn, motioned me back from the anteroom to rejoin the directors of Maison de Vere.

I halted. Everyone was standing champagne goblets aloft, a magnum opened sitting in an ice bucket in the middle of that 18th century masterpiece of an oak monastery table.

'Bravo' and 'santé' was the toast to me. I was dumbfounded and then smiled greatly relieved.

Albert spoke first as Charles handed me my goblet.

"Caterine every director commends you highly for your proposals. They've been adopted unanimously. You'll be asking yourself why the theatricals? There are two reasons:

Number one, you've caught every one of us out at some time or other by your wicked sense of humour. As for the Ming, I still haven't recovered. This is pay back time."

"And secondly you could not be allowed to set up the coffee today as you would have seen the champagne on ice in the kitchen."

I burst out laughing and raised my goblet.

"Gentleman today I have learned a lesson."

Every pair of eyes regarded me.

"How I've benefited from teaching you a Scottish sense of humour, *merci, santé,* and slainthe."

I was staying overnight with Maman in Montparnasse after the board meeting. It was an opportunity to indulge in one of our 'tête à têtes' and also talk about baby Yves. Maman had just returned from visiting him.

"He's just gorgeous" she smiled "and of course Rodrigue and Elisée are ecstatic. Félicité is still in charge. What was that incident you mentioned when you and Gildas went to the hospital after his birth?"

"It was hysterical." I replied.

"We were seated with Rodrigue and Elisée in her room, baby Yves sound asleep, when a nurse brought in some coffee. Félicité announced.

"Of course the birth of my brother has given Papa and Maman a lot of trouble. When I was born, being a girl, I did not."

We burst out laughing.

"*Mon Dieu*," said Maman "what a character she is."

"Yes," I agreed, "the nurse nearly dropped the tray."

The phone bell rang. It was Gildas, about the board meeting.

"Bravo chérie but I'd no doubts. Before I speak to Maman, I must tell you I've changed my plans. I'm leaving twenty-four hours earlier on the Saturday next weekend.

Kevin Marples phoned requesting two extra days duration to revise budgets and asked me to extend the visit returning on the following Sunday."

Gildas voice was terse I knew the mood!

"I told him absolutely not. I'd no intention of invading two weekends. Therefore, I leave on Saturday, then work through the Sunday and I return on the Friday as planned. Now when will you be home tomorrow?"

I confirmed my TGV train time to Saint Pierre des Corps and then passed the phone to Maman. Before we retired for the night she said.

"You're very happy I can see that but the sixth sense still lingers, am I right?"

I nodded, "Images wander and waver impossible to explain."

"Remember what I told you: an asset and a curse. Concentrate on the asset if you can although I know that it's not so simple, after all it's based around instinct, uncontrollable. From my experience with trained concentration, the happier thoughts can prevail."

"I'll try Maman. I have so much good fortune."

We embraced and wished each other 'Good Night.'

How my thoughts returned to haunt me.

When I arrived at Tours Saint Pierre TGV station, I received a surprise. Standing waving to me on platform 2, head and shoulders above everyone else, Gildas! I stared in disbelief. He was smiling his sexy smile, striding towards me kissing me on the forehead.

"Edmund gave me a lift, he's visiting his parents for the weekend. The family home is just north of Tours." He told me.

"Right we're going out for dinner to our favourite restaurant. Now where's your car?"

We drove southeast from Tours, Gildas at the wheel of my cabriolet, a drive of about 20 minutes not far of course from BeauRobert.

This was the restaurant of the dinner we never made that night we learned we were in love. It was a small auberge nestling in the Cher valley but its reputation had grown with the stature of its proprietor, Marius Maurice.

He greeted us personally; we had become friends and he had spent evenings with us at BeauRobert. Of middle height, medium build and modest looks, there was no mediocrity about his food for it was his passion. Aperitifs enticed you, the menu a seduction process and after tasting the wines your love affair was complete.

"Gildas, Caterine, welcome," he bounced towards us, full of bonhomie, showing us to our special table in the alcove, claret curtains draped in velvet at either side.

We chose his mushroom starter with its exquisite sauce on a bed of spinach. Next I decided on a turbot in basil and Gildas the seafood. Marius made a few accompanying suggestions and Gildas discussed the wines. We reached for our aperitifs and Marius's plate of hors d'oeuvres.

Suddenly, I realised, looking at my watch.

"Why, it's exactly a year since that weekend." I began.

Gildas grinned. "Yes, the dinner we never made! With apologies to Marius I still prefer the other 'courses'."

He said it in English and I laughed. It did not 'pun' in French.

We used both languages in our dialogue, similar to my family upbringing, I knew Gildas's parents had spoken in English as well as their mother tongue with their children. Therefore it was a natural tongue for Gildas, Elisée and Frédéric plus essential for international commerce and communication.

It was a gourmet meal a special evening. Gildas had arranged our local taxi service to return to BeauRobert. My car would be collected on Saturday.

Returning to BeauRobert we walked in the grounds and entered the walled garden to sit on the terrace. The evening was warm and welcoming. Dalliances of moonlight masked memories of the garden for some moments. Then, you would remember what you had forgotten as first the lilac and then the hydrangea bushes emerged from the shadows. Suddenly, the rose garden's profusion of plants with its floral canvas flooded into sight. It was nature's game of hide and seek: the garden loved it playing with the moon.

Gildas placed his hand over mine on the wild cherry terrace table. He looked at me with those bewitching eyes and I returned his gaze, a look we knew well.

"You know I was annoyed when I phoned you at Maman's?"

"Yes," I answered, "but unsure why."

"It was Marples' suggestion to extend the visit a further two days, unnecessary and quite unjustified. What incensed me more were his reasons for that extension."

Gildas stood up and walked to the terrace railing, his tall broad frame obscuring one corner of the oak abri.

"He told me that it would give us an opportunity for two more nights of fun away from our wives. He had laughed coarsely down the phone line."

There was silence.

"Heavens Gildas. Do you mean to tell me you turned down such an opportunity?" I teased him.

Without smiling Gildas said.

"I replied and I quote: ' Kevin Marples, you've not been honoured as yet to meet my wife. She's indeed a rare creature, extraordinarily beautiful, highly intelligent and extremely talented. Also, she's a personality who graces my life making it both stimulating and fulfilling. Consequently, I've no desire to leave her for five minutes, never mind five days'."

"Gildas," I was stunned "what an accolade."

Gildas was not given to comments of this nature outside the family.

Between ourselves especially, it was a game of check and checkmate. Only last weekend sitting together at the pool he had said.

"Chérie, such an unusual hair colour but better if darker red, closer to mine, a shade more aristocratic," and he grinned.

I pondered and then replied.

"Perhaps your hair is acceptable but not your feet. Just size nine shoes at six feet four inches quite out of proportion. At your advancing years now, you'll soon topple over."

I moved but not fast enough, however I held on dragging him with me into the pool.

Gildas laughed as I recalled the banter of the previous

weekend and we retired to our apartment, our love affair and for me a dreamless sleep.

It was the prelude of the nightmare to follow.

The week prior to Gildas's departure seemed to pass in a frenzied phase.

I was in Paris finalising details for 'C.C.' with the individual de Veres directors. Each was appointing a team to tackle the projects planned for the period after the main French vacations in August.

We were targeting one of the larger and one of the smaller châteaux on a geographical and chronological basis. This plan had been devised by me, designed to maximise the de Vere in-house talents but economise on outside time involved. Nevertheless it was a massive undertaking: carpets to curtains, furniture to furnishings, porcelain to paintings, and so much more. It was exciting and every member of the de Vere personnel from Albert, the directors, the auctioneers and valuers, to the porters and administration staff were imbued with enthusiasm.

Albert had already invited everyone to a reception when the château contract had been announced. He informed them of the inevitable expansion plans and the prestige for Maison de Vere, not to mention the revenue riches. He was a born leader, a taskmaster but his team responded to his tenacious orchestrated overtures!

Then an unexpected event occurred. Frédéric phoned Gildas asking if he could stay with us on Thursday evening. He had a few days holiday and had taken the opportunity to meet nephew Yves again spending two nights with Rodrigue and Elisée on the Tuesday and Wednesday.

Gildas phoned me at Montparnasse with the news.

"Chérie, does that cause a problem, although I knew you'd be back at BeauRobert on that Thursday."

"Not at all," I responded. "I'd love to see Frédéric again." I hesitated.

"Is something wrong?" as I detected some concern in Gildas's question to me.

"Yes, but not his health I made sure of that, he just said he wanted our advice on a personal matter."

Looking at Frédéric over dinner on Thursday I felt how like yet unlike Gildas and Elisée he was. In some ways he shared both and none of their features. His hair Elisée's chestnut, strong facial bone structure like Gildas but not quite as tall, about six feet two inches and a slimmer build but still powerful. The eyes as bewitching, this time Icelandic blue and an extrovert personality but not tonight.

We talked about many subjects over dinner, family, business, his medical commitments and promotion to junior consultant in obstetrics at his Paris hospital, but Frédéric was distracted.

Several times, Gildas and I exchanged knowing glances. Over coffee in the salon library, finally he told us.

"It's Charlotte. I asked her to marry me last weekend and she dropped the bombshell." Frédéric swallowed hesitating.

My earlier anxiety turned to foreboding.

"She was born with a malformed uterus. I know the condition, inoperable, which means no children."

Frédéric stood up to hide his distress and Gildas and I exchanged a further look of shared sadness. I left it to Gildas to respond; not, I hope, out of cowardice but more compassion. He had grown up with Frédéric, I had not. Gildas also stood up, walked over to Frédéric putting his arm round his brother's shoulder.

"Frédéric, I'm going to ask you a question, a brutal question. Do not hesitate before you answer it."

I held my breath. I already knew what the question was.

"Whom do you love most and who is more important in your life Charlotte or a fictitious future child?"

Frédéric answered immediately.

"Charlotte of course, but" he stopped and my heart sank. The brothers stood facing each other.

"Your 'but,' Frédéric says it all."

I left them together, my coffee remaining cold in my cup. Frédéric's sob sending sorrow deeper into my soul.

Gildas appeared in my study nearly two hours later; he was emotionally drained and almost dropped down on my sofa set against the wall.

I had decided to try working, concentrate on some task, anything to distract my thoughts from that shattered young man.

Gildas said.

"I've never seen Frédéric so distressed. He loves Charlotte, no question about that. You know Frédéric: Elisée and I always teased him a blonde one week, a brunette the next and no doubt someone in-between but nothing serious until now."

"Where is he?" I asked.

"I put him to bed with a very strong malt." Gildas smiled thinly, "the Scottish and French recipe but as you know that only numbs partially the pain tonight. Tomorrow reality re-emerges."

"But Gildas so many other options are open today with the advancement of medical science and failing there, adoption. They both love children so much. I remember Frédéric with the doublet at Elisée's wedding and Charlotte talking to me so animatedly about her younger brothers." I broke off at Gildas's solemn expression.

"That's the impasse," he sighed "Charlotte will not consider any use of medical science, 'abuse' as she put it to Frédéric, to produce a child. He of course, will not accept adoption."

"But have they discussed these options sensibly. Can't they reach a compromise. For example, a medical trial first with adoption second?"

"Caterine, don't you understand, they're at war!"

I was silent as Gildas stood up and walked to the patio window. It was now after 10.30 pm, the night dark but we could discern some nocturnal life from outside; small animals, the major inhabitants of the walled garden with their spasmodic scurrying movements in search of some satisfying supper.

"Do you know why they have these principals?" I asked quietly, still seated on my maroon leather chair swivelled round now from my desk to face Gildas.

"According to Frédéric, Charlotte considers her body has failed her once already. She won't contemplate a second or further failures. As for Frédéric," Gilda's sighed as I rose up to join him at the window. "Frédéric is prejudiced because of someone he knew. Actually, someone he knew well and detested. Someone in the du Gilbert family who was adopted, my late wife, Isabella."

Outside suddenly, the nocturnal activity ceased. The light of the moon vanished. Although it was high summer and the evening warm and mellow, a draft swept through the room. It affected both of us, Gildas, hand chilled as he took mine.

We retired to our BeauRobert apartment, our showers and our four-poster bed. Both deep in thought, our minds attuned but our bodies not. By tacit consent this was not a night for any form of lovemaking.

This is where I finally failed.

On reflection I can see it now: the threat he posed, with my instincts I should have sensed it. Instead I heard the alarm bells ringing but ignored their warning chimes and so created the other and the greater crime.

Chapter Eighteen

On Friday morning Gildas and I shared breakfast in our apartment as usual, the freshly baked croissants or boule left in the traditional French bread box by Agathe on the coffee table in the smaller salon.

Today, it was for both of us a more subdued occasion. Gildas helped me clear the cutlery and crockery, drying them for me, in an unusual gesture as normally, I left them to drain in the second sink.

"Gildas you're on another planet. Can I do anything to help with Frédéric?"

"Sorry, Caterine" he replied looking disturbed.

"Would you mind if I went out on the horses this morning with that young brother of mine. I think he needs a breath of fresh air preferably through his brain."

"Good idea!" I smiled feeling more relaxed, see you at lunch."

A telephone conference call was planned for this morning with Albert and the de Vere board at 10am. I glanced at my watch 7.30am. That gave me sufficient time to attend to correspondence with e-mails to Sabine to confirm my itinerary for the following week in the Loire valley and prepare my response to the items allocated to me on the Board's agenda.

Firstly my luxury. I prepared a thermos of my special coffee ready for the conference call and then I set to work.

At. 12.10pm I replaced the receiver and stretched, breathing a sigh of relief, The conference call had been a battle but I knew I had won round number one. Everything had been reasonably straightforward until the last item, AOB – any other business. Then I had introduced my specialist subject and most importantly a deadline for the Board's decision. My tactics were perfection for several reasons:

It was ten minutes before noon – stomachs beckoned.

It was a Friday before a Monday national jour de fête.

It was a summer weekend traditionally for families to absent themselves from the cities and de Vere Board members were no exception.

It was a subject raised by me on previous occasions, which had caused a division.

It was a relief to everyone I was not present to analyse and dissect these divisions.

Albert, I knew well would not be amused and also not surprised. However I still had to prepare my case to win.

I walked round the gardens to the kitchen to call on Agathe. What a superb cook she was. We chatted often together and exchanged recipes although I knew she had many more than I. Before Gildas and I were married during our engagement, we had both agreed that I should acquaint myself better with the staff members, tenant farmers, the estate managers, gardeners etc at both Saint Roche Rivière and BeauRobert. Each time this had been achieved with pleasure on my behalf and I hope on theirs. There were many incidents I could recall but Agathe's was particularly poignant for me.

On that occasion last summer, I had wandered round to the kitchen one morning when I knew from Gildas that Agathe enjoyed her 'coffee mug' as she called it and knocked on the kitchen door. On opening it she looked astonished stuttering,

"Madame la Comtesse," dropping to a curtsy, fumbling with her apron; and I was only engaged!"

"I am sorry what's wrong?"

I had been taken aback and then remembered the former Comtesse du Gilbert, Isabella. But how to handle it?

"Agathe," I had answered. "There's nothing wrong. I've just called to see you."

She had looked at me dumbfounded, still almost seated in this ridiculous curtsy legs withering on the kitchen floor. I had taken her arm to raise her up. She had started to protest about helping her but I had forestalled her comments asking her to make some coffee, adding,

"Agathe, I mean a mug of coffee, here, one for each of us at your oak kitchen table."

She stared at me astounded.

"Do I have to repeat myself Agathe?" I had said smiling.

She had shaken her head and turned to the preparation of now two 'coffee mugs.'

As she set them before us I had added,

"Agathe, you address Le Comte as Monsieur and so I'm Madame. If you ever curtsy to me again or address me in more formal terms, I'll sabotage every one of your secret recipes." I lifted my mug 'santé'!

To my horror Agathe had burst into sobs but that was quickly resolved.

On this occasion when I entered her domain Agathe was cleaning some vegetables picked from the kitchen garden for lunch. We chatted for a few minutes; she was looking forward to seeing her family in Orléans tonight on this holiday weekend.

I climbed the stairs opening the door to the smaller hall. There I met Frédéric still in his riding gear, how attractive he looked. I smiled to myself. More like Gildas than I had thought.

"Caterine, bonjour." He strode towards me and kissed me on both cheeks.

"Please accept my apologies for ruining what should have been a special family evening. It was very selfish of me."

"Nonsense, Frédéric, no apology. Who else can you confide in but your family. That's what brothers and sisters are for. Gildas and I are concerned only for your happiness."

As he stepped back I gasped.

"What's wrong Caterine you look as if you've seen a ghost?"

"The gloves," I stuttered helplessly still staring at his left hand in which he was clasping Gildas's driving gloves.

"Mon dieu, Caterine I know I shouldn't use them for riding but I had no others with me."

He grinned, "But it's not a crime is it?"

"No," I attempted some feeble laughter. "I thought at first they were Gildas's."

"Heaven forbid! He'd only use his in the car as would Elisée. Don't you have a pair?" he added surprised.

I shook my head.

"Then you must ask Gildas to order some for you, exclusive to the du Gilberts you know."

"Yes," I replied with a forced smile.

"Well, I'm off to shower, pack, and change for lunch. Then it's back to Paris. I'm on duty from tomorrow. If you are looking for Gildas he's still in the stables."

And he disappeared up the stairs.

Slowly, I walked out of the château and passed the east wing heading for the stables. Gildas I could see quite clearly now mounted on Pascal and trotting round the paddock. He waved halted and dismounted, leading Pascal to his box.

"Caterine, chérie," he greeted me.

"Is there a problem?" I inquired as Gildas removed the tackle and began brushing Pascal.

"A loose shoe, I'll speak to Roland after lunch." Gildas replied, brushing vigorously, Pascal standing patiently enjoying the attention!

Roland was one of the tenant farmers who was also a qualified blacksmith.

"Have you seen Frédéric? He was going to change and I must too."

"Yes, in the hall," I replied hesitating, "I didn't know you, Elisée and Frédéric had the same driving gloves."

"Pardon? Oh yes a family tradition. I must order a pair for you, I'll" he stopped.

"Mon Dieu, Caterine, you're not still thinking about that incident at Klaus. For heavens' sake use some common sense. Come on or we'll be late for lunch."

As we walked back to the west wing two factors filtered through my mind. Why had this incident irritated Gildas so much and how had he known the owner's name. I was positive I had never mentioned it and certainly not his Christian name, Klaus. Either way in the earlier conversation Gildas had shown no indication of knowing him.

After Frédéric departed, just before 3.30pm, Gildas and I returned to our respective studies for a couple of hours and then while Gildas completed his packing, I saddled up Avril and went for a trek in the woods.

It was a good idea and cleared my mind. Maman's words echoed from the past 'a curse and an asset. Concentrate on the asset.' Emerging from the woods I spurred Avril on for a short gallop and then cantered back to the château. My decision was made I would concentrate on the asset.

Gildas and I sat out under the oak abri beside the swimming pool. It was a perfect June evening. We laughed as always at the antics of the swallows flying swiftly and deftly like spitfires with their incredible manoeuvrability but unlike the famous aeroplanes they deliberately dipped their undercarriages in the pool water to cool off!

They shared a characteristic with those war time pilots for the swallows showed no fear; determined, continuing this practice whether we were in the swimming pool or it was empty.

Gildas had opened a bottle of champagne. He raised his goblet and gave his toast

"To a rapid return!"

"Agreed," I smiled at him thinking how handsome he was. This evening he wore cream coloured chinos and a matching short sleeved shirt with buttoned down epaulettes. On each pocket his personal monogram 'GduG'.

He echoed my thoughts.

"You look as always so extraordinarily beautiful. Is that a new dress?"

I had chosen emerald green silk a simple design by Jean Le Marr but with a sexy zipped split which could be adjusted according to the effect desired!

"Darling," I laughed. "You bought it for me on our honeymoon in Zurich instead of that hat. Thinking of the price tag the hat would have been a less painful option." Suddenly I shivered.

"Are you cold, Chérie?" Gildas asked surprised.

"No, I'm not. I don't understand it." I replied.

Gildas grinned, "You're standing too near the ice bucket wanting more champagne" he said and we laughed. He picked up the bucket, champagne bottle inside and we strolled through the gardens in the warm evening sunshine to dinner. Strangely, I still felt cold.

As Agathe was now en route to Orléans we dined in our apartment very simply: a green salad starter tossed in roquefort dressing, sorbet, and then tuna steaks in a wine sauce on a bed of ratatouille. Neither of us wanted dessert so we wandered out to the terrace for coffee and cognac.

"Did you make any progress with Frédéric," I inquired.

"Not much although he has agreed to contact Charlotte and call a truce after their battle. I'm sure he'll ask her out for dinner. But after that" Gildas shrugged his shoulders.

"Well," I replied "that's better than I expected. Now, what time do you want us to leave for Saint Pierre tomorrow?"

Gildas replied with an almost imperceptible hesitation.

"I don't chérie, I'm taking my car and leaving it at the station."

"Pardon." I stared at him. "For the whole week? But you never do that. If I can't take you Felix drives you. Why the change?"

I became concerned but Gildas was smiling.

"No more questions or you'll spoil my surprise."

I relaxed, "What are you up to?"

"You'll know soon enough." He replied.

By now the tide had fully turned I was marooned too late for any escape. Time like that tide was moving fast, time was in fact running out until my imprisonment complete, isolated on my island state.

Chapter Nineteen

I watched Gildas's car from the château entrance steps of BeauRobert as he drove down that enchanting driveway: the acacias and oaks beckoning him onwards. This time away from, not to our home. I waved a final time, sighed and turned towards the gardens walking for over an hour wandering deep in thought.

When I returned, it was nearly 10.30am.

Felix met me crossing the larger hall.

"Madame, you received a call from Madame Cameron. I took the liberty of saying you were in the gardens. She asked if you would return her call at your convenience."

"Thank you, Felix. Did she say from where she was phoning?"

"Yes, Madame. She said she was at home."

I went to my study and picked up the receiver pressing their direct number on the dial. Donald answered and it was the usual hilarity. We had arranged another dinner in Paris in April staying again in Montparnasse but Shona's Mum had been rushed to hospital with peritonitis and it was cancelled. Fortunately, she had made a full recovery.

"Gildas is in the US for a week" I explained to Shona "after that we are both in France. When are your free for a weekend at BeauRobert?"

"Mid July?" suggested Shona.

"Fine," I said checking Gildas's commitments on the wall calendar.

"I'll confirm on his return. Now how's your mum and what's the gossip?"

The call lasted an hour but it was one of the telephone numbers at special rates so not too expensive! As I replaced one receiver I picked up the other when the house phone rang. It was Felix.

"The blacksmith has arrived Madame, about Pascal."

"I'll see him at the stables immediately, thank you Felix."

After a very light lunch I went for a ride on Avril and a swim in the pool, swallows still suddenly diving in front of me or even behind as was their whim. Stretching out on the sun lounger under the abri I thought to myself what a hedonistic lifestyle of a day! My evening was also effortless. I was dining with Edmond, Gildas's veterinary colleague and his wife Roseline. We had become a friendly foursome. It was to be an earlier meal than usual as they were driving to the south of France on Sunday and leaving before dawn.

I was reading again after many years one of my favourite novel's Flaubert's 'Madame Bovary' and had just put on Tchaikovsky's No 1 piano concerto when the house phone rang again. It was Felix and very agitated, a personal matter. Less than a minute later he arrived in the smaller salon.

"It's Yvette's brother, Madame, he's been in an accident in Spain and taken to hospital in Saragossa. I think it's serious. May we leave tomorrow? We can stay with friends overnight en route and arrive there on Monday. Only it means you are alone here, with Agathe being absent. I don't think …"

I interrupted him, "Felix first of all sit down. Now what details do you have?"

Felix replied, stuttering, very distressed.

"Not much Madame; just that his lorry crashed and his injuries are serious. We've the hospital's emergency number to keep in contact."

"Right, pack now, as quickly as possible. You leave when you are ready."

"But Madame, that's not possible. We've our duties and .. "

"Felix that's an order, I'll meet you and Yvette at the garages."

They were packed in minutes, meeting me as arranged, Yvette in tears. I put my arm round her.

"Felix, let me know any news and I handed him my car keys. The tank's full, safe journey."

He looked at me dumbfounded.

"Madame, I was taking my little car. I can't accept this offer," he began.

"Another order Felix," I replied. "My car is faster and more comfortable and you've driven me in it often. There's plenty of transport here if I need it; the four wheel drive, the estate van, Monsieur's 'Classic' or I might even borrow your car and get it dirty!"

For the first time there was a flicker of a smile on their faces. Felix's car was always spotless and polished weekly. They drove off still in shock at their mode of transport.

Before leaving for the village and Edmond's, I had not received a call from Gildas but we had not fixed any time for him to phone, both of us knowing the vagaries of travel. My evening spent with Edmond and Roseline was very amusing. Obviously, we shared a common bond with animals and recounted numerous anecdotes. I told them about Felix and Yvette.

"Caterine, aren't you concerned about being at BeauRobert alone?" Roseline asked me.

"Yes," added Edmond, "surely you could ask one of the estate staff, husband and wife to stay over the weekend."

I looked at. them astonished.

"Mon Dieu, what could happen to me? Are you expecting to read some lurid headline in the national press next week? Comtesse raped at château?"

I burst out laughing and they joined in.

"Nevertheless Caterine I think you should reconsider," said Edmond.

I looked at him and answered.

"Edmond, may I ask you two questions?"

"Certainly." He replied somewhat perplexed.

"Are either Felix or Yvette of bodyguard stature and when was there any crime, even of a minor nature committed in this village?"

"You're right," Edmond smiled "the idea's quite ridiculous."

When I arrived back at BeauRobert it was exactly 9.30pm.

I locked up and went to Gildas's study. Downloading the computer I found an e-mail from him. All was well. He had phoned while I was at Edmund's. He must have forgotten I was dining there. That was an unusual aberration and puzzled me a little.

As I turned off the computer I heard Leah's miaow coming from the smaller salon. This was uncharacteristic unless she was disturbed.

I hesitated, then opened the connecting door from Gildas's study. The lights were dimmed not as I had left them. I gasped startled as a figure emerged from the shadows: a male figure, very tall and very handsome, known intimately to me. I stood transfixed, then stuttered.

"But you're supposed to be in ..."

He interrupted me.

"But I've returned Caterine, La Comtesse du Gilbert and he bowed. It was a formal bow, hand across his waist and as he stood straight again, I felt fear flood my being and trepidation touch my soul. I stared in shock, in horror at the du Gilbert gloved hands.

I was now gripped by terror. There was evil in this man, satanic evil. I could smell it now but recognised by me too late. I was trapped alone. Quickly, I glanced round but I already knew the answer. The salon door key to the smaller hall was not in the lock neither was the key to the French window sortie to the lakeside. They had been there after I locked up.

Before I could utter another word he touched the wall light switches, without turning round. He knew this room so well.

"Allow me Madame," he addressed me. "I've brought you a present Caterine, La Comtesse du Gilbert, may I present...."

Light flooded the salon. In the middle sat another figure in a strange chair. Another figure whom my stunned, numbed mind slowly recognised; the perfection of the profile, the black heavy hair falling like the hood of a silken cloak onto her shoulders, as of many years ago; at the British Embassy, at David's wedding, in a photograph in a newspaper article. A figure who was dead. Dead after a riding accident, lost for eight months and then her remains found and buried, buried in the family vault in the chapel at Saint Roche Rivière but alive. Isabella, the true Comtesse de Gilbert!

The room swam in front of me. I was fighting for control, images, painful images moved morbidly through my mind. Papa's accident, David's operation, and finally the headstone on the grave at Saint Roche Rivière with the words, Isabella, La Comtesse du Gilbert and the dates. R.I.P.

She was alive. I was dead, dead in mind body and soul. I was standing looking in a mirror reflecting a nightmare, life and death in images together fighting against each other with life desperate, struggling for survival; images, grey at first, coming slowly into focus in black and white, then developing into a lurid kaleidoscope.

I regained control and saw it was the gloved hand I was

seeing again as it turned that strange chair, strange to me because it was a wheelchair.

The act seemed to take some time as if in slow motion, the chair turned out of its perfect profile forty-five degrees, until she sat facing me.

It was the worst disfigurement I had ever personally witnessed. Nausea engulfed me as my eyes saw that sight to which my mind would have preferred to be blind. The face looked like a waxwork: a waxwork of which one side only had been completed the other side pulp waiting for the craftsmen to create again and to complete the perfection. Two eyes stared at me: the one was human ebony the other a black plastic shell. She said nothing and I realised she was heavily sedated. No words had been spoken since that fateful introduction. Silence stood like a sentinel between us.

It was pierced by the ring tone of a phone, his mobile phone. He removed it from his monogrammed jacket pocket and punched in a reply without speaking. My body was now starting to shake in shock as all the ramifications reared, like those haunting spectres I had suffered over months in my mind. Suddenly I realised I was losing control. I forced myself to breathe slowly, deep breathes. My mind mastered my body and I began to think fast, furiously calculating the options, my brain engaged while his was distracted.

Out of the fading light, two figures emerged to stand at the locked French windows. He produced the key, unlocked the door and let them in. I did not recognise these uninvited guests. I had never seen them before in my life. A man and a woman walked towards him, the man bowed and the woman bent her knee in a curtsy. They were simply, even poorly dressed, not staff, more like peasants.

They moved immediately the only sound their shuffling round Isabella's chair, fussing with and adjusting the rug. Then they stopped and turned awaiting his command. To my amazement he conducted the conversation in a language I was completely unaware he knew; sign language the communication of the orally impaired. I watched and I understood.

"Take my sister back to her home. Look after her as you have always done. Do nothing until you receive my instructions, nothing, nothing at all. Au revoir."

The woman nodded compliance, curtsying again while the man answered in the slightly slurred speech of the born deaf addressing him with his full title and making a further bow. Then with a minor squeak of the wheelchair, all three were gone.

His sister! My god, I thought, so that's how he concealed her.

We regarded each other like two gladiators in the Coliseum, planning our strategy to gain supremacy. He knew his strengths and I knew mine. I stared at this evil man again, at those bewitching eyes set in a handsome face, a man with a powerful body, a man of stature, wealth, intelligence, repute, recognised for his eminence. A man of power now wielding more than one kind of power over me. How he had woven his spells so subtly in my mind, that I had become confused, mystified at times. Demented by demons and then uplifted, lost in my love affair, deliriously denying this deception. Blind.

I waited. He removed the du Gilbert gloves and addressed me.

"Caterine you are a beautiful woman, an extraordinarily beautiful woman but you know that already. Many men have uttered these words to you as I have in the past also."

"I remember well when I used that expression at Saint Roche Rivière. It was to Donald, actually as we watched you with Rodrigue and Elisée. You were wearing emerald green at the christening of Félicité, your hair was shimmering like a rare gold, your body was magnificent and your face with those violet blue eyes, 'incredible'. I say this to you because I want you to know how I value you as a rare creature. Apart from your beauty you're highly intelligent and talented. I want you to know also that it was not my intention to cause you unnecessary distress tonight. However, the truth couldn't be concealed much longer for reasons outside my control."

I had my response ready.

"Why didn't you tell me before, when we met again at BeauRobert?"

"Are you mad?" he looked astonished. "That would have ruined everything. She was my secret. My plans at that time uncertain, waiting for events to unfold. And then followed an unexpected development for me: a love affair, the engagement and that unforgettable wedding here at BeauRobert, the legal consecration was very important to me albeit I knew it was false.

Desperately, I wanted that wedding to take place, although I knew I deprived you of your right to become La Comtesse de Gilbert but always I wanted you. Believe that, always, even more now."

He had opened the door of opportunity and ruthlessly I grabbed the handle.

"Actually," I replied returning his gaze "that's not important to me, the title is meaningless as is the marriage." He looked shocked.

"What do you mean? That not being married is unimportant. I can't believe you, knowing you as I do."

"Then," I replied walking towards him "you are a fool. It's you I want. You, I've always wanted, your body I crave and you whose life I wish to share."

I kissed him slowly, languorously.

He responded immediately and putting my arms around his neck I reciprocated that response.

"This turn of events means nothing to me if I have you."

"*Mon Dieu*, I've been blind" and he moved his hands up

over my breasts, as I moved mine down already aware of his erection. I broke off

"Not yet! Let's have a drink and tell me the whole story about Isabella."

I turned and walked to the rosewood commode.

"Cognac?" I inquired and he grinned.

"Thank you."

We talked for another hour caressing each other, my refilling his cognac several times, mine also but topped up with soda. At last plans were in place. He pulled me towards him again. Hands moving over me, his mouth kissing me more urgently, down my neck his body throbbing, erection high.

"Darling, I've a better idea." I said leaning over to kiss him again softly enticingly. I took his hand.

"Let's go into the garden, I want to undress for you under the moonlight. Would you like that?"

He stared at me.

"Christ! What a woman!"

We walked together hand in hand through the study and out of the patio doors onto the terrace.

"Wait here until I skirt the shrubbery and then as I slowly strip off my clothes, walk towards me, but take time. When you reach me I'll be completely naked," I giggled "at your mercy!"

His eyes were just a little more glazed now but followed me, mesmerised by my movements. I was standing opposite him, unbuttoning my shirt, dropping it on the lawn. Putting my hands behind my back, I unhooked my brassiere in a gesture I found ironically familiar and raised it up over my head.

I heard his intake of breath the cognac perhaps playing its part. I watched as he started to walk towards me. We were now only 15 metres apart. I undid the button of my knee breaches and pulled down the zip lowering them slowly over my thighs, letting them fall to the ground holding his gaze and stepping out of them, now totally naked.

He quickened his pace, arms outstretched.

"Ma chérie," he cried out and was gone.

Gone to Hell down the shaft of the old disused well.

I waited. I waited for many minutes slowly pulling on my clothes. Silence, I walked over.

The night time breeze rustled through the shrubbery otherwise silence still. I looked down: 26 feet deep and 8 feet of water, the shaft narrow but wide enough for the passage of a human body. I lifted up the loosened tarpaulin and replaced it.

Adieu, Professor Philippe Martine, adieu !

Chapter Twenty

Suddenly I felt nauseous, legs weak, almost paralysed: it seemed as if I had been at a dress rehearsal for some Molière play, which despite major misgivings by the theatre manager was a success, aims achieved in the principal role, mission accomplished. Now, however, it was the first night, the performance, and I was the major player acting the central character on whom the cast depended: but I was suffering stage fright, terrified in the wings, my hands hot and clammy, my brow breaking out in sweat, mouth moistureless, pulse throbbing, faint, feeling so faint.

A scuffle in the night time shrubbery reawakened reality. Without a backward glance at the well, I walked forward towards the terrace, the open patio door and as I already knew my analysis for my destiny.

A drop only remained in that cognac bottle but I grabbed its neck and emptied what was left into my mouth: it tumbled down my parched throat and I spluttered almost choking in the sting of the undiluted spirit.

"Scream! If only I could scream" I thought as I collapsed on the sofa, bottle left at a drunken angle on the tapestry rug which covered the floor.

It seemed only minutes but probably some time before my brain engaged again. I remember I walked to the apartment kitchen to make myself a flask of my special coffee; then I sat down and cold bloodedly dissected the last few hours.

During that time spent with Philippe I uncovered all the facts, as plied with several cognacs, his tongue loosened. Initially, however, he was hesitant. After pouring out our drinks I placed the goblets on the Louis X1V table and sat down beside him moving over to kiss him again enticingly.

"Philippe, you know now what I said was true. It was you I wanted, not Gildas."

"Yes, but you still married him. Why?" dark brown eyes analysing me in a steady stare.

With my reply I attacked.

"And why not?" I cried. "You never phoned me although you promised you would."

I stood up, angry, upset, and turned to face him. "How do I know you're being truthful. This is probably an act. Trying to win my affection just for tonight." I turned away in distress.

Philippe jumped up and caught my hand pulling me against him replying

"I never phoned you because that 'shit' stopped me."

"What do you mean?"

"Your 'husband' my cousin Gildas," he spat out the name.

"I don't understand," gazing at him in astonishment.

"Gildas phoned me in Zurich. He was castigating, telling me you were appalled by my comments to your staff about the time taken over the project; plus other 'innuendos' particularly to the coloured girl. What a pleb, she was. I can't remember her name if she ever had one."

"Sabine," I replied quietly, temper wanting to erupt but calmness critical.

"Gildas lied." I snapped.

"I knew nothing of this. Bloody Hell, what a bastard he is. He separated us deliberately."

I looked at Philippe again and placed my arms round his neck.

"We must make plans for our revenge. Isabella is one factor but I have another. You've always loved BeauRobert and wanted it for yourself. Am I right?"

Philippe nodded.

"Then," I smiled. "Between us we've a lethal concoction which dare not pass his lips."

Philippe was now staring at me.

"What do you know?"

"Ah, later. Firstly, tell me about Isabella" and he began.

"Isabella asked Gildas for a divorce: a divorce from her life of Hell to marry me. But he refused wouldn't countenance it. The attendant publicity, scandal, the slur on the family name, all that was repugnant to him."

"God," I thought, "her cold blooded strategy to keep her title and her lover!"

"She phoned and told me. We'd arranged a meeting that evening and I was already in France. Isabella was distraught. I tried to calm her but that wasn't possible. She was very highly strung. We agreed to meet earlier in my manor house adjacent to Luçay Christian. It was rocky terrain unsuitable for fast riding, the ground hazardous."

"Isabella ignored that, I'm sure and pushed on in a frenzied furore. My assumption is that her horse stumbled; a flawed stirrup leather, the one she used in her haste to saddle up broke and she was thrown, one foot remaining trapped in the other stirrup, dragged along that gravelled ground unconscious unable to protect herself. Her helmet saved her brain but not her beauty and eventually not her mind."

"When I found her she was still unconscious. The injury to the right side of her face," he stopped, "I can only compare it to a brutal burn, if possible even worse and the eye was gone; there remained only an empty socket where the ebony had been. With all my skills that damage I couldn't repair."

Philippe paused taking up his goblet and a gulp of the cognac. I lifted mine but never even sipped, my mind still analysing options and playing for time.

"But darling, you could have left Isabella there to be found. You did not. Instead you took her away. I assume to Switzerland and ensured she was cared for. That was a generous gesture."

By this time I had replenished his cognac generously for the third time. At my remark, he laughed and turned to look at me as I sat again on the sofa.

"Chérie indeed I would have left her there, she and I were finished together, she was a disfigured wreck!"

"Why did I not leave her? Why did I take her to Switzerland and install her in that remote chalet with a peasant couple, one mute and one deaf but medically skilled?" We looked at each other and I answered him in one word.

"Gildas!"

"Exactly, Caterine. Isabella was my ace of spades. Her disappearance caused him months of anxiety, uncertainty and unwelcome publicity. I phoned him and then visited Saint Roche Rivière to offer my assistance. I must admit I relished his suffering. Then I waited, plans uncertain but ready to play my hand when the cards favoured me."

His arm was now round my shoulder and I moved closer.

"Bravo darling, but then a body was found." I looked at him confused. "Surely it could be proven it was not Isabella?"

Philippe smiled. "That was the masterstroke. Into my hand was dealt the trump card: ironic and fortuitous. The body found was Caucasian and approximately Isabella's age but badly decomposed. Everyone else reported missing during that freak snowstorm in La Touraine had been recovered; for the three who died, bodies identified, only Isabella remained unaccounted for."

"Further, known to only close family, Isabella had been adopted. It was arranged very discreetly in Switzerland. Oncle Matthias and Tante Emilie travelled extensively on his business. One year they left France together and returned with a baby. That baby of course was Isabella. Her natural parents never sought nor wishing to be found and so no DNA!"

"But Philippe what about other identification?" I asked.

He finished the cognac and I rose to replenish it and mine: his undiluted mine mainly soda.

As I sat down again, he lent over to kiss me, his hands on my breasts, murmuring softly.

"Philippe darling, later, tell me what happened."

Reluctantly he continued.

"I moved fast. Isabella's dental treatment, minor as it was took place in Switzerland. I had a means of access to the records." He grinned. "They were blitzed from the computer memory!"

"Brilliant." I gasped.

"As for the local police here" he shrugged his shoulders, "there was compelling evidence. The only person reported missing not found and along or nearby that ditch where the remains were discovered, her whip, her helmet, the damaged stirrup leather and her mobile phone. The evidence appeared conclusive. Remember also, Gildas is someone of great influence here, a man of power, wealth and stature. The police, unwilling to inflict more distress, stir painful memories naturally closed the case."

"Of course," I said thoughtfully. "So what did you decide to do about Isabella after this development."

"Wait even longer." Philippe replied.

"Wait until Gildas remarried. He had to. He would want an heir. I must admit my patience was stretched, he took much longer than I anticipated until you appeared."

I giggled as he kissed me again.

"It's getting late," he said glancing at his watch. "Let's have some fun!"

"Soon darling, you haven't heard my secret yet. One more cognac each and I moved to the rosewood commode with our goblets.

"By the way, how would you have coped if you'd been absent from Switzerland and Isabella became ill or died?" I inquired.

"Oh plans are in place. She has papers, forged obviously, registering her as my sister. I have a local *notaire* known and obliged to me. That poses no problem."

He hesitated.

"Philippe, what is it?" I sensed some fact unknown to me.

"Isabella's dying, Caterine. The cancer which destroyed her mind when she first saw herself in a mirror after the accident has now physically invaded her body."

"*Mon Dieu,*" I gasped shocked. "How long?"

Philippe stood up walking towards me eyes just a little glazed and replied.

"A few weeks, two months at maximum."

"So that's why you brought her here tonight but Gildas had already departed."

"Yes," replied Philippe "a day earlier than my information from Klaus Lundberg. He's a family friend from Switzerland."

Now the jigsaw was nearly completed. But some intricate pieces were still to be placed in position.

Philippe grinned now.

"However, I thought I'd still pay a call on you perhaps persuade you to entertain me as you'd be lonely, alone."

I handed him his cognac smiling flirtatiously.

"And how did you know I was alone?"

"Well, Agathe's aunt works at Luçay Christian sur Loire and I discovered from the staff of Klaus that she was on weekend leave. Afterwards, it was simple to arrange for Felix and Yvette's absence. A very efficient 'phone service' will update them on the patient's condition."

He laughed uproariously goblet raised in victorious triumph. How I maintained control I know not. Loathing, linked with hatred on a gathering chain of venom filled my being; but I had to ensure he won no laurel in this gladiator's arena.

Remaining calm I raised my glass.

"Bravo, again darling. *Saluté*!"

"Thank you," Philippe responded with a mock bow. "Felix and Yvette will be hunting around Saragossa for a fictitious hospital without a patient," he laughed coarsely again.

I glanced out of the window. It was dark, but the moonlight reflected on the water, shimmering shadows forming strange shapes like past spectres in my mind.

"One factor, darling, still puzzles me knowing your intelligence."

"What's that?" He asked standing beside the walnut armoire, brandy goblet aloft. "Well," I said thoughtfully, "your original intention was to confront Gildas and me together here with Isabella. Surely you knew that was a dangerous strategy. His reaction would be shock, horror certainly but then fury. Gildas would have summoned the police, your guilt indefensible and ..."

Philippe interrupted me smiling sardonically.

"I think not. My loyal servants, simple people, understand that Isabella my 'dearly beloved sister' was abandoned by her husband after an accident he caused, that he believes her now dead. Of course, they're unaware of his name. They were told that I'd saved her by chance and intend one day to bring her husband to justice when I have sufficient evidence.

My case to Gildas would be presented as follows:"

"One, both servants are prepared to swear in a court of law

that it was Isabella's husband who hid her away in that remote chalet and his instructions they followed. Two, in Switzerland, I have in a safe deposit box, a secret dossier. When that dossier is revealed to the *notaire* obliged to me, he will authenticate it. It includes correspondence typed on Gildas's computer and other false but condemning evidence. The planning has been meticulous. Well, what do you think?"

I could not answer at first, stunned, paralysed, praying for some sacred power to restore my loss of speech. Silence stirred the room. Recovering, I turned to face Philippe.

"But Gildas will accuse you. How you found Isabella. The police will investigate."

I hesitated struggling for words. Philippe drained his glass.

"Gildas will not call the police. Why? To him any investigation would be an anathema: a court case, the scandal, slur on the du Gilbert name, suspicions about him, innuendos, gossip. Elisée and Frédéric to consider and of course under other circumstances you. I know Gildas and he'll know another factor."

"What?" I whispered.

"The media coverage, the publicity, press deductions; he, the Comte du Gilbert with his stature, wealth and eminence could not accept his wife as a disfigured wreck, mind demented, no chance of heirs to his inheritance. No, Caterine, he will not challenge me. He had the motive. I had not!

We will negotiate. Easier now with Isabella's limited time. She'll be cared for and he'll grant me my wish which is exclusively in his power: to change my name to du Gilbert."

Suddenly my calmness returned and my resolve.

"And over these years no discovery of Isabella in Switzerland." I said thoughtfully.

"No, not by anyone. Initially she was unrecognisable. The du Gilberts are known in France but Gildas never wanted to be a member of any European celebrity culture. As for Isabella and me we maintained a low profile in Switzerland. Anyway the Swiss mind their own business usually in Swiss francs!"

I laughed in an attempt to hide my distress as he joined me.

"Not even your notaire knows who she is?"

Philippe replied irritated.

"No, I told you, she's registered as my sister. Now tell me what you know to add to his pain?"

It had to be said. Now with all Philippe's revelations, I had no choice. It was my final ploy to gain his total trust.

Pulling the one curtain still remaining open I shut out the lake and turned to face my adversary, smiling with hatred in my soul.

"I'll threaten to reveal publicly Gildas's partners. Did Isabella never mention them to you?"

Philippe was dumbfounded.

"Partners, other women, Gildas with mistresses. No, she said nothing. I'm astonished." His words were slightly slurred.

"Philippe," I replied "with other women I could compete, but not with men!"

He stared at me in total shock.

"Gildas a homosexual. Mon Dieu ! I don't believe it. He staggered a little backwards.

"No," I said "bisexual but given the choice prefers a man."

It was my trump card, a lie of course, a ruthless lie. Unsuspecting, slightly drunk and wanting me I led Philippe out to the garden and I murdered him.

On that Saturday, the day Gildas drove down the driveway en route for Tours, Saint Pierre des Corps as I waved 'au revoir', Felix met me in the gardens, looking concerned as I was going for that walk.

"Madame, may I have a word?"

"Certainly Felix, is there a problem?"

"There is Madame. I don't understand it. The new cover for the old well doesn't fit, too small; yet here are the dimensions, confirmed in writing to the manufacturers. I've just phoned them and they've apologised for the error but Monday's a jour de fête. This means the next delivery will be Tuesday. It's quite out of order, Madame," Felix added agitated.

I tried to calm him, inquiring.

"The tarpaulin's still in place, isn't it Felix and so it's safe for any animals in the garden."

"Of course, Madame. As you know we've only small animals there because of the wall, but it's not load bearing for humans, not possible. With the upper structure supporting the winding system for the chain and bucket now removed, it's unrecognisable as a well, and the ground was excavated at that side as it's a lower level, barely covered by the tarpaulin. Frankly, it's highly dangerous. If anyone walked towards it especially in the dark it's likely he would slip under the cover, the ground subsiding. Mon Dieu!"

Felix shuddered, passing his hand over his brow.

"Don't worry Felix," I reassured him, "no-one will be in the garden but me and all the staff have been informed as a precautionary measure, I know."

"Yes, Madame, at Monsieur Le Comte's instructions and in writing to all members of staff living in or out, even the tenant farmers, although only the gardeners are affected and they are not returning until Wednesday."

And that's how I planned my strategy round that well.

Philippe would have raped me. I have no doubt about that. He had me trapped in the west wing, all doors locked, he, the Master Jailor, having ensured I was alone: Felix and Yvette departed in distress on a hollow mission.

I had seen his intentions on his face, in those evil eyes after that horror scene before the wheelchair left and he would have raped me not once but many times. I was under his control through Saturday night, the whole of Sunday, until he chose to take his leave and of his sexual predilections I knew nothing.

At first, I had considered escape through Gildas's study and the walled garden, the southern gate: but he would have caught me, a powerful man, an ex international rugby player. My chances were nil.

The second option was to pretend passion, endure the rapes. I could not.

I knew also he would be spitting on my child, the child of my lover and me, growing now in my womb, my surprise for Gildas on his return.

And so, I chose the only option: Death down the well.

Adieu Professor Philippe Martine. He is dead. However, she's alive Isabella la Comtesse du Gilbert, Gildas and Caterine adulterer and mistress expecting a bastard child but Isabella cannot live long, a few weeks, two months at most. She is in a remote Swiss chalet with two servants under an assumed name. No-one else knows her true identity not even the notaire, only the deceased Philippe and me. And I am alive. Life has defeated death in that battle.

Isabella's jailors have been ordered to take no action until they receive instructions from a dead man.

Gildas is absent and ignorant of all these events as are Maman, David, and Alix as well as Rodrigue, Elisée and Frédéric, with all other family members and friends.

The chances of discovery are remote. During the time I have reflected, I have analysed this case again and again for flaws.

There are none.

Philippe disappears, a prominent man, the finest plastic surgeon in Switzerland with numerous commercial interests, but many accidents could have befallen him and often men of eminence wish to evaporate, assume another identity. It was not unique.

Further, he had no recent connection with BeauRobert. In the unlikely event he was traced here I would not deny it. As far as I knew, being in the area, he called to see Gildas. With his cousin overseas, he left his regards to us both promising to phone and departed, as I understood, returning to Switzerland on the following day.

That was plausible, not open to question.

But if I do not tell the truth about the events of this evening; if I remain silent, can I live with this lie? I remembered Papa's words "always be honest or you commit a greater crime; you lie to yourself."

But if I am honest, our happiness is forever destroyed. Gildas will search for Isabella. I recall so exactly his words "I blame myself for her death" just as I did about Papa. After all Isabella is still his wife and he is an honourable man. Under these circumstances, positions reversed, I would take the same action, without hesitation. Our marriage is already illegal, a sham, but known only to me and I have our child to consider.

Finally, if I reveal the truth, I condemn myself for the crime I have committed.

Philippe was an evil man. When I reflect on his callous calculations and suffering to which Gildas was subjected; plus Philippe's false accusations, flawed witnesses, secret fatal file and his lascivious intentions for me, I have no regrets. He deserved his death.

The legal system, however, would disagree. Philippe should have been put on trial and the jury decide his fate.

My thoughts were tormented, tortured by my failure to predict these events, anticipate developments and forestall the future. I held the key to that door on destiny's path but left it unturned in the lock.

Professor Philippe Martine was the threat, a man obsessed with the du Gilbert family, a member of it certainly, a cousin, but by marriage only, not a bloodline, not bearing the du Gilbert name. He was like a soldier in the ranks failing to gain his commission who cannot aspire to future promotion and challenge the general himself, a man of whom he was insanely jealous, Gildas du Gilbert.

The images I had seen which delved deeper and deeper: those fearful phantoms, haunting spectres were not from Gildas, nor figments of my imagination but from Philippe, a warning about the peril he posed: the association between Gildas and him, family connections, dual friendship as children, their shared love of BeauRobert, and the major clue, the catalyst – Isabella. All were common factors but I failed to connect the links.

How blind I had been!

One factor had puzzled me, the gloves.

I had asked Philippe when I saw them placed on the coffee table.

"I thought these were exclusive to the du Gilberts" I had said to him in mock surprise.

"They are," he had replied. "That's why I had them copied for me."

Then on looking at them more closely I had seen the GduG crest was missing. It could not be falsely replicated.

The man was demented.

But I'm not, although I should be.

I stood up and walked through our private apartments so treasured by Gildas and me where we had shared our love affair.

I passed our bedroom, the arched hall, to stand eventually in my study, curtains still open: the wind around was gaining momentum, splatters of raindrops covered the panes of glass on my patio door.

Suddenly, in the distance, the rumble of thunder a few miles away and then predictably minutes later a flash of lightening rent the night sky.

As I watched the storm advanced towards me threatening in its intensity. The depth of my dilemma deepened. To tell or not to tell: to be honest or forever live a lie.

Was there a choice? The decision was mine alone. I was the only witness. Maybe the gods could help me to decide.

With a mighty roar Mars decreed as his thunder rocketed around BeauRobert. In a flash of the following crooked lightening, I found my answer.

Adjusting the drapes, my hand surprisingly steady, to ensure they were perfectly closed, I turned to extinguish my antique, oil table lamp.

The final verse from that Wordsworth sonnet of the imagination which had eluded me now stirred in my mind.

"Some say that here a murder has been done,
And blood cries out for blood: but for my part,
I've guessed when I've been sitting in the sun,
That it was all for that unhappy Hart."
And what cause the Hart might have to love this place.
And come make his death-bed near the well!"

Calmly, I retired to bed my decision made.

Chapter Twenty-One

June 1998

Silence was my decision: to reveal nothing of that horrendous night and the murder I committed to save my sanity and my soul. To salvage a life for Gildas, for our unborn child and protect my beloved husband from the threat of treacherous blackmail for deeds he had not committed.

I used Donald Cameron's bible: the technique he taught me to compartmentalise my mind. That Saturday evening became the 'INCIDENT'. It was locked away in an area of my mind to which I threw away the key.

On Tuesday of the following week Felix and Yvette returned to BeauRobert. I had already received a phone call to tell me what I already knew from Philippe's disclosures. I intercepted them at the main door, as he was driving to the garages.

"Please come in. I've coffee and a snack ready. You must be very tired." I said smiling.

'Thank God' I thought they had returned safely from their ordeal.

They stared at me in astonishment and then followed me into the smaller salon.

"Madame" Felix began "I don't think you should be preparing food for us."

"Rubbish" I replied opening my special thermos "this is the 21st century not the 18th."

Shell shocked they sat down as I poured out the coffee.

"Now tell me, after this debacle which has caused you so much distress, do you wish to take further action, inform the police?"

"No Madame, definitely not" Felix replied exchanging glances with his wife.

"Yvette and I have discussed everything. Whoever set this up must be known to us although we are unaware of having any enemies: but also we are seen to be perhaps by some in a privileged position."

"Pardon, Felix, I don't quite understand" I interrupted him, surprised.

"Well, Madame" he continued "Yvette, myself, our children, my parents and grandparents have all lived at the du Gilbert estate under the family's patronage. Monsieur le Comte's late father took the unprecedented decision to offer staff the opportunity to purchase their tenanted properties at subsidised prices, sectioning off the area of land on which these properties were built so that the ground was included in the sale. Everyone to my knowledge accepted creating if you like "a little estate" within a much larger one. It was radical thinking at the time; perhaps some in the locality considered it too generous, which created resentments."

Felix coughed suddenly embarrassed.

"I think I've said too much."

"Not at all Felix" I replied re-filling the coffee cups. "I'm very interested but what's the relevance?"

"If Yvette and I reveal the facts of our sudden departure on Saturday and our distress it will only give the culprit satisfaction. We'd prefer to say we visited Yvette's brother's family in the holiday weekend."

"Why not" I raised my cup of coffee with an internal sigh of relief.

During the night on that Monday, he returned again: the crooked man this time was transformed. He was a person of stature, over 6' tall and of athletic build with a smiling face which I knew well, Papa's face. I woke up screaming as it was engulfed in flames.

Over the following few days before Gildas arrived I made my preparations, long walks, riding on Avril, sensible diet although I had no appetite and sorting out my mind. The bible had never failed me. I could not give it reason now. By the Saturdays' afternoon of Gildas' return I was ready. As it happened I was unprepared.

Mucking out the stables, I found myself grabbed from behind and lifted in the air.

"Gildas" I shrieked immediately recognising his touch, his masculine smell and his laughter.

"I've missed you so much" he murmured as he kissed me pulling me down with him onto the hay.

Avril must have regarded us with amusement at our antics in her stable before she yawned and concentrated on her lunch.

"They're just gorgeous. I can't believe it. Where did you find them?" I exclaimed.

Gildas smiled "Just north of Tours, that's why I needed my car on this trip. So you're happy with my surprise present?"

We were sitting together in Gildas'study on the floor playing with two Weimaraner puppies, a dog and a bitch; 10 weeks old their unique silver grey short haired coats were gleaming in the reflected light from the midsummer sun which had spread its rays through the study windows.

"Thrilled" I replied "but however tall they grow, the cats will still be in charge!"

Gildas kissed me on the forehead in that loving gesture and we made our way for lunch.

Over coffee Gildas said:

"You know I was really grilled by that breeder about the dogs' care and well being: it was very reassuring that she took so much interest in their future home. In fact she's phoning to make an appointment in a month's time to check on their development."

"What!" I exclaimed "but you're a vet."

"Yes, but I didn't tell her. It would have been unfair, spoiled her speech." Gildas grinned "anyway the puppies are a welcome addition to the BeauRobert household."

It was the perfect opening and I seized it.

"Yes, chéri, but not the only one."

There was silence.

Gildas having finished his coffee had walked over to the window in the smaller salon overlooking the lake.

I smiled to myself and waited.

Turning round, he stared at me, green eyes mesmerising.

"Are you telling me you're pregnant?"

"Oui Monsieur. We've given ourselves a honeymoon baby."

What a night that was.

Two weeks later in mid-July the inevitable happened.

It had to be and I had to be prepared. I was.

On the Saturday morning I had received a call from Albert de Vere to clarify some logistics for the following week then Céline spoke to me.

"What news, Caterine. Both of you must be thrilled!"

"Thanks Céline, we are but I'm not sure about Albert, I've promised him my commitment and Sabine, as my assistant, is advancing in qualifications. He won't be deserted by me during this pregnancy or afterwards."

"He knows that Caterine and also something else."

"What's that?" I inquired interested.

"Only women can have babies and he was an advocate of equal opportunities. He has no defence! If you're free next Saturday, come over for dinner, about 8.00pm? and stay overnight."

"Love to" I replied still amused as I replaced the receiver.

The door bell clanged. For some reason it seemed an unusually ominous sound, my sixth sense alerted me and that department of my mind slammed shut.

A few minutes later Gildas and I were sitting in the library with Klaus Lundberg. He explained everyone's concerns.

"How can Philippe just disappear, Monsieur. It's not possible. He and I have always been close, the son I never had." He paused very agitated, his head now in his hands.

"M. Lundberg" Gildas replied standing up, let's have some coffee and you articulate the facts."

He rang for Felix and the coffee appeared within minutes. I remained silent.

"Well" Lundberg continued draining his cup "Philippe was on a three weeks vacation which I already knew. He had told me he would spend time in France and his London residence. I received a call from the managing director of his parent company Claude last night. You will I'm sure know that apart from his medical practices he had numerous commercial interests – property, leisure investments, etc. You are his cousin and close I understand?"

"Yes" Gildas nodded "but more so in earlier years but please tell us what this director said about some 'disappearance'. What did he mean?"

Lundberg without asking refilled his cup of coffee.

"Philippe was due to return yesterday, Friday morning, for a board meeting of the parent company. He failed to arrive – the director phoned his London home, the property here, plus his Swiss residence: staff replied but no Philippe. Attempts to reach him by mobile or e-mails have failed: that's when I received Claude's call. No-one, family, friends or staff have heard from him over that vacation period. Where is he?"

Lundberg looked distraught, but he continued:

"I checked at Philippe's manor house near here. One of his cars was in the garages, but that means nothing. Usually he kept one there for the times that he flew to Tours. However his preference was to drive directly from Switzerland."

"Do you know what his travel plans were on this occasion?" Gildas asked.

"No, as I said we had little time together."

"Perhaps we can help with some dates here" Gildas replied turning to me.

"Chérie?"

I then reiterated to Klaus Lundberg what I had already told Gildas soon after his return from the States.

"Philippe appeared here unexpectedly one week ago looking for Gildas. As he was in the USA, Philippe paid his respects and left."

Lundberg stared at me.

"Can you remember exactly when that was?" he asked.

"Certainly, it was one week ago today exactly: the Saturday Gildas flew to the US. I had dined earlier with friends in the village and he arrived just after my return, about 9 pm I think."

Klaus stood up.

"Why that's the day after he left Switzerland and settled in his manor house. I saw him for only a few minutes on the Friday as ironically I had commitments with family in Geneva."

Turning to face me he continued.

"But he must have talked about his plans for his visit, his vacation, spent some time here surely. He was a relative after all."

Before I could answer Gildas interrupted.

"M. Lundberg, Caterine was not a member of Philippe's fan club and justifiably. During the work she undertook at Beau Robert for the château contract her staff were treated with some contempt by my cousin which caused distress not just to them, a loyal professional team, but to both of us. Naturally, however, we are concerned for Philippe's well-being. We shall begin our own enquiries and inform the local police of his visit here. After that it is a matter for the authorities."

Lundberg regaining some composure, nodded agreement.

"Yes, of course. I'll tell Claude of my visit."

We all shook hands and Gildas accompanied him to the main door.

Alone I closed my eyes, temples throbbing, mouth dry.

The next challenge would be Gildas' inquisition. That I had to survive.

That inquisition never happened.

Over lunch where I toyed with my food, Gildas was relaxed about his cousin.

"Certainly, this so-called 'disappearance' is out of character for Philippe. He's usually meticulous about his professional and commercial interests; in my opinion he's become too much of a playboy, in recent years. I notice Lundberg never mentioned his South American properties."

"Pardon," I looked up startled "what properties?"

Gildas attacking his side salad with vigour replied

"Well, I've no details but Philippe told me once he'd invested in Brazil. That information slipped out after several cognacs. I'm sure those properties still exist. He could be there."

I hesitated before asking.

"Gildas, what action will you take now? You mentioned the local police."

"Chérie, it's a formality. We'll inform them of Philippe's

visit and then it's up to them and the Swiss authorities. Frankly I never really liked Philippe, not to be trusted. I preferred his brother Jacques although I wish my cousin no ill will. Subject closed. Now how's my gorgeous wife, her expanding tummy and the weekend plans?"

That vulnerable door in my mind which had threatened to open during Klaus Lundberg's visit manufactured itself a bolt and padlock.

Unfortunately, eventually someone found the keys.

Chapter Twenty-Two

It was a quieter August for my work being the main French holiday period plus the massive influx of foreign tourists made is impractical to invade the châteaux when the proprietors and staff were already waging war albeit winning financial victories.

At the beginning of that month, Donald and Shona spent a weekend at BeauRobert. David, Alix with the twins and Julian had flown out to Australia three weeks previously to see Uncle Fergus, Aunt Bebe and our Australian cousins.

"The children are so excited" Alix had told me on her last phone call before their departure. David thinks we should pack three straitjackets for the plane journey!"

I chuckled "maybe two parachutes for both of you?"

"Great idea" Alix exclaimed "we'll aim to jump when we're over Bali!"

"When are you meeting up with Maman in Perth?"

"Not sure yet" Alix answered "as you know she's travelling between Sydney and Adelaide to stay with her university pals. It's to be confirmed."

"Courage et bon voyage" I added as we said our goodbyes.

Donald and Shona were in their usual high spirits when they arrived on the Friday afternoon.

"You're looking super" Shona said as we all hugged each other in the main hall.

"Yes, indeed, lovelier than ever" Donald added.

"With this girth? You must be joking. I think I'm giving birth to an elephant!"

"I hope not Chérie, the gestation period can be 21 months." Gildas added eyebrow raised.

The fun and laughter continued all weekend.

On Sunday evening before dinner, Shona spoke to me as we were sitting by the pool. Our respective husbands were still changing after an energetic game of tennis; the original courts, lain in disrepair for years, has recently been renovated. Of course I was in no condition to make up a foursome!

"I think I might be pregnant too, Caterine, as I've missed a month, unusual for me."

"Shona, that's brilliant. Does Donald know?"

"Not yet. I don't want to anticipate anything and be disappointed. We'd love a baby."

I kissed her. "I'm sure you're right. Let Gildas and me know as soon as it's confirmed."

On Monday morning Gildas drove them to St Pierre des Corps and the TGV to Charles de Gaulle from where they were flying direct to Scotland. We would meet again in September at the Château Ball.

Gildas and I spent most of that day in our studies catching up on work completely unaware of the shock awaiting us the following week.

"Well Caterine no need to ask how you are, glowing I would say" smiled Gustave our local GP.

"Ready for your scan?"

I nodded, very excited but also apprehensive.

Gildas turned to Gildas whom he'd known from childhood.

"Just remember, when you see the image, this little individual will have only two legs, not four!"

As they looked at the screen consternation registered on both their faces and glances were exchanged.

"What's wrong?" I said quickly, trying to stay calm.

"What's wrong with my baby?"

Gildas, holding my hand, squeezed it.

"Nothing wrong Chérie, it appears" he hesitated and I looked up in alarm.

"Christ Almighty," he exclaimed "There's three of them!"

My visit to the surgery lasted much longer than planned!

By the time we returned to BeauRobert shock had not even registered, we were numb.

I remember, I almost collapsed in the smaller salon onto the sofa after Gustave's examination confirmed there were three heartbeats. It was triplets!

"There's no family history, Gildas, of multiple births, none at all."

Gildas was still standing beside me after guiding me to that claret coloured Louis XV sofa.

"But Alix had twins, Angus and Alexandra, there must be something in the genes. I know there is no evidence in the du Gilbert's or any side of the family."

"That's the point" I replied "the twins' connection is from the McCallum family. Alix's grandmother gave birth to twins, girls, nothing on the Sinclair side."

It was now noon. Glancing at his watch Gildas made a decision walking over to that handsome sideboard in the corner of the room.

He returned with two goblets, one contained a small cognac with soda for me and an undiluted cognac for himself.

"Normally, we don't indulge at lunchtime during the week. Both of us aware of the habits of too much alcohol, also you've taken only the infrequent glass of wine since you learned you were pregnant."

He handed me my goblet adding:

"This however is an exceptional occasion for three reasons. One, to salute our triplets, two, to savour the grape and three, to save our sanity. Cheers!"

"All right" I replied as I took a sip, replacing my glass on the walnut table.

That's when we looked at each other and realisation struck.

"Mon Dieu" Gildas exclaimed "considering the number of times we made love each day, it could have been sextuplets!"

I spluttered on my next sip of cognac.

Over dinner we discussed some of the ramifications. Gildas to my surprise was very anxious for me.

"Don't be ridiculous, Chéri. I'm thrilled. Of course the news was a shock but just think, one pregnancy and an instant family."

"Yes, I know, but as I said."

I interrupted him.

"Frankly, I consider us very blessed. There are thousands of couples, desperate for children and unable to have any for one reason or another. As for us, we've also no financial constraints. Look at our good fortune" I continued waving my hand "surrounded in luxury plus St Roche Rivière and all our investments. Even if everything collapsed around us, we can both work in our respective professions, earn a living" I stopped, a little breathless.

Gildas was smiling.

"All right Chérie, I've got the message. Bravo. It was quite a speech. Come and have coffee in the smaller salon and an early night: this news has been intoxicating!"

The following day I phoned Maman in Scotland just returned from Australia.

"It was an outstanding success, Caterine, and a memorable reunion with the family in Perth. Angus and Bebe organised a farewell party for us. Many of the guests you would remember from our visit after your Masters graduation."

"Now" she continued "how you are and when's the scan?"

"I had it yesterday and everything's fine, although we received a little surprise."

"What do you mean? Are your dates wrong?" Maman asked.

"No, not at all. It's the fact I'm expecting triplets!"

There was a pause.

"Caterine, even considering your often caustic humour, I don't find the remark funny."

As Maman continued I signalled to Gildas beside me and passed him the receiver. He confirmed what I had said. To our amusement the line went dead!

Initially we kept the news within the family and then our closest friends. Maman arrived at BeauRobert the weekend following my phone call. After loving embraces in the main hall she stood back to look at us.

"Well Petite you are definitely glowing. Gildas I think the shock's been too much. You're the one requiring a doctor!"

Laughing together we wandered out to the garden.

Everyone was thrilled for us.

David, Alix, Frédéric and Marie-Thérèse.

At the beginning of September I told Albert de Vere. For once he was speechless.

"Before you ask the obvious questions, please let me anticipate answering them."

Albert nodded.

"Crazy as it may seem, I intend to continue working, assuming" I hesitated "there are no complications at the births."

I had been unsure how to phrase this. As an intelligent man with two healthy children he would understand the innuendo.

"Why? There are several reasons. One, with the award of the Château contract to de Veres, a contract spanning several years, I am in actuality working mainly from home, hence 'on hand' for my children. Two, Sabine as my assistant is gaining in qualifications as a major anchor for us in Paris. Three, I am fortunate to be able to afford a nursery staff at BeauRobert to assist in caring for the triplets. Finally a message from Gildas to you."

Albert reacted: "What's that?"

"Tell Albert we both need to work to maintain not only our financial security with three children to educate but to retain our sanity!"

Albert stood up, put down his coffee cup and came over to embrace me albeit standing further back than usual!

"You're a great girl; how lucky it was to find you. I wish you all the happiness in the world to you and your expectant family. Stay as long as it's possible at de Vere."

How ironic his words became.

"Well, that's settled" Gildas said that evening as we sat in the library. "Albert's reassured."

"How's Frédéric?" I asked suddenly "any news about Charlotte in his phone call today?"

"Nothing, they've decided obviously to remain apart. As you know they had a reconciliation for several weeks but it couldn't be sustained. Maybe better this way although he's fragile emotionally albeit not showing it."

I was silent for a while, thoughts in turmoil. It seemed madness but I had to ask the question.

"Gildas, how long did you have a mistress in Paris?"

He turned round from sorting some volumes out of order in one of the bookcases.

"Paris, a mistress! I've no idea what you're talking about!"

My heart sank. Surely he could not deny it.

Then I told him about Alix's remarks at Elisée's wedding.

"I did not ask you before because I assumed she'd disappeared from the scene, after our marriage."

Somehow I felt vulnerable. To my horror Gildas burst out laughing. That made me angry.

"I don't find this subject amusing especially as you've not denied it. Alix told me Frédéric and Elisée were aware of her existence, a member of the Château committee, I think.

"Well" I asked standing up with difficulty at my increased weight "What's your answer?"

Suddenly, for the first time in my pregnancy I felt unwell, a little dizzy and staggered. Gildas literally ran from the other end of the library, catching me and gently despite my protests insisting I lay back on the couch with my feet up and then giving me some water.

He knelt down beside me.

"Darling, I'm sorry. Are you all right?"

Placing his hand on my tummy he said:

"I think there might be a battle for space without your knowledge."

Sipping the water I replied.

"I shouldn't have asked now. I don't know why."

Gildas lent over to kiss me.

"Caterine, everything is literally "kicking in" if you'll excuse the pun; also we're both upset about Frédéric and Charlotte. I think your hormones are playing numerous games.

How do you feel now?" he asked obviously concerned.

"Much better" I replied smiling "but would still prefer some explanation about your French mistress."

"OK" came the reply "perhaps I should start at the beginning."

"When I was sixteen Papa introduced me to a 'teacher' in Paris, well educated and highly professional. We shared many lessons together adapted by her according to each pupil's predilections."

I stared at Gildas as the message registered.

"After that experience I forgot these teenage fumblings at parties. I enjoyed two relationships, one at nineteen and the other at twenty two, both lasting nearly twelve months and finishing amicably. Then, as I've explained, Isabella and I married meeting again after a teenage romance, making a commitment to each other for all the wrong reasons; then the disaster. When I was widowed, during that period I had one other relationship" he paused "best forgotten".

"But where in all this is your other girlfriend? I don't understand" I asked trying to absorb the facts and these women in Gildas' life about whom I had been ignorant.

"The 'other girlfriend' was Amélie Bayard: a member of the Château committee certainly but never a lover of mine. I don't know how Elisée and Frédéric made that assumption."

"Well, what exactly was your relationship? Don't tell me you were 'just good friends'!" I replied incredulously.

Gildas walked over to one of the bookcases, touching those leather bound volumes in an affectionate manner and then turning back to me gave his response:

"Actually yes."

I stared at him "Gildas, your brother and sister didn't believe that, tell me why I should."

"Because they believed some idle gossip. From me you'll receive the truth."

"Amélie was widowed, the wife of a close friend of my parents. Anticipating your reaction I can confirm she was much younger than him, over 20 years difference in age.

Most people thought she had married him for financial gains. In fact that was erroneous. Although never disclosing anything publicly she was independently wealthy from a family trust. Their relationship was a veritable love affair.

After her husband's death she made a substantial contribution to various charities and those châteaux ineligible for French government support."

I was stunned.

"But why didn't she disclose those donations, her financial independence and also why did you have contact with her which inferred, at least to Frédéric and Elisée, you were very close?"

"Amélie was in a different class: above innuendo and gossip. I think the speculations amused her. As for our relationship I found her highly intelligent, with a droll humour and formidable personality. Actually you and she have a lot in common except I never found out if she and I shared our sexual rapport!"

I picked up the cushion at my side but before I could throw it at him Gildas grabbed it from me.

It was the beginning of another adventurous evening!

Chapter Twenty-Three

The Château Ball loomed in September and the vulnerability I had sensed the previous month re-emerged with a vengeance.

During my visits to de Veres for business discussions and conferences I had also seen Marie-Françoise at D'Aquin about my gown for this year's Ball. We had agreed black was inappropriate a colour associated with elegance – not my mode this year!

White was just too obvious, emphasise my girth and the triumphant violet of the previous year was not an option. Therefore we decided on my favourite jade: it was a Grecian design, bodice in Belgian lace caught under the bust with a voluminous chiffon skirt predominantly in the selected jade but dropping in folds of turquoise and aquamarine.

The day before we left for Paris to stay at Montparnasse overnight, as usual on the evening of the Ball, I dressed myself up to show Gildas.

"What do you think?" I asked turning round.

Looking up from his paperwork in the library after dinner he replied:

"It's lovely Chérie" without much enthusiasm.

I felt deflated, especially as I was aware that in recent days he had seemed distracted, not his usual self.

Doubts began to invade my mind, increasing my vulnerability. Words and remarks from the past. For example from Sabine.

"With his stature, wealth and looks, women must fall at his feet."

And Marie-Françoise "Gildas du Gilbert, the enigmatic dream of all my contemporaries."

Perhaps now he was growing tired of me, the sexual attraction fading ; my body in its pregnant state unattractive, the love affair a tenuous one for him not the depth of mine. Suddenly I felt very uneasy. The answers to these questions were received at that Château Ball.

To my surprise Gildas had arranged for us to arrive in our car at the rear entrance of the venue.

"I didn't think you'd want to be exposed to the glare of the press flashlights" he said registering my reaction.

I now became concerned about his reasons, a sense of disquiet. However Gildas seemed almost relaxed when we installed ourselves at our table to be joined by various members of the du Gilbert family plus Donald and Shona.

They were ecstatic having phoned us earlier in the month with the news that Shona's pregnancy had been confirmed.

"We're so excited, Caterine, only problem morning sickness. Have you a cure?" she asked me smiling, eyes sparkling.

"Well Maman recommended a brand of herbal tea but I'm not sure which one. Strangely I never suffered from that common pregnancy symptom. Give her a phone, Shona, and she'll tell you her elixir!"

Before the buffet was announced I was standing with Gildas, Elisée and some of their Parisian friends near the entrance foyer. It was an animated group, some of them not well known to me.

Suddenly Elisée gasped, a look of horror on her face.

Startled I followed her gaze to see Johnny Roxford, heir

to that British dukedom and a valued client of mine at de Veres, with an elegant blonde companion. Instinctively I turned to Gildas on my other side and was shocked at his expression.

"Gildas, Caterine" Johnny hailed us hurrying over hand in hand with his partner "how are you both? May I introduce…"

A low transatlantic drawl interrupted him.

"Don't waste your breath, Johnny, the Count and I have already met under very unpleasant circumstances."

Silence prevailed. All conversation ceased as she stood centre stage; exceptionally beautiful in a shimmering white silk gown displaying a deep décolleté, her honey coloured hair was swept up into a classic chignon.

Large feline tawny eyes stared at those sea green ones.

I was ignored totally and Gildas' expression had become impassive. Johnny grasped the situation instantly.

"Well, let's all have a memorable evening" he said with an ironic grin sweeping his companion away.

Typically everyone started talking at once to cover up the embarrassment. Taking my hand Gildas said:

"Darling, let's dance" and ushered me onto the floor. Fortunately it was a waltz allowing me to move slowly if not with much dignity.

I knew of course, as I remembered his words "when I was widowed I had a relationship best forgotten". She was the one.

When we returned to Montparnasse it was nearly 2 am.

After that confrontation and Gildas' recent distracted air I had decided to take action, fight my corner and in this match find out the score.

"You must be very tired Chérie. We should have returned earlier but you insisted on remaining. Why?"

"Several reasons Gildas, but first of all tell me about her."

"Yes" he nodded "that request is no surprise."

He opened Maman's cabinet and poured himself a large cognac. At the water he offered me I shook my head.

I waited as he collected his thoughts.

"Her name is Francesca Rawlings and she's a concert violinist, highly talented. She and Elisée were students at the Conservatoire in Paris. We were together for nearly 12 months during which period she sacrificed a part of her career so we could spend more time with each other. Then I asked her to marry me and she accepted."

My fears realised I sank back on the sofa in emotional pain. I had been right. He was still in love with her and she rejected him. My temples started throbbing and that compartment of my locked mind suffered a physical blow attempting to prise the doors open; but the bolt and padlock held.

Standing now at the windows of the Montparnasse apartment Gildas drew the new chintz drapes.

Sighing, he continued as I sat like someone becalmed, isolated, filled with trepidation for what lay ahead.

"We were never officially engaged. Forty eight hours later I withdrew that proposal of marriage; a gesture of which I'm not proud. I should never have asked her to marry me. It was said in a moment of extreme" he stopped and I could imagine exactly what kind of moment that might have been.

Nevertheless I was stunned, trying to absorb the facts, realising to my massive relief that I'd been wrong.

"But Gildas, what did you say to her, the reason for your change of mind?" I stuttered.

"I told her the truth. Brutal maybe at the time but I could only be honest" Gildas hesitated and turned to look at me.

"I told Francesca that it would be dishonourable of me to enter into marriage with her when I knew I was still in love with another woman. Of course she was unaware at that time who that woman was. She won't be now."

"My God" I exclaimed "I got it so wrong this evening. I thought you were still in love with her."

Gildas stared at me, "What the Hell do you mean by that remark?"

"Well, your expression, the one on your face when you saw her with Johnny. It was wracked with emotional disturbance."

"That wasn't love. It was hate. I detest that guttersnipe. She's venomous. Attempted to destroy the du Gilbert family name."

"How?" I almost whispered the word rarely having seen Gildas so enraged.

"Francesca decided to wreak her revenge; her social circle in the musical domain were told her version of events which passed into general circulation in Paris. Her tale was that I had withdrawn my proposal of marriage after discovering her antecedents were coloured, from Martinique."

I gasped "But she's American surely?"

"Her father certainly but her mother French. I can assure you she has no connection to Martinique even through her maternal line. It was a blatant lie. A poisonous tale to discredit my family line. You know the du Gilbert motto, written of course in old French but translated states: 'Morality prevails creating equality'."

I was reared to respect that honour as were our predecessors; no differentiation or prejudice between culture, colour or creed.

Chérie, I shouldn't dwell on the past and spoil our evening together."

"Gildas" I smiled "I posed the question."

"All right. Come on let me take my gorgeous wife to a very comfortable bed."

On December 15th our three babies arrived, two weeks early. I was lucky with a relatively short labour and the first two "popped out" within three minutes of each other – a boy and a girl: shouting out in protest at their abrupt removal from their sanctuary in the womb. They appeared most displeased, a healthy sign.

Baby number three was a different prospect: stubborn, preferring cocooned in that comfortable state. Why leave it to emerge into the unwelcome environment of an increasingly alien world?

Gildas still holding my hand as I struggled on said:

"Darling, everything looks fine, but it might be better to have a Caesarean now."

He kissed me in that familiar loving fashion on the forehead absorbing all the birthing sweat.

Looking back I cannot remember what caused it but it reminded me of our love making and my back arching our third baby, a second boy arrived in the world with even more protests than his older siblings. As it happened that marked his style all his life.

After Gildas and I held our three healthy children together in our arms it is impossible to describe our emotions. Even ecstatic is not enough.

The following weeks were mayhem but joyous ones; family visits and friends, congratulations galore and just afterwards in January to relax in a different family life. Now we had our own children to care for and contribute to the strong bond built with David, Alix, Elisée and Rodrigue.

Gildas and I had discussed various options and decisions made we set up a nursery in the upper West Wing of BeauRobert above our suite – divorced from guests' slumber but very accessible to us.

Agathe's niece we discovered was a qualified nanny with five years experience in the echelons of Parisian society. She wanted a change. A boyfriend in the village enhanced her desire to move!

Gustave found us a trainee nursery nurse.

Gildas and I felt very blessed with these arrangements. Just details had to be confirmed.

About six weeks after the birth of our instant family we sat down in the smaller salon just simply to relax and discuss future plans.

"Well" Gildas said smiling "the system's settled in, you and I feed the babies at breakfast time plus sorting out the nappy requirements. Patricia takes over for most of the day with the nursery maid and we repeat our performance in the evening. Seems to work!"

"It's brilliant. You've found it so easy to cope I must admit. I'm surprised and very appreciative of your efforts."

"Chérie, this is simple. As Gustave told me before your first scan I'm used to dealing with four legs – the admin is halved!"

"All right Einstein" I replied laughing "employ that brain and find the collective name for our family. We can't use the triplets that's commandeered by David and Alix."

Gildas hesitated then answered:

"As they arrived all at once, I think we should go up a degree – I suggest "the treble". OK!

Chapter Twenty-Four

At the end of that January before I returned to de Veres full time, Donald and Shona spent a weekend with us at BeauRobert. Usually we would have travelled to Scotland to see them but with 'the treble' that was not possible.

"They're just gorgeous. What can I say?" Shona repeated after Gildas and Donald left us alone in the nursery "and I just love their names"

"Do you? Why especially?"

"They're traditional, yet modern with an international identity. Guy, Gabriella, Géraud, all the Gs. By the way why was that?"

Shona turned round still standing by the cots.

"To save money changing the family logo!" I grinned.

"You're looking great Shona" I continued "is the baby due in April?"

"That's right. Donald's like a little boy running around in his organising mode: painting rooms at home that were in perfect condition, he's changed the nursery furniture layout twice and his Mum and Dad are being hounded about their arrival date in Scotland to coincide with the birth. It's a mad house!"

"Well Shona, that's just the reaction of an expectant father. It's we women who actually control events!"

After dinner of broccoli soup, sole in a herb cream sauce, salads and a choice of desserts, we sat down in the library for coffee.

"Heavens" Shona exclaimed "that meal's put on a few more pounds; which I can ill afford!"

Some banter began as usual.

"By the way Donald" Gildas asked "why did you take so long to achieve this pregnancy. That letter I gave you before you and Shona married laid out specific instructions for copulation. The advice which you requested from me."

Shona and I were suppressing our laughter.

Donald looked serious:

"You're right Gildas it would have occurred earlier but there were two problems."

Gildas waited eyebrow raised.

"One, I couldn't read your handwriting and two, the diagram was upside down!"

Just a few minutes later the convivial scenario changed. It was an incident glossed over at the time among true friends but which returned to haunt all of us a few months later.

"Gildas, I owe you a fiver on that bet over the wine."

"I'm not surprised I won with my connoisseur's knowledge" Gildas replied.

"Rubbish. Just damned good luck guessing the year!"

Donald pulled out his pocket book which looked as if it belonged to the dark ages.

"My God" Shona asked "where did that come from?"

"Darling, you know the one I received from Dad and Mum as a Christmas present's been returned, lining torn. Why they buy these designer labels I don't know, waste of money."

As Donald opened the wallet something else fell out. It was a photograph and it fell face up on the walnut table.

The photograph was of a woman on a beach.

The woman was naked.

The woman was me.

No one uttered a word. Donald picked up the photograph, turning it the face down.

"An interesting photograph of a beautiful woman with whom I had a love affair. Then we parted but remained close friends. She then married a man who also became my close friend. Then I met another beautiful woman, this time it became a love affair for life."

Donald stood up and handed the photograph to Gildas.

"It belongs to you."

He turned to Shona:

"Darling, it's time for bed."

After they left Gildas asked me:

"Is that the only one?"

"Yes" I swallowed nervously "it was taken on the Cameron's private beach in Barbados. We had been fooling around in the water …"

"Caterine, that doesn't interest me. It's the past. We're our future." As he took my hand we left the library and crossed the hall to our suite.

In early February I was back in full harness with de Veres. The château contract was advancing well. Naturally there had been a few hiccups, two legal disputes, albeit minor, but generally for a project of his magnitude relatively few commercial problems.

At the first board meeting I attended in March I notated on the minutes my personal project which I had discussed during that conference phone at the Château.

It was rejected but this time by a smaller margin.

Afterwards Albert spoke to me in his office.

"Caterine, why this obsession with a UK base and particularly in Scotland? We have a reliable agency through Montaigue Smyth a Fine Arts House you nearly joined as a graduate. They pay us a handsome commission for the items they handle for us."

"Handsome, rubbish. They're swindlers, with extortionate gains. We're the losers on profitability for the items that pass through Montaigue Smyth's agency in London."

Albert stared at me.

"But commerce is based around profit. It's the business world. What's changed with Montaigue Smyth even if they're taking too high margins?"

"Albert, in my opinion de Veres should establish a UK office with headquarters in Edinburgh. The detailed analysis for this is contained in my report. With careful planning and shrewd investment I am confident we can become a major UK player and destroy those bastards."

"That's strong language from you, Caterine" he replied taken aback.

"When you see what I've written, I'm sure you will concur with my proposals!"

April began with a flourish, the gardens' floral displays showing earlier than usual promise.

Gildas's commitments were more onerous than ever particularly with the main project to film that classical novel at St Roche Rivière.

The 'treble' were thriving under strict supervision from Nanny Patricia and utterly spoiled by Gildas and me when she was absent!

I remember the date exactly when we received that call. April 16th 2000. Returning from the garden I was arranging some flowers in the smaller salon. Another bunch lay in the kitchen to give to Yvette for her house.

Hearing Gildas' voice on his study phone I glanced at my watch. It was exactly mid-day.

That call confirmed that Donald and Shona's baby had arrived on time – a boy, born dead.

A distressed Duncan Cameron had phoned Gildas.

"There was no warning. That perfect little fellow never drew breath. They're distraught."

The following morning neither of us could make a decision. What should we do? As I stared at my reflexion in the bathroom I was horrified to see large blobs of mascara all over my face stained from last night's tears as Gildas and I had clung together again as our initial reaction of numbness then shock translated into emotional reality at that tragic news, when we were unable to sleep.

"What the Hell" I said to myself as I scrubbed off the mess "how can I justify such inane vanity when our closest friends have just lost their precious longed for baby."

Even more poignant was the fact that Shona had always teased me when we were teenagers.

"Heavens, Caterine. Unlike every other woman in our 'crowd' you don't experiment with make-up but perhaps just a stick of mascara to emphasise those long fair lashes in your right hand pocket?"

After much discussion Gildas and I decided to write.

"Normally, after a death a chore I loathe" Gildas muttered pacing his study that same morning "but at the moment the other choices are not options."

The letter was brief.

Dear Donald,

We care as your dearest friends.

A phone call was too impersonal and to have flown over would have intruded on your privacy and your grief.

We are here for both of you at any time when you need us.

To you and Shona our love.

Gildas and Caterine

Neither of us expected a response. The only healer was time: but three weeks later there was a major development.

"Mr Cameron" Felix announced as Donald appeared almost staggering into the library where we were seated with our aperitifs before dinner.

"Donald" both of us cried out.

"Merde, what's wrong?" Gildas exclaimed striding over to catch him as he stumbled.

"Caterine" he turned to me "a large brandy."

My hand shaking I managed to fill one of the goblets.

Donald looked awful: he must have lost at least 6 kilos from his lean 5'10" frame.

I came over with the brandy, placed it on the table and attempted to embrace him.

"Don't touch me, Caterine" he shouted "don't dare touch me."

Shocked, bewildered, I stepped back.

"Donald, sit down and let's talk." Gildas said helping him onto the sofa.

I made the only decision I could, I left the room.

I must have been dozing and woke with a start hearing Gildas' voice.

"Come on Chérie, that sofa's not comfortable, it's bedtime."

"But what happened?" I asked. "What's wrong?"

"Nothing that can't be solved. Let's wait till morning."

He picked me up and carried me to our room.

At breakfast I drank my coffee but toyed with my croissant.

"Caterine, you have to eat, no dinner because of the circumstances and now no breakfast."

"But I don't understand why you won't tell me" I replied "we're so close."

"Donald himself must tell you his reason for coming here. It's his catharsis."

He came to the smaller salon just before 10 o'clock. I felt

nervous and very apprehensive but he walked over and embraced me holding me for several moments saying

"I'm appalled at my reaction to you last night. Please sit down and I'll try to explain."

"To put the facts into logical terms I'm faced with the ordeal of two deaths – the loss of our baby son, physically and that of my wife, mentally."

I found at first I could not reply.

Donald stood up walking over to the south facing window with its view of the lake.

In an act of irony the swans were revelling in the mild April temperatures, baby cygnets in tow.

"Is Shona in a depression? That's understandable but with your support she'll recover. The experience you both suffered is horrendous, unimaginable."

Donald turning from that scene of family harmony interrupted me:

"Caterine, Shona is in emotional purgatory. She believes I'm still in love with you."

I stared at this man, my university professor, my mentor who became my mate steering me on the career path I craved. A path I needed to ascend to atone for responsibility I felt for Papa's death; then my lover but ended years ago.

"But that's not true" I began as Donald held up his hand in that familiar gesture of student days when every lecture class was immediately silenced.

"Yes and no". He responded "Gildas saw it in Barbados when you spent that weekend during your honeymoon and Shona thought the same although she never told me."

Remembering Gildas' words to me on the BA777 flight back from Barbados I stayed silent in turmoil and trepidation of what his next words would be.

"Both were right in one aspect but wrong in another. It's ironic that the visit you and Gildas made to Barbados was the defining moment when I severed those ties to you. Of course we loved each other during the two years we spent together and we may have married if you had not decided against it. Actually you made the right decision albeit the one I had anticipated."

"I don't quite understand what you mean" I replied.

"Actually it's quite simple but then in emotional trauma everything becomes complicated. On reflection now I was in love with an image, a painting in my mind which I strove to recreate and present in triumph to the Fine Arts world. That's why I chose de Veres for you: a young house gaining in reputation whose merit was recognised by rapid promotion, disregarding age."

"What can I do Donald to help you convince Shona it's all untrue?"

"Gildas and I discussed it until late last night as you know. Time will help. The loss of the little fellow" he stopped eyes closed for a moment memories revived

"Caterine, drastic as it sounds I think you and Gildas must banish yourselves from our lives."

With great sadness that is exactly what we did at Donald's request.

As it happened Maman was staying with us the following week. After I told her about recent events she answered:

"Give them time, Petite, to find their peace again together. I'm sure they will."

Late spring moved to summer. The 'treble' were more demanding than ever and almost a comedy with their antics in the nursery. Although only six months old Gildas and I concluded they had a radar communication to keep everyone guessing. This was particularly significant in the nursery.

As usual Gildas and I attended to that early feed and then changed the nappies. Nanny Patricia albeit in her late twenties had insisted on using the non disposable variety "much better for the environment and easily washable" she had informed me. I concurred.

However, after six months of coping with three babies she found herself in difficulties. Suddenly Gildas and I discovered to our amusement a charge for one of the major brands of disposable nappies appeared on the nursery accounts. Patricia came to see me.

"As you know Madame we've checked with Doctor Rimbaud and the babies are fine. It's just" she hesitated "their spasmodic bowel movements cannot be timed. It's playing havoc with the laundry arrangements."

"No problem Patricia" I replied "You organise the nappy purchases according to your requirements" turning away to hide a smile.

Gildas burst out laughing when I told him. We were sitting in the smaller salon together, our two Weimaraner puppies, Jaeger and Fuerstin, as we named them dozing in contentment at our feet.

Our four cats, the two Persians and two tabbies were ensconced on the opposite sofa each in their individual beds. As it happened that sofa was from Louis XV epoch and in claret velour. Definitely superior feline mode!

Chapter Twenty-Five

Despite our good fortune with the treble the remaining part of the year manifested itself in various degrees of family crises.

At the end of June Uncle Fergus phoned us with the sad news. Aunt Bebe had died suddenly from a stroke.

"Thank God there was no suffering. It was very quick."

"I've spoken to Véronique and David's called. Both insist they're flying out for the funeral service. I've told them it's too long a journey." His voice broke and I handed the receiver to Gildas, better this conversation now man to man.

So it was decided. David and Maman flew out to Perth on a very sad journey to attend my aunt's funeral.

Maman called me two days after the service.

"I'm staying on Petite, just for a short time. Catriona, your youngest cousin's unwell with a chest infection. The doctor's here now and suspects pleurisy but with antibiotics she'll be fine."

"Stay as long as you need to, Maman. How's uncle Fergus?"

"Bearing up" Maman replied "but who knows what's in the mind. And he's very concerned now for Catriona with her medical finals only a few months away. At least if I prolong my visit I can give both of them support."

"All right" I replied "Love from all of us."

The following morning Gildas handed me an envelope.

"What's this?" I asked.

"Perhaps open it and you might find out."

"Martinique, our honeymoon location" I gasped, then the dates registered.

"But that's in two weeks time. I'm not organised and the babies, we can't leave them."

"Caterine, they're in very good hands here and Elisée is coming to stay to reassure you. She insisted. There's only one problem."

"What's that?" I asked alarmed.

Nanny Patricia will have two other youngsters to contend with but at least not requiring disposable nappies!"

What a special two weeks that was, reminiscent of our honeymoon and just as sexy!

On our final evening we dined at the restaurant we had always favoured, smaller than the other two, less ostentatious, Gildas raised his champagne glass.

"A toast to us and the treble."

We touched glasses. Santé!

Little did we realise the miseries to follow.

"Well" Albert said "I've read your report, actually several times. It's devastating. Where on earth did you receive all this information?"

"A colleague of mine from university. He joined Montague Smyth six months ago, after working in the US since graduating."

I was seated with Albert in my Paris suite of offices the week after returning from Martinique.

Clutching his cup of coffee which I had prepared for him he stood up.

"This information warrants a criminal investigation."

"Correct" I answered.

Albert, coffee cup in hand paced my lounge area.

"But who's going to investigate it?"

I replied "What about you?"

"Are you mad Caterine?" Albert stopped abruptly "It could cost me de Veres. No I won't risk it, absolutely not!"

"If you won you'd inherit their client base and our UK headquarters would be secure, flooded with business demands, clients clamouring for services."

Albert raised his voice.

"I repeat, Caterine, absolutely not. What's happened to your commercial judgement which I've always relied on? You must have been affected by the sun in Martinique" he muttered about to leave.

"No, Albert, I've been affected by this further information in my pocket."

In a gesture similar to Gildas one month ago I handed the managing director of de Veres an envelope.

Our subsequent discussions lasted a further hour.

The Château Ball held as usual that month proved to be a less dramatic event then the two previous years and passed without incident.

Maman spent a week with us at BeauRobert at the beginning of October and we received the latest news about our Australian cousins.

"How's Uncle Fergus now?" I asked her as we sat on the terrace in the walled garden.

"Better but still in sorrow, as you and I understand too well.

"That's great news about Catriona passing her exams" I said. "I'm sure you were an instrumental part of it staying on for over two months. Uncle Fergus must have been very grateful."

"He was and Catriona but I didn't do anything special, just some emotional support and an extra pair of hands. Like Papa he's not very practical domestically, couldn't boil an egg." She grinned. "But he can now, even graduated to a passable version of my seafood casserole."

"Heavens" I replied "he'll soon be conducting cookery classes on Australian TV."

"I can't believe how Guy, Gabriella and Géraud have grown since I last saw them in June, it's incredible!"

I laughed "you're right Maman, according to average statistics for weight and length they're off the scale, but as you know, both the du Gilberts and Sinclairs family members are tall. The treble will inherit that gene, I'm sure."

Suddenly Maman changed the subject.

"How's Shona? Any contact from her or Donald?"

I stood up not wanting her to see my distress and walked to the end of the terrace.

"Donald phones Gildas from time to time" I hesitated "but from Shona nothing."

"That's sad, very sad for all of you. Let's hope time will employ its substantial powers to heal the breach."

The following few weeks were hectic, conferences at St Roche Rivière, plans for a family reunion at Christmas, the Château Contract on-going and a crucial meeting with Albert de Vere.

We met in his suite in mid-November at 10.00 am.

It was a Friday morning and I had spent that week at the Paris headquarters although having no contact with Albert as he was in London for a Fine Arts conference.

"Well, Sabine" I smiled at my protégée and now friend "thanks again for coping so brilliantly here while I've been indulging myself in motherhood at BeauRobert."

"That's nonsense, Caterine, you don't indulge in anything for yourself and babies are hard work. Phew triplets! I couldn't believe it when you told me!"

"I'm very blessed with all the help I have. Fortunate to be able to afford it."

We were seated in the lounge area of my office, coffee on the table. As our work had started at 7 am and it was now 9.30 I considered we needed a break.

"How's Antoine and his veterinary studies?"

"Brilliant Caterine. He's loving every minute of it and very happy, passing everything with flying colours."

"Actually" she looked embarrassed "Maman and I heard from him yesterday. He has been chosen for the French national team at swimming. He wouldn't have had the opportunity unless Gildas had awarded him that scholarship with all its advantages plus membership of the Sports Complex."

"Sabine" I reminded her "your brother was awarded it by the university on merit. Gildas just presented it to him!"

Sabine nodded smiling.

That was when the phone rang and Albert requested that meeting.

As I entered his offices I thought he looked tired, face pale, drawn, lacking its usual vibrancy.

"Albert" I announced before sitting down "you need a long weekend with Céline, probably without the children."

"Caterine, you must be psychic, I phoned Céline from London. We're off tomorrow for two weeks. We need time for ourselves. As for the youngsters."

I interrupted him

"No problem Albert. Call Céline and tell her Gildas and I will collect them tomorrow. We're staying overnight at Montparnasse this evening as Gildas has business in Paris. You both know they love BeauRobert and will be well cared for."

Albert stared at me "You're actually serious? With those triplets to cope with?"

"Of course" I replied surprised "I've lots of help and Gildas loves children. They're more than welcome. I was just saying to Sabine this morning that we are very fortunate to be able to afford the nursery staff."

"Caterine, even alone you could have coped financially. You must be one of the best paid Fine Arts directors in Europe and deserve it. Thank you from me and Céline in her absence for your offer to care for the children but grandparents whom we prevail on rarely have stepped into the breach!"

"I'm sorry Albert, presumptuous of me!"

"Nonsense Caterine, it just displays that character and attitude I recognised at your interview with me and confirmed by your progress after joining de Veres."

"What's that?" I asked bemused.

"Difficult to sum up" Albert paused

"On the upside: determination, dedication, high intelligence and outstanding talent. On the downside: raw ambition, a certain arrogance at times, unwilling to admit error and a wicked sense of humour which in certain company would fail to be appreciated. In other words an individual not lightly to be challenged. All of that I recognised during the interview and experienced during your career at de Veres. Finally on the inside: these elements I learned also as I came to know you better: a person with an uncanny rapport with and judgement of people whatever colour, culture or creed. Your staff hold you in high respect and would defend you even if you were in the wrong. A woman of integrity, generous of spirit, with a heart of gold."

There was silence as I stared at Albert stunned, dumbfounded.

"Mon Dieu, Caterine, I've rendered you speechless – unique."

"I'm not sure how to respond" I stuttered sinking now into the sofa.

Then my humour reasserted itself.

"You forgot to mention my temper!" I smiled

"No, I didn't" he replied "but you've never allowed it to manifest itself in your commercial dealings. I assume Gildas copes with it. God help him, although he seems to be surviving well!"

"Finally, and the reason I asked for this meeting is because at the Fine Arts conference I heard rumours, about Montague Smyth's activities. I consulted my closest colleagues in the Art World and as your report inferred embezzlement could be a charge imposed on them, Evidence however is slim and who would take action against such a major institution of such stature. Let me ask you a question."

"Yes," I replied, "what is it?"

"Can you guarantee your university colleague will stand by these statements in a court of law?"

"That answer must come from him."

"All right! This challenge must wait a little longer. I'm going to enjoy my holiday.

Chapter Twenty-Six

Christmas was a marvellous family reunion. Maman, David, Alix and the triplets, Rodrigue, Elisée plus their two children and ourselves with our 'treble' who had celebrated their combined first birthdays earlier on 15th December. That had been a low key affair at our request, Gildas and I had agreed that Christmas was the most appropriate time for everyone to visit BeauRobert if they wished.

"It's the holiday time, unburdened by commitments" Gildas grinned "if everyone agrees we'll offer purgatory here. All hands on deck!"

Actually the system worked well with much hilarity.

Everyone 'mucked in' and the 'treble' incredibly well behaved.

The only person missing from the Christmas celebration was Frédéric who was holidaying in the Caribbean.

"I hope you don't mind" he had told Gildas.

"Of course not. You're a free spirit. Enjoy yourself."

How ironic those words became.

On 2nd January, after celebrating New Year at a party in the village, life returned to some normality.

I discussed the domestic duties with Agathe and Yvette

while Gildas talked to Felix and the other staff members.

"I suggested he cut back and I'd employ someone to 'understudy', Felix was shocked, even angry."

"May I ask Monsieur le Comte if my standards have fallen in recent months? To my knowledge they have not."

"That was his response, chin up, back like ramrod, face expressionless." Gildas laughed as he repeated their conversation.

"So Felix is re-installed as head of staff with a generous rise! My father was right. He told me 'don't ever underestimate Felix. He's a force to be reckoned with.' It's all those years with the du Gilberts!"

Just before midday I was passing Gildas' study when I heard his phone ring and then his welcoming tones.

"And a Happy New Year to you too, young brother, now how's Barbados and your news?"

It was Frédéric, obviously. I smiled to myself: a super holiday I was certain. After all he was young, single and very attractive.

Picking up a magazine in the smaller salon I waited for Gildas' call to offer my season's greeting to Frédéric. It never arrived.

When Gildas appeared his face was ashen, expression grim.

"What's wrong?" I gasped standing up "is Frédéric ill?" I remember stuttering.

"No, Caterine, my brother's in excellent health. In fact, he's just got himself married."

I was relieved.

"That's a surprise but not bad news. Who is she?"

"You're right in that it's not bad news. It's disastrous. Frédéric has just married Francesca and she's pregnant."

Rodrigue and Elisée arrived later that afternoon. On receiving Gildas' call they had dropped everything, bundled the children into their estate car, with a hurriedly packed suitcase.

When Elisée saw Gildas in the library she ran over breaking into tears.

"It's my fault. You wanted to tell Frédéric about Francesca, the history, and I dissuaded you."

"My dearest sister, that's nonsense, it was a joint decision. Frédéric was spending a year in Australia at that time on his gynaecological course. There was no need to alert him to my relationship with her" Gildas replied still enfolding a distraught Elisée in his arms.

Rodrigue stared at me shaking his head visibly distressed.

"But she does not love Frédéric. It's her revenge on you."

"Yes, Elisée. I suppose it is. And she's been clever. Told our brother that I took her out 'a few times'. How she knows the du Gilbert family, even met Caterine at the Château Ball."

There was combined silence, as the implications permeated.

"Come on, we need some fresh air" Gildas announced 'let's stretch our legs and sharpen our minds!"

During that walk Elisée gave me the background to Francesca as the men stopped at the stables.

"I thought we were friends at the Conservatoire but it was a ruse to meet Gildas. Naturally I invited her to Saint Roche Rivière on several occasions. Her reaction to Gildas, unlike my other friends, was cool even distant. I realise now it was deliberate. Then she sent me tickets for her debut concert. You know she's a classical violinist?"

I nodded.

"And brilliant, Caterine, skipped 12 months at college."

"I don't recognise her name" I replied "that surprises me."

"Her career is based in the US, she rarely performs in Europe."

"Well" Elisée continued "after attending that debut concert

Gildas asked her to have dinner with him. That's where she was exceptionally cunning. She turned him down."

"I see, alert his curiosity."

"Exactly. I mean I know he's my brother and I'm prejudiced, but he is very attractive and good fun even without all this" Elisée replied gesturing to the estate. "But, Caterine" she added hastily "he's never been conceited, quite the opposite. In fact I don't think Gildas realises how attractive women find him. Why, nearly all my friends were crazy about him." She stopped staring at me in horror "Mon Dieu, Caterine, I shouldn't be saying this to you. You're his wife!"

Her expression lightened the atmosphere and I laughed.

"It would appear I'm the lucky one, landed the jackpot."

Elisée, expression still serious, answered:

"No, you both did."

We wandered along in silence for a while, then heard the horses. Gildas and Rodrigue trotted past us.

"We thought we needed more strenuous exercise, see you in an hour." Gildas called as the horses broke into a canter and disappeared from view.

Dinner that evening could have been a disaster for Agathe, as our first courses remained untouched.

Gildas then took charge.

"Right, it's time for action. I have a plan but revealed only after dinner's eaten. None of us was reared to waste food, especially when millions in the world are starving. Bon appétit!"

The message was well received, we responded accordingly.

The weekend following all of us gathered again at BeauRobert. It was 'déjà vu' but the atmosphere was different with the plan in place.

"I don't know if I can go through with this" Elisée muttered nervously "I'm no actress."

"None of us are, Chérie" Rodrigue replied putting his arm

round her should but Gildas is right, she must not triumph."

As Elisée nodded we heard the car arrive.

"Frédéric, Francesca, our hearty congratulations" Gildas said striding over to greet them.

Francesca was, as I remembered, classically beautiful, coolly elegant, the natural blonde hair swept up in her traditional chignon.

She was wearing a vermillion coat-dress edged in navy, tied at the neck with a silk bow in the same colour of blue. Signs of pregnancy were not as yet evident.

"Well, thanks to my family, no introductions necessary for Francesca" Frédéric replied grinning. He looked bronzed and happy. My heart sobbed for him.

"Just one" Gildas interrupted.

"Francesca, you've not been introduced to my wife."

Frédéric turned in surprise.

"But I thought, chérie, you met at the Château Ball."

"Only from a distance" Gildas replied.

"Francesca, it gives me great pleasure to present Caterine."

It is unbelievable that you can embrace someone but not touch. That is exactly what happened.

Those feline tawny eyes flickered over me with contempt, even disdain.

It was war. We both knew it.

I retaliated with what I hoped was a gracious smile and said:

"Gildas and I are delighted to welcome you to our home, BeauRobert."

Lunch was a masterpiece of acting perfection. We had all rehearsed our parts and delivered that performance.

Rodrigue, after Gildas'lead, was the star of our supporting cast, keeping Francesca entertained.

"I've only met her infrequently at Saint Roche. It's easier for me than Elisée." He had told Gildas when he had outlined his plan.

"We must treat her as if the past doesn't exist. Take her by surprise and leave Frédéric in ignorance and peace. She shall not triumph." Gildas had declared "it's vital."

Over coffee Frédéric described their plans.

"As you know I take up my obstetrics consultancy at Boston General at the beginning of February. We're driving to Fontainebleau later this afternoon to spend a few days with Francesca's mother, then to Paris at my apartment. We're letting it initially for my first year in the US and then decide on future plans. The tenancy's in place.

That means we arrive in Boston mid-January."

"Where are you staying initially?" Gildas asked.

"That's where we're fortunate. The hospital's providing us with accommodation, albeit temporary until we can find a house. They've been very generous in the details of the contract."

During Frédéric's remarks I had watched Francesca again as I had studied her during lunch. They had been exceptionally attentive to each other and she almost seemed to flirt with him; albeit cool with us, she laughed at Frédéric's comments, touching his hand occasionally, once or twice whispering in his ear.

"My God, Frédéric" I thought "you're out of your depth."

At last at 5 pm they left for the two hour drive to Fontainebleau. Farewells said and after a final wave of hands from the BeauRobert portails, Gildas, Elisée, Rodrigue and me returned to sit this time in the smaller salon, the cats and dogs joining us as almost simultaneously we sank into the sofas.

Gildas spoke first.

"My thanks to all of you – brilliant efforts. I know Francesca very well (I winced and then discarded my thoughts about their intimacy). It is the first time I've seen her unnerved, disconcerted; although it saddens me that my brother's wife had to receive such treatment from the du Gilbert family."

There was silence as Gildas walked towards those darkening shadows descending in early January from his favourite window with its view of the lake.

"Let's hope their new life in the United States brings them happiness and for all of us peace."

In many ways his words were fortuitous, although Gildas was unaware of them at the time.

The treble revelled in the garden where we had sectioned off a play area for them on the southern side. Gildas and I took much pride and pleasure in watching them all toddling around, full of their individual antics.

Guy being the eldest was rallying the troops. Gabriella, however, unknown to him we considered was actually in charge of the parade.

As for Géraud, he just stood in line, quietly smiling to himself; maybe he was the youngest but as the years proved, the wisest of them all.

One Friday in early summer Gildas collected me at St Pierre des Corps after I had worked at de Veres headquarters in Paris for that preceding week. I knew immediately on seeing that tense expression on his face that he had a business problem – it always manifested itself that way.

"What's wrong?" I asked as he relieved me of my briefcase and emergency overnight holdall, striding in his characteristic mode to the station car park more hurriedly than usual.

"I've an urgent meeting tonight at BeauRobert, I'll explain why en route."

"When is it?" I asked as Gildas swerved the car out of our reserved space and headed south."

"At 7.30 pm" Gildas replied.

I glanced at my watch: the time was 6.30 "Gildas, take the faster route via Loché sur Indrois. It saves 20 minutes at least, otherwise you'll be late which you know you'll hate. Especially as you've been reminding the staff recently about time-keeping."

"I don't like that road, always suffered delays on it."

"But that was years ago. It's much improved. I use it often. Turn off the route nationale at the next slip road" I reassured him.

Gildas followed my instructions and immediately we were cruising along the country roads at the standard 90 km/h with literally no traffic.

"So why this hasty meeting and at BeauRobert, that's not usual. Normally they're held at Saint Roche's offices."

Gildas, after checking the rear mirror answered:

"That young manager, appointed a month ago is an imbecile. He wrote out a cheque for some minor work to a building company of whom I don't approve – charlatans. It's on record not to use them."

"Left now, Chéri, you know the route" I interrupted.

"Yes" Gildas replied "you were right glancing at the car clock. It's quicker and much less traffic."

"Well, this idiot employed by St Roche Rivière Estates sent a cheque to that construction company for 50.000 Euros not the 5.000 Euros they were due, of course the cheque's been cashed."

I gasped "but the bank has instructions, over a set sum to verify with your offices."

"Unfortunately Francis was on holiday. His temporary replacement told me and I quote

'With respect Count du Gilbert you're wrong, there are no instructions, from experience I have often found that individuals of your background are not well informed on matters of finance.'

"May I ask what your background is?" I replied to him

"Naturally, I have an honours degree in banking and accountancy from Bordeaux University."

I swallowed "What was your response?"

"Let me tell you that whoever paid your fees wasted their

money. You should have joined the incompetency faculty. All accounts of Saint Roche Riviere Estates at this branch are closed forthwith. You will receive written confirmation within the hour."

It was at that point we both saw it as Gildas swung his coupé to the left and the shortcut through the forest –diversion!

"Bloody Hell, Caterine, I knew this idea was madness. I seem to be dealing with idiots this week!"

I retaliated of course and words ensued. The rest of the journey was continued in silence.

Though Gildas made a call to BeauRobert it meant he was late for his meeting by nearly 40 minutes.

That evening, after giving the children a late supper myself, much to nanny Patricia's disapproval at their altered bedtime, I retired to our suite and cooked a toasted snack. Gildas was still ensconced in his meeting at 10 pm.

Unusually for me I felt tired. After a hot shower I went to bed and a fitful sleep.

When I awoke at 6 am, Gildas had already left for St Roche. There was a hastily scrawled note on that white starched family notepaper. It surprised me.

"Sorry chérie I was so late last night and ill humoured earlier. I'm taking you out to dinner tonight, at 9 pm."

Smiling I kissed the notepaper and prepared my breakfast.

As always the dinner was exceptional.

"Let's have our brandies at home" Gildas suggested.

"Agreed" I replied.

On entering the smaller salon I noticed a large jade box on the walnut armoire.

"What's that?" I asked Gildas as he poured out our cognacs.

He glanced over, looking surprised after handing me my glass, then he walked over and picked up the box.

"Heavens, I'd forgotten. A small present for my beautiful accomplished wife and mother of my three children. Please open it. I trust you'll approve."

"This is one of your jokes" I grinned "it's probably full of those empty boxes in decreasing sizes you gave to Rodrigue on his last birthday. The one he told you he did not want to celebrate!"

Still smiling I lifted the lid and stared at the contents in total shock, recognising them instantly.

"Gildas!" I stuttered eventually. "These were in the de Veres auction. Sold to a telephone bidder, overseas, name undisclosed. Paid a king's ransom!"

"Correction, chérie, a queen's ransom, for you."

Inside that jade box was an exquisite suite of emerald and diamond jewellery – necklace, bracelet and earrings, belonging originally to the royal family of France and of course a perfect match for my engagement ring.

Still stunned I stared up at my husband.

"You're worried about what I paid, am I right?"

I nodded overwhelmed.

"Well, let me explain the history. Several years ago Papa and Maman attended the Château Ball as normal, staying with close friends in Paris. On the following day when they went out, the apartment was raided and the safe's contents including my mother's jewellery, diamonds, sapphires, family heirlooms taken. The gems were never recovered. Papa received the insurance compensation.

As the paperwork was concluded just two weeks before their plane accident the jewellery was never replaced. Consequently, the funds, invested in a UK property portfolio to which I have contributed, appreciated handsomely."

"To this value?" I asked astonished.

"Even more" Gildas replied grinning "but don't worry the portfolio's still in place. I sold one apartment in central London and for the balance made a personal donation. From contacts I heard this jewellery was coming up for sale and I asked Albert to make enquiries. With his business acumen he ensured de

Veres handled that transaction. No doubt I've just paid him, and actually you, a handsome commission!"

"What can I say? How can I thank you for the magnificence of a gift like this?"

"First of all, cancel those tears and secondly wear the emeralds tonight."

"Tonight! You mean put them on now?" I asked.

"No, chérie, later and I'll dress you in them when you enter our bedroom after your shower, without your peignoir!"

As it happened we found we had to make some interesting adjustments to our love making to accommodate the gems.

On the following day, after lunch, Gildas received a phone call from the bank manager, Francis.

"He's back from holiday this morning and requested a meeting, today if possible."

"Have you agreed?" I enquired just returned from the nursery and a hectic hour.

"Yes, as a courtesy to him. I confirmed 3 pm but I'm not changing my mind." Gildas replied walking over to the window in his study overlooking the garden.

There was a significant silence.

"Gildas, I rarely criticise your judgement but on this occasion I think you're wrong."

"Why?" turning towards me.

"You have accounts for your various enterprises with all the major French banks, mostly at head offices in Paris. This account in our local town is minor and with a private bank which, after deliberation, you personally patronised. I remember your words when Francis contacted you for that first meeting. 'I'm impressed. He's young and innovative, the board he's established deserve a chance and like Papa's custom I want to encourage local investment.' Agreed you'll have a court case, time consuming but you will win, evidence concrete and undisputed, costs awarded. Francis was not guilty, absent on holiday, his first with his wife and children in three years. I have met them often at the local market.

The temporary who replaced him insulted you certainly, a fool, but he'll be replaced and lessons learned.

I liked Francis and his wife. Please re-consider your decision."

"From you, Caterine, sentiment in business" Gildas regarded me eyebrow raised.

"To me, on this occasion, it's not sentiment but a matter of conscience. Many other businesses and commerce in the region were sceptical when they established that private bank. Your patronage paved the way, they were flooded with new accounts. If you remove yours the sheep will follow. I, however, will not be one of them, my account will stay."

Gildas changed his mind!

Chapter Twenty-Seven

In early summer, all was peaceful. The treble were healthy, happy, giving Gildas and me joy and pleasure as we monitored their progress, either cackling with laughter or growling in protest at each other's explorations in their adventure land.

Eighteen months old now – it seemed unbelievable. Most weekends were spent with haphazard outings round tracks on the BeauRobert estate, buggies in tow.

They still maintained their radar control, each demanding relief from their walking efforts on sturdy, rapidly expanding legs at measured intervals.

"This is ludicrous" Gildas gasped collecting Guy and Gabriella from a stumble into the forest, after some rabbits.

"No, it's not" I panted as I grasped Géraud on a similar mission. "They're playing games."

And so it continued all their lives.

"It's a girl" Frédéric announced to Gildas in his June phone call "no name as yet, we're still deciding. She's a healthy 8 lbs and Francesca's fine."

Gildas having taken the call, gave me the news.

"Well, Frédéric's happy that's the important aspect."

"Yes, you're right, my brother's overjoyed and I suppose we should share in that. I'll phone Elisée."

Two days later we received another phone call from Donald. This time I answered it.

"Shona's given birth to a girl. We're thrilled. Her name's Catriona and all's well."

"Brilliant" I replied "give them a kiss from both of us."

We sent a card with our love. It was acknowledged with a photograph of the baby but no call from Shona.

That upset me.

"There's no more you can do" Gildas told me "she's made her decision to walk away."

Later that day I went for a wander, alone in the grounds.

I can remember the date exactly, Saturday 30th June, when I received that urgent text message from Maman. Immediately I phoned her mobile.

"Caterine, Alexandra's seriously ill, meningitis. I'm in Jimmy Black's car en route to the airport. Should arrive in Zurich mid-afternoon. David and Alix are at her bedside at Zurich central hospital." Her voice faltered "it's the more serious strain". Before I could reply the connection went dead.

I ran out to the garden and told Gildas who was sitting with the children in their play area.

"What can we do? I feel helpless. God Almighty, she's only eleven."

"We can move." Gildas replied glancing at his watch.

"There's a private flight from Charles de Gaulle to Zurich, in three hours time, a business connection for the banks. Get Patricia here for the children while I try to book you on it. Then grab your overnight bag and I'll drive you to Paris."

Taking a taxi from Zurich airport to the hospital I found myself shaking.

"This is unacceptable" I told myself. "You're no help to anyone in this state."

Deep breathes followed and some emotional control.

The staff were extremely sympathetic and one of them accompanied me to Alexandra's room. Before I could enter, my brother emerged.

"Caterine, how did you get here?" He was ashen, distraught.

"Never mind that, how is she?"

"She's fighting for her life and she's losing."

I grabbed him as he fell into my arms.

It was a traumatic 48 hours but David was wrong. Alexandra won.

When she emerged from the coma, she was heavily sedated and confused. Her long corn coloured hair soaked from the sweat of the fever but those arresting grey eyes, though dull reflected new life.

"Where am I?" She mumbled. "Papa, Maman, what's happened?"

After David and Alix kissed her, Alix said.

"You've been ill chérie but you're going to be fine. Now try and take some rest."

Suddenly turning her head and recognising me, Alexandra asked:

"Aunt Caterine! Am I in Heaven?"

"No my dear niece, you're still in Zurich but Uncle Gildas and I want you to come and stay with us and all the family at BeauRobert, very soon."

"They nearly lost her. It was touch and go." I told Gildas when he collected me at St Pierre des Corps on the following Wednesday.

"I know chérie, after what you said on the phone I called Frédéric who told me the only chance to save her was that experimental drug. That's why the specialist persuaded David and Alix to try it."

"So, that's why the decision was taken so swiftly. How can

I thank you and Frédéric. Your actions saved her life."

"No Caterine, it was medical science. We just helped it along!"

I put my hand on his knee as he drove me home, tears in my eyes. How the gods had favoured me in finding a husband like Gildas.

August was a month of celebration and a family reunion at BeauRobert.

Alexandra was regaining her strength playing with the treble, young Angus and Julian joining in the fun.

Rodrigue and Elisée spent a long weekend with the children enjoying tennis on the renovated courts, water polo in the pool and rides on the horses in the estate grounds.

"We've been blessed" I said to Maman as David, Alix and Gildas helped us organise the picnic.

"Indeed we have" she replied finishing her glass of Chablis "or maybe not" looking alarmed pushing back her chair abruptly.

"What's wrong?" I asked in astonishment.

"I've forgotten my scones and I smell trouble."

Laughing together we ran to the kitchen. Fortunately it was not the burnt offering she had feared and heartily devoured by all the family with lashings of jam and cream.

The following months were demanding and rewarding as Gildas and I strapped ourselves into our professional harnesses: also an interesting development occurred with Montague Smyth. After a board meeting in early September, Albert invited me to join him in his offices.

"Why the secrecy?" I asked him. "What's happening?"

"Montaigue Smythe" he replied "your bone of contention."

"You're taking them on, I'm surprised. We agreed to differ."

"Actually, the company's troubles will go public tomorrow in the national press."

"How do you know, Albert?"

"From one of my colleagues after the information you provided me in that envelope. Of course, I never revealed any of it but that knowledge allowed me to pose interesting questions which raised eyebrows. Further suspicions led Montaigue Smythe into a trap carefully laid."

"What exactly do you mean by that Albert?" I asked intrigued.

"The details are unimportant; but the consequences are significant: the public exposure of embezzlement and forgery will result in a lengthy court case. It will destroy Montaigue Smythe eventually and open the market for de Vere's expansion as you anticipated. Further it will crucify the bogus reputation of someone I detest."

I was taken aback. "At Montaigue Smythe, who is he?"

"No, Caterine" Albert replied "at Dunns, my original auction house a man who tried to crucify me after my early appointment to the Board of Directors. Next weekend as a gesture of my personal appreciation of your efforts, the cave of BeauRobert will receive the gift of an exceptional case of vintage champagne."

On the Friday of that week as I was working at a château in the Creuse, I called at Saint Roche Rivière. I suppose I was curious about the film production taking place.

"You should visit when you're in the area" Gildas had suggested the previous week "it's fascinating."

Parking my car in the rear forecourt, I wandered round observing all the activity. Two security staff had requested my pass at the entrance gates and then apologised on recognising me.

"Here it is." I announced smiling "you're rightly doing your job."

I remembered my first visit here for Elisée's wedding, how awesome it had been with all its Renaissance splendour, plus my petulance over that Impressionist painting. What a child I had been rectified by David's reprimand.

Walking through the entrance hallway, a woman emerged from the grand salon, instantly recognisable. Dark, sultry, more striking even than her photographs, the American actress playing the leading role in the 'movie'.

On seeing me, she stopped abruptly.

"I've not noticed you before" she said eyeing me somewhat cagily "are you one of the extras?"

My humour asserted itself and I decided to have some fun.

"You could say that" I replied. "How do you think the film is progressing?"

"OK" she answered "but it's such a bore hanging around while the minor roles have to be rehearsed."

"But a superb venue, such a French classical background and ancestral history to reflect the mood of the novel" I remarked.

"Is it? Well not for me." She glanced round. "It's too old with those ghastly pictures on the walls and bits of faded cloth hanging down."

"My God, the tapestries!" I thought to myself "what a Philistine!" and was about to walk away when she continued.

"But not the owner. I met him this week, a French Count. He's young, 30s, and what a dish to look at. As for his body. My God! It won't be long before I'm parking my slippers under his bed!"

I was incensed but replied calmly.

"You're mistaken, mine are already in place."

She stared at me.

"Bloody Hell! How did you manage that so fast. He must be paying you."

With immense control I retained my composure.

"Another error. Let me explain the circumstances. I share with great pleasure the Count's bed. As it happens I'm his wife, Caterine, la Comtesse du Gilbert" and I left.

It gave me some satisfaction to witness the shock and horror registering on her face.

On that same evening after dinner we were sitting chatting in the smaller salon when Gildas' phone rang.

"Damn" he muttered looking at his watch "I hope there's no problem on the estate tonight!"

When he returned a few minutes later he said:

"That was Enrique, the film director, he told me about your encounter with Madeleine."

"How did he know?" I answered taken aback.

"The producer was in the grand salon with the senior technician checking some lighting details. Apparently the film crew are appalled at her comments. Enrique has decided to fire her."

"What?" I replied shocked. "But he can't do that."

"Caterine, of course he can. He controls the reins. Why didn't you tell me of those insults?"

I stood up and walked to the walnut armoire, deep in thought.

"Actually, because when I reflected on the incident I was to blame."

"Don't be ridiculous, Caterine."

"I'm serious, please let me explain."

"Madeleine is young, uneducated from a deprived background in New York; but she fought hard to improve herself taking menial jobs to finance night school studies and acting lessons. As it happened she was a natural, a rare talent. This is a major opportunity for her. She cannot lose it on my account."

Gildas stared at me incomprehensively.

"Where's your blame?" He asked.

"Because I played games with her. She assumed I was an 'extra' on the set and I didn't deny it". Albert's words came back to haunt me 'a wicked sense of humour, Caterine'.

"If I had introduced myself properly on that first encounter, this crisis would never have occurred. Please call Enrique back and explain the circumstances. Yes, she was foolish to make these statements to a complete stranger and of course I was enraged about her comments about you, but that's the world in which she lives: a fantasy land filled with celebrities some genuine but the majority false. I do not want her career crucified by poor judgement on both our parts."

On the following weekend, as agreed by Gildas and me, we received four guests for dinner at BeauRobert, the film director Enrique, the producer, the senior technician and Madeleine. As they were shown into the library by Felix I saw that she was very nervous and for her demurely dressed, no vision of that exceptional décolleté.

"Monsieur le Comte, Madame la Comtesse » she began « I want to express my deepest apologies for my conduct. »

Gildas interrupted her "that's forgotten. My wife informs me it was a mutual misunderstanding."

"Exactly" I replied. "Also I'm Caterine and you all know Gildas. Now let's enjoy our evening."

After an awkward start everyone relaxed.

Just before dinner I went up to the nursery to see the children, all asleep even Géraud!

As I returned to the smaller hall Madeleine emerged from the salon. I smiled at her.

"What a palace!" She exclaimed "How special to live in a home like this. I wish I knew more about the history. Could you recommend a book for me to buy?"

"If you're really interested, I'll do more than that."

"What?" She answered in surprise.

"Before you leave we'll make a date for you to return. How long is the film location time?"

"Six months at least" she replied "but I don't understand, return where?"

"To BeauRobert, I'll give you some basic guidelines on the French châteaux family history, paintings and furnishings then lend you some books which you can read on set."

"My God!" She exclaimed. "You don't sound like a countess, you're just normal." then clamped her hands over her mouth in horror.

"Best compliment I've received in years" I laughed and she joined me as we went into dinner.

Chapter Twenty-Eight

The following six months as I recall passed in the proverbial blur.

The film production had been extended for a further three months for technical reasons.

"I'm not worried" Enrique had told Gildas "fabulous location ."

Madeleine and I had established a surprising rapport. I had discovered she was intelligent, absorbed facts quickly and very keen to learn. She had borrowed a library of books from me, returning each one on time and replacing it by one she had bought new, ordered through my suppliers. Her commitment and enthusiasm roused my admiration. When I told him Gildas groaned.

"Mon Dieu! Don't invite her to stay at BeauRobert on a permanent basis. Both our reputations will be ruined!"

Christmas of 2001 was a quiet affair; we had received numerous invitations, as usual – to David and Alix in Zurich, to Rodrigue and Elisée in their French manor house (Maman was spending this festive season in Australia). One other invitation had concerned us.

"I know it's a lot to ask, with the triplets, but we'd love to see you. Francesca and I would fly over but Rosalie's hip is still in traction."

"How's she progressing?" Gildas had asked Frédéric.

"On target, no problems with the treatment. I'm confident it will be resolved by February."

After the discussion with his brother Gildas said to me:

"What should we do?"

"I don't know chéri. I feel guilty we haven't seen their baby, now six months old, but circumstances were against us initially. Then Frédéric phoned us about this displacement of the hip diagnosis. That little Rosalie required hospital treatment. Thank God, there seems to have been no complications!"

"Yes" Gildas muttered as he walked over to the walnut sideboard.

"My only concern is that Frédéric, the innocent one, has been immersed in multi-faceted du Gilbert guilt."

Gildas contacted Frédéric and suggested we wait till Rosalie's treatment was completed in March, when all of us, treble included, would fly to Boston.

"Brilliant" Frédéric replied. "It'll be a family reunion."

How his joy would turn to despair.

Towards the end of those hectic six months, in March, I was seated at my desk in my Paris office. I recall it was a Friday afternoon; the weather was the finest of springs in the French capital, warm and fresh with a welcoming sun sending rays of pleasure into my offices, the gods' good omen for the months to follow.

"Come in" I answered on hearing the knock on my door. Initially I did not look up assuming it was Sabine. She was due for a meeting on some valuation disputes.

"Caterine, may I come in?"

On hearing that voice the signature I was writing scrawled across the page and I stood up.

Racing round my desk, as she ran from the door, we

embraced each other. There was nothing to say. That was enough.

"I've discovered an exciting new restaurant" Donald declared as he, Shona, Gildas and I sat in the Montparnasse apartment.

This reunion had been arranged by Gildas and Donald. Shona had wanted to contact me for months but at the last minute her courage had failed fearing this time I would reject her.

"No way" Gildas had reassured Donald when he had phoned to enquire. "It would be a huge relief for Caterine if we could meet and I have a plan."

Between them they organised this weekend in Paris staying in Montparnasse just like old times and dining handsomely in one of Paris' finest restaurants, not as new as Donald had imagined.

"It used to be a private club, members only, with discreet arrangements in its hotel adjacent" Gildas informed us. "Established in the mid-19th for the benefit of its patrons and their mistresses."

"Just one question, chéri." My husband looked up from studying the menu as two other pairs of eyes regarded me quizzically.

"Are you familiar with the boudoir décor?"

It was a special weekend stirring happy memories of yore.

At the end of that month Gildas called me in Paris from his office at Saint Roche Rivière. It was on the week before Easter, the 27th.

"Caterine, I'm about to start the Board Meeting here but I've just received an e-mail from Frédéric."

"It's Rosalie, a problem?" I asked anxiously.

"Absolutely not, she's 100%, treatment a success."

I sighed with relief as Gildas continued:

"Frédéric said he's made a last minute decision to attend

some medical conference in Paris and asked if it's OK to stay at BeauRobert next weekend that's Friday 3rd April. By the way he's alone."

"Thank God" I muttered to myself.

"No problem Gildas, as far as I'm concerned. We've no commitments socially and if I had they would be cancelled for your brother."

We saw Frédéric's car arriving in the April sunlight, the early evening shadows reflecting on it as the vehicle passed by the lake.

To our surprise, he did not drive to the garages as usual and came to an abrupt halt at the main door.

Gildas and I rushed forward to greet him and then halted in shocked horror on those elevated entrance steps.

Frédéric stood there haggard, eyes stark, his striped business suit hanging on his muscular frame. He must have lost six kilos.

"Frédéric" Gildas exclaimed racing down those steps.

"You're ill! For God's sake, what's wrong?"

But Frédéric put up his hand, staggering backwards, warding off Gildas' efforts to help him.

"Not ill or maybe in my mind."

Gildas and I waited alarmed, witnessing his distress.

"I know everything. Can I still stay at BeauRobert?"

"Frédéric, my brother" Gildas replied moving forward to embrace him "this will always be your home!"

Suddenly I realised Frédéric was not alone.

Running to the back of the car I opened the door and removed the sleeping child.

"Don't worry about Rosalie. We'll look after her."

Sitting, the three of us in the smaller salon, Frédéric explained events.

"Francesca never loved me. Of course you both knew that and Elisée. She wanted revenge against the du Gilberts.

345

"Where is she now?" Gildas asked "is Francesca in Boston?"

Frédéric laughed hysterically.

"My dearest wife is ensconced with her lover, multi-millionaire American businessman with all the toys: private plane, yacht, apartments in Manhattan and Monaco plus a Berkshire estate. She's been cheating on me for months."

Gildas and I were stunned, numb in disbelief.

Frédéric continued, standing up and pacing the room.

"I'd suspected for some time and then found the evidence. She didn't deny it. That's when I discovered her ultimate treachery. God help me I wanted to kill her." Voice choking he was unable to continue, tortured memories invading his mind.

Gildas stood up pouring all of us a brandy. Handing his to to Frédéric, he put his arm round his brother.

"Do you want some rest now? You're exhausted mentally and physically."

"No, Gildas, thanks. I have to say this now."

He took a gulp of his cognac.

"Currently, we're legally separated with divorce proceedings in place. I'm returning to live in France as my Boston contract has expired. Although the hospital requested I renew it, I politely declined."

Gildas and I exchanged glances the same thought in our minds.

Frédéric stood up nursing his goblet of brandy and walked to the window looking out on the lake.

There was silence for several moments. That's when Gildas posed the fearful question:

"And Rosalie?"

His brother turned round almost surprised.

"She's staying with me of course, in case you were wondering and don't want to ask, she is my daughter. I have indisputable medical evidence."

My heart sobbed for him.

"Frédéric, just be warned. Francesca may have agreed custody, but you know her now, venomous. She could maybe change her mind."

"No chance Gildas, she doesn't want our baby, never loved her. Her only reason for getting pregnant was to trap me. She told me during that night of confrontation in our Boston apartment."

"I knew with your old-fashioned code of du Gilbert, knew you would have to marry me. I have no interest in the child. She would be an impediment, more accurately a crippled impediment to my future lifestyle."

"That is when I nearly tried to kill her but some common sense prevailed in my unhinged mind."

"Christ Almighty, the woman's inhuman" Gildas cried out.

I ran over to Frédéric and hugged him tears streaming down my face. He clung to me fighting his own display of distress.

Eventually he said:

"And to think I walked away from the one woman I really loved for that shit of a whore!"

None of us had any appetite, but while Frédéric showered I prepared some pasta with a ratatouille sauce and an avocado salad. Afterwards a cheese course with Scottish oatcakes.

"He must eat" Gildas said to me. "How's Rosalie?"

"Still sleeping, also exhausted" I replied.

"When Frédéric's ready I'll take him to the nursery and then we can have dinner."

Over coffee I asked Frédéric about his future plans.

"Well, Caterine, Gildas, I must admit to some dereliction from the truth. There's no medical conference in Paris but I do have interviews for various jobs, not all of course in the capital. That will take about two weeks."

"Then we'll take care of Rosalie for you" I said. "It will be a pleasure."

"Absolutely" Gildas agreed. "You won't have to worry about her."

"I would normally accept your offer with grateful thanks but I'm taking her to Fontainebleau on Sunday."

"Fontainebleau! Who lives there to look after her?" We both exclaimed.

For the first time since his arrival Frédéric smiled.

"Someone who loves her very much. Someone who insisted Rosalie stays with her while I attend the interviews. Ironically, Francesca's mother, Yvonne."

Gildas and I stared at him nonplussed.

"You see, she and her daughter never enjoyed a harmonious relationship. Francesca was much closer to her father, also a concert violinist, but without his daughter's prodigious talent remaining in the strings division of the orchestra. So he lived his dream in her. I hope both of you don't mind on this occasion."

"Of course not, if that's what you want" I replied.

"But I do have a favour" Frédéric smiled again, looking more like his former self.

"All being on schedule I'd like to return with Rosalie on the 19th. Perhaps Elisée, Rodrigue and their children could join us that weekend."

"I'm sure that will be a priority for everyone." Gildas answered "a family reunion. Anything else?"

"Actually yes, an imposition I'm sure. In the week following I'd like to fly back to Boston, clear out the apartment, tie up some loose ends at" he hesitated "the lawyer, Can Rosalie stay here? The problem is, I'm not sure of the time scale, but maximum three weeks. Obviously, if you need extra help in the nursery, I'll pay for it."

"Frédéric, it'll give us all great pleasure to have your daughter with us at BeauRobert. As for the payment, well, as I shall be attending to her personally on many occasions, just one question" I replied.

"What is it?" He enquired bemused.

"Can you afford my fees?"

For the first time since his arrival, Frédéric laughed.

As it happened Frédéric's stay in the US lasted just over two weeks.

"I'll return on Friday, mid-afternoon. Looking forward to seeing everyone." He had told Gildas in a phone call.

I took action on receiving this information.

On the day of Frédéric's arrival back at BeauRobert, I had a late appointment at the headquarters of a legal firm in the centre of Paris.

Although five minutes early I was shown immediately into the junior partner's offices.

The lawyer stared at me in shocked surprise.

"Caterine! But the name here is Sinclair."

"Yes, Charlotte, I made the appointment in my maiden name."

She knew immediately.

"This is about Frédéric and the answer's no!"

"Charlotte, as a lawyer and I understand one held in high regard surely it is customary for the accused to be allowed to plead her case."

When I arrived at BeauRobert, Charlotte was with me.

On seeing her enter the library Frédéric was speechless, his facial expressions reflecting first shock then joy.

Closing the door we left them alone.

"How did you manage it?" Gildas enquired. "Personally I thought the chances of persuading her were nil."

"A lot of debate, even argument, but in the end it was summed up in one question and its reply."

"What was that?"

"I said to Charlotte. I have opened the case and now you must close it. My final summation is simple, I have outlined the facts and also his feelings for you. Ask yourself one question 'Am

I still in love with him?' If you are don't condemn yourselves to be prisoners of unhappiness through selfish pride."

Some time later they joined us in the smaller salon hands clasped tightly, faces radiant albeit watery eyed! Frédéric began:

"What can we say to both of you for bringing us back together? It's just to let you know our plans. Once my divorce is finalised, we will be married and bring up Rosalie as our child and then" he paused to look at Charlotte, she nodded "once we have established a secure family base for Rosalie it is our intention to adopt a baby, a baby from Martinique."

To quote an old adage 'there was not a dry eye in the house!'

On a Sunday at the beginning of June Gildas and I were sitting in his study discussing recent events.

"Put on the TV chérie, I want to see the result of that tennis final. As I told you my university team is defending the title."

As it happened we turned into the end of the news bulletin.

Suddenly the newscaster interrupted his prepared script.

"Reports are coming in that in the early hours of this morning a mayday call was received off the cost of Sardinia from a yacht. It has been confirmed that the yacht belongs to multi-millionaire businessman Brent Aster. Coastguards alerted the rescue services who raced to the location indicated by the crew but the vessel could not be found; however wreckage has now been sighted in the area.

On board this luxurious yacht registered in Monaco were Mr Aster, a number of guests still to be identified and his current constant companion Francesca Rowlings, former classical violinist and separated from her husband, Frédéric du Gilbert. He is a member of the French family dynasty. The couple married less than two years ago and have a baby daughter. Rescue services are continuing to search the area, but, as yet no survivors have been found."

Gildas and I stared at each other then moved.

He phoned Frédéric and I Elisée and Rodrigue.

Fortunately both members of our family were at their homes. When we returned to the smaller salon, Gildas said:

"Frédéric had not heard the news, he couldn't speak, shocked. But I told him to get out of the apartment with Charlotte and Rosalie before the media ghouls strike. He's on his way. What about my sister?"

"Rodrigue answered. They're disappearing to his parents' former farmhouse, out of the public glare. 'Hopefully the hype will last only a few days' were his words to me."

Gildas walked over and kissed me on my forehead.

"We're safe here, chérie, at BeauRobert."

"Are we? I hope so. How dreadful to have to hide like hunted animals from the amassing pack where none of us bears any guilt."

"That's the world we live in now. As we've discussed often our life has more advantages than most in that we can afford our guardians of privacy: some, certainly, gained from heritage in the châteaux buildings, the mainstream from hard work, endeavour, assiduous stewardship."

"I know, Gildas, from what you explained to me about your grandfathers' shrewdness. Otherwise much of the du Gilbert inheritance would have been lost."

"Yes, definitely: but why such intrusion of our family's personal lives I've never courted a high profile status, in fact detested it. I've attempted to invest and encourage local enterprise and provide employment in the area. You've agreed with these principles, funded studentships at de Veres and of course our joint donations to conservation work in Africa for endangered species."

"It would appear, Gildas" I replied "that our thick walls hide more than our privacy. But this is our choice. None of our families court the glare of publicity."

Later that afternoon Frédéric arrived with Charlotte, carrying Rosalie in her arms. We gathered together in the smaller salon.

"Any news? We've checked the radio en route here but no update."

"Not so far, Frédéric, no further developments."

What could we do waiting for more information about that yacht?

Gildas and Frédéric went for a walk in the grounds, while Charlotte and I spent time with Rosalie; she had just started to walk and stumbled around the cushioned play area which we had originally set up for the treble.

Fortunately they were absent, now two and a half years old, with Nanny Patricia at a nursery party in our local village.

"Heaven help her" I said to Charlotte in an attempt to lighten the proceedings.

Charlotte gave a smile in response.

On the 6 pm news bulletin, it was headlines.

"It has been confirmed that the yacht belonging to multi-millionaire Brent Aster, which sent a distress call off the coast of Sardinia in the early hours of the morning sank rapidly as the result of some freak accident, causes unknown. Sadly all on board perished trapped in their cabins: next of kin have been informed and an investigation is underway. Brent Aster was an entrepreneur...."

Gildas walked over and switched off the set.

Frédéric had his head in his hands. Looking up he said: "My God! We parted in bitterness and acrimony but what a way to die!"

There was silence. No-one could speak. All of us wrestling with our individual thoughts.

Frédéric contacted Francesca's mother that same evening who explained that the authorities had been searching for him.

The following day he drove to Fontainebleau to see her.

"Naturally she's very distressed but calm." Frédéric told us on his return.

"You see, I could have predicted this. If not a yacht, a fast car or a plane" Yvonne told me. "We may not have been great mates but I loved her. The saddest part for me is that for all her prodigious talent, her beauty and material assets, I don't think Francesca ever found happiness."

"Yvonne asked me to be in charge of the funeral arrangements. Francesca's to be buried in a remote village in the Pyrénées where she spent many holidays as a child. The only people present will be Yvonne, Francesca's brother and family, plus me." He looked at Charlotte.

"Perhaps now Francesca will find peace."

The tragic circumstances prevailing of Francesca's death meant there was no impediment to Frédéric and Charlotte marrying.

"It seems untimely, Charlotte and I have discussed it."

"Why?" Gildas replied to his brother as all four of us sat in the library. It was the end of July four weeks after that funeral service in the Pyrénées.

"After all, there will be no official announcement."

"I know" Frédéric replied "and Charlotte and I want to make our personal commitment to each other as soon as possible. It's just the last four weeks have been very harrowing and I fear further intrusion."

During July, Frédéric had been plagued with media and press attention in Paris either outside the hospital where he had been appointed Head of Obstetrics or at his Montmartre apartment, where Charlotte could never, of course, be seen. Rosalie had remained at BeauRobert during this period, where they spent time with her at weekends.

Eventually Frédéric abandoned Montmartre decamping to Montparnasse, seemingly forgotten by the press where he and

Charlotte could arrive and depart discreetly by means of the underground car park.

"Come on Charlotte, let's find Rosalie, put her in the buggy and go for a walk, clear our heads."

When they returned a decision had been made but before plans were put into place Frédéric made a courtesy visit to Yvonne and explained the circumstances.

"Take your happiness when you can find it, life's too short to wait." She had told him.

"I agree" said Francesca's brother whom Frédéric had met for the first time at the funeral.

"One life has already been wasted. Don't make it another two."

Therefore, in early September Frédéric and Charlotte were married in a simple service in the private family chapel at BeauRobert. It was attended only by closest family members plus Donald and Shona.

Duncan and Iona Cameron offered Frédéric their home in Barbados for their honeymoon, secluded and away from any possible media glare. It was accepted gratefully. As agreed there was no official announcement of the marriage. The press would find out at our chosen time.

Chapter Twenty-Nine

The two years following Frédéric's marriage to December 2004 were happy times.

On that first Christmas following the treble's third birthday we had 'full house' at BeauRobert. Ten adults who included uncle Fergus flown out from Australia to see us and nine children. What a party!

On Christmas Eve as the adults were seated in the grand salon awaiting our champagne cocktails, a tradition of the festive season, uncle Fergus stood up adjusting his tie somewhat nervously. Clearing his throat he said:

"I'd like to make an announcement."

There was silence as all chattering ceased.

"Recently I asked Véronique if she would do me the honour of becoming my wife and she accepted making me a very happy man. I hope you will join me."

Before he could finish there was cheering as everyone stood up, then spontaneous applause and mayhem as everyone gathered round to kiss both of them warmly and offer our congratulations.

Maman looked flushed and Uncle Fergus non plussed.

Eventually order was restored and I disappeared to the kitchen returning with their 'engagement' present.

They were both rendered speechless.

Their 'present' was a massive wedding cake in Scottish tradition in three tiers with the greeting:

To Fergus and Véronique

Congratulations and our love

The du Gilbert and Sinclair families

Glasses raised, Gildas gave the toast.

"To you both, many happy years together!"

Later that evening Maman spoke to me in her suite.

"I knew you'd be happy for us although Fergus was a little nervous about it. Your cousins in Australia reacted exactly the same way as you did."

"Of course, they would." I said as I kissed her. "It's a blessing to see you both happy."

Maman smiled "we realise I cannot be Bebe and he cannot be Angus, but we get on very well with a similar sense of humour. Both wanting to travel, it seemed impractical to have separate rooms."

She hesitated, the aquamarine eyes as vital as ever.

"I told Fergus marrying me was unnecessary. He was shocked. 'Véronique' he replied 'you may be French but I'm Scottish. Marriage it will be!'"

We collapsed together in mirth.

The treble were a constant joy to Gildas and me, now in the spring following Maman's marriage to Uncle Fergus in Martinique in January, attending the local nursery school.

Gildas and I decided they should stay in the village environment until they were six which meant two years also at the primary school.

"I've no guilt at not paying fees" Gildas informed me as Grandpère built it from his own funds!"

Then it was our intention to apply to a relatively new school established near Tours.

"It's co-ed and very progressive with an exceptionally wide curriculum" Gildas informed me, run by a 'benign' disciplinarian.

Languages covered include Russian, Chinese, Japanese and Arabic. The scientific range is extensive touching on nuclear physics and meteorology, but literature, history and geography are also high on the agenda as are music and sport. Each pupil must choose one subject from each of the categories and teaching standards are exceptional."

"I don't want them coerced Gildas, pushed beyond their capabilities."

"They won't be. Every child is assessed regularly and has an individual tutor with whom the pupil can consult on any concerns: also it is 50% boarding and 50% day school, the latter being our choice. The difficulty is being accepted as the entrance exam is demanding. We'll visit the school next week and you can tell me if you agree we should apply for three places."

Over the following 18 months we were busier than ever: me with de Veres and the Château Contract and Gildas with his numerous enterprises.

The movie now completed at Saint Roche Rivière, we were invited to a private preview in Paris.

It was spellbinding. The château offered a stupendous setting to that great love story and the sensitivity of the photography lent an ethereal quality to its image.

After its launch worldwide, the film received global accolades and at the Emmy awards it hit the jackpot winning Best Picture, Best Director, Best Photography and I was especially delighted to learn Best Actress. Madeleine's future career was secured.

To my surprise I received a personal note from her thanking me again for her 'further education'. Enclosed also was a book on mediaeval art. "You expressed interest in this volume not in your collection. It gives me great pleasure to offer it as a token of my appreciation."

I was taken aback at her thoughtfulness and very touched.

"Time like the wind goes hurrying by and the hours just fly" to quote a poetic phrase.

Suddenly it was January 2005.

Sitting in my offices at de Veres, Albert enquired:

"How's the Scottish project , Caterine, still on schedule?"

"Absolutely" I replied. "Next week I'm flying back to Edinburgh, visiting Glasgow also, to analyse the property options; all going to plan I hope the headquarters and sales distribution will be up and running by the summer; that would mean an official opening of the Scottish Division of de Veres in September, exactly as planned!"

Albert placed his coffee cup on the table and stood up, walking to my window with their outstanding views of my favourite European city, Paris.

"Caterine, we've known each other since you graduated and my family have been friends of the du Gilbert's for several decades. These are important connections and loyalties. Let me ask you. How does Gildas regard this Scottish venture? After all, you'll be absent for six months at least."

I stared at Albert, taking a final sip of my coffee.

"He's very supportive. We've discussed it thoroughly and anyway I'm only absent during the week, spending every weekend at BeauRobert. Why do you ask?" I enquired somewhat puzzled.

"Perhaps, concerns: after all you have a young family, triplets no less, now five years old, demanding much commitment. I think perhaps you should reconsider this task. I can appoint one of the board."

I interrupted Albert, temper roused.

"You're implying I'm neglecting my children. That's somewhat arrogant from a man who worked 18 hours a day to establish de Veres. Where were you when Céline was nursing two babies born 14 months apart? Where were you when she had to cope with four hourly night time feeds, nappy changes and those quirky infantile moods? Where were you when she organised the smooth running of a household to create a relaxed atmosphere for you and your potential clients to visit your home and discuss the opening of valuable contracts?"

I glared at Albert.

There was a long silence.

"Thank you Caterine for those incisive words."

I felt appalled. Certainly Albert and I had experienced our differences, some head to head encounters but always but always fought in a fair contest. In this one I had been unjust.

"I apologise Albert and appreciate how concerned you are for me and my family." I shook my head continuing:

"My temper and outspokenness. Never controlled it all these years. You were the man who took the gamble, gave me the career opportunity I craved. I owe you so much."

Albert spun round rotating his swivel chair to face me. He was grinning.

"Actually you're right in everything you said, including the gamble. It seems to have paid off handsomely for both of us!"

On impulse I went over and kissed him on both cheeks.

The following week, peace made with Albert, I flew from Charles de Gaulle to Edinburgh to continue the planning for my Scottish project over the forthcoming months.

In March during one of my stays in Scotland Gildas called me on a Thursday evening.

"The treble are fine, chérie, more demanding than ever. I'm soaked! They chased me round the play area with three water pistols against my solitary one from which the little devils had removed the water!"

I laughed "Gildas, you should have checked your 'equipment'."

"It's always in working order" he retorted. "You can test it out. I'll be waiting in the summer house on your return, champagne chilled."

I smiled as we said 'au revoir'. Only four days apart but I missed him so much.

Arriving at BeauRobert on the following evening I drove to the garages, depriving Felix of his chauffeur treat. I left my luggage to be collected later and raced through the walled garden to the summer house, exhilarated, so happy to be home.

Gildas was waiting, his tall broad frame obscuring the variegated ivy plants at the rear of the spacious glass vaulted entrance.

"Chéri" I began then halted in stupefaction at his unfathomable expression.

"What's wrong? The children?" I stuttered, fears aroused.

"Guy, Gabriella and Géraud are in great spirits. Unfortunately I'm not. Please sit down and let me explain."

Elation deflated, confused, I sank onto the chintz cushions of the wicker suite.

"A few hours ago there was a discovery at BeauRobert raising questions which must be answered."

It was over! The key had been found to that padlocked compartment in my mind. It burst open a veritable Pandora's box to plague our personal world.

"Caterine" Gildas' voice penetrated my desolate thoughts. "Please tell me what happened on that fateful night when Philippe called here six years ago."

And so, strangely calm, even detached, I recited my lines like a well rehearsed actress on the stage.

At the mention of Isabella, Gildas staggered backwards as if struck by a massive whiplash.

"Alive, still alive" he whispered, shock and disbelief written in capital letters like some tabloid headline all over his ashen face."

"Yes" I replied "but with only weeks to live, dying of cancer."

Gildas sank down on the larger wicker armchair opposite

me which thudded against the stone wall protesting at the sudden arrival of his weight.

Continuing my description of events, my status shifted and I became one of the audience studying and analysing the performance horrified by the exposure of greed, jealousy and betrayal but demanding more, the maximum value for the ticket price I had paid.

Before I had finished Gildas stopped me, holding up his hand like a final gesture in military terms to dead comrades. He already knew the fatal result.

I found that I was unable now to look at him and stared at the worn grey flagstones on the summer house floor, hope vanquished, the future bleak.

Suddenly my body started to tremble as I felt his touch, strong arms embracing me, pulling me against him as his mouth moved gently over mine.

"Why didn't you tell me chérie. To suffer such agony, terror, absolute Hell, then bear that burden all these years. I don't understand why you didn't tell me."

Staring at Gildas, I felt myself suspended in a void, between desolation and hope. The reality returned with a vengeance.

"Because I murdered him."

Gildas stood up gazing out onto the wild rose garden. Turning round he said:

"Did you push Philippe down that well?"

"You know that wasn't possible with his physique." I answered automatically like a robot.

Once again I sensed I was elsewhere, floating in time, searching, seeking my real world. The atmosphere was eerie. Gildas' sea green eyes stared ahead, beyond me to another icy horizon in the reflected light.

"I bloody well wish you had" he replied voice raised high.

"Gildas, I'm confused and I think I'm going to vomit."

My stomach was churning, my legs weak. Putting my head

down to alleviate the nausea, drops of sweat fell onto the flagstones which despite their weight danced up in front of my eyes; suddenly I was drifting along a country lane lined with crooked men pointing their staffs at something or someone in the distance on a hillock.

"Caterine, chérie. I'm so sorry, forgive me, take a sip of this." Ironically what Gildas had given me was cognac. At the same time he placed a handkerchief packed with ice against my forehead and then lifting my hair, against the back of my neck. Some minutes later I felt better – nausea and dizziness receding.

Before I knew what was happening, I was carried, despite protests to our suite, helped into a hot bath and once I was refreshed we would eat, Gildas told me.

"But I'm not hungry, I'm still confused."

"Then the vapour should clear your brain. If not I will afterwards" was his reply.

Suddenly, as I soaked in that steamy, bubbling water I knew he still loved me and that he was on my, no 'our' side.

After a light supper of which I ate little, we sat together hands clasped sipping some Chablis.

Gildas explained the events which had occurred earlier that day.

"I had decided to have the old well examined by the Water Board; its source had been contaminated for some time and then dried up completely two years ago. The site I had thought could be put to more ecological use. The senior engineer, Fabrice, phoned me at my Saint Roche office. As I had known him from primary school in the village plus many football matches together, against opposing teams, we had an established rapport."

Gildas stood up, stretched, placing his wine glass now empty, on the armoire.

Fabrice told me that the well structure was still in good

order, water source eliminated by geological developments but sound enough to in-fill with no subsidence dangers in future. He confirmed an official report would follow. One matter had troubled him. His assistant had found what appeared to be human remains and some other items. He said.

"I'm no fossil expert but they've been placed in an excavation box while the sundries are in a sealed bag for you to examine now under Felix's care."

"Frankly" Gildas continued "although taken aback the news didn't bother me and I put it out of my mind."

"How do you feel now? Would you rather we left this till the morning?" Coming over to put his arm round me, kissing me gently.

"No" I confirmed voice steady "as you said during dinner, we put confront this catastrophe together, better now."

Gildas nodded.

"Returning to BeauRobert I was reminded by Felix in his inimitable fashion of the developments as the custodian of the box and bag. The former we know about but in that bag was a mangled mobile phone, discoloured and caked in grime but still discernable in its distinctive gold plated jacket. I recognised it as Philippe's."

There was a few moments silence.

"And that's how you knew."

"Yes."

"But could not understand why I kept it a secret."

"Correct."

"Then you must have suspected I'd had sex with Philippe and in some midnight masquerading there had been an accident, all of which I had to conceal."

"Do you actually believe what you're saying?" Our eyes locked.

"No" I whispered "but what did you think?"

"I thought Philippe had raped you and in revenge you had

summoned a 'Boedicea' power and actually thrust him down the well!"

Indeed in every respect it was an extraordinary night.

On the following morning, when I awoke, I was horrified to learn from my bedside clock that it was nearly 10.00.

Then I saw the tray on the walnut inlaid table containing freshly squeezed orange juice, morning croissants, a flask of coffee and a note in that starched, white, monogrammed notepaper. I giggled at the contents, like some silly schoolgirl. Trials and tribulations lay ahead but in a sense my mind had been set free, unfettered and this time my lover was by my side.

That Saturday afternoon Gildas and I sat down to plan our strategy.

"Chéri, before we have our discussions" I hesitated. "Please tell me, would you have searched for Isabella?"

"Definitely not. There was no doubt she was being well cared for. She had made her decision unfolded in events, no longer my responsibility. Since you've asked that question let me answer another one. Philippe orchestrated his own demise. You were trapped at the mercy of a powerful man with iniquitous intent the details unknown to you, torturing your mind. But you used your wits, kept a cool head. Yes, brain defeated brawn on that occasion. And you played your trump card, plied him with cognac. If Philippe had not been drunk he would have skirted that well instinctively, he knew these grounds so well. But he was disorientated, intoxicated by drink and by lust."

"Caterine, Philippe killed himself."

I stared at Gildas. Suddenly I felt the tears pricking my eyes. Blinking quickly was no help to stem the flow as sobs wracked my body and the Hell of that night manifested itself in raw emotion.

My lover was there, gathering me in those strong arms,

stroking my hair, murmuring loving words. For the first time in six years I felt free.

An inquest had to be held. The human remains with DNA testing were identified and the mobile phone was conclusive evidence.

Gildas, however, put plans in place, discreetly used his influence, a rare intervention from him, consequently media interest was nullified, proceedings from the inquest aroused no press headlines.

It was held in May near St Roche Rivière, the family château on the Creuse which was still Gildas' official residence. Implications were, to outsiders, that events had taken place there.

After the usual formal preliminaries, some witness statements were taken, all perfunctory. Then I was called.

"Madame la Comtesse" the coroner addressed me.

"Please explain the events of the evening in question when Professor Martine visited the family château."

I replied with my carefully rehearsed response.

"Philippe Martine called to see my husband. As Gildas was absent in the USA on business that wasn't possible. After paying his respects to both of us, Philippe left."

"At what time was that Madame?"

"About 9 pm" I replied. "As it happened I had just returned from dining with friends in the village."

There was a pause as the coroner consulted his notes.

He recommenced.

"Madame. I understand Professor Martine was a member of the du Gilbert family. It that correct?"

"Yes" I answered. "A cousin by marriage of my husband."

"And yet you did not invite him in?"

"No, I did not."

There were some murmurings in the courtroom.

The coroner coughed replying "I see."

In fact he did not see at all!

It would seem unusual and certainly discourteous not to have invited Philippe into our family home.

The coroner addressed me again.

"Finally, Madame, did Professor Martine prior to taking his leave not give you any indication of his vacation plans?"

It was the opening I desperately needed otherwise I had to try and create it, a much more difficult task.

"I don't think he could have informed me of them even if he had wanted to."

There was silence.

The coroner looked up from his script peering at me from his unflattering bifocals.

"Why was that Madame?"

I sighed "I regret to say that Philippe was drunk, very drunk indeed."

Verdict. "Accidental death".

It was the perfect solution.

The French press and media practically ignored it, a footnote only in Le Journal.

As for the Swiss, they were appalled that their eminent plastic surgeon had fallen from grace. Philippe was granted an obituary column highlighting his career, his death referred to as "a tragic accident in the grounds of an ancestral estate in France."

As for the Sinclair and du Gilbert families: Gildas played the same trump card he had used with the French national press – anger.

"I hate to lie but the truth is not an option." He had told me. Therefore it was agreed. Before the inquest he had phoned everyone with the remarks:

"Bloody idiot, arrives late evening, drunk out of his mind. Caterine handles the situation impeccably to avoid trouble.

Then Philippe takes that shortcut known to him through

the walled garden to his manor house. Disorientated, he tumbles onto the temporary cover and oblivion. Now, there's an inquest, probably mountains of publicity through no fault of any member of our family. Christ! I informed everyone of the well problem and in writing. Then Philippe buggers it up!"

A few days after the inquest, Elisée and I met for lunch in Paris.

"I thought that was a lovely idea for you and Gildas to renew your wedding vows recently with our families present. It was very romantic."

Smiling ironically to myself I replied:

"It was Elisée, a memorable ceremony."

As my sister-in-law chattered on, I recalled Gildas' words on the morning of that day.

"Let's think of our previous visit to the altar as our wedding. Today is our marriage."

I returned to reality at Elisée's voice.

"We're all so relieved there was no major media attention. After Isabella's disappearance we were besieged for months. You've no idea, it was a continuous nightmare!"

Elisée halted abruptly, hands raised in distress.

"What am I saying? Gildas told Frederic and me how much you suffered after your Papa's accident. How thoughtless of me!"

"No need to apologise. That's all in the past. I've learned in my life not to look back. It bears barren fruit. Let's enjoy our lunch."

As it happened the following week I had bad news at de Veres.

The second survey I had commissioned as a precaution to check the building premises I had selected in Glasgow for the Scottish headquarters were damning: the rafters were riven with dry rot.

"The damage is terminal" I told Albert.

"Can it not be treated in time for the opening in September?"

"No way. I have to find alternative premises. That's far from easy at this late date."

"Albert regarded me keenly.

"I agree Caterine, but it was your project. The responsibility is yours to find a solution."

After dinner in our apartment, staff on leave, Gildas and I discussed the options.

"How long will it take" he asked me in his practical manner.

"Three weeks at least and you're in the US. The children are our priority. I can't leave them for that time even with such reliable staff. I'll postpone the Scottish opening."

"Nonsense. That's unacceptable. Let's explore other options."

Further discussions ensued, a phone call was made and we found our solution.

They arrived four days later and were welcomed lovingly.

"It's a dream I envisaged – custodian of BeauRobert for a month and no bill to pay with my cherished lady by my side. We'll stay as long as we're invited."

As we sat together in the library I felt very blessed. Gildas and me, Uncle Fergus and Maman. The treble would be safe in their caring hands.

During the following months I worked relentlessly. Numerous calls and e-mails to Maman at BeauRobert and Gildas on his US tour to promote the French Châteaux as Ambassador for the committee.

All was well and most importantly our children healthy, safe and thoroughly spoilt.

Packing my case prior to returning to France, I smiled to myself. Marchmont, my family home in Perthshire had profited well from my Scottish enterprise. De Veres had paid a handsome rent for me to use it as my commercial base; much more economical and practical than any hotel.

Suddenly I heard the crunch of gravel in the driveway. Surely not Jimmy Black with more eggs, there was no-one to eat them, I thought.

I ran downstairs, nearly tripping over in haste and into the gardens.

He stood there tall and very handsome, known intimately to me, and was grinning.

"Gildas" I shrieked "It's not possible."

"Yes, it is" he replied striding towards me and gathering me in his arms.

"We're spending a night here and then travelling back tomorrow from Rosyth to Zeebrugge by boat. It's all arranged."

What a journey that was!

Once on board the ship we reserved our table at the à la carte restaurant and retired to our executive cabin. It boasted a full size double bed with other well appointed facilities.

Gildas removed the champagne he had ordered from the refrigerator.

"This is a celebration indeed" I remarked observing the year."

"Correct" he replied "to toast a mission accomplished in Switzerland."

"You've been already? I know we discussed it but when? What happened?"

There was a slight movement; the ship's voyage was underway.

Gildas gazed from his armchair onto the promenade deck, the Venetian blinds angled to welcome the setting sun but to conceal ourselves from the other passengers taking advantage of that early evening stroll.

He continued.

"Some phrases you had used during your bizarre narrative

describing that night in 1999 had buried in my troubled mind but now resurfaced.

"Lawyer obliged to me, the mention of a secret dossier and a couple, both aurally impaired."

"Casting back I remembered two brothers in the village with whom I had played at football when I was a teenager. One was academically bright and the younger born deaf. Papa had intended to help them with their further education when Philippe's father stepped in: a man in total contrast to his son. With their parents' blessing he installed them in Switzerland. The elder I knew had become a lawyer, of the younger brother I had no knowledge. After discreet enquiries with the executors of Philippe's estate I was confident no dossier existed with them. Based on my hunch, I traced my former football team mate: a renowned lawyer in the banking home of the Swiss gnomes, Basle! Roughly this was our conversation."

"Monsieur le Comte!" He greeted me.

« Come on Clément, it's Gildas. How are things – prosperous I must assume."

Clément had grinned, greetings now warm.

"Yes, Gildas, I'm a very fortunate man. You haven't changed. Despite inheriting the title, just like your Papa, no pomposity! What can I do for you?"

"Philippe, my late cousin, you were close to him, I know, albeit not his official lawyer."

"Yes, Gildas, his Papa set me up. I owe that family a great debt, as does my brother. Philippe's death in that tragic accident must have been a great shock to you and your family."

"It was Clément. The staff and my wife had no indication he would decide to take that short cut to the north gate. I am here however on Philippe's behalf. We had an agreement that if he pre-deceased me, I would take under my auspices the confidential dossier held in these legal offices in his name. This is why I have made the appointment today."

Clément hesitated:

"What's the problem?" I asked him.

"Well Gildas, Philippe's instructions were to retain this dossier until he authorised its release."

"Absolutely right. I am authorising it as his power of attorney. If you doubt my credentials I can produce the necessary papers; but that will take time. You know me, my identity indisputable and I am willing to sign a document of release of this dossier. That way you have honoured your legal obligations."

Clément paused then made his decision.

"Of course, Gildas. Give me a few minutes and I'll have the release papers drawn up while I locate the dossier. Meanwhile my secretary will bring you coffee."

Gildas stood up to stretch his legs.

"You bluffed him, double bluffed him in fact. And he returned with the dossier, which you signed for" I asked incredulously.

"Yes, indeed" Gildas replied refilling my glass "also I received more information about his brother."

"Feel a bit guilty, Gildas. We've lost touch although I receive a Christmas card. He's still living in that remote area in the Alps with his wife."

I found that village and Isabella's burial place with its pitiful cross.

As Frédéric said and I repeat his words about Francesca "we parted in bitterness and acrimony but what a way to die."

"And the dossier, Gildas" I hesitated "did you read it?"

"Indeed, I did : typed by Philippe on my personal computer; it would have destroyed me, my family and all the work undertaken by Papa and my grandfather. It was a crucifixion. Let that bastard rot in Hell!"

The Saturday of that weekend we arrived at BeauRobert after the six hour drive from Zeebrugge, at 4pm.

Maman and Fergus had left two days earlier to pursue their travels with air tickets purchased by us (despite their protests) and our heartfelt thanks.

After greetings from Felix, we raced to the children's playroom and spent the following two hours with them running round outside, tossing tennis balls for one of our 'catching' sessions and then all five of us mounted our cycles and chased round the 'sentier de randonnée' marked out on the estate.

For Gildas and me laughter had returned to our home and to our life. It was an essential ingredient to our love affair and our happiness.

On the Saturday evening, the treble installed in their bedrooms asleep, we set up the plans discussed over dinner on the boat.

Consequently, an invitation was issued to our family and close friends.

The du Gilbert

Gildas and Caterine

Une soirée

Saturday 27th August 2005, 18.00 hrs

At BeauRobert

More details were enclosed about accommodation facilities, paid by us nearby. Family and close friends would be staying in the château.

On the following day we received a surprise before our salad lunch on the terrace.

Sitting on the walnut armoire in the smaller salon was a magnificent bouquet of blooms, incorporating lilies, delphiniums and carnations.

I knew it was not from Gildas. Always he sent me roses, my favourite flower. Maman was somewhat of an expert on this subject and I had learned much from her, considering myself her natural heir.

Gildas had found this amusing over the years and insisted

I attempted to identify the species he had chosen. Usually I was forced to consult the rose encyclopaedia!

Looking at the attached card, it read:

To Monsieur and Madame

Welcome home

Sincerely,
The staff at BeauRobert

Gildas and I stared at that card and then at each other. We were rendered speechless by such a gesture with its implications of their concerns for us.

How fortunate to have the support of such a staff. We were very touched.

On the day of the Soirée, Gildas and I were fully occupied making final checks on the arrangements.

What an evening: it was an unusual blend of people. Gildas and I had decided to invite those we trusted most. Those individuals who had supported us and defended us over recent years. Hence, there were many members of the estate staff from Saint Roche Rivière plus those from BeauRobert, including Felix, Yvette and Agathe with her husband. Plus not forgotten, the porter at Montparnasse!

We kept the proceedings informal, a buffet provided for obvious reasons by outside caterers, to release the members of staff from preparing any food on that day. As a surprise however I cooked several haggis which I had stored in our private freezer with 'neeps' and 'tatties' which was well received to my astonishment!

If I remember correctly it was 3 am when Gildas and I staggered into bed. It was also a pleasure to reflect that the caterers would arrive at 7 am to clear up the mess!

The opening of de Vere's Scottish headquarters passed smoothly in September and Gildas with me settled into a more mundane daily programme which suited us admirably over the following three months.

Christmas plans had been confirmed at the Soirée.

Consequently on 23rd December, I flew with my husband and the triplets to Zurich. It was the children's first plane flight and they were very excited, hopping from one foot to the other asking innumerable questions at the departure lounge at Charles de Gaulle.

I noticed we were attracting some attentive looks from other passengers, perhaps not surprising. There was Gildas, with his burnished copper and me, strawberry blonde; then our treble, Guy sporting auburn waves, Gabriella pulling at her long straight blonde locks and Guy with a head of jet black curls. What a motley crew!

After the chaos of our arrival, with four adults attempting to restrain the antics of three older cousins sweeping the younger ones into the air in welcoming waves, Alix and I settled down finally in the dining kitchen for a coffee and a chat in their new home. David and Gildas had taken everyone into the garden for a game of rounders, or at least an apology for it.

"I love this house, Alix. It's private, secluded but only 20 minutes drive from Zurich with spacious grounds and" I hesitated "gracious, yes, that's it, gracious living."

"Well put, Caterine. That would eloquently describe this property. David and I were very fortunate to secure its purchase. In fact, we exceeded our planned budget, but not excessively" Alix grinned. "It was love at first sight – a coup de foudre!"

"No wonder" I replied "and in practically 'walk-in' condition!"

"Absolutely. Of course, there are some parts of the décor we will change eventually, but that's personal taste. I'm looking forward to planning the gardens again but that will take time. They have been neglected by the previous owner, who created them and refused any extra assistance as he grew older. This terrain was his 'baby', but he forgot that the 'baby' could not always be 'bottle fed'."

I laughed at Alix's analogy.

It was a traditional Christmas. Presents under the handsome fir tree positioned in the large wood panelled hall were eagerly ripped open on the morning of 25th. Gasps of surprise emanated from everyone.

Unusually perhaps for this time of year, a ceiling was put on the amount spent on everyone's gift from and to each other including to the children.

The rule was that each adult could spend a maximum of 20 euros on any present. Each child, five euros (from their pocket money) and each teenager 10 euros.

Then a contribution was made form the du Gilbert and Sinclair families to joint charity and environmental projects from funds normally spent by the majority of families on Christmas gifts.

It worked out well with presents ranging from anti-wrinkle cream from me to Gildas and for Alexandra from Angus, a dunce's hat.

How happy we all were, unaware of the sorrows to follow.

On 26th, after breakfast I meandered with Alix through the semi-neglected rose garden. We discussed ideas for replanting and sat down together on an old stone seat near a former arbour.

"I have to say Alix, Gildas and I have been shocked by Alexandra. She doesn't look 15, so sophisticated and great fun with it. Of course, neither of us has seen her for several months but, even so, she's maturing rapidly, a young lady already." I smiled.

"A young monkey, you mean. She's too confident, high

handed. Yes, she's bright academically but, for example, last night, she was aggressive with Gildas on the European Union constitution. She should have backed off. After all he's her uncle and far more knowledgeable."

"Is he, Alix? Maybe. The point is Gildas enjoyed that round table discussion. He welcomed Alexandra's challenges as did I. They were logical, well thought out and deserved merit."

Alix stopped before uttering her reply.

"You mean by that statement you agree with Alexandra's conclusions?"

"Not necessarily" I responded. "Let's just say if I were in the Glasgow University debating chamber, I would lend weight to her cause."

Gildas and I returned to BeauRobert on 28th. We spent the following days with work and our treble. The traditional New Year Party took place in 31st. We all cheered. Roll on 2006.

Chapter Thirty

The year began routinely: the Château Contract had become a permanent de Veres' project, like the Forth Bridge. You started at one end and when you had finished it was time to return to the beginning again!

In the middle of January, I spent time in Edinburgh and Glasgow to satisfy myself about the progress of the Scottish operation while Gilda flew to the US again for a week on a marketing promotion for Saint Roche Rivière and discussions on some new projects he was planning.

Then at the beginning of February Alix 'phoned:

"Is it still possible to come and see you on that weekend before the school break?" She asked.

"Of course, it's in the diary."

"Thank God" she replied "we need a change of scenery."

"What's wrong? You sound upset." I said concerned.

"It's Alexandra, she's had a boyfriend for several months but concealed it from us."

"Not a clever move, certainly, but she's 15 "

Alix interrupted me.

"That's part of the issue. She told him she was 18 and he believed her. David and I are furious at her deception to us and to him. For the present she's under house arrest! I'll give you the details when we meet. Also she will be the only one accompanying us. Julian's visiting friends and Angus is on a football tour."

"OK" I replied. "See you in two weeks."

The change in Alexandra was instantly noticeable on their arrival. She was pale, subdued and that exceptional complexion had developed some spots. I knew she had been wrong to betray her parents' trust but she and I had a certain rapport. Perhaps because she had spirit and was like me a bit of a rebel. I felt sorry for her.

After the usual family greetings I plunged in.

"Alexandra, why not run down to the stables and saddle up Avril. Jack's there grooming the horses. You know him well. He'll ride out with you."

"Can I, aunt Caterine? Can I really?" She answered face lighting up. Then she glanced at her parents.

David frowned but he knew the initiative had been taken. He would have been churlish to refuse.

He nodded adding: "Back here in two hours."

Alexandra's response of "yes Papa" was uttered as she raced away in a hail of gravel in the direction of the stable block.

As all four of us entered BeauRobert, David turned to me.

"Devious, dear sister and typical. You haven't forgotten your old tricks!"

"David" I stared at him wide-eyed "how could you accuse me of deception? I was just being hospitable to my niece."

The "Alexandra conundrum" however was more complicated than Gildas and I had imagined.

Sitting in the library over coffee, David and Alix explained.

"Her boyfriend came to see us at the end of last month with a reluctant Alexandra in tow. Of course, neither of us knew anything about the relationship. We've since discovered two school friends have been providing alibis. Alix and I were incensed." David said, expression grim.

"And also disappointed" Alix added. "Alexandra's high spirited, even rebellious at times (I smiled to myself) but she's always taken her responsibilities seriously, generally level headed, never given us any cause for concern till now."

"Frankly" David continued "I think after the meningitis scare, when we nearly lost her, we've overtly indulged her without realising it."

"You're being too self-critical" Gildas interposed. "It's her first serious boyfriend, always an emotional time. Who is he anyway and what did he say to you?"

"Well" David replied "here's the pocket history and also his reaction to events. His name's Pierre Merendez and he's 24. Born in Switzerland but orphaned as a baby he was brought up in South America by his mother's family. He was educated there initially and then in Switzerland, hence he speaks five languages fluently. Attending university in Geneva he qualified as a lawyer. Currently he is employed by one of the most prestigious legal firms in Switzerland. I know one of the partners. His description to me of Pierre was 'a gifted court lawyer, highly talented'. It would appear his star is in the ascendancy."

"And his response to the relationship with Alexandra" I prompted David.

"Shocked at the discovery of her age and surprisingly the same reaction as us. He told Alix and me in Alexandra's presence 'horrified, is the only way I can express my feelings when I found out. And also very disappointed. A young lady whom I held in the highest regard and had grown to love had deceived me, betrayed my trust in her and also her parents.' At this point Alexandra had started to sob quietly sitting in the corner of the conservatory. Pierre added 'I want to assure you that during our relationship there's been no impropriety of any kind. Alexandra, please confirm that statement to your parents.' All our daughter could do was nod unable in her distress to answer." David concluded standing up and walking out over to the east window with its view of the woods, visibly upset.

"So what's happening now?" Gildas asked turning to Alix.

"Before we could make any comments, Pierre put forward his." She replied.

"I have no doubts of my love for Alexandra and my wishes for her to share in my future life. At my age I can be confident in these feelings but at her age she cannot as I've told her. My suggestion is we separate for several months. At least till her 16th birthday in June. As it happens I am being promoted and will be spending a period in London. It gives Alexandra time to go out with other young men. If you, as her parents, are agreeable it gives both of us time for reflection."

"He seems a sensible young man" Gildas said.

"What is he like, though as a person I know time was short in his company, but what were your impressions?"

David replied. "Articulate, obviously benefiting from a first class education, he stayed on at our invitation for dinner. He was exceptional company, witty with a vibrant personality and incisive mind."

"Plus one other factor David omitted" Alix added.

"What's that?" I inquired gathering up the empty coffee mugs.

"He's gorgeous to look at, the archetypal tall, dark, handsome: straight out of a Hollywood movie!"

"Mon Dieu!" I answered. "What a stunning couple they must make! From what you've told me I can't see Alexandra changing her mind."

That evening before dinner, Alexandra came to see me in my study where I was sorting out some papers.

"You'll know all about it I suppose, Pierre and everything." She sighed.

"Yes, my dear. You seem to have dug a hole for yourself and him."

"I know I was wrong, aunt Caterine, but it all happened so quickly. We met in a coffee shop in Zurich. I was rushing out as he came in and we collided. The contents of my handbag strewn all over the pavement. I was furious and called him a clumsy idiot." She grinned continuing "Pierre did not like that telling me it was my fault and an argument ensued. To annoy him, as I thought, I changed languages from German to English then French and finally Spanish, but he equalled them. When he started in Portuguese I had to admit defeat."

"Quite an encounter." I smiled. "What was his next move?"

"Well, a crowd had gathered by this time.

Taking my arm Pierre said: "It would be in both our interests to settle this dispute inside."

"That was the beginning" Alexandra said. "I know I'm young and I want to study Fine Arts, as you did, and establish a career, but Pierre and I've discussed everything. He's ambitious too. But we want to do these things together, not apart. The world's changed, time's short. Mum and Dad won't agree but I've told Pierre I want to share his flat, live with him as a couple when I'm sixteen. That way, time will tell us if it's a long term commitment. What do you think, Aunt Caterine? I mean you've been around."

Alexandra stopped abruptly, hand over her mouth in horror: "Heavens! I didn't mean that as it sounds. I love you so much and admire all your achievements."

"Alexandra" I laughed going over to give her a hug. "I'm not in the least offended and for what it's worth, here's my advice."

By her 16th birthday in the first week of June, Alexandra had not changed her mind, nor had Pierre.

She phoned Gildas and me at BeauRobert with a request.

"Aunt Caterine, would you and Uncle Gildas do something for me?"

"Of course, my dear, if we can."

"You know Pierre and I are back together. I'm so happy about everything and so is he. It's fabulous."

She stopped breathless with enthusiasm.

"Young love" I thought smiling. "How simple life seemed then!"

"I discussed your advice with him, what you suggested last February and Pierre's in total agreement. We will enjoy the coming year as boyfriend and girlfriend, spend time with our different sets of friends from both age groups. It will give me time to explore the depth of our relationship. To live together, it's too early. We must wait."

"That sounds very sensible, Alexandra. What do Dad and Mum think?"

"They're very pleased and I think relieved." She laughed then rushed on bubbling with happiness.

"As it happens, Pierre has business in Tours next Thursday and staying with friends near BeauRobert that evening. Could he call in to see you? He's heard so much about you, would love to see the château."

"Delighted" I replied. "Tell him to come at 6.30 pm for an apéritif. Gildas and I look forward to meeting him."

"Thanks, Aunt Caterine, just brilliant. I know you'll love him, he's gorgeous."

Smiling at her lively chatter, I replaced the receiver and made a note in the calendar. I would tell Gildas tonight.

On the following Thursday the door bell rang at precisely 6.30 pm. Felix used the house phone as Gildas and I were on the terrace.

"Monsieur Merendez has arrived. I've shown him into the library." He confirmed.

Somewhat curiously, we went to meet Alexandra's boyfriend for the first time.

For the rest of my life that rendez-vous would be indelibly inked on my mind.

As Gildas and I entered the library, Pierre had his back towards us, no doubt admiring that view from the east window of the woods, which bordered the lake.

He was, as Alix described him, taller than David's 6'2" with exceptionally broad shoulders. In my mind a vague recognition stirred but I brushed it aside.

On hearing us he turned round smiling in greeting and for the first time in my 36 years I nearly fainted as in shocked horror I recognised a ghost. Simultaneously, Gildas stiffened beside me.

The young man took several strides towards us.

"Monsieur, Madame, I'm delighted to meet you at last, especially as I've just found out we're family. I'm the son of Philippe Martine."

Gildas recovered first gripping the outstretched hand and I received the traditional French greeting.

"This is quite a shock Pierre. Please excuse our initial reaction but Caterine and I are unaware my cousin had any children, never even knew he had married!"

By now I had recovered my composure outwardly but mentally was still reeling from the physical presence of this man. He could have been his father's twin.

"I'm not surprised by your reaction. I found out only six months ago who my father was and just last week the du Gilbert connection." He paused for a moment, appearing disturbed.

"Pierre, how inhospitable of us. What can I offer you to drink?"

"Whisky, Monsieur, please."

"A malt?" Gildas inquired, offering him a choice.

"The Spey Valley one, thanks." Pierre replied then continued.

He repeated what David had told us about his background and concluded:

"So I never knew my father or met him. From my mother's family, no information, only that he was paying for my education which was privileged: primary school in Brazil, followed by secondary education in Geneva and my law studies split between United States, UK and Switzerland. Then six months ago I was informed by members of my father's trust that, subject to several legacies, I was the sole inheritor of his estate, I was flabbergasted, especially on receiving the details."

He turned to Gildas. "I'm sure you are aware, Monsieur, that my father was a very wealthy man."

"Yes Pierre, and please call us Gildas and Caterine."

"Thank you" he replied smiling sipping at his malt. "Also on learning of the connexion with the du Gilbert I discovered about my father's tragic accident here. It must have been a total shock for you and Caterine."

Gildas replied.

"Indeed, it was. No one could have predicted Philippe would choose that short cut through the walled garden to the north gate."

Pierre shook his head, walking over again to the window.

"It's bizarre. Isolated by my father all my life and then suddenly discovering who he was, a man of eminence and then the tragic circumstances of his death."

At the same time I discover I've been bestowed a fortune by him, never need to work again in my life! Of course, that won't happen, I've always been ambitious and I must pave my own path, prove to myself what I can achieve to and for myself."

There was a moment's silence.

Turning back from the window, Pierre added:

"You know the strangest part of recent events is the fact I have no image of my father as a person. Therefore I find difficulty in recognising some sentiment in his death. Does that sound ungrateful? Even callous? I have asked myself many questions over recent months, one of which repeats itself. Would I be better off if my father instead of leaving me his vast wealth on his death, had bestowed to me his love during his life?"

Gildas and I had no answer to give him.

After chatting for another 30 minutes, Pierre took his leave.

"Perhaps it's more appropriate if you explain to Alexandra and her parents the family connection. Please do that for me.

"The next time we meet I hope it will be with your niece. She's the best thing that's ever happened to me."

Over dinner I said to Gildas.

"I almost feel sorry for him. Why did Philippe ignore him especially when he took care of him financially. I assume from his statements Philippe was a multi-millionaire."

"I'm sure he must have been although, obviously, I don't know the details. Academically he was extremely clever, skipped two classes at primary school; his reputation as a plastic surgeon was unparalleled plus this commercial acumen, a rare combination of expertise."

Gildas frowned and I waited for his further analyses.

"I recall my father's words many years ago about Philippe – 'a brilliant mind, bordering on genius, I wonder sometimes if that is a dangerous frontier' – I remember asking him what he meant by that statement – 'the finite division between sanity and insanity' – was his response."

Gildas put down his dessert spoon and looked at me directly, eyebrow raised in that quizzical fashion.

"You and I know how he tried to destroy both of us. A man obsessed with many elements of the deadly sins. In summation a flawed genius, a man with a demented mind."

The week following Pierre's visit I was driving round the département 36, the Indre, looking at some of the lesser know châteaux on the contract.

This region had always appealed to me, out of the tourist domain and off the beaten track. It was an area of undulating terrain and lightly wooded, benefiting from the border on the National Parc de la Brenne.

This Brenne parkland with its thousand lakes boasted an environmental treasure trove, where the species of mankind and animal worked together and lived in harmony creating products of quality from their endeavours. It was a lesson to the noisy, polluted, industrial world: how to create in tranquillity and enhance the environment.

On the Friday evening I received an e-mail from Shona and phoned her.

"How are things?" I asked a little anxiously.

"I'm fine Caterine, blood pressure stable and this baby very active which I enjoy despite the kilos. I probably shouldn't tell you but we're having a boy. I decided to find out this time."

"Shona, I'm so happy for both of you, as is Gildas about this pregnancy; and a little boy! You must be thrilled."

"We are Caterine, Donald's even looking out his old rugby boots! Now, about my e-mail. Can you and Gildas meet Donald on Thursday in Paris? He's got some business there and would like to have dinner. I'm hors de combat, at six months' pregnant I prefer to remain at home! If you can see Donald, just confirm a.s.a.p."

Gildas and I met Donald at one of his 'restaurants' on the left bank and returned to Montparnasse for the night. There was no point in Donald opening up their Montmartre flat just for one overnight stay.

Over coffee and some discussions on the British and French government failures, Donald asked:

"By the way, I didn't know Philippe Martine had a son."

Gildas and I stared at Donald in stupefaction.

"How do you know?" I whispered. "Gildas and I found out only this month."

"I saw him in my club last week" Donald replied. "Of course, I did not know who he was but I couldn't mistake him, the image of his father, so I checked the register. There it was, Suite 109, Pierre Martine."

"But he doesn't use 'Martine', he's known by his mother's family name, 'Merendez'," Gildas interrupted.

"Well not at the club" Donald responded. "Of course, it's not a club now, more a private hotel. Anyway he seems to take after his father, never liked the man, not to be trusted" and he picked up his brandy goblet.

"What exactly do you mean by that statement?" I asked concerned.

"Simple answer, Caterine. He was there with an older man and three women, all sharing their suite, what is described in the press as 'upper class call girls'. Always amuses me. To my mind a prostitute is a prostitute, the only difference is the price."

"You're wrong Donald." I exclaimed "there must be another explanation."

"What's bothering you? You can have no interest in Martine's son."

"Yes, Donald, we have. He happens to be Alexandra's boyfriend and the relationship could be serious." Gildas replied.

Donald stared first at me and then Gildas.

"I suggest you tell David and find a means of separating them and fast."

Gildas phoned David on the following evening from BeauRobert.

"What did he say?" I asked anxiously.

"Surprised, taken aback but also cautious, his response was

that Doanld's been mistaken. Anyway we can't do anymore tonight. Let's have some dinner."

At 11.00 pm as we were listening to a Wagner CD when the phone rang and I answered it.

"Caterine." My brother's voice resonated down the line. "I nearly made an ass of myself tonight. I asked Alexandra 'I didn't know Pierre was in London again last week. Some friends saw him'. 'That's right', Alexandra replied grinning 'with some beautiful young ladies.' Apparently, Pierre's father bought a model agency, originally up market, now rapidly declining, Alexandra was informed of all the details. Pierre fired the management and has hired a new team. He told Alexandra that he and the chief photographer would be interviewing some models at his London club, international names. It would cost money to place them on the books but that's par for the course. I must re-establish the agency in the upper league.'

"Caterine, please tell Donald to check his facts before making false allegations. Love to all the family."

Gildas' comments when I told him of David's conversation were couched in diplomatic terms.

"Donald must have received misguided information from some jealous frustrated old fogies!"

Laughing together we walked with Gildas' arm round my shoulder to our BeauRobert apartment.

In July, at the beginning of the children's school holidays we organised a weekend at BeauRobert for all our family plus Albert, Céline and their son and daughter.

It was an exhausting weekend: swimming, water polo, tennis, riding round the estate plus one essential ingredient, cycle practice!

"Remember, gentlemen" Gildas announced before dinner on Saturday. "We've the charity race in the middle of September. Here are you sponsorship forms. I provide a magnum of champagne for the race winner and one also for the participant who raises the largest fund for the charity."

"What's this about?" Pierre asked bemused.

David explained:

"It's Gildas' sadistic punishment for all so called volunteers, a cycle race south of Argenton sur Creuse an area not known for its even terrain."

There were groans from the men while the female members of the assembled company smiled knowingly.

"You obtain a range of sponsors to pay two euros per kilometre and suffer an afternoon of agony."

"What's the distance?" Pierre enquired.

Albert added his voice: "Just 25 kms! Last year after suffering Hell on that saddle, I hobbled into the office for a week and I'm a regular cyclist with my Versailles club. It's purgatory!"

Everyone laughed.

"I'd like to volunteer" Pierre offered "I haven't cycled for a while but I used to be very keen."

"Bravo Pierre, here's your form." Gildas said handing him the race details.

Over dinner I observed as I had witnessed all weekend how attentive Pierre was to Alexandra; plus those private glances and delicate touches between them. I had no doubt they were in love.

The August month in France was very hot with scarcely any rainfall and surprisingly few thunderstorms.

Unfortunately the verdant grass suffered despite valiant efforts from the gardeners and ourselves to water regularly and use innumerable bags of mulching.

"I think if this global warning continues we need to consider a new irrigation system and change some of the plants to deeper rooted varieties." Gildas said exasperated one evening, noticing one of his climbing ivy plants withering.

"The problem is the governments know it's happening but take no action. God knows I've raised the subject at various conferences and forums, to little effect. It's frustrating. David agrees with me."

"Sorry chérie. Forget my moans. Let's get changed, I promised the treble some fun in the pool. There I can literally cool off."

A few days later I received an e-mail from Alexandra. It read.

"Dear Aunt Caterine,

I need your help. There's a family crisis. Pierre has received an offer of a job in Brazil: junior partner with one of the major legal firms in the country; he was head hunted for the position, a dream opportunity for him. He's asked me to marry him and set up home in Sao Paulo but Dad and Mum are against it. They tell me I'm too young, studies uncompleted. But Pierre's just returned after checking everything out. He's been given a luxury apartment, free for three months and there's an American University where I can continue my studies. Also he receives a generous living allowance, never mind his salary – mega bucks!

But he must sign a two year contract. Pierre wants to take this opportunity.

If I don't join him, I'm breaking my commitments but if I do I risk a family split, a disaster.

Please speak to Dad and Mum. I'm desperate for your support and that of Uncle Gildas.

I love Pierre and I love Dad and Mum, owe them so much too, but it's a lifetime choice for both of us.

I must go with Pierre, take my chances, live my life.

Xxxx Alexandra."

For several minutes I sat in my study holding that e-mail in reflection. Then after checking my watch I phoned David at the head office of the Mercantile Bank in Zurich, on his private line, a rare occurrence.

My brother answered immediately and hearing my voice knew the reason for my call.

"So Alexandra's told you." David sounded weary and I became even more concerned.

"I'll call you later if that suits you, when is the best time?" I asked him.

"It makes no difference, Petite. Alexandra's made her decision." He hesitated and I felt a sob in my soul at his use of that childhood family name for me.

"Alix and I have tried every argument, every persuasion, exhausted all our energies. We've even begun to think that we are wrong to make our protests. She's young, far too young, no experience of life. What if the marriage is a failure or, God forbid, also coupled with a child. Of course, she can return to her family and welcomed; but she will have lost so much opportunity in her life."

"What has been Pierre's stance in all this?" I inquired.

"Alexandra sees him as very sympathetic, however, Alix and I see him as impatient; but who are we to be prejudiced. You, Alix and myself pursued our careers relentlessly. Heavens Alix was still taking on translation work at eight months pregnant, despite my protests.

In the ultimate analysis, Pierre seems mature, level headed and certainly far from penniless; also he's determined to succeed on his own merit which is creditable. Sadly we must give Alexandra our blessing and let her go."

Gildas had been in Dusseldorf during the events staying overnight, returning the following evening about 7 pm.

I reiterated what had transpired.

We were sitting in the smaller salon, together, as I'd poured out our coffee.

"I don't see frankly that David and Alix have any other option, do you?"

Gildas hesitated, standing up to draw those claret velour drapes observing the diminishing evening light.

"That depends" he answered "on how to interpret the development of recent events."

"I don't understand what you mean." I replied handing him his coffee.

"Let me explain; some factors have been disturbing me on this whole subject over recent months. If you agree I suggest the following action."

I was taken aback, even shocked, but agreed Gildas should phone Donald.

He returned from his study after nearly 20 minutes.

"I was right in that Donald has the contacts. He'll organise the plan tomorrow and reckons we should have the conclusion in two to three weeks."

After finishing our coffee we went to the children's bedrooms to kiss them a second good night. It was a ritual from Gildas and me although the treble were unaware of it lost in their dreamy slumberland.

Exactly 19 days later Gildas received a document by courier and a phone call from Donald. It was 15th September, a Thursday, and I was working in my study. I can remember I was irritated as my computer was causing me problems. Oddly enough for all my appreciation of advanced technology and intense interest in science at school, I distrusted computers except for basic functions. This adversity had always amused Sabine.

"But they're brilliant Caterine, accurate and save time."

"Do you think so? I disagree. Accurate? That depends on the facts fed into them. Time saving? Sounds plausible until time lost when they crash down often with massive information loss. And third, they're a headache in two major areas."

"What's that?" Sabine asked taken aback.

"Eye strain and breach of security."

Gildas came in and sat down on my leather sofa, handing me the document. His facial expression was sad, even despondent.

"This is not pleasant reading." He confirmed.

In fact, it was damning. The report from those private investigators who had followed Pierre Martine   .

After an initial page outlining the instructions they had received and legal implications, it read as follows:

1, Mr Pierre Martine (also know as Merendez) is a member of the private club/hotel in London, aforementioned. It is a reputable establishment of long standing.

2, In this establishment he conducts various business meetings for the law company with whom he is employed in Switzerland, also aforementioned. These meetings take place on a regular basis during weekdays, mainly lunchtime appointments.

3, During the visits to London Mr Martine spends long hours in his legal work It has been observed that he arrives at the London headquarters of his office at 7 am and often departs as late as 9 pm.

4, At weekends, it has been observed that Mr Martine and also on some weekday evenings ....

I read on in horror and disgust.

"To sum all this up, he lives a life of sexual debauchery among prostitutes and pimps and Klaus Lundburg leads the way; and yet, Pierre met him only six months ago when he discovered who his father was. That I don't understand." I said tossing the document down onto the chair vacant beside me.

"No, it's surprising, but for whatever reason Philippe never revealed the existence of Pierre or his marriage which ended in divorce. Donald provided me with further information not revealed in the report as technically it's hearsay."

"Pierre and Klaus spoke mainly in German together but the investigator posing as a club member spent several years in Austria and so he understood. Alexandra was not targeted, thank God, as you and I suspected. That meeting in Zurich was sheer coincidence much to that bastard Lundburg's amusement. However one fact is indisputable, these sexual practices are not new to Pierre. He was overheard telling Lundberg that if he was over in Brazil, quote: 'you have my address. I'll be delighted to provide you with the names of some elite escort agencies with some delectable practices!' What a life Alexandra would have spent, entrapped in this deprived world." Gildas concluded.

It was decided that after David's arrival, on that Friday evening when he was staying just before the Saturday race, I would leave him with Gildas in the smaller salon where my brother would receive the reasons why Gildas had instigated the investigation and then give him the report.

That is exactly what transpired and making an excuse about putting finishing touches to dinner which was being taken in our apartment, I disappeared into the kitchen.

When I re-entered the smaller salon about half an hour later, David was standing at the window which looked over the lake.

He turned round and I ran over to hug him.

"I wish there had been another way."

David held me close for several moments then said to both of us:

"You must know Alix and I have delved deeply to find a means, any logical reason to deter Alexandra from going with Pierre to Brazil; and there it lies on that document . But it will grieve me greatly to give it to her. She'll be devastated. My lovely, vivacious daughter will be taken asunder, broken hearted."

Gildas and I glanced at each other, knowing David was right.

"A man who has everything, youth, health, outstanding

ability and recently untold wealth. How could he possibly be attracted to such debauchery?"

Gildas looked at his watch.

"David, we have another task tonight. I arranged to meet Pierre at the local auberge for a beer ostensibly to discuss race tactics. In fact I've reserved a room for him and that's where we confront him with this report , if you agree."

My brother nodded ."When ?"

"We're due there in 20 minutes"Gildas replied.

They left together in silence and returned within the hour, expressions grim. I did not ask what had happened.

It was a sombre meal.

Uncharacteristically, my brother failed to finish his main course.

"I apologise, Caterine, to waste such well prepared food but I seem to have lost my appetite."

"Don't apologise, it's not surprising. Dessert or just coffee?"

"Coffee, thanks.But let me phone Alix first to let her know the score."

Gildas and I watched with sadness as my brother left the room a dejected figure .

"What happened ? What was Pierre 's reaction ? "I asked anxiously.

"Laughed in our faces." Gildas replied.

"I don't love these women. They're my toys , playthings , my sexual amusement.

Come on don't tell me you haven't similar diversifications when a wife cannot satisfy you ."

Pierre had grinned then adding "All men do!"

"David went for him but I managed to get between them before battle began .One fact's certain, Pierre leaves for Brazil next week, alone."

When David returned after his call to Alix, we drank our coffee with only a few attempts at conversation and retired to bed.

The following morning after a later than usual breakfast, to compensate for no lunch before the race, Gildas and David departed.

To relieve any hunger pangs I had packed a snack for them of mixed fruit including bananas, chocolate and bottled water.

"We should return about 6.30 pm" Gildas said kissing me in that loving fashion on the forehead. If we're delayed, I'll phone."

Waving 'au revoir' I returned to our apartment kitchen, cleared the dishes off the breakfast table and loaded the dishwasher. Then I started to prepare salmon en croûte for the evening meal. As I placed the pastry I had prepared in the fridge, the phone rang. Answering it, I heard the news I had hopefully anticipated. Gildas and I were having another baby. Smiling to myself, I replaced the receiver. He would be as thrilled as I was, our family complete.

I remember I moved as in a dream toward my study and then halted in disbelief. How had he known?

On my leather sofa lay a bouquet of roses, twenty four red roses and a note on that white starched family notepaper. Of course, as I realised, it was a happy coincidence. The note contained two poems: the first was one of the Scottish bard's 'naughty ones' quoted at private parties and it made me laugh, typical Robert Burns.

The second was a Wordsworth sonnet "To a Lady" but Gildas had substituted another nomenclature. It read:
"Countess! The songs of spring were in the grove
While I was shaping beds for winter flowers,
While I was planting green unfading bowers
And shrubs – to hang upon the warm alcove,
And sheltering wall; and still as fancy wove
The dream, to time and nature's blended powers
I gave this paradise for winter hours,
A labyrinth, Countess! Which your feet shall rove."

I sank down on that sofa, smelling the fragrance of the blooms and then startled I recognised the variety, it was the darkest of all the roses with the richest of aromas. Its name, 'Deep Secret'. Had Gildas really believed I was pregnant? I smiled again to myself picking up the bouquet to arrange the flowers in a vase. Tonight when he returned I would discover the answer.

The afternoon I spent with the children who had stayed overnight with school friends in the village. It always amazed me how often we had received invitations for the treble from other parents to joint their family activities; it was an onerous task to cope with triplets!

The September day continued warm and balmy; the sun seemed in a lazy mood slumbering behind floating clouds failing to find the energy to shine.

I must have been affected by the mood because my eyes slowly closed in sympathy and thoughts drifting into warm memories and halcyon days.

"Caterine! Caterine!" I heard the call and awoke to see my brother's anxious face as he gathered me in his arms.

"I'm sorry" I mumbled "must have fallen asleep" yawning still only half awake.

Looking up, about to ask who had won, the expression on his face finally registered with me. Perhaps in the recesses of my mind I already knew.

"Where's Gildas ? "I asked quite calmly. "Why's he not here?"

"Don't worry, Petite, he'll be all right. His bike was found further up near the river, almost undamaged. They're looking for him now. Probably he tried to find help, after it happened. It was in a remote area." David rambled on but I heard only silence.

In my mind I saw the images.

That white starched family notepaper, written in that

distinctive hand, a bouquet of the deepest red and most fragrant roses named 'Deep Secret' and a man tall and very handsome known intimately to me.

They searched for days, even weeks.
But my beloved Gildas was never found.